THE LAW
OF
THE HEART

THE LAW
OF
THE HEART

BORIS STARLING

Text copyright © 2021 by Boris Starling
All rights reserved.

Published by Lake Union Publishing, Seattle

www.apub.com

Amazon, the Amazon logo, and Lake Union Publishing are trademarks of Amazon.com, Inc., or its affiliates.

ISBN-13: 9781542028110
ISBN-10: 1542028116

Cover design by The Brewster Project

Cover illustration by Jelly London

Printed in the United States of America

A NOTE ON THE TITLE

In 1912, the year that North Korea's Eternal President Kim Il Sung was born, an English physiologist concluded two years of experimentation by publishing his theory that 'the strength of the heart's systolic contraction is directly proportional to its diastolic expansion'.

That man was my great-grandfather, Ernest Starling, and the theory – one of the foundations of modern cardiac medicine, which every doctor knows as well as they do their own name – became known as 'the law of the heart'.

I have long wanted to use it as the title for a love story. I hope this one is worthy of it.

A NOTE ON NAMES

North Korean names are written surname first, the opposite of most Western practice. Almost all North Koreans have a two-part forename, spaced and capitalised rather than hyphenated as is the case in South Korea. For example, North Koreans refer to Kim Il Sung, South Koreans to Kim Il-sung.

PART I

Revolution of Thought

'It is like a running blaze on a plain, like a flash of lightning in the clouds. We live in the flicker.'

Heart of Darkness, Joseph Conrad

1

Pyongyang, December 2015

A circle of light against the darkening sky: the coal stove, pulsing a dull orange and reflected in a window on which snowflakes whirled a silent tattoo. No electric lamps to brighten the room because there was no power. At this time of year, you were lucky to get three or four hours' electricity a day.

'Comrade Park, what transgressions have you made against the Revolution these past seven days? What transgressions have you made in thought, in word, and in deed?'

Min couldn't see who had spoken. In any case, it didn't matter. The weekly confessions were made and received by the entire collective. There were a dozen people crammed in here, seeking each other's warmth without making it too apparent, for even to acknowledge the coldness of the room could be construed as criticism of the regime. They wore uniforms of identical dark green: trousers for the men, knee-length skirts for the women. The deep red of their epaulettes and collar flashes seemed to glow slightly in the light from the stove.

Min glanced at Choe Yun Seok. He had watchful eyes and too much hair growing out of his ears. They worked in pairs, one man and one woman, and she'd been partnered with him ever since she'd started here two years before. He smiled and nodded at her. She cleared her throat and took a breath.

All day she'd been dreading this moment and thinking of ways to postpone it, but now it was here she suddenly wanted to get on with it and get it over: the reality could hardly be worse than the anticipation. Besides, she was a performer of sorts: it was part of her job. *So perform.*

'Comrades,' she said. 'I have appraised the week that has passed. In order to correct my faults, I must cleanse myself of the repeated sins that accumulate and slow down our beloved Revolution. I – I have fallen short of the standards of vigilance expected of a tour guide for the Korea International Travel Company.'

They all knew what she'd done: that was why Yun Seok had encouraged her to confess in the first place, because if she didn't do so then someone else would just denounce her, and that was much worse. Min hurried on. 'Yun Seok and I' – he was expected to take any fall for this just as much as she was, of course – 'were escorting a group of American tourists. We took them to Mansu Hill to show them the statues of our Great Leader Kim Il Sung and our Dear Leader Kim Jong Il.' She glanced towards the far wall, where twin pictures of father and son hung. Such pictures adorned every room in the country, and by law nothing could be placed higher than them. 'Of course we encouraged the Americans to take pictures at this most sacred of sites. We failed to notice that others in the group were mimicking the poses of the Great Leader and the Dear Leader in a mocking and disrespectful way. Yun Seok and I were insufficiently alert to the antics of these uneducated barbarians. Though my thoughts were full of love for the Great Leader and the Dear Leader, and though I had repeatedly communicated this to the tour party, my actions left much to be desired. We will review our handling of the situation and ensure this transgression never happens again, with reference to lessons personally handed down by the Great Leader, the Dear Leader, or preferably both.'

Her shoulders slumped as she finished. She felt suddenly drained. Yun Seok patted her on the forearm and leant across. 'Well done, Min Ji,' he whispered. Formal and well mannered, he was one of the few who used her full name. Most people just called her Min: as a small child she'd insisted that her name was simply that rather than Min Ji, and it had stuck.

She and Yun Seok were the oldest and youngest in the room. He had been a guide for more than twenty years, which made him practically old enough to be her father. He'd already told her that if they handled this well they'd get a slap on the wrist and no more. Min hoped very much that he was right.

The other ten discussed the case among themselves. Min had worked there long enough to know the men who left their gaze lingering on her a little too long and the ones who didn't, the women who spread rumours like a farmer scattering seeds and the ones who didn't. She knew their likes and dislikes: she knew them as much through what they let slip in the margins as through what they said. And so she knew they'd all be weighing up two contradictory factors: that someone else's misfortune was as often as not your opportunity, but also that this could easily happen to any of them and that a little mercy now would be remembered next time around.

Min looked out of the window while they talked. She loved the city more than usual when it was still like this, softened and smoothed under its white blanket. Even now, snow still evoked the same sense of delighted wonder in her as it had done when she'd been a child, dragging a toboggan up to the top of Moran Hill over and over so she could sledge back down again, oblivious to her parents' impatience, to the cold, to anything but the sense of speed from being so low to the ground and the high tinkle of her laughter as she crashed into soft, welcoming drifts.

In the distance she could see the vast bronze statues where the incident to which she'd confessed had taken place. Yes, she *had* been distracted by one of the Americans asking her to take a photo of him, but that was no excuse. She *should* have been more alert. It had been drummed into her, into every Pyongyang child, from their very first day at school.

'What do the Americans do in the southern zone of our great nation, children?'

'They kill our brothers with tanks and spear our sisters with bayonets.'

'What else do they do, children?'

'The Yankee imperialists brand their prisoners with hot irons, set wild dogs on women, and wrench out children's teeth with pliers. They began the war and begat the tragedy by which our nation was divided in two and our people have had to endure the pain of living divided.'

'When should you trust an American, children?'

'Never!'

Min had met many Americans and was always polite to them. She asked where they were from, and remembered names at once meaningless and exotic: Nebraska, Tallahassee, Delaware. They seemed pleasant enough, she had to admit, but that was surely only because they were hiding their true natures while they were here.

The chatter between the guides quietened. They had reached a decision.

One of them – maybe the one who'd first asked Min about her transgressions, maybe not – stood up.

'We congratulate you, comrades, for these admissions, which are so essential to the progress of each of us. We have also taken into consideration Comrade Choe's lengthy service and the consistently excellent feedback which Comrade Park receives for her enthusiasm, knowledge and presentation. The collective has therefore decided that Comrade Choe and Comrade Park should forfeit their next three scheduled tours from Europe, and should make alternative arrangements with the Chinese embassy.'

The tour company's offices were in a building so brutalist and grey that it would have leached colour from the rainbow itself. Outside on the pavement, Min and Yun Seok walked in silence for a few moments, each of them instinctively sensing how many people were around and how close they were: in other words, assessing the chances of their conversation being overheard. It wasn't that they were about to discuss anything particularly sensitive: it was just that such checks were what everyone here did as a matter of instinct, everywhere and all the time.

Their breath billowed in lung-shaped plumes as they spoke

'The punishment is reasonably mild,' Yun Seok said. He spoke precisely and slowly, as he always did, as though he took every sentence and twisted it in the air so he could examine it from all angles, inspecting and weighing the words before releasing them into the wild. Once she had asked him whether he had enjoyed his breakfast that morning, and it had been a good half-minute or so before he'd replied 'perhaps'.

'You did well,' he continued now. 'Everyone there likes you.'

That wasn't quite true, Min knew. She thought of the man who'd repeatedly asked her out when she'd first arrived at the KITC fresh from college, and who'd become all huffy when she'd said no. Eventually Yun Seok had taken the man to one side, and after that there had been no more problems. Min still didn't know what Yun Seok had said, but she'd seen the flash of steel on his face as he'd steered the man out of the room. She'd never seen Yun Seok like that before, or since.

She dragged her attention back to the here and now. 'They also knew it was your first offence,' Yun Seok was saying. 'The confession should always come from the junior member, who has more of the Revolution's lessons still to absorb.'

'But the Chinese—'

'I know. I know.' The Chinese comprised the vast majority of foreign visitors to Pyongyang, but few guides enjoyed being assigned to them. Sometimes they got drunk, chased women and spent less in the hard-currency shops than Westerners did, which in turn meant less commission for the guides. 'It won't be a long period. Three weeks, perhaps four.' He gave a quiet double cough, a point of punctuation to fill the pause. 'Everyone in that room has experienced similar disciplinary protocols, and without exception they have become better citizens as a result.'

Min considered this as they walked. The buildings towered above and around them, huge monoliths in white and grey marching towards the horizon. The Taedong ran sluggish and dark, and the willows on the bank bent low under the ridged lines of snow on their branches. A poster of strong hands crushing an American soldier beneath his own nuclear bomb splashed red and yellow through the monochrome.

A bus was pulling up.

'This is mine,' Yun Seok said. 'See you tomorrow.'

'You too. Say hi to your wife and kids.'

'I will.'

It was a running joke, sort of, since Min had never actually met Yun Seok's family. She knew that he was married, had two teenage sons and lived out in east Pyongyang near the rubber factory. But that was pretty much all she knew about him. He wasn't unfriendly: he just didn't talk much about his home life or show any interest in hers, though when she organised staff picnics on the weekends or after work on summer evenings he came along dutifully enough.

Yun Seok waved at Min and climbed on board the bus. It had ten red stars on the side, with each star signifying 50,000 km safely travelled. It made Min proud to think how frugal and durable the bus was, unlike all the throwaway rubbish with which the Americans and Japanese crammed their landfills. This bus had been the equivalent of all the way to the moon, and more.

She watched the bus set off again, skating uncertainly along tracks already made by the vehicles ahead and round a tram stranded by the power cut. She passed the Pyongyang University of Foreign Studies, where she'd learned English, and ducked down the steps into Three Revolutions station. No problem with the electricity here: the lights were blazing and the steady stream of passengers coming up through the turnstiles indicated that the trains were running fine. Min bought a token, received a grunt from the man behind the till in return for her pleasantry about the snow, passed through the steel blast doors, which could be closed in an instant if need be, and stepped on to the escalator.

A month fending off lecherous telephone salesmen and looking after minor government officials who got so drunk they soiled themselves. That wasn't what being a tour guide was: not for her, at any rate. Being a tour guide was showing lucky tourists the very best of Pyongyang and making sure their stay was as interesting and educational as possible. Being a tour guide was the commendation slips she received from them and which she filed away in a drawer at home. *'Our guide Min was wonderful, so informative and helpful . . . Min was the best guide we could have asked for. Nothing was too much trouble for her . . . Min is a natural storyteller and really brought things alive for us . . . Please say a special thank you to Min, whose knowledge and pride in her work really added a huge amount to our experience in Pyongyang . . .'*

One month. One whole, long month. Not to mention the failure that it represented, whatever Yun Seok said. All her hard work, all her good behaviour, not just on the job but throughout school and university too – all of that, undone in a moment.

She shook her head. A month was only a month. It could have been worse. Think of the good things. She was lucky to be Korean and even luckier to live in the greatest city in the world. Where else could boast a metro system like this, for example: stations deeper than any others in the world, not a speck of litter or graffiti (unlike the pictures she'd seen of the New York and London subways), and mosaics of the Great Leader striding towards a sunlit future with soldiers, engineers, mechanics, cleaners, cooks, farmers, and housewives following eagerly in his wake? Nowhere else, that was where.

She boarded a westbound train, catching a glimpse of her reflection in the window. She'd been told often enough how pretty she was, but she could never quite see it herself. Her hair was perfectly straight and jet black above sleepy dark eyes. Her mouth was small and full, a little plump bow of red. High cheekbones tilted down towards a sharp chin. Maybe everyone found their own faces as unremarkable as she did hers.

She let the gentle swaying of the carriage leach some of the anxiety from her. Stations came and went. Triumph. Renovation. Construction. Golden Fields. It wasn't until the last that she realised she was humming, and even then it was only because a soldier was glaring at her. It was an unspoken but universally recognised rule of the metro that you travelled in silence.

Restoration: her own station, and the end of the line. The train stopped, the doors opened, and she joined the throng heading up the stairs and out into the street. The buildings here were newer than in the city centre, and they looked it too: a series of huge cylindrical residential towers and wave-shaped housing slabs rather than the brutalist Fifties cubes, as though an alien race had landed.

If living in Pyongyang itself was denied to many of Min's fellow countrymen, living out here on Restoration Street was denied to many of her fellow Pyongyangites: a privilege within a privilege.

Tower Two had forty-three floors. She went through the main entrance, across the lobby, pressed for the lift, waited a minute, realised it wasn't coming, and took the stairs to the third floor. When they'd first moved here, she remembered, she'd been upset not to get an apartment on the higher floors where the view across the city was much better. Now she was glad they hadn't, with the lift being out of order so often. It was one thing for her, young and fit, to walk endless flights of stairs, but quite another for her grandmother, and increasingly for her parents too.

She could tell the moment she opened the door that only Cuckoo was home, because the radio was on so loud that the sound was beginning to distort at the edges. '*The Korean Workers' Party has hailed as a hero a thirteen-year-old boy in Hyesan who denounced his uncle for seditious statements . . .*'

Cuckoo had her back to the door. Min hurried across the living room to turn the sound down: down but not off, of course, because the radios broadcasting constant government news were hard-wired into the walls and only went off for good when the power did. You had to be very brave or very foolish – and in this country the gap between the two was perilously slim – to clip the wires: ten years in prison, maybe more, if they caught you.

'*"If you go against our Supreme Leader I will smash your dog head," the boy told his uncle. "You are not a person. You have become a monster. You have become a class enemy and opened your bloody mouth."*'

Cuckoo only turned her head towards Min when she heard the sound drop.

'Hello, darling girl,' she said. 'Good day at work?'

'Not really, no.'

'Why? What happened?'

So Min told her, from start to finish and nice and slow so Cuckoo could hear it all. Getting things out in the open meant thinking them through in the round. Cuckoo listened as she always did, with her head to one side. That was how she'd got her nickname, from someone who thought the pose looked like that of the bird. She was halfway between eighty and ninety in a country where few made it past seventy-five, her face was ridged like contour lines on a map, and her hair grew ever sparser and whiter, but there was nothing wrong with her memory or her comprehension.

'Sounds like a lot of fuss about nothing,' she said when Min had finished. 'Yun Seok's right. Do your time and forget about it. A little setback like this is hardly the end of the world. Might even do you some good, golden girl.'

'Do you think I should mention it at dinner tonight?'

Cuckoo laughed. 'Don't be daft. You know what your parents are like. Your mother will fuss, your father will try to get involved. Remember how he was about your school reports?'

Remember? How could Min forget? Unless she'd finished literally top of the class and had been awarded 'exemplary' for her attitude, he'd berated the teachers to their faces as though it had been their fault rather than hers.

'It can be our secret.' Min smiled and took Cuckoo's hand in hers. It was warm enough in the apartment, but even so Min could feel the cold on the old woman, and when she took her hand away again she saw the liver spots dotting the skin stretched thin and tight like parchment.

Cuckoo saw Min's expression, because Cuckoo didn't miss a damn thing. 'Just my bones, dear. You know what they say. Men age like a fine wine, but women age like a glass of milk.' She laughed again. 'Your mother would like this to be my last winter.'

'My mother would like nothing of the sort. She's devoted to you.'

'She tolerates me, and you know it. If I try to help too much, she gets annoyed because I can't do things as fast as I used to. If I keep out of the way, she thinks I'm being lazy.' Cuckoo didn't add what they both knew: that Han Na, like every wife in the Democratic People's Republic of Korea, had no choice when it came to taking in her mother-in-law. It was 500 years since the Ri dynasty had enshrined the policy that families took care of their elders, and it remained true to this day. Korean families were born together, Korean families lived together, and Korean families died together.

'Well, *I'm* devoted to you. And you'll probably outlive the lot of us, old woman.'

Cuckoo kissed Min on the forehead. Min was, she knew, the only grandchild Cuckoo had ever known, and Min herself had only barely known any other grandparents. They shared a bedroom to this day, the two of them, as though they were sisters rather than grandmother and granddaughter. Like the rest of the apartment, their room was spotlessly tidy: twin beds made up with hospital corners, wooden floor polished so hard and bright that Min could practically see her face in it, and all of it Cuckoo's doing, of course. Min's parents slept in the other bedroom, and there was also a kitchen, a living room and a bathroom. Simple beige furniture throughout. A German tourist had once told Min that this was how poor people lived in his country, and it had taken all her willpower and good training not to call him a liar to his face.

The front door opened. It was Han Na, Min's mother, clutching a thin plastic bag of shopping in one hand and trailing a line of snow from the other. 'Hi, hi,' she trilled. 'Sorry I'm late. Huge queue at the store. The delivery lorry hadn't arrived.'

13

'That's the second time this week,' said Cuckoo. 'They should sort it out.'

Han Na gave the tiniest shake of her head: *not here. Not even here.*

'Honestly,' Cuckoo added. 'You people. Afraid of your own shadows.'

'Not another word!'

Of all Han Na's house rules (and they were all hers, whatever Chul Woo said: either he agreed with them or he was wrong) this was the most unbreakable: there was to be no political criticism whatsoever, not even the tiniest bit, within these four walls.

Cuckoo glanced at Min and made a mock-scared face. Min tried not to laugh.

Han Na clapped her hands together. 'Come. This *onban*'s not going to make itself, and I bet Chul Woo will be famished when he gets back.'

Min watched as Han Na bustled over to the kitchen. She was riding ever lower, Min thought, as though gravity was gradually but inexorably twisting her downwards. Yes, Han Na looked tired – everyone did in winter – but the redness in her cheeks wasn't just from the cold, she'd given up attempting to conceal the badger's stripe of grey in her hair, and there was a hint of turkey wattle round her neck that Min was sure hadn't been there this time last year.

Onban was a traditional Korean stew, and they set to making it while chatting about this and that, three generations all together. Cuckoo cooked the rice, Han Na sliced the mushrooms and chicken, and Min ground the mung beans into *bindaetteok* pancakes. Han Na kept glancing towards the door, and Min saw the nervousness she held within her: what time would Chul Woo come home, and what kind of mood would he be in when he did?

The answer to the first was always the same: whenever he pleased. The second was as hard to grasp as mercury. Yesterday Chul Woo had chewed Min out for slurping her soup too loudly, but the day before she'd ribbed him mercilessly about going bald and he'd laughed along as though it were the funniest thing in the world.

'He was like that even as a little boy,' Cuckoo said, as though reading Min's thoughts. 'Sunshine one moment and thunder the next.'

At that very moment they heard Chul Woo's key in the lock, and from the set of his face as he came through the door they all knew tonight was thunder, as indeed it seemed to be more and more these days. Han Na opened the fridge and pulled out a bottle of Taedonggang beer. Chul Woo shook his head even as he was taking off his coat. 'Something stronger,' he said.

She poured him a double measure of Paekrosul brandy which he drank so fast that it could hardly have touched the sides: but when she offered him another, he shook his head irritably. 'Let's eat.'

He kicked off his shoes on the way to the table, listing uneasily to one side in the brief moment when he had one shoe on and the other off. The stack heels again, Min saw, though she could never understand why he bothered. He was no shorter than the average man in Pyongyang, and he still looked good for someone in his early sixties. His eyes were alert and darting behind rimless glasses, and he was trim enough beneath his black polo neck. Cuckoo was right about the ways in which men and women aged, Min thought. Maybe the amount of housework each of them did had something to do with it.

They sat in their usual positions around the circular table: Han Na nearest the cooker, then Min, then Cuckoo, then an empty space, and finally Chul Woo. Han Na served the *onban* and they began to eat. She and Min batted innocuous questions at Chul

Woo which he returned with such monosyllabic indifference that eventually they gave up. He picked at his food.

'We've worked hard to make this,' Cuckoo said suddenly, 'so eat up. And cheer up too, while you're at it.'

Chul Woo glared at her. 'Stop treating me like a child.'

'Then stop behaving like one. You've been a misery-guts ever since you started this new job. If you can't handle it then you should have said so.'

'Sssh.' Chul Woo lowered his voice. 'It's not the kind of thing you say no to. Not if you value your career. And your family.'

Min took Cuckoo's hand again, part sympathy and part warning – *leave it now.*

They finished dinner in silence. Chul Woo got up with a glass of blueberry wine and left the women to clear away and wash up.

Table empty and dishes washed, Min went through to the living room. Chul Woo was sitting at his desk, his back to a wall comprised almost exclusively of monuments to his work and vanity. He had directed more than fifty films, and they were all represented here in some way or another: posters of *Comrade Kim* and *My Village at Sunset*, reel tins for older movies like *The Forest Sways* and *When We Pick Apples*, VHS boxes for *Nation and Destiny* and most of the others, and finally DVDs for the ones like *An Emissary of No Return*, which he'd made recently.

He had what looked like a large map open in front of him. When Min looked closer, she saw that it was a schematic diagram covered with his scribbles.

'Jucheland?' she asked.

He nodded without speaking. Jucheland was a theme park he'd been put in charge of building, even though he'd hardly even been to a theme park before, let alone designed one. But somewhere along the line it had obviously been decided that a film director's vision was the only thing that could make this theme park special.

16

Films had sets, didn't they? Films were spectacle. So Chul Woo had been approached, and now here he was.

'Anything I can help with?' Min continued.

She clocked the glance Chul Woo shot at the twin pictures of the Great Leader and Dear Leader on the far wall: a glance that she knew was both cause and explanation. Whatever was vexing her father had come from the Supreme Leader or as near to him as made no difference, and one did not criticise decisions that came from the Supreme Leader, just as one had not criticised decisions that had come from the Dear Leader before him and the Great Leader before *him*.

'We Koreans are one great family with the Supreme Leader as father,' Chul Woo said. 'Only he can carry us forward. We do not know everything he knows, which makes us incapable of understanding the true glory of his master plan. In the fullness of time we will come to comprehend everything that isn't clear now.'

He turned back to his schematic. Conversation over.

The radio burbled away in the background. '*Our socialism is the people's hall. It is socialism centred on the popular masses of the people's philosophy.*'

Min didn't say anything. Of course she didn't say anything. No one in this country said what they meant: you didn't survive for long if you did. *The birds and the mice can hear you whisper.* That's what Han Na had taught her when she was a child. That was why there was no criticism of the Supreme Leader within these four walls, just as there had been none of the Dear Leader before him and the Great Leader before him.

And once you started thinking like that, you applied it to absolutely everything: because you never knew who was listening, and you never knew what they might or might not deem inappropriate. If ever you wondered whether or not to say something, that was your answer right there. You could only think it. They hadn't found a way of breaking into your thoughts.

Yet.

Later, in bed, Min stared into the darkness and ran through the nightly catechism in her head. *Thank you, Supreme Leader, for your guidance. Thank you for our great national family. Thank you for granting us the items so many still aspire to. Thank you for the five chests: for the wardrobe, the bookshelf, the cupboard, the shoe closet and the quilt chest. Thank you for the seven appliances: for the TV, the fridge, the washing machine, the electric fan, the sewing machine, the tape recorder and the camera.*

She heard Cuckoo come into the room and settle herself into bed.

'Goodnight, dear Cuckoo,' Min said.

'Goodnight, sweet Min.'

The sheets rustled as Cuckoo tried to make herself comfortable.

'I'm dying, you know,' Cuckoo said suddenly.

'Don't say that.'

'It's true.' Cuckoo knew it with the same certainty that every living thing knows their place in the endless cycle. She knew it the way a newborn lamb knows to suckle its mother, the way a sunflower turns its face to the heat and light as they pass overhead, the way an ageing gazelle knows that the herd will run on ahead and the lion will take the hindmost. 'It's not imminent, don't worry. I'm slowing, not stopping. I'll still be here tomorrow, and next week, and next month. But this is my last winter.'

Cuckoo was no stranger to death: few people were in this country. But other people's deaths were always different from your own, no matter how they came about: young or old, peaceful or violent, expected or sudden. You could endure any number of other people's deaths, but only one of your own.

'Are you afraid?' Min said.

'Not yet.' Cuckoo knew she wouldn't die forgotten, as she had her family with and around her, but she also knew that every death is a journey that must fundamentally be taken alone, and that there'd be a real loneliness of the heart in taking that journey.

'Angry?'

'No.' Cuckoo wouldn't become angry, either, no matter how close it came. She wouldn't just be fine one moment and dead the next: the decline would be gradual, she would lose many things before she lost life itself, and this would cause her anxiety and distress whether she wanted it to or not.

She didn't know whether she'd suffer or be in pain, but then again she had known both many times over and had endured them, so the prospect didn't daunt her as much as it might have daunted someone else. She didn't know what, if anything, lay beyond death. Long ago, before the schism, she had been at least nominally a Christian, but there was no religion in this country any more and hadn't been for a very long time, since a man of flesh and blood had arrogated the divine rights of worship and flawlessness not just to himself but to his son and grandson too.

Min got out of her bed and into Cuckoo's, seeking comfort quite as much as offering it. Cuckoo laughed softly, but when Min kissed her on the cheek Cuckoo's tears were warm and wet against Min's skin.

This is how I live, Min thought, wanting to hold on to things as they were for as long as possible. This was her life. And within its own confines, and today's setbacks notwithstanding, it was pretty good.

This was her life, treading the tightrope between what she could and could not say and knowing as instinctively as breathing how to keep her balance.

This was her life, with their little unit of four where everybody slotted into their roles as snugly and uncomplainingly as jigsaw pieces.

This was her life: from home to work and back again, week in, week out.

This was her life, today as it had been yesterday and would also be tomorrow.

This was her life, safe and easy and repetitious.

This was her life in the workers' paradise, and nothing would disrupt it.

This was her life before he came.

2

The door of Moritz's office was open, so Theo went straight in without knocking. Moritz was talking in fast German on his mobile while typing furiously on a laptop. He swatted the air with one hand, a show of being busy. Theo shrugged, pointed to the open door, and stood his ground.

Moritz ended the call and sighed. 'Since you're here, I was about to ask you if—'

'I'm resigning.'

Moritz blinked twice, removed his glasses, pinched the bridge of his nose, and looked at Theo again. 'Shut the door, sit down and tell me what's up.'

Theo closed the door, sat opposite Moritz, and tried a smile. Words tumbled in his head. He waited for them to resolve themselves into some sort of order and cleared his throat. 'I've had an offer from another company and I want to take it.'

'B&M?'

'Yes.'

'Figures. They're about the only ones who could afford you.' Moritz clicked his tongue against the back of his teeth. 'That'll make it awkward tonight.'

'The awards? Yes.'

An electronic ping signalled the arrival of an e-mail on Moritz's desktop. He glanced at it and then back at Theo. 'How much are they offering?'

'That's confidential.'

'Tell me.'

'It's not about the money.'

Moritz rolled his eyes as though humouring a child. 'It's always about the money.'

'I've found my employment here extremely rewarding and fulfilling, and I really appreciate the opportunities, but they're . . .'

'. . . the market leaders and they've made you an offer you can't refuse.'

Theo looked out through the glass partition at the rest of the office. Naked brickwork ran below gunmetal beams, less a design choice than a legal requirement in riverside warehouse premises. There were elaborate models of rollercoasters everywhere he looked, either in cardboard and plaster on the large island in the centre of the room or endlessly twisting on his colleagues' screens. He saw half a dozen people hard at work, and wondered how many he'd keep in touch with once he'd gone.

What could he tell Moritz? The truth, perhaps, except he wasn't sure he even knew what the truth was himself. There was something he could hardly make out, let alone name: an itch beneath his skin which came and went, a prickling across his shoulders which intimated that where he was right now was not where he really should be.

He turned back to Moritz. 'They're the market leaders and they've made me an offer I can't refuse. But it's more about the opportunities than the money.' He didn't add 'really, it is': the phrase was always either redundant or dishonest.

Moritz steepled his fingers and regarded Theo across the top of them. Moritz was always neat, Theo thought: dressed all in black because he said it was easier that way, rimless glasses with dark-red arms, and silver hair cropped tight to his skull.

'Will you do me a favour, Theo?'

'Depends what it is.'

'It's to do with what I was about to ask you when you came in. A meeting. A meeting I'd like you to come to. I always wanted you to come to it, actually, but I was also always going to tell you at the last minute because – well, you'll see when you get there.' Theo opened his mouth: Moritz raised a hand. 'Please. I know you want to leave. You know I want to keep you. I know you have a non-compete clause in your contract. You know a first-year law student could pick that one apart. So – come to this meeting with me, and you may reconsider, and then we can talk maybe equity or partnership or something. Maybe not. But at least come. Will you do that?'

Theo thought. He'd figured Moritz would try to talk him out of leaving, of course, but he'd presumed it would be in the confines of this office. A meeting that he'd always wanted Theo to attend but had never mentioned? It sounded weird.

But intriguing, too.

'Yes,' Theo said. 'Yes, I'll do that.'

It was three days before Christmas, mild and drizzling, which meant that neither the street decorations nor the shopfront displays could make Theo feel remotely festive. Even the baby blue of Tower Bridge's suspension cables seemed dull and muted. Seagulls circled lazily on invisible helices above barges moored in low-tide mud.

'Two hundred and fifty years ago,' said Moritz, 'this place was full of pirates.'

'Still is,' Theo replied.

'Yes?'

Theo nodded towards the skyscrapers on the north side of the river. 'Sure. They just use computers rather than cutlasses these days.'

They went into Bermondsey Tube station and caught a Jubilee line train going west. Long before Theo had ever been to England, let alone London, he'd been obsessed with the Tube map: the cleanliness of its design, its stark bright colours, the way it imposed calmness and order on the chaotic reality it represented, the shapes of elephants and bottles and dolphins, which he'd found hidden in the criss-crossing of its lines. He'd been given a poster of it when he was eight or nine, and whenever he'd moved into a new bedroom that poster had been the very first thing he'd stuck on the wall, even though – especially because – it had been torn at the corners with all the times he'd had to pull it off one place and put it up somewhere else.

The train rattled and swayed through the tunnels. Theo caught a glimpse of his face reflected in the blackness of the window. He was all autumn colours: hair cascading in thick loose spirals of fire brick, eyes shaded somewhere between moss and pine, and freckles spotted across his skin in faded chestnut. He looked tired, he thought, but then again he often thought that.

Moritz was frantically tapping out an e-mail on his smartphone, even though he couldn't possibly have reception down here – or maybe he did, given that networks were putting Wi-Fi into stations now. The carriage was almost full, and Theo was pretty much the only person not staring with glazed eyes at a glowing thumb-swiped screen.

Moritz finished his e-mail, picked up a discarded copy of *Metro* and flicked through it. 'Busy Christmas?' he asked, and it was a moment before Theo realised he was talking to him.

'Oh, you know. This and that. You?'

'Back to Frankfurt. Whole family there. Brothers, sisters, cousins.'

'You all get on well?'

'Yeah, very well. Luckily. It's madness, never a chance to sit down, but I love it.'

Theo felt a pang of sharp envy in his flank.

The train slowed. Green Park. 'This is us,' Moritz said.

Theo followed him out of the carriage, trying to work out where they might be going. The Ritz? Perhaps it was a big client. But Moritz was making for the Piccadilly line.

The posh stops – Hyde Park Corner, Knightsbridge, South Kensington, the ones where wedge-shaped supercars prowled and growled and where shopgirls were as thin as the clothes rails they tended – came and went. By the time they got to Earl's Court, Theo was equal parts mystified and intrigued. The line terminated at Heathrow. They were going to pick someone up from the airport. That must be it. But if so, then why not send a cab?

Another stop, another hydraulic hissing as the doors opened. 'Acton Town', said the sign. Moritz nudged Theo, got up and left the train. Theo followed.

Acton Town?

It might as well have been a different city. The ticket hall was a monument to brutalism and the shops that lined the station arcade were past their best, if indeed they'd ever had one: a dry-cleaners, a kebab takeaway, an empty café, and a minicab office spilling bored drivers. 'It Could Be You', shrieked a Lottery sign. Not if you understood statistics it couldn't, Theo thought.

They passed unremarkable terraces where estate-agent boards sprouted like mushrooms after rain. A large road ran up ahead. Theo saw the sign. 'A406 North Circular'.

'Not long now,' Moritz said.

He turned right on to the North Circular. Traffic lights held and released cars in spurts of brake lights and billowing exhaust plumes: metal snakes of frustration and impatience, a rush hour that had over the years elongated itself into a rush day.

Theo had once attended a lecture on traffic modelling and found it fascinating, all the ways in which individual behaviour designed to increase journey speed ended up having the opposite effect on the collective. Cutting someone off just ensured that everyone went slower. Like most things, it was illogical only if you didn't understand the science behind it.

They walked for a couple of minutes. Moritz squinted into the distance and pointed towards a house on the other side of the carriageway. 'There,' he said.

It was a large but ordinary-looking house, with black gates and an empty flagpole on the paved area out front. Moritz waited for a gap in the traffic and crossed over.

The black gates slid silently open as they approached. Theo broke stride for a moment. Someone was watching them, and he wasn't sure he liked that. Moritz didn't seem bothered, but then again Moritz had some idea what was going on here.

A black Mercedes was parked next to the flagpole. A person-alised number plate: PRK 1D. They walked towards the front door, which like the gates seemed to open of its own accord. Moritz paused to usher Theo through ahead of him, and as Theo stepped across the threshold he saw the small brass sign that said 'Residence and Office. Embassy of DPR Korea'.

An embassy? *An embassy?* Most London embassies were grand Georgian mansions in Belgravia or concrete Mayfair fortresses, not suburban homes off the North Circular. And DPR Korea meant the Democratic People's Republic of Korea . . .

North Korea.

Surprise – *what the hell?* – gave way almost instantly to realisation – *so that's why you wouldn't tell me where we were going*. Moritz had known Theo would have questions: lots of questions, maybe too many. Better to present this as a fait accompli and deal with those questions later.

'Trust me,' Moritz said, as though reading his thoughts.

The door closed behind them. A middle-aged Korean man in a cheap suit was standing in front of them. 'Mr Schuster. Mr Kempe.' The Korean man pronounced the words with exaggerated deliberation, as though he had spent some time practising them.

'Ambassador Hyon,' Moritz replied. 'Thank you for seeing us.'

Hyon shook first Moritz's hand and then Theo's, bowing slightly each time.

'Please.' Hyon led them into a small room off the hall, where a simple table was set with sachets of coffee and teabags. Hyon gestured for Theo and Moritz to sit on one side of the table. He took the other side, beneath the watchful twin gaze of Kim Il Sung and Kim Jong Il set high on the wall above him. Theo saw that the portraits were set at an angle, the top edges further from the wall than at the bottom, so that the faces seemed to look down on them rather than just out at the room.

Hyon poured the coffee and tea himself, pulled a piece of paper from his jacket pocket, scanned it quickly as though reminding himself of something, and then set it down on the table and smiled at them.

'Let me get straight to the point. I have been authorised to ask you to build a rollercoaster in Pyongyang. This rollercoaster will be in a theme park named Jucheland which will showcase the incredible talents and achievements of the Democratic People's Republic of Korea under the Juche philosophy of self-reliance as brought into the hearts of the Korean people by the Great Leader. Mr Kempe, you designed the H5 rollercoaster at Europa-Park, is that right?'

'Yes, that's right.' It had been Theo's first major rollercoaster, and perhaps the one he was still most proud of, not least for the technical challenges he'd had to overcome. He'd named it H5 after hang-gliders' slang for the master level in their sport, because the coaster made its riders feel like they were flying: they lay flat on their stomachs suspended below cars which themselves hung from rails above them, and the ride contained two heartline inversions and three different loops.

Hyon smiled. 'I rode that one myself last year. It was unforgettable. That's why I recommended you for this assignment.'

Perhaps, Theo thought, he should have seen this coming, but he was still trying to get his head round the surreal nature of this whole meeting. He felt as though he was a pace or two behind the others, and it unsettled him. People did this the whole time: obfuscated, concealed. Engineering didn't, or at least it didn't do so deliberately. The solution was always there if you were smart enough to find it.

Theo had long ago learned to read upside down. It had been a useful skill when trying to glimpse his school reports while his father was going through them, and it was still a useful skill now. Below 'H5 – Europa-Park', Hyon had written six names: B&M, Intamin, Gerstlauer, Mack, Vekoma, and Zamperla. Two Swiss companies, two German, one Dutch, and an Italian: presumably the ones the North Koreans would approach if Theo turned them down.

'As you may know,' Hyon continued, 'our glorious capital contains some of the most impressive architecture in the world. The Juche Tower is taller than the Washington Monument. Our

Triumphal Arch, similarly, towers over that of Paris. What's the tallest rollercoaster in the world?'

'Kingda Ka at Six Flags Great Adventure,' Theo replied instantly. 'One hundred and thirty-nine metres.'

'This one will be taller.'

Theo and Moritz were past Hammersmith on the way back into town when Theo finally spoke.

'Why?'

'Why what?'

This was Moritz's way, sometimes, to answer a question with one of his own. Theo had long since stopped finding it annoying. 'Why North Korea?'

'Why not North Korea?'

'Because there are so many easier places to build a coaster.'

'Like where?'

'Like everywhere else.'

'That's the point! Everyone else builds everywhere else. This'll set us apart, give us a USP. You know: oh, Leuschner Piesk, they're the crazy ones who did North Korea. Europe? North America? Easy. But *this* – this makes us special.'

'What if I say no?'

'Why would you say no?'

'Because I don't want to end up in a prison camp, for starters.'

Moritz snorted. 'Don't be stupid. Why would you end up in a prison camp?'

'Why did that poor American kid end up in one?'

'Which American kid?'

'It was in the papers the other day. Not just him, either. There've been a few over the years. Arrested on some bullshit, given a show trial and carted away. There's a reason the US government warns against travel there.'

Moritz did a quick Google search on his phone and showed Theo. 'Look. That kid tried to steal a propaganda poster. And the ones before him, they were trying to bring Bibles in from China.'

'And they ended up in jail.'

'Yes. That's what life's like in places like that if you break the rules. But if you *don't* break the rules – and you won't – you'll be fine. I know several people who've gone there, and they've had no problems at all. Quite the opposite. They've been given guides, there's no street crime, they stay in the best hotels. It's like, I don't know, Dubai or something.'

'It's nothing like Dubai!'

'I mean in terms of what you can and can't do. In Dubai you can't kiss or drink in public, so while you're there just don't do that. Different restrictions in North Korea, but same principle. Find out what you're not allowed to do and don't do it. Besides, you'll be an honoured guest. You could see how much the ambassador wants you to take the job. And you'll do it so well, you know you will.'

'I'm not allowed to do it anyway.'

'Why not?'

'His list of rival companies. No Premier. No S&S. No Americans. I'm an American citizen.'

'You're also a British one. That's how we'll register you.'

'What's to stop me moving to B&M and just taking on the project once I'm there?'

'Your innate decency.' Was Moritz being sarcastic? Theo couldn't tell. 'Seriously,' Moritz continued, as though he'd sensed Theo's uncertainty. 'You *are* a decent person. You do what you say and say what you think.'

'You mean I'm tactless?'

'Sometimes. But always honest.'

'I'll consider it and let you know.'

'Come on, Theo. Think what this could be. This could be your Fallingwater, your Sydney Opera House, your Guggenheim Museum, your Reichstag dome. Listen to your heart.'

'Listening to your heart is no way to make decisions.'

'You want a new challenge? Fine! Here it is. Something maybe only you could make properly.'

Theo fancied himself immune to flattery, if only because he knew his own worth when it came to what he did. He couldn't be flattered by lies, as he would recognise them as such, and he couldn't be flattered by the truth as he knew it already.

'This could be the most extraordinary thing you've ever done,' Moritz persisted.

'Or it could be a total shitstorm.'

Moritz sucked his teeth. 'It could be. But how will you know unless you try?'

'You want me to do it for you.'

'Of course. But I also want you to do it for *you*, and that's the truth.'

London in all its diversity came swarming into the carriage when they stopped at Earl's Court: half a dozen French schoolchildren, a blinking dowager who looked mildly alarmed at the very prospect of public transport, a couple of dirt-spattered builders and a woman with green and white braids in her hair.

'I'll think about it,' Theo said.

The issue hung unspoken and heavy between them all afternoon, and it only began to dissipate once they got to the ballroom of the Grosvenor Hotel and Moritz was in his element once more: people, chatter, a party. *Theme Parks Today* magazine sponsored an annual awards ceremony, which they rather optimistically referred to as 'the Oscars of the rollercoaster industry', and this year it was London's turn to host.

Theo hated events like this as much as Moritz loved them. He watched Moritz work the room – a hug here, a shoulder clasp there, roaring laughter and a joke – and envied him his ease with people. Moritz even greeted the B&M table like long-lost brothers: no hint whatsoever that he knew or cared that they were trying to poach Theo from under his nose. Theo gave them a watery smile from a safe distance and hoped none of them would ask what the exact situation with Moritz was, not because it would make him uncomfortable but because he didn't want to be distracted while weighing up his decision.

He wouldn't even have come if he wasn't up for an award. More precisely, if he wasn't up for the biggest award of the night, Best New Ride. Even more precisely, if he wasn't trying to retain the title he'd won for the past two years (no one had ever done the hat-trick before, as far as he knew, although he'd never actually bothered to find out). And most precisely of all because it had been written into his contract: attendance at any awards ceremony where he was shortlisted was obligatory if Moritz deemed it so.

Leuschner Piesk had taken three tables, which meant the entire company workforce and their spouses or partners too. Theo, having neither, had invited Sophie, who as usual arrived half an hour after he'd told her to. There had been a time when he'd factored this in and given her start times to events half an hour earlier than they actually were, but she'd cottoned on pretty quick and soon enough they'd gone back to the previous arrangement: her late, him trying not to get too exasperated.

'Sorry, sorry,' she said as she leant in to kiss him. 'Got caught up at work. Had to do a bit of legal magic to get out of it.'

'Legal magic?'

'Left it till tomorrow.'

He laughed when he realised she was being serious.

Sophie's skin was alabaster white and her hair kobicha brown, which in some lights made the leap across to black. There was something fight-or-flight in her watchful level blue gaze, and she seemed at once very strong and very fragile.

They staggered the awards between courses, running the low-profile ones first: Best Landscaping, Best Carousel, Best Hallowe'en Event, and so on. Dessert and coffee were on the tables by the time they got to the sharp end, and now the cheers for the winners were becoming ever louder, reflecting not just the more prestigious nature of these awards – Best Dark Ride, Best Water Ride, things that involved decent amounts of both imagination and engineering – but also the fact that most of the audience knew free booze when they saw it.

Theo sipped at his wine and watched Sophie talking to Moritz. The sooner this whole thing was over the better. Everyone acted all blasé about winning, but Theo actually meant it. He genuinely couldn't have cared less. Awards were subjective comments on an objective process. If he did his job, which invariably he did, then by definition the coaster would be a success. Besides, winning meant making a speech.

'And now, last but very much not least, the one you've all been waiting for,' said the MC. 'Best. New. Ride.' Cheers sputtered from a few tables. Theo felt the shifting of bodies around him as people began to pay attention.

'This year was an exceptional year for new thrill rides,' the MC continued, 'which made the choice particularly difficult. All three of our nominees push the boundaries of current technology.' Short film clips began to play on the screen behind him. 'Valravn by Bolliger & Mabillard at Cedar Point. The world's tallest, fastest, and longest dive coaster. Riders descend down a seventy-metre ninety-degree drop before being thrown through three inversions. Mako, also by Bolliger & Mabillard, at SeaWorld Orlando. Themed to the speed of the mako shark, this features a series of huge camelback hills and an insane hammerhead U-turn, and gives riders great amounts of airtime. And Vapour Trail by Leuschner Piesk at La Ronde. Small cars allow for tighter turns, including a plus-ninety-degree dive and a heart-dropping five-hundred-and-forty-degree downward helix.'

The crowd applauded. The MC opened the golden envelope. Theo wanted to be at home reading a book, watching TV, anywhere but here. Sophie squeezed his hand.

'And the winner is . . .'

The MC held the moment long enough for the catcalls and whistles to start. Of all the garbage that talent shows had unleashed on the world, Theo thought, this was one of the worst: the artificially long pause.

'. . . Vapour Trail, designed by Theo Kempe for Leuschner Piesk!'

Fixing his expression exactly equidistant between smile and grimace, Theo led the Leuschner Piesk team up through waves of applause. The audience were giving him a standing ovation: they, the ones who actually knew what it took to succeed in this business, and him, the first person to win it three times in a row. Perhaps, he thought, he'd been a bit harsh on the whole process after all.

He climbed the steps to the stage and looked out across the room, letting his eyes focus into the middle distance so the crowd became an amorphous mass. The MC handed him the trophy, a double helix of wood and steel after the two main types of rollercoaster. Steel coasters were faster, taller and quieter; wooden ones swayed more and had a certain old-school charm: both appealed to hardcore enthusiasts.

Theo took the speech from his pocket. His hands were shaking. 'I'm very honoured and humbled. Thank you. This is the best job in the world and I love doing it.' He handed the trophy to Moritz and stepped back among his colleagues, hearing nothing of what Moritz was saying but wondering how he could get the audience to laugh as loud and applaud as long as they were doing.

When the awards were done and the band had struck up once more, people came from all over the room to congratulate Theo. The B&M guys were gracious in defeat and said he'd thoroughly deserved it. Moritz, his face a high flush of wine and excitement, said, 'Hands off my superstar', and everyone laughed a little too loudly. A couple of rollercoaster enthusiasts – 'Bob and Jen Hornung from Tulsa, Oklahoma, ridden one thousand two hundred and seventy-six coasters, all-American record' – dragged him into communal selfies and said they'd won tickets in a special magazine draw and goodness they were so honoured and he was like the Rembrandt of rollercoasters.

'The Rembrandt of rollercoasters,' Theo repeated. 'Thank you.' And even as he spoke he realised he'd had enough of tonight in every way. It wasn't just that he didn't want to be here any more: it was that he *couldn't* be here any more, he no longer had the energy for even one more minute. The problem wasn't Bob and Jen Hornung from Tulsa, Oklahoma, who seemed extremely nice and who could clearly talk rollercoasters all night long. The problem was him.

'Will you excuse me just a moment?' he said, taking Sophie's hand and walking across the ballroom.

'What's up?' she asked when they were out of earshot.

'I'm going.'

'I'll come with you.'

They found a taxi within seconds. Theo gave the cabbie Sophie's address followed by his own, and they clambered into the back.

'Thanks for coming tonight,' he said as the locks clicked shut.

'Not at all. I enjoyed it.'

'You did?'

She nodded at the trophy. 'I always enjoy seeing my friend do well.'

Theo glanced out of the window and saw a couple walking arm in arm along the pavement. They both looked to be in their fifties, and there was nothing special about them other than the way they were together: the easy manner in which their bodies shaped themselves to each other as they walked, the half-smile on his face as he leant his head against hers, the unconscious rhythms of two people with the kind of connection that the world simply disappeared around them.

He and Sophie had met on their first day at university. They'd stood next to each other in the matriculation photo, Kennedy and Kempe, and had been friends ever since: her the loud, popular one, him the nerdy introvert. One drunken night they'd made a pact to marry each other if neither of them had got hitched by the time they were forty. At the time it had seemed to Theo like a rather sweet affirmation of their friendship, but as years had passed and the deadline had begun to loom larger – only five years away now – it had begun to appear more and more as an admission of failure. *Everyone else has got on with it, we're the last two on the shelf, how about it?*

Theo worried that Sophie would take it literally, if only because deep down he felt that he should too: a pact was a pact, after all. But equally he knew that if they really wanted to be together, they would have been by now. They'd slept with each other a dozen times or so, whenever he was in the country and she was between boyfriends, and always with a sense of familiarity: comforting, unexciting, never awful, never wonderful, and never enough for him to want to build on it, which he knew said as much about him as about her and probably rather more.

'How's what's-his-face?'

'Dan?'

'Yes, him.'

'We finished last week.'

'Why?'

'He said I wanted to move things too fast.'

'Did you?'

'No. He's just anoth— just a commitment-phobe.'

'I'm sorry.'

'Liar.'

'I'm sorry if you're upset, I mean.'

'I'm not.'

And there it was, in their usual half-spoken code: the invitation.

'Stay with me,' she said abruptly.

It was midnight. Theo was sitting on the edge of her bed, pulling on his trousers. He turned and looked at her. She had never asked him that before.

'I have to go,' he said, and it sounded weak even as he said it.

'You *choose* to go.'

'That's not fair.'

'Isn't it? You never stay. You leave. You *flee*.'

'I don't.'

'You do. Why?'

A car alarm wailed in the distance.

I don't trust that your feelings are genuine. I don't want to ask you because you'll say of course they are, but there's no way of knowing that for sure, and so I'd rather just assume they aren't than risk finding it out for real.

'I don't know why.' He took her hand. She didn't pull away. 'What's this about?'

With her other hand, she dabbed at her eye. 'I don't know either.' She tried to laugh. 'Don't worry, I'm not about to declare undying love or anything. I just thought . . . that it would be nice to wake up with you for once. For you to stay, and reach for me in the morning, and maybe stay in bed a while, and talk, and hold me, and laugh with me, and have breakfast, and not always act like this is something *shameful*.'

'It's not shameful.'

'It feels that way sometimes.'

'I don't mean it to.'

'I know. But it does.'

Theo felt a lurch in his gut, as though he'd driven over a hump-back bridge at speed. He always hated these conversations, the raw laceration of his failings until he felt as flayed as a Renaissance anatomical drawing, picked apart and unravelled, a multitude of threads fluttering like prayer flags in the breeze.

'That's not fair,' he said, and the words sounded even more of a lamentable whine than they had the first time. It *was* fair. He kept himself boxed off in concentric circles of avoidance. It was fair, and he knew it full well.

'You know what I'd love to see you do, even once? Be the one who cares more. Not necessarily with me, but with anyone. Be the one who isn't so detached, who can't bear to leave things. It's not a badge of honour, to keep yourself at arm's length.'

'Of course I care.' *And I walk out because it's easier to leave than to be left.*

'You . . . You make things, places, for men and women to behave like children.'

'I do it well.'

'You do it *brilliantly*. But they're strangers. You don't know them. And yet their happiness is your reason for getting up in the morning.'

'The challenge of making something which will make them happy is my reason for getting up in the morning. If I make it well enough, they'll be happy. Their pleasure is the confirmation I've done my job. Nothing more.'

'You know what it is? Your heart pulses in five-four time. Irregular, inconsistent, asymmetric. That's what it is.'

He didn't say anything. He didn't have to. She was right, and they both knew it. He lay back and leant his head against her shoulder. She kissed his crown, the way a mother would kiss a child who had come to her bed after a bad dream.

The trophy was on the floor beside her bed. It was already engraved with this year's win: Vapour Trail. Last year had been Desperado; the year before, Challenger. He knew every inch of them, just as he knew every inch of every coaster he'd ever made, and he loved them all equally. Theo's coasters weren't just rails and girders and cars: to him they lived and breathed and laughed and cried, they were every single person who rode them because the only thing that made people feel more alive than the fear of dying was the relief when they hadn't.

The trophy caught the glow of Sophie's bedside lamp as he turned it in his hands. The double helix. Wood and steel. Life and love. Risk and reward.

'So what's next?' she said. 'No, don't wince. Not us. What's next for you?'

'My next project?'

'Yes.'

'Depends on whether I move firms or not. If I stay where I am – North Korea, perhaps.' She laughed. 'I'm being serious.' The smile retreated from her face. 'They want me to build the tallest coaster in the world.'

'What did you say?'

'I told them I'd think about it.'

'You should have told them to take a hike.'

'Why?'

'*Why?* Because North Korea has one of the worst human-rights records in the world, that's *why*. Some of the cases I've seen – Jesus, Theo, they'd turn your stomach. There's no justification for going, not unless you're providing some sort of humanitarian aid. Otherwise you're just collaborating with that awful, awful regime.'

Theo tried not to sigh too obviously, but it slipped out anyway. Once upon a time, when they'd both been younger, he'd seen her as a crusading justice warrior. She fought the fights that had to be fought in the places where they needed her most. He'd loved her ferocity and passion for the underdog. But somewhere along the line, passion had given way to hectoring. She'd get on his case whenever he'd take a job abroad. Riyadh? Have you seen the way the Saudis treat women? Beijing? Maybe read about the Uighurs before you go. Mexico City? If you want to stop cokeheads from getting better all across the US, go ahead. Tiny barbs that had become a little bigger each time.

'No, don't sigh.' There was an edge to Sophie's voice now, half-shrill and half-hardened. 'You have a responsibility.'

'Maybe projects like this are the best way to engage?'

'You must know how weak that sounds.'

'You can't know the reality of a place until you've been there.'

'The reality! They'll show you what they want to show you, nothing else.'

'If I don't do it then someone else will.'

'So let them.' She looked at him. 'You can't, can you? You couldn't bear someone else to get something like this.'

40

'You don't understand.'

'No? I'm glad I don't, then. Go. I'll save you the trouble of wondering if you're fleeing. Go. Get out. And only ring me if you choose not to take that job.'

There was a certain silence specific to Christmas Day in the city: not just an absence of people, gone to visit families strewn across the country or cooped up in flats overcrowded with distant relatives, but a slowing, a hushing, a solitary day where the frantic bustle eased and no one hurried.

He'd run first thing, as he always did: got up, drunk two cups of coffee, laced up his Asics and gone out the door. He liked to run first thing because that meant it was done and dusted for the day, and also because he loved the feeling of a city waking up to a new day, loved being out on the streets with a ragtag army of fellow vampires: street cleaners, refuse collectors, cab drivers, partygoers for whom late night had become early morning.

Today, of course, there had been none of these.

He would ring his own family at lunchtime, as he always did (the time difference with Vermont meant that any earlier risked waking them, which wasn't to say he wasn't tempted). They would go through the motions of being interested in his life, as they always did, and he would wait for them – one of them, either of them – to hold out an olive branch, as they never did. The conversation would last perhaps five minutes in all, maximum: and that would be it for another twelve months. Same time next year, no one ever said, as to give voice to the farce would be to acknowledge its existence.

Before and after that, his day yawned empty.

'Otto,' Theo said, 'what do you think I should do?'

Otto regarded him evenly through a horizontal pupil and swam to the back of the aquarium with lazy flicks of his tentacles.

'Will you answer me if I give you some food?'

Again Otto's unblinking eye from behind seaweed fronds. Theo opened the tank and dropped a jar full of shrimp and crab into the water. The jar's lid was on, but Otto had worked out how to open it weeks ago. He swam back towards Theo, catching the jar with one tentacle, unscrewing it with another, and reaching for the food inside with a third.

Theo could watch him all day. Many people found themselves freaked out by the fact that octopuses were so different from humans – they could squeeze themselves through tiny holes, grow back arms that had been cut off, taste through their skin, change colour, shapeshift, and had a mouth in their armpit – but for Theo all this was what made them so fascinating. They were genetic divergents: they were aliens.

Otto finished feeding, swam over to two halves of a coconut shell, curled up in one and pulled the other over his head.

'Otto. Talk to me.'

Theo rolled up his sleeves, lifted the lid clean off the tank – it was heavy, as it had to be, since octopuses were world-class escape artists – and put his arms into the water. He waited a few moments, and then Otto pushed the top coconut half off himself and oozed over.

'What should I do?' Theo said.

Theo in his world, bones and gravity and people: Otto in his, malleable and weightless and alone. Theo wondered what it would feel like to swap, for an hour, a day, a lifetime.

Otto's eight arms twisted and reached for Theo's two. Theo felt the suckers against his skin, tender but insistent in their slipperiness, examining and caressing him in the same movement. This was where most people would have pulled their arms away, Theo

42

knew, but he kept his right there. It was, he felt, as though Otto were trying to divine his intentions through what he could taste and feel in Theo's body: to show Theo a truth that no amount of rational questioning could ever uncover.

Sophie was with her family in Surrey. Or was it Sussex? He thought about ringing her, but that would come across as too needy: and besides, he still hadn't decided whether or not to go to North Korea. He'd told her she didn't understand, and she didn't, but he knew too that it was partly his fault for hiding too much of himself and then blaming her for not seeing him properly.

Otto pulled away, gradually unpeeling his suckers. Theo could see little red circles where they'd clamped on to his skin, scores of tiny red hickeys. Otto looked at Theo again, and in his gaze Theo saw acceptance, even approval.

Bolliger & Mabillard were the best manufacturer in the world. They'd offered Theo everything he wanted, everything he'd asked for and plenty he hadn't: salary, bonuses, equity, holiday pay, perks, the lot.

this could be your Fallingwater

Everything he'd *thought* he wanted.

your Sydney Opera House

But everything he needed?

your Guggenheim Museum, your Reichstag dome

Theo remembered a quote he'd read: something about the definition of madness being doing the same thing every time and expecting a different result.

this could be the most extraordinary thing you've ever done

He dialled Moritz with still-wet fingers, wanting to do it now – an impulse decision, heaven forbid! – before he began to second-guess his sudden certainty.

I want you to do it for you and that's the truth

'Theo!' Moritz's voice came through the phone loud and sudden, shouting to be heard above the background hubbub. Theo heard the high, delighted shrieks of children and the low rumbling of a man laughing, and for a moment he felt unexpectedly and fiercely alone. 'Merry Christmas, my man!'

'I'll do it. North Korea. I'll do it.'

'You will? Ah, man: that's the best Christmas present. Thanks. You won't regret it.'

'I hope not.'

'You won't. Listen, I have to go – it's pandemonium here – but I'm flying back tomorrow so let's talk then, yes?'

'Good,' Theo said, but Moritz was already gone. Theo dried off his arms and turned the Nespresso machine on.

This was his life, full and feted and yet still missing something.

This was his life, giving total strangers an experience they'd never forget while holding off anyone who threatened to get too close.

This was his life, and it had been touched by many people and yet also by none, not where it really counted.

This was his life, safe and secure and calibrated as closely as his coasters.

This was his life, and it would not change unless he changed it.

This was his life before he went.

3

Min was clearing up after supper when a knock came at the door, so loud and sudden that it made her jump. She glanced at the clock. It was exactly nine o'clock. People didn't knock on one's door at this hour without a good reason, and a good reason as often as not meant a bad reason.

She went over to open the door, wiping her hands dry on her trousers as she did. Three unsmiling men in the olive uniforms of the Ministry of People's Security stood in the hallway. Her stomach turned a quick involuntary flip-flap. Had she done something wrong? Had Han Na, or Chul Woo, or Cuckoo? If so, then what? You could transgress a thousand ways without even knowing that you'd done so.

'Ah,' said Han Na from behind her. 'Right on time.'

Min realised what the men were here for, and breathed a sigh of relief which she tried not to make too obvious. Every apartment block was designated an *inminban*, a people's group. Everybody had to belong to an *inminban*, and every *inminban* had a head, an *inminbanjang*. Han Na was Tower Two's *inminbanjang* – the post always went to a woman – and it was her job to keep an eye on everyone in her building.

A good *inminbanjang* – and bad ones didn't tend to last too long – knew everything about everyone. She knew what they did, how much they earned, who their family members were, who they loved and with whom they feuded, and what they possessed, down to the last spoon. She knew who the informers were, because they informed to her. She knew the relevant laws backwards and could quote them verbatim: Article 32 of Political Directive No. 944 'requires the relevant agency's approval when accommodation is provided for another person in one's own house', and Article 33 'requires anyone who detects abnormal situations including any conduct violating laws to report to the relevant agency'.

In other words, inform or risk being informed on yourself.

And every now and then – at random intervals, of course – the *inminbanjang* would team up with officers of the *Bowibu*, the State Security Bureau, and conduct raids on every apartment in the block. These raids were designed to flush out people and things that shouldn't have been there – anyone staying over without the requisite permission (citizens should be in their own beds in their own homes unless they had a good, officially mandated reason not to be), or contraband (anything from South Korea, for a start).

'Don't wait up,' Han Na said to Min as she stepped past her into the corridor. *Inminban* searches went on till the small hours: there were thirty apartments in their block, and every apartment took at least ten minutes to search, not because they were large – quite the opposite – but because all possible hiding places had to be checked. And all this had to be done by torchlight, as the *Bowibu* always cut the power before a search to prevent people from ejecting DVDs from their machines (though equally, of course, it would almost certainly have gone off sooner rather than later anyway; and in any case, most people watching contraband videos did it with a USB stick these days).

Han Na led the three *Bowibu* men away. One of them, the youngest, turned to look at Min as he left. His face was extraordinary, she thought: a tangle of shifting lines and planes, of crevasses and creases. Cheekbones like raised daggers, sad eyes of slate grey, a bent nail of a nose and skin like rawhide over the peninsula of his chin. When he smiled at her, horizontal lines like cat's whiskers bloomed and faded across his cheeks.

Min arrived at work twenty minutes early, but even so Yun Seok was already there. He was always there, or so it seemed. He knew the ropes better than she did. Never be late, never be off sick, never be complacent, never give anyone a chance to block your promotion or ease you backwards, even – especially – after you'd been censured, because when you were down was when they would force you down still further. He knew the old proverb – the absent one is always wrong – and he knew its essential truth too. It was no coincidence that the Korean word for 'place of work', *juntoojang*, was also the word for 'battlefield'. They were all serving the state, but everyone was also out for themselves. And why wouldn't they be? Who wouldn't want to do their bit for the motherland any way they could?

If she had expected Yun Seok to be there, she hadn't expected Chul Woo, her own father, to be there too. Chul Woo ushered them into an empty office and closed the door behind him.

'I understand that you have both forfeited your next three European tours.'

Min had no idea how Chul Woo knew this – she certainly hadn't told him – but life in Pyongyang was all about connections, and he had as many as anyone.

'However, I have been authorised to offer you an assignment which does not contravene that stipulation. This is an assignment which has been arranged and funded by the SAC.'

The briefest expressions of surprise floated across both Min and Yun Seok's faces before they rearranged them back into the necessary blankness. The SAC was the State Affairs Commission, and its reach went right to the top.

'There will be no financial advantage from this trip to either of you. But it was deemed – that is, I made a strong contention with which all the involved parties agreed – that your experiences with the wayward photographers last week would make you extra vigilant on an assignment like this, and that you were therefore the ideal pairing to be entrusted with it.'

In other words: *I've put my neck out for you, so don't screw this up.*

Min knew that this was a test not just of her and Yun Seok as a pairing but as individuals too. Guides worked in pairs to keep an eye on each other as much as the visitors. It was imperative that they would not be manipulated or compromised by foreigners and their wily tricks. Even though she was very much Yun Seok's junior, she was still required to fill in a form appraising his performance every month. He would certainly have been doing the same about her, and probably much more besides.

'An American is coming to design a rollercoaster for Jucheland,' Chul Woo continued. 'You will look after him for as long as he's here, and for all that time you can consider yourselves seconded to the SAC. Since he's travelling and working alone, you won't be obliged to stay in the same hotel as he does, as you are with your normal tour groups. You'll be able to stay at home as usual. Needless to say, you must give him the best view of our great country and take good care of him, but always remember this: he is an

American. And what do the Americans do in the southern zone of our great nation?'

'They kill our brothers with tanks and spear our sisters with bayonets,' said Min and Yun Seok in perfect synchronicity. As with her confession the previous month, Min made sure to pitch this at just the right tone: loud enough to be vehement, not so loud as to embarrass someone performing it with noticeably less zeal.

'What else?'

'The Yankee imperialists brand their prisoners with hot irons, set wild dogs on women, and wrench out children's teeth with pliers. They began the war and begat the tragedy by which our nation was divided in two and our people have had to endure the pain of living divided.'

'When should you trust an American?'

'Never!'

Chul Woo smiled and looked at his watch. 'His flight lands in half an hour.'

Theo should have been in Pyongyang just after breakfast. It was only an hour and a half's flight from Beijing, where he had overnighted, but the delays had grown like crazy: an hour, then another hour, then two more, then three more, and finally another hour just for luck, so it was eight hours later than scheduled that the plane actually took off. For Theo, that had meant eight hours of irritation, discomfort, and the mild panic he felt whenever things didn't happen the way they were supposed to.

The clerk at the Air Koryo desk in Beijing blamed the airport ground staff, though every other flight seemed to be leaving on time. The pilot's intercom briefing was conducted entirely in Korean, so he could have been discussing K-pop for all Theo knew, and when he asked the stewardess why they were so late she gave him a synchronised swimmer's smile and a Trappist monk's silence.

Air Koryo handed out the *Korea* pictorial magazine, the *Pyongyang Times* in English and *Rodong Sinmun* in Korean. The first two at least helped Theo not just to identify the girl band playing loudly on the overhead monitors as Moranbong Band, but also to discover that they were the local equivalent of Little Mix. Moranbong were playing to what seemed the world's worst audience: thousands of expressionless soldiers in identical uniforms, all sitting ramrod-straight and still. Only when an outsize image of Kim Jong Un appeared on the giant screen behind the band did the audience leap to their feet and applaud, and only when it vanished did they stop clapping. They even applauded in unison, Theo saw, as though their hands and arms were pistons and valves all working in perfect precision.

The video faded into a brief snowstorm of static before beginning again. Theo watched, almost hypnotised despite himself: one of the singers' mouths contorting itself into shapes, the keyboardist's fingers dancing across black and white keys, the blur of drumsticks and guitar strings, the blank soldier faces, the applause, blank faces again. Four minutes, snowstorm, repeat. Tape loop.

Only when he swallowed and heard the noise of the engines suddenly louder in his ear did he realise they were descending. He looked out of the window. They were over what looked to be a small town, probably a satellite settlement outside Pyongyang. Open land gave way to housing blocks in pale pastels, the delineation between the two as straight and marked as though done by ruler. There were almost no cars on the roads.

When Theo craned his neck, however, he saw the lazy meandering of a river, and a flame-topped obelisk, and sun shards shattering on the glass front of an enormous pyramid, and he realised with a start that this was it, this was Pyongyang. No urban sprawl, no gridlock snakes flashing angry red brake lights.

They should have had a sign at Beijing departures, he thought. *Please put your watch forward one hour and back sixty years.* The plane landed with a feather-light bump and taxied to the stand. It was the only aircraft on the apron. To one side was the terminal building, as shiny and new as if it had just been pulled from its packaging. Everywhere else was a vast expanse of tarmac and snow bound by barbed wire.

Theo had a sudden urge to turn back and demand to stay on this plane until it returned to Beijing. This was too strange, too far outside his comfort zone. Maybe he shouldn't have rung Moritz so impulsively on Christmas Day. Maybe he should have listened to Sophie.

A posse of Chinese businessmen were bumping him in the back to make him exit the plane, and almost before he knew it he was walking with everyone else along the airbridge into the terminal building. It was as though he was seeing the world through a skein of gauze. His body still thought it was the middle of the night. He felt adrift, cut free without sight of harbour. He liked parameters, a horizon line, anchor points: oriented here, tethered there, triangulated. He had none of them.

He was still some way from the passport control booth when a uniformed man approached him. 'Mr Theo Kempe?'

'That's right.'

'This way. Please.' The man gave him a smile in which metal teeth and enamel ones ran approximately fifty-fifty. Theo followed him down a corridor which smelt of disinfectant and into a windowless room. His suitcase was already there, lying open and empty on the floor with its contents arranged on a table: neatly arranged, Theo noticed, in fact so much so that he could practically have photographed it for one of those what-to-take-when-you-go-on-holiday

51

shots. It was an unnervingly impressive neatness, especially given the speed with which they'd have had to get his suitcase off, opened and sorted: and in an obscure way it pleased him, to see his own neatness replicated here. Of all the places to find a kindred spirit . . .

'Any weapon ammunition explosives killing device?' the man asked.

'No.'

'Drug exciter narcotics poison?'

'No.'

'Handphone cellphone other communication means?'

'I have an iPhone and a MacBook.'

'Show me, please.'

Theo fished them out of his bag and passed them over. The man wrote down the serial numbers of both devices in what looked like a school exercise book before handing them back.

'Publishings of all kinds?'

'Yes.'

'Please.'

Theo had bought a couple of English-language paperbacks at Beijing airport. He took them out of his hand luggage and handed them over. The man flicked through them and handed them back. Apparently satisfied, he began to repack Theo's suitcase for him. When Theo stepped forward to help, the man waved him away. He packed fast and neat, with a valet's instinctive eye for best use of space. Then he stamped Theo's passport and, still carrying Theo's suitcase for him, led Theo through the customs area, into the arrivals hall and over to a middle-aged man and a young woman in dark-green uniforms with red epaulettes and collar flashes. They were both wearing hats with a red star on the front.

They stepped forward and bowed in perfect unison.

'Welcome to the glorious capital of the Democratic People's Republic of Korea,' said the man, handing him a bouquet of flowers. 'I am Yun Seok. We will be your guides during your stay.'

Theo didn't know whether he should bow back to Yun Seok. He sort of half-leant forward while shaking Yun Seok's hand. The man who had checked Theo's baggage handed his passport to Yun Seok. Yun Seok tucked it into the inside pocket of his jacket and gestured to the young woman. 'This is Min Ji.'

She gave him a smile that didn't reach anywhere near her eyes, and also handed him a bouquet.

'Welcome to Pyongyang,' she said.

There was a driver, Nam Il, who wore outsize glasses and spoke no English. Not much Korean either, Theo thought, if his taciturnity was anything to go by. Yun Seok rode shotgun, with Min alongside Theo in the back.

Precious few vehicles on the highway meant that the ride into town was quick. To Theo, Asian cities were either sleek anime-tinted metropolises jagged with neon and tech or chaotic clamorous dirt bowls swarming with mopeds and street traders, but either way they flashed images of colour and energy as fast as he could process them. Not here. Traffic was light. Uniformed women stood inside painted white circles at intersections and waved candy cane-striped batons at any car that came past: as much, Theo thought, from joy at finally having something to do than any great necessity to control traffic. There were bicycles – in this cold! – buses and trams, but relatively few private cars, and the ones Theo saw were mainly shapeless Chinese saloons. Nor were there any advertising hoardings: only the propaganda posters flashing reds, yellows, and blues behind their bellowed messages of pride and glory, lantern-jawed soldiers and farm workers wielding bayonets and scythes with equal intent.

Min swivelled slightly to face Theo. 'Where in America are you from?'

Such a normal question, and yet for Theo such an unanswerable one. He'd grown up a military brat, shunted from base to base whenever his father had changed jobs. They'd moved twenty-five times in eighteen years.

Where was Theo from?

Lakenheath in the flatlands of East Anglia, where his father had been posted as an air-force mechanic and where he'd not just met a local girl but also persuaded her to follow him from pillar to post? Altus, Oklahoma, where Theo had been born? Kirtland, New Mexico, the only place in his childhood where he'd spent more than a year? Offutt, Nebraska, where he'd had the most fun? Durham's ancient cathedral and the northern English winters, where he'd gone reluctantly to university, because having a British mother made it cheaper, and found that despite himself he'd loved it? All of those, none of those, or perhaps the interstates on which every summer he'd travelled squashed in the back of his parents' station wagon on the way to a new place, a new home, a new school?

It was his father's career that had taken them all round the country, the names of the air-force bases like placeholders on a map of Theo's past, waypoints on a treasure hunt where the gold remained out of reach until the end of time. Schriever, Malmstrom, Ellsworth, Barksdale, Tyndall, Goodfellow. Snowbound Montana winters and swampy Louisiana summers, freshening Colorado springtimes and crisp Dakota autumns, but deep down always the same place, where everything and everyone stopped at five o'clock on the nose to listen to the national anthem, where wives and children were segregated according to the ranks of their husbands and fathers, where some of those same husbands and fathers beat those same wives and children behind closed doors and no one said anything, where post was checked and phone calls listened to, where anything and everything was subject to rules and regulations.

Where was he from? Everywhere and nowhere, that was where.

'I moved around a lot as a kid,' Theo said. 'My dad was in the air force.'

A small walnut of muscle appeared beneath the skin of Min's cheek. Yun Seok, turning in his seat, shot Min a warning look. Min swallowed, nodded, and smiled at Theo.

'Is there a problem?' Theo said.

'No.' Yun Seok's expression was that of a sphinx. 'No problem.'

'There is a problem. I saw her face. She didn't look happy.'

'I assure you, Mr Kempe, there's no problem.'

The tyres thrummed on the highway. Theo realised that they would stonewall him until he gave up. He shrugged and looked out of the window. They were passing a building the size of a super-tanker, an entire city block of monolithic grey brutalism. Theo had seen similar in windswept former Soviet cities: architecture as war, the total sublimation of individual to state. But the building's roof was a cascade of Korean toppings, lozenges and diamonds and pyramids stacked and spilling like children's toys. It was a strange mix, and he wasn't sure whether it worked aesthetically, but he noted it all the same: one day he might use it in some design or other, either directly or as an abstract through several layers of change. He was a magpie, as all designers were. Hadn't the architect behind the Sydney Opera House been inspired by sails? Or was it shells?

'National in form, socialist in content,' Yun Seok said.

'And inconsistent in design.'

Theo could, he knew, have made approving noises. That was what his brother would have done. It was military-brat survival strategy 101, learned almost by osmosis: don't be awkward, get people to like you, don't fight the new environment, work out what they like to hear and tell them that. How do I get accepted? How should I be? What do you want me to be? It had worked for Neale over and over again because he had made it work, but Theo had always refused. It's fake, he'd said. There's no point being fake just to get people to like you. Well, Neale had replied, since no one likes you anyway, it's not a problem you need to worry about.

'Your hotel!' Min exclaimed suddenly. 'Yanggakdo International!'

She was pointing to a dour rectangular tower rising from an island in the river up ahead, though her tone suggested that the Hanging Gardens of Babylon had materialised in front of them.

'One thousand bedrooms,' Yun Seok added proudly. 'Eighty-seven thousand, eight hundred and seventy square metres total floor space.'

'We will be with you all times you are not in the hotel,' Min said.

'When you are in the hotel, you stay there until we arrive,' Yun Seok added.

'I can't just walk around?'

'No.'

'What about running?'

'Absolutely not.'

'Why not?'

'For your safety.'

'Is Pyongyang a dangerous city?'

'Not at all,' Min said. 'There is no crime here. We work to a socialist ideal.'

'If there's no crime, then why do I need to worry about my safety?'

Min looked at Yun Seok. Yun Seok looked at Min.

'It is better that way,' Yun Seok said.

The car turned right, and the Yanggakdo slid out of sight.

'Aren't we going there now?' Theo said.

'Very important visit first.'

We will be with you all times you are not in the hotel. When you are in the hotel, you stay there until we arrive. In other words, round-the-clock surveillance, not just the assigned guides he'd imagined: and Theo couldn't stand that, not for any longer than a few days, certainly not for as long as it would take to design a rollercoaster. He liked being on his own and doing what he wanted when he wanted, not having to second-guess an army of watchers.

He liked to run, *needed* to run, especially when he spent so much time cooped up in a small office in front of a computer, feeling scrunched and stale and antsy. Leaden skies hiding the sun as though through spite, rain falling without rest or imagination, twilight before teatime: all these pushed down on his soul like a blanket, and the best way through them was to get out there, finding the rhythm where footsteps and breathing were perfectly matched, where the frustrations and toxins came out with the sweat. A shaking out, an uncoiling. Being deprived of that . . . even the thought of it sat low like a stone in his stomach.

'Very important visit where?' he said.

'You will see.'

'Why not tell me now?'

'You will see.'

Jet lag, fatigue, apprehension: Theo didn't know whether it was any, all or none of these, but he felt a snap within him just the same.

'Can you turn the car around?' he said. 'I've changed my mind. I want to leave.'

'We will soon be at the important visit.'

'Did you hear me? I want to leave. I want to leave the country. Please take me back to the airport.'

Again Yun Seok and Min exchanged glances. 'We are not allowed to take you back to the airport,' Min said.

'Then find someone who will allow it.'

'That will take some time.'

'Fine.'

'So in the meantime we should make this visit and go to your hotel.'

She'd outmanoeuvred him, and the little smirk she gave showed that she knew it.

Nam Il, who'd seemed to pay no heed whatsoever to the argument, pulled over and parked the car. Theo saw two enormous bronze statues, so kitsch that despite himself he had to stifle a sudden urge to laugh.

'The Grand Monument on Mansu Hill.' Min's voice sounded reverent. 'Eternal President Kim Il Sung and Eternal General Secretary Kim Jong Il.'

Of course. The first two generations of the world's only communist dynasty.

'OK,' Theo said.

Min, Yun Seok and Theo got out and walked towards the statues. Kim Il Sung was the one on the left: soft-faced, curiously effeminate and sexless, almost androgynous. He was dressed in a suit and overcoat and was smiling with one arm outstretched, a gesture that seemed to Theo halfway between hailing a cab and giving a Nazi salute. Kim Jong Il was wearing a parka over a two-piece jumpsuit, which gave him the look of an Elvis impersonator seeking shelter from a rainstorm.

'The Eternal General Secretary's parka coat is a symbol of revolution and a witness to history,' Yun Seok said.

There was a crowd in front of the statues: men and women in black and white, rapt in silent communal devotion but also somehow detached from one another, like figures in a Lowry painting.

Theo, Yun Seok and Min climbed the steps to the plinth. Beyond the statues, Theo could see straight down a long, clear axis that arrowed all the way across the river to another monument: a hammer, a sickle and a calligraphy brush raised high in three clenched stone fists. The whole place felt less like a city than a stage set, everything designed and choreographed to the millimetre for maximum visual impact: less like somewhere to live and work than a mindset, a manifestation, father and son ubiquitous and omnipotent. Paintings. Stage sets. Did anyone actually live here? Theo had a sudden fanciful idea that the crowd, the traffic ladies, even Min and Yun Seok and Nam Il themselves were all actors, and at the end of the day they'd all sit round over a drink and laugh at how they'd hoodwinked the stupid foreigner.

It was only up close that Theo could get a real sense of the statues' size. They must, he thought, have been about—

'Twenty-three metres high,' Min said.

'Come,' Yun Seok said. 'You must pay your respects.'

Theo stiffened. He'd had a gutful of paying his respects as a child: at five o'clock each afternoon on every base he'd ever lived, he'd had to stop whatever he was doing, face the Stars and Stripes fluttering high over the buildings and bow his head as the 'Last Post' was played. Respect had to be earned, he thought, not simply assumed.

He was just about to tell Yun Seok, politely but firmly, what he could do with his respects when he felt a hand on each elbow, surprisingly strong against his resistance, and before he could stop them Min and Yun Seok were bowing and taking him with them as they did so.

Min gave him a *there-that-wasn't-so-hard* look as they straightened again. Then she and Yun Seok produced flowers from nowhere as though they'd been taking lessons from Penn and Teller – the very same flowers, he realised, they'd handed him at the airport

– and as a threesome they laid one of the bouquets at the Great Leader's bronzed feet and the other at his son's.

They went back to the car.

'Now we go to the hotel,' Yun Seok said.

'You liked the monument?' Min asked.

'Very much.'

'The craftsmen who worked on it were radiant with the glory of their task. The image of these great ones and of the current Supreme Leader must never be defiled. If you have a newspaper with their picture, you must not fold the paper across the picture, you must not sit on the paper, you must not crumple the paper. Also, you must not make any negative comments about any of these leaders nor joke about them at all at any time. Do you understand?'

'Yes. I understand.'

'Do you have any questions?'

'About what?'

'About anything.'

Theo said the first thing that popped into his head. 'How much do the statues weigh?'

'Why do you want to know?' Min sounded as though she thought he was enquiring about some top-secret detail of the country's nuclear programme.

'Measurements are always of interest to me.' They were more than that, he thought: they were his vocabulary. Height, length, velocity, acceleration, G-force and airtime: he could no more do his job without these than a chef could cook without ingredients or a chauffeur drive without a car.

'I'll find the answer and let you know as soon as possible,' Min said.

'As soon as possible,' Yun Seok emphasised.

The fruits of last night's *Bowibu* inspection were laid out neatly on Han Na's kitchen table. Not the contraband itself, of course – no stacks of illicit DVDs, banned books or South Korean chocolate bars – but the money from the bribes taken for not confiscating them. Han Na had her share, just as the *Bowibu* members would have theirs. As for the punishments handed out to those who couldn't pay, well, that wasn't the *inminbanjang*'s problem. That was decided by the *Bowibu* and the courts, though the two were effectively the same. Sometimes people received community orders, though since everyone was supposed to work for the community at all times it was hard to see how these could be classed as punishment.

On rare occasions, people – usually repeat offenders – just vanished. Gone to the mountains, that was what it was called: when someone just disappeared one day and was never seen again. No warning, no explanation, no trace. Gone to the mountains. When Min had been younger she'd thought this kind of thing romantic, even heroic: someone renouncing life in the city to go and live as a hermit in the high peaks, far from civilisation. Only when a classmate had told her, aged fifteen, what the phrase really meant had she discovered the truth, and even then she hadn't truly believed it until she'd asked Cuckoo.

Chul Woo, being a film director, was allowed to see films and shows not available to the general public. He had a pile of DVDs on the table, and Min glanced at the topmost one. Five people smiled up at her from the cover: a young woman in a short tartan skirt and four young men in jackets and ties. Min didn't need to read the title to know what it was: *Boys Over Flowers*, about a poor but headstrong girl called Jan-di who'd won a scholarship to an academy where she had to choose between four rich, handsome students.

It was insanely popular in the South, and therefore totally banned in the North. She'd never seen it, but she'd heard so much about it from her friends, most of whom hadn't seen it either. The few who had, however, were obsessed, and the others absorbed the details as though by osmosis. Of course, the ones who claimed to have seen it might have been lying, and if questioned by the authorities would have certainly admitted to lying, whether those lies were true or not, in order to save their own skin. So for all Min knew nobody might have seen it, or everybody, or an indeterminate number in between.

Min heard the door opening and instinctively put the DVD back on its pile.

'Hi,' said her mother, shedding hat and gloves as she came across the room. 'How was your day? What's the American like?'

What was the American like? Min thought. He'd seemed like something come from the forest, hair and eyes coloured by nature. An insolent face, superior and slightly serpentine. His father had been in the air force: the same air force Cuckoo had told her about, all those American bombers that had flattened not just Pyongyang but every other city in the country. A million people killed, in Hoeryong and Huichon, Kanggye and Kointong, Sakchu and Sinuichu, and everywhere else besides: death from the skies, day after day after day, as though they would not stop until there was no one left to kill. He'd worn a copper bracelet on his right wrist – men didn't, *shouldn't* wear jewellery – and he'd smelt of toothpaste. He'd demanded to be taken back to the airport. And he'd asked her how much the statues weighed. How should she know how much the statues weighed? More to the point, who could she ask without revealing that she didn't know, just in case she was supposed to have known all along?

She'd disliked him on sight, and not just because she'd been waiting eight hours. She'd seen that Yun Seok had disliked him too. But she'd found it easy to be polite while nurturing her dislike: that kind of Janus face was second nature to all those who lived in this country. What you did was not what you said: what you said was not what you thought. So she'd given an insincere smile and welcomed him to Pyongyang anyway.

She shrugged. 'Tall. Asks stupid questions. Behaves like an idiot.'

Han Na nodded sagely, as though she expected nothing else of Americans. Min felt momentarily deflated that her mother didn't ask why Theo's questions had been stupid or his behaviour idiotic: Min would have enjoyed the retelling of them.

'Well, make sure you're back from him in good time on Sunday,' Han Na said.

'Why?'

'There's a young man coming round.'

It was parents' responsibility to arrange marriages and decide who would make a good match for their offspring. Han Na and Chul Woo had introduced Min to perhaps half a dozen young men since she graduated 'plenty of women your age have been married two or three years already by now' – but none of the meetings had been quite right, and a couple had been downright excruciating. Min still shuddered at the memory of an engineer with bottle-top glasses and a terrible stammer who'd never looked her in the eye and had taken half the afternoon to get a sentence out, and the stand-up family row that had followed when Cuckoo had suggested they choose a candidate who was at least halfway plausible rather than one who was so clearly wasting everyone's time.

'Who's this one?'

'This one, as you so dismissively call him, was here last night.' It took Min a moment or two to remember: the young *Bowibu* agent with grey eyes and a tangled face. 'His name is Hyuk Jae. You'll like him.'

Those last three words sounded to Min more like a threat than a prediction.

Sleep usually came easily to Min, but not tonight. The water supply was off, so she'd had to wash in cold water from the bath, which she'd filled that morning as a precaution, and when Cuckoo had heard her tossing and turning in the darkness, she'd said, 'You know what? When you can't sleep, it's because someone's thinking of you.'

Now Cuckoo's sleep was measured in the rise and fall of her breathing. Min gave up the struggle, got out of bed, and padded through into the living room. The fridge hummed. The power was still on, rather surprisingly. Perhaps the electricity system had finally been upgraded. The state had been promising it long enough.

A shaft of moonlight slanted across the pile of DVDs. Min hesitated before taking the top one, putting it in the machine and turning on the TV. She kept the volume so low that she had to sit close to the screen to hear, but she didn't want to wake anyone: particularly her mother, who would lecture her on the immorality of watching illegal programmes, her father's privilege be damned.

Pressed almost up against the screen, Min felt she could practically step across into the world of Jan-di and her four suitors. It was Seoul at night, and Jan-di and one of the four (Min didn't really care which one) were down by a bridge. They were just sitting on the grass, and suddenly the bridge started squirting jets of water through multi-coloured lights so they looked like falling rainbows.

This moonlight rainbow fountain was the most beautiful thing Min had ever seen. There was music, too, but she didn't dare turn the set up any louder than it was. She backed the DVD up a little and watched the bridge squirting rainbow jets for a second time. And a third, and a fourth, and a fifth: colours dancing across the screen, prisms of light caught and shimmering between falling droplets, reds and yellows and greens and purples so vibrant they practically pulsed.

When Min finally went back to bed, she stared into the darkness and dreamed about that bridge.

4

The alarm filtered gradually into Theo's senses: a two-tone siren which seemed to come from every direction at once. He woke at first slowly and then all at once, his stomach lurching, and tried to work out where it was actually sounding. It was both loud and distant, and he realised that wherever it originated, it wasn't in his room.

He got out of bed and looked out of the window, tilting his head this way and that. It was coming from both left and right, front and back, and he realised that the sound was city wide, piped through speakers on street corners. An air-raid siren, except how could there be an air raid? There'd been nothing in the media about increased tensions or the usual sabre-rattling which seemed to surface now and then in this place.

The sirens stopped and in their place came loud music, martial and interlaced with a man shouting what were surely propaganda slogans. It wasn't an attack warning, Theo realised: it was the city's communal alarm clock.

This place. This crazy place.

Time to get up.

'What about my return flight?' he asked in the car.

'We are seeking guidance on that issue,' Min said.

'You mean you haven't done anything about it yet.'

'Please, Mr Kempe. At least come and see the site first.'

Taesongsan had seen better days, to say the least. The existing rollercoaster track, filthy and patched with rust, looked down almost apologetically on to a shattered carousel. A plastic horse lay on its side, the colours of its bridle fading to dirty white. Weeds forced their way through the cracks beneath the dodgem cars.

There were few sights sadder than abandoned fairgrounds, Theo thought. They'd been built with love and care, and that's how they should have been maintained too. If he listened carefully, perhaps he could still hear the laughter and the delighted screams, echoes held in the broken-down site. And where there had been those once there could surely be again one day. In spite of himself, almost, Theo felt a familiar quickening: a challenge, there to be risen to.

'This is Chul Woo,' Min said. 'He is the park's director.' She hesitated a moment. 'He is also my father.'

Chul Woo gave Theo a handshake so perfunctory as to be borderline rude and rattled off something in Korean.

'The rollercoaster man,' Min translated. 'He is pleased to meet you and looks forward to helping you realise your design according to the wider requirements of the park. There are many aspects to this park, and they must all be accorded their proper place in the hierarchy.'

'Ask him if he's worried that the rollercoaster will dominate the park.'

'I cannot ask him that.'

'No. You *won't* ask him that. Tell him I've had this before, park designers trying to marginalise me. I know what I've been tasked with, and I know what I need to achieve that. I'm happy to work with him in a genuine spirit of mutual cooperation, but if he thinks he can sideline me he has another thought coming. Tell him that.'

'If he agrees, will you stay? No more return flights?'

'Tell him that.'

Once again she'd outmanoeuvred him. She nodded, apparently satisfied, and turned back to her father. They spoke for half a minute, perhaps, fast and over the top of each other, and eventually Min said, 'He agrees.'

'He said a lot more than that.'

'He said he agrees.' She held his gaze, challenging him to find her even more infuriating than he already did: and when Theo looked away first he felt as though he'd suffered some obscure form of defeat in a game whose rules he didn't even know.

Chul Woo brought out the plans for the new park, to be built on the ashes of this one. There would be three main sections, named after the Three Revolutions: technology, culture and ideology. Each of these three sections was itself to be subdivided into three zones, the exact details of which were still being worked out. At the centre point where all nine zones met would be a revolving statue of all three Kims: the Great Leader, the Dear Leader, and the Supreme Leader.

'Jucheland,' said Chul Woo emphatically, as though daring Theo to disagree.

Min translated for Theo as Chul Woo continued to speak. 'We're going to tear this place down and start all over again. Fifty acres of blank slate. It's going to be the best theme park in the world. It will be a monument to the guiding principles of self-reliance which make the Democratic People's Republic of Korea the greatest nation in the world. We must give our all in the struggle to unify the entire society with the revolutionary ideology of the Great Leader, Comrade Kim Il Sung. We must honour the Great Leader, Comrade Kim Il Sung, with all our loyalty. We must make absolute the authority of the Great Leader, Comrade Kim Il Sung.'

Theo knew that other people seeing these plans would have laughed at how kitsch and overblown they were, at least to Western eyes. He didn't care. For a start, all theme parks were overblown in one way or another: that was the whole point of them. Besides, he was looking at the schematics from an engineer's point of view: seeing the paths between zones, the efficacy of the central hub, the possibility of rides and shows on the perimeter to attract guests, shops near the exit to catch the punters before they left, watch out for pedestrian bottlenecks over there, and so on. These weren't his specific areas of expertise, but over the years he'd picked up and absorbed enough to know at least the basics. He'd bombarded park designers with questions and they'd almost always been happy to answer: they were all obsessives, just as he was, and they could talk theme parks all night and most of the next morning too.

Most of all, of course, Theo was looking where and how he could route the rollercoaster. A coaster as tall as the one they wanted needed a lot of track, not just vertically but horizontally too. Tall coasters meant long drops. Long drops meant high speed. High speed could only be scrubbed off by time and distance.

Theo looked at the plans, and then round at the dilapidated funfair, imagining not what it was now but what it could and would be when it was finished. He couldn't yet see how the coaster would look, but that didn't worry him. Designs tended to come to him in pieces – an incline loop, a sidewinder, a wingover – rather than all at once, as though he were less a painter conjuring a picture from nothing than a restorer gradually uncovering what had been there all along. Some of the best coasters he'd made had taken a long time to formulate themselves in his mind. The ones that came easily never turned out to be that special.

'I can work with this,' Theo said.

Min translated. Chul Woo smiled and said something which Min translated back. 'Good. And the timetable is no problem for you?'

'No one's mentioned a timetable.'

Again the brief conferring as Min switched between languages. 'September the ninth.'

Theo laughed. 'It doesn't take nine months to design a roller-coaster! I'll have a couple of options sketched out in the next few weeks.'

Chul Woo shook his head when he heard Min's translation.

'No,' she said to Theo. 'September the ninth is when the whole park opens.'

Theo thought all weekend before coming to a conclusion. He rang Moritz and, getting no answer, left a voicemail message. He looked out of the window at the vast pyramid that rose high above every other building across the other side of the river. It brooded over the skyline like . . . well, Theo knew enough Orwell to remember the four ministries shaped just like this building. The Ministry of Love, which enforced its writ through fear, the Ministry of Peace, which waged endless war, the Ministry of Plenty, which rationed everything, the Ministry of Truth, which did nothing but lie. Miniluv, Minipax, Miniplenty, Minitrue. War and peace. Freedom and slavery. Ignorance and strength.

Theo looked at the pyramid for long minutes, as he did every day. No one went in, no one came out. He had never seen anyone do either. There were no lights on inside, not that he could see. A building that enormous, and totally empty? It seemed that way. But how could that be possible, even in a place like this? The glass panels on the outside looked new enough. It wasn't derelict. And when he'd seen the pyramid at night it seemed blacker even than the other buildings against the indigo skyline, as though it were sucking the very darkness into itself.

That darkness fell fast in Pyongyang, and faster still without the transition into twinkling streetlights at the end of every city day. It was like night falling on the African savannah: absent one moment, present the next. No lemon oblongs of light at office windows, no advertising hoardings in rippling neon, hardly even the twin cones of car headlights. A cityscape suddenly swathed in black, a darkness studded only by a single glow: the flame atop the Juche Tower, edifice to the nation's creed of self-reliance.

With darkness came silence. A couple of men walked past at least a hundred yards away on the other side of the river. Theo heard them talking as clearly as if he'd been standing next to them. The streets could hum during the morning and evening rush hours, but outside of those Pyongyang felt to him like a ghost town. No traffic, no people, no sirens, no music. It was as though the city had been switched off. The only place still working, or so it seemed, was this hotel.

Hunger knocked. It was early for dinner, but he hadn't eaten since breakfast: just sat there, turning things over in his head. He left his room, walked down the corridor and pressed the button to call the lift. The doors opened immediately and he stepped forward—

—only to realise just in time that there was no lift there!

Theo was on the edge, lurching in his stomach as he wind-milled his arms to stop himself from overbalancing and going straight down the shaft. He grabbed hold of the doorframe and pushed himself back away from the edge, catching a glimpse of the top of the lift cabin a couple of hundred feet below. Certain death. Welcome to Pyongyang. Sorry about the splat.

He sagged against the wall, his breath coming in quick shallow pants. Even as he did so, he realised that a small, dispassionate corner of his mind was interested in the physical manifestations of this state of shock.

The lift doors slid shut again as though nothing had happened.

Theo pushed himself upright on badly shaking legs, took one of the armchairs from the corridor and dragged it in front of the doors. It wasn't much of a barrier, but it was better than nothing. When he finished he slumped in the chair until his heart rate was down from gallop to canter.

Theo figured he should report it. He went back to his room, tensing his legs with each stride until the shaking began to diminish, and dialled reception. No answer. He hung up and tried again. Still no answer. He slammed the receiver down and yelled. 'Dammit! Your lift tries to kill me and you don't even pick up the phone!'

He took the stairs all the way down to reception: or rather, to what he thought was reception. He must have counted a floor or two short, for the one on which he found himself had some corridors blocked with large stretches of carpet stacked in rolls, and others where toilets and lamps were lined up like sentries. Unhinged doors leant against each other: exposed wires poked blindly from the walls. They were clearly doing some serious renovations here. Theo went back the way he'd come, and three flights of stairs later he came out at reception as he'd intended.

There was a bar next to the lobby on the ground floor. The barman was wiping glasses with a cloth, even though the glasses were perfectly clean and perfectly dry.

Theo opened his mouth to ask for a drink, but the voice that spoke was not his own.

'Now *here's* a man who looks like he could use a beer.'

He was in his seventies: jug-eared and rheumy-eyed, with grey hair that rose and fell in waves and thick black eyebrows like twin stripes of tar.

'Mark Peploe. Glad to know ya.' A thick chunk of Texas in that accent. And he was right: Theo could do with a beer, and the company too.

The bar was sectioned into booths of what looked like wood and felt like MDF. They took their drinks and headed for the far end. Peploe lit a cigarette – a Raison, green packet with a cat picture on the front – offered Theo one, and shrugged at the refusal. His index and middle fingers were stained dark tobacco yellow.

'You're the rollercoaster guy, huh?'

'That's me.'

'I figured. Word gets around. How's it going?'

There were several possible answers to that question, Theo thought, but he wasn't sure Peploe would be much help with any of them.

'I've barely started, to be honest.' He hoped that would be sufficiently non-committal. 'And you? A diplomat?'

Peploe barked a short laugh. 'Hardly.' Theo opened his hands: go on. 'Long before you were born,' Peploe continued, and the condescension in those five words let Theo know that this guy was now going to talk all about himself and not ask a single further question in return, 'long before you were born, I was a US soldier stationed on the border down at Panmunjom. Frontline of the Cold War, it was: that, and Berlin. Late 1962, a couple of weeks after the Cuban Missile Crisis. I was twenty-two and full of attitude. I had an argument with my superior officer, thought "screw this", and walked across the DMZ to the North.'

'You defected?'

'Sure did. The North thought I was a spy to start with.' He rolled up his sleeve and showed Theo a mound of dull red scar tissue. 'They cut out my army tattoo with a pair of scissors. Gave me a savage infection. No antibiotics, of course. I almost died. Took me six months to convince them I was on the level. They brought me to Pyongyang, gave me an apartment, a wife too. Been here ever since. Almost fifty years.'

'Fifty years? You must really love it here.'

'I hate it.' The bonhomie was still there, but now there was a harder edge beneath it too: something floating beneath the surface, half-glimpsed like a shark in heavy water. '*Hate* it. Always have. Every damn day of it.'

'So why not leave?'

'They won't let me go. They won't give me a passport. I can't go nowhere. Fifty years for one mistake made when I was real young and dumber than dumb. I knew nothin' 'bout nothin' back then. Shit, the US army could have told them that. The last report I got before skippin' said: "Private Peploe's a chronic complainer who's lazy and resistant to authority." Yeah. Safe to say Uncle Sam didn't shed too many tears when I hightailed to the North. Though no one here ever calls it the North, obviously. The Democratic People's Republic of Korea, even though it's not democratic, it doesn't belong to the people, it's not a republic, and it doesn't cover all Korea. Not that they like to hear you say any of that, of course.'

They chatted for a while: which was to say that, as Theo had figured, Peploe talked and Theo listened. Theo was a captive audience, and Peploe was making the most of it. He told tales of life here in Pyongyang, the old hand showing the newbie the ropes. It was a role Theo could tell he had played before: his stories were a little too pat, their telling too well honed. A performance wheeled out for every newbie in town.

Eventually Peploe drained the last of his beer, wiped his mouth with the back of his wrist, and stood up. 'Gotta shoot. How long you here for?'

73

Now that, Theo thought, really was the question. 'Not sure, yet.'

'Well, a while at least, I hope. Can always use the company.'

It was only after Peploe had gone that Theo realised he'd neither paid for the beer nor even offered to. A captive audience who ended up with the bill, that's what Theo was. Well, it wasn't him who was paying in the end, was it? He had another beer, and then a burger. It was half past seven by the time he headed back to the lifts, though not without an involuntary detour when he got lost and found himself going through a service door which led out to the garbage collection area at the back of the hotel. A kitchen worker stacking bins out there looked directly at Theo, and his face went through half a dozen expressions in less than a second, a raft of emojis made flesh: surprise, bewilderment, alarm, fear, confusion and finally self-preservation as he averted his face.

Theo backed up uncertainly and found the lifts at the second time of asking. When the one working lift finally reached his floor, he saw a couple of workmen fixing the broken doors of the other. They hadn't moved the chair he'd put there. They were just working around it. Odd. Illogical.

It wasn't until Theo was back in his room and saw the darkness through the window again that the realisation came to him. If there wasn't enough electricity for the whole city, or anything like the whole city, then *of course* they would ensure that the foreigners got first dibs, the better to keep the reality hidden from them.

And the principle didn't just apply for this hotel: it applied *within* this hotel too. The floors he'd passed on the way down to the lobby weren't being renovated: they were being *stripped*, to keep the inhabited floors like his looking good. As long as a small proportion of the place – the one that people saw – was shipshape, then the rest could go to hell.

Now Theo realised something else too. Reception hadn't answered when he'd rung them to report the lift doors. No one else had tried to use the lift from this floor, or else they'd have moved the chair he'd put there.

So how had the maintenance men known to fix it?

He'd shouted in frustration right here in this room. *Your lift tries to kill me and you don't even pick up the phone!* That was the only way they could have known. But he'd already hung up by then. And still they'd heard what he'd said.

How? There was only one way how. His room was bugged.

No. He wasn't having this. It was bad enough that he wasn't allowed out of this hotel without minders and had to be accompanied everywhere. But not to have privacy even in his own room was beyond the pale.

If there was a bug, he'd find it.

He prised the cover off the phone. No sign. He checked on the underside of the table and chairs. He lay flat on the floor beneath the bed, examined the slats holding the mattress in place, ran his hand round the frame. Not there either.

He stood up. It could be anywhere. In the light fitting, behind the mirror, inside one of the picture frames . . . *Be systematic. Be organised. Think where you'd hide a bug if you were the one planting it.*

The phone rang, loud and sudden enough in the silence to make him jump. He looked at his watch. Bang on eight o'clock. He picked up. 'Moritz?'

'Please stop searching your room.' A Korean voice.

'Fuck off!' He slammed the phone down.

It rang again immediately. He snatched it up. 'Stop spying on me!'

'Spying on you?' Moritz gave a soft chuckle.

'Yes. This place . . .'

'Theo, are you all right?'

'No. No, I'm not.'

'What's up?'

'I can't do this, Moritz.'

The pause that followed wasn't delay on the line. 'Why not?'

'This place is too weird.'

'How is it too weird?'

'How *isn't* it? It's a freak show, the whole damn place.'

'Just concentrate on your work. That'll block everything else out.'

Theo didn't know how much to tell Moritz. He wanted to say that in essence he liked the challenge of this one but he wasn't sure he could get it right, not in a place like this which so persistently knocked him off kilter. He was used to things taking time to come to him, but this was different, this was a blankness in his mind, and if he couldn't get past that then what was he? Because if he wasn't a coaster designer, he didn't know what he was for.

'The work can't be done,' he said eventually.

'Why not?'

'The park's due to open on September the ninth.'

Another pause, more freighted than the last. 'Why so soon? And so specific?'

'It's their National Day. The ninth of the ninth. Nine zones in Jucheland.' Theo smiled through the beat. 'I quite like that bit of it, actually.'

'Nine months isn't impossible.'

'It is.'

'No, it's not. We've built coasters in that time before.'

'Sure, once we've had everything else signed off. But not in parks which haven't even been started.'

'By "everything else", you mean the blue-sky stuff?' The blue-sky phase of any theme park was when overall concepts were hammered out. The running joke was that the process always happened exactly the same way. First, the creatives asked the engineers for things. Next, the engineers told the creatives their demands were impossible. Then the engineers proposed their own alternatives. Fourth, the money men took one look and declared these alternatives way too expensive. Fifth, everyone started again. And finally, when everyone's time, money and patience had run out, that was the point at which a park opened to the public.

'Yeah. That, and all the preliminary stages too. Feasibility studies, investor capital, permits, licensing. We haven't done any of those yet.'

'Because we don't need to! You want something – workers, materials, anything – the North Koreans'll give it to you. Simple as that.'

'I don't know.'

'I do. Otto says hi, by the way.'

Theo had left Otto with Moritz: it was one of the conditions he'd put on doing this, that Moritz would look after Otto as though he was his own.

'How is he?'

'Very cool. I can spend hours watching him. When the sunlight hits the tank in the morning it puts his shadow high on to the wall, like he's just hanging out up there.'

'Tell him I miss him.' Theo wondered whether he'd ever said that to or about a human being, whether or not he'd ever expressed a simple 'I miss you': and since he couldn't remember having done so he could only presume that he hadn't.

'I will.'

'Thanks.'

'Please, Theo. It'll come to you. Just give it a bit longer. I've seen you like this before on projects, and they've all come good in the end.'

'You haven't seen me quite like this.'

'That's 'cos there hasn't been a project quite like this.'

'True.'

'So we're good?'

'I— OK, yes. We're good. I'll give it a bit longer, at least.'

'Great. Thanks. Talk soon.'

The line went dead, and in the near-silent hum Theo wanted to tell the listeners *actually, no, I think I might go crazy if I have to spend nine months here.*

It had made Min obscurely sad, seeing the Taesongsan Funfair like that. They'd been there as a family several times when it had been open: eating candyfloss and bashing into each other in the bumper cars, her and Cuckoo in one and Han Na and Chul Woo in the other, Cuckoo spinning the steering wheel this way and that like a fiend and everyone guffawing and shrieking with every impact. Happy times.

It wasn't just that the funfair was gone: it was also that Theo had seen it like this, not as it had been then. She felt ashamed. She wanted to show him the best of this city, not a place that looked like the American cities she saw on TV, all smashed up and neglected. She should have anticipated this, she felt, and prepared an explanation as to why the place was the way it was: that the neglect was somehow deliberate, or even the fault of the Yankee imperialists. Perhaps she could have said that the Americans had originally built it with substandard materials and lack of care, or that the decay was a result of the unjust, immoral sanctions they were imposing on this country.

In any case, Theo wouldn't be around for long. She'd seen the look on his face when she'd told him that the entire thing had to be done within nine months, and had heard him muttering on the way back to the hotel that it was an impossible timetable. He'd tell them he couldn't do it and go back home, and then she and Yun Seok could go back to their usual gig of Western tourist groups and commissions in the hard-currency shops, and in years to come they'd see this as a mildly strange interlude and laugh about the strange American who'd wanted to leave almost before he'd got here.

There was a knock at the door. Han Na was out of her seat in a flash, welcoming Hyuk Jae in, offering him tea, trilling in the high voice she always used when she was on edge. 'You remember Min, of course you do. She's been so looking forward to this, I can hardly tell you. Let me take your coat. Sit down, please.'

Hyuk Jae was still wearing his *Bowibu* uniform, even though it was Sunday. Maybe he was doing it to appear smart and professional. Maybe he didn't have any other clothes. Min looked at him, trying to examine him without making it too obvious. Was he different from the others? Or was this just a game of musical chairs, where she would end up with whoever happened to be standing there when the music stopped?

Out of the corner of her eye, Min caught a glimpse of Cuckoo trying not to laugh.

Hyuk Jae sat on the sofa next to Min, leaving a good metre of clean air between them. Han Na brought tea, poured it and sat down opposite, next to Chul Woo. It wasn't exactly intimate, Min thought, but then again it wasn't supposed to be intimate. It was an interview, more or less, just like one would have for a job, with the background checks already taken care of.

Hyuk Jae cleared his throat. 'I used to see you come out of the apartment block,' he said, 'and I thought to myself: she must be the most beautiful girl in the world.'

He said it artlessly, too clumsy to be anything other than sincere.

'How long have you worked for the *Bowibu*?' Min asked, as much to cover her embarrassment as anything else.

'Only six months. I was in the army before that.'

Then he was off, on safe ground as he could talk all about himself: how his father and grandfather had both been career army officers – his grandfather a major-general, his father a lieutenant-general – how he'd wanted to follow in their footsteps because there was no greater honour than defending the fatherland against external enemies, and how he'd reached the rank of *sojwa*, major, before being transferred to the *Bowibu*, which was of course just as great an honour because it meant defending the fatherland against internal enemies.

There was something missing there, Min thought. A light had dimmed in Hyuk Jae when he'd spoken of the *Bowibu*, and she realised that his transfer from the army had not been voluntary, no matter what he said about it.

Hyuk Jae didn't ask Min what her career plans were. He didn't have to. If they were to be married then Min would be a *Bowibu* officer's wife, and that would mean following Hyuk Jae wherever he was posted. Right now, of course, Hyuk Jae was living in Pyongyang, so Min's life wouldn't change that much. But he could be relocated at any moment, and if he was then she would have to follow, no questions asked. And if they were to have children, which they would – only cold people didn't have children – she would have to give up her job to look after them. That went without saying.

It was not so much a conversation as a monologue, with Min prompting Hyuk Jae now and then as though he were an actor who'd forgotten his lines. Han Na watched with ill-disguised approval, and when Hyuk Jae told Chul Woo how much he loved his films, Chul Woo practically preened himself like a cat. It was, Min thought, one of her father's most obvious and least appealing characteristics, that he rated people largely in terms of how talented they thought he was and how effusive they were in saying so.

Hyuk Jae left after what Min thought was about two hours but actually turned out to have been not quite forty-five minutes. Han Na had barely shut the door behind him when she turned to Min with a big smile. 'What a nice young man.'

'He was very polite.' Min couldn't think of anything else to say.

Han Na cleared the tea away. Cuckoo came to sit next to Min.

'What did you think of him?' Cuckoo asked quietly.

'I thought – that he's a man of good standards and decency.'

'He's a crashing bore, that's what he is.'

'He'd never hurt me.'

'He'd never excite you, either.' She kissed Min's cheek. 'And you deserve better.'

5

The winter dragged on, and the weeks with it. Day after day Theo, Min, and Yun Seok sat in silence: silence, that was, apart from the revving of the bulldozers and the metallic clanging of the rides being dismantled outside, and the shouts of warning or remonstration from the men operating the machinery, and the whirring of the electric heater, which was neither loud enough to drown out the exterior sounds nor powerful enough actually to warm the tiny cabin.

To start with, Theo had asked if it was entirely necessary for them to sit in here with him while he was trying to design the rollercoaster. Min had told him that they were here to look after him, and if it was peace and quiet he needed then that was fine and they wouldn't make a sound. Theo had stopped asking after the third time, and had just given them his back.

It wasn't the engineering he was struggling with: it was the design. A rollercoaster needed to tell a story to get the riders involved. Expedition Everest at Walt Disney World's Animal Kingdom was a runaway mine train looking for the yeti. Busch Gardens in Tampa Bay had Cheetah Hunt, set on the African savannah with the track leaping high and crouching low like a cheetah. The Smiler at Alton Towers was ostensibly part of a big scientific experiment. He wanted something specifically North Korean which wasn't being used anywhere else in Jucheland, but neither Min nor Yun Seok were any help, let alone Chul Woo.

Most of all Chul Woo, come to think of it. When one day Theo sprayed a line of paint on the ground to mark out the rollercoaster's path and tethered balloons on steel hawsers at various points along that line to show its height variations too, Chul Woo came to the hut and gestured angrily at the balloons. Min translated for Theo as Chul Woo spoke.

'He says the coaster is too long.'

'Tell him it has to be that long if it's to be that high. The speed has to run off gradually. I can't just drop it from a hundred and fifty metres and hit the brakes.'

'He says it's dominating the park rather than being a part of it.'

'Tell him to do his job and I'll do mine.'

This brought a flurry of invective from Chul Woo.

'He says you need to be reminded who's in charge,' Min translated eventually. But Chul Woo had already stalked off, gesticulating angrily in Theo's direction, and Min knew that though her father could shout and scream, in reality there was little he could do about it. The order for the rollercoaster to be as tall as it was had come from on high, and in this country that only meant one place, or more accurately one person.

Every night Theo would eat alone in the hotel. Sometimes Peploe was in the bar, but more often there was no sign of him, which suited Theo well: he looked forward to seeing Peploe only as a respite from the monotony, and the pleasure of Peploe's company began to pall roughly two minutes into any meeting.

Theo's hotel room was now as familiar to him as his own apartment back in London. What had once been novel had become commonplace: the way the designers had never seen a shade of brown they didn't like, with a chocolate bedspread on top of beige sheets and taupe chairs against burned-umber wallpaper; the way the TV had ten channels but only the three North Korean ones seemed to work; the way a female newsreader in an elaborate pink-and-black dress hyperventilated over footage of Kim Jong Un as the Supreme Leader climbed aboard a gunboat while ecstatic sailors threw themselves into the sea, and visited a factory while a phalanx of officials scribbled every word he said into their notebooks, and pressed a button to launch a missile while generals watched in awestruck rapture.

Theo could have gone home, he knew. He could have abandoned the project, maybe even left Leuschner Piesk altogether as he'd planned. B&M would almost certainly have offered him that job again, and if they didn't then any other company would jump at the chance of having him on their roster. But he hadn't. He'd chosen to stay here and stick it out because – well, why?

Because he was loyal to Moritz, because he hated not seeing things through, because he relished the challenge of designing the tallest coaster in the world and the ego involved in that. Because of all these and none of them too. There was something more, deeper and half-hidden beneath the surface, that grasped his ankle whenever he thought about packing up and whispered at him to stay.

Min watched Theo's computer screen as images of rollercoasters appeared and disappeared, span round in circles or flipped on their heads. Theo would press a key or move the mouse, and suddenly a part of the rollercoaster on screen would rear up or plunge downwards, stretch itself like an elastic band or squash up like a crumpled can. Sometimes Theo would flick between two or three separate designs on screen as though shuffling playing cards.

He told her that he was using CAD programmes in 3D, and showed her how it allowed him to design and adjust not just how the ride would look but how it would behave: stress analysis on parts and riders, algorithms to make bends as smooth as possible, clearance envelopes to ensure that passengers couldn't be hurt, ballistic envelopes to see where any falling objects could land, collision-detection procedures, speed and G-forces and braking, fault-tree analyses and everything else.

He told her all this, and she couldn't have cared less.

He seemed to her so self-possessed, so alone. Everyone here did everything together, and the only place that was really yours was inside your own head. There was no such thing as a loner in this society. But this man with his computer and auburn hair, he was one. He carried himself as though there was an invisible force-field around him, as though to admit the slightest dependency on another person would have been to confess to a dreadful weakness.

More importantly, at least in the short term, he was showing no signs of leaving. Min had been convinced he'd give up and go home when he'd found out that he had to do the whole thing in nine months, and he still didn't seem entirely happy with things, that was for sure: but he was still here, and he'd stopped asking about flights and passports. How could Min get rid of him without being blamed for it? Perhaps she should discuss it with Yun Seok, but if so she would have to couch her words carefully: this was a project authorised by the SAC, of course, and any attempt to deliberately undermine it would land her in big trouble.

No, she thought. They were stuck with him. She would just have to make the most of it.

'You know who he sounds like?'

Min was almost asleep when Cuckoo spoke. The words materialised out of the darkness, so unexpected that Min wondered for a moment whether she'd dreamt them.

'Who's "he"?'

'The American.'

They had spoken about Theo over supper. Min smiled to herself: this was typical Cuckoo, to pick up the thread of a conversation hours later, sometimes even days or weeks on, and run with it as though there'd been no interlude whatsoever.

'Who does he sound like?'

'Your father.'

'He's nothing like him.'

'No?'

'No.'

'He sounds like him.'

'In what way?'

'That self-possession you talked about: the way you say he keeps himself from the world. Your father does that too.'

'That's different.'

'In the way it comes out, maybe. But deep down? I wouldn't be so sure.'

'There's no comparison.'

'He's an American, not an alien. There's always a reason why people behave the way they do.' Cuckoo shifted in bed, propping herself half-upright on one elbow. 'Did I ever tell you about the time your father came back home in the middle of his army service?'

'I don't think so.'

'Right. He must have been twenty-two, twenty-three.' Every man in those days had to join the armed forces, and for an entire decade to boot. 'He had a week off. He arrived with his clothes hanging off him, as usual – the army never gave them enough to eat – but this time he was absolutely silent too, and that was a new one. I asked him what was wrong. "Nothing," he said. But I saw how gingerly he walked and how he winced when he sat down. So I asked him again, of course, and this time he yelled at me to shut up, stop interfering and leave him alone. Then he went into his room and stayed there for three days.

'I had to go to work, of course, so I left him as much food as I'd managed to stockpile in his absence, and every evening I waited out his silence and listened to the radio. "Esteemed Comrade Kim Jong Il has been elected to the Political Bureau of the Workers' Party's Central Committee, with special responsibility for organisation and guidance. Announcing the election, the Great Leader, Comrade Kim Il Sung, said that if there ever came a day when he himself could not carry out the final victory of the Korean Revolution, then his son would do so."'

Cuckoo's impression of the radio newsreader was so perfect that Min coughed a laugh.

'Then on the third evening, once he'd finally come out of his room, he was picking at his food when he began to cry. My instinct was to rush over and hug him tight, but I knew he'd just shrug me off. So I closed my hand over his and squeezed lightly, just enough for him to know that I was there and that I'd listen if he wanted me to. Gently, he removed my hand and lifted his shirt over his head. His torso was striped pink and purple, like streaks of a sunset through clouds.

'"I was too slow on a march." His voice was so soft that I had to lean in close to hear. "So . . ."

'"Too slow or not," I said, "your superiors shouldn't be doing this."

'"My superiors?" He huffed a short, bitter laugh. "It's not my superiors."

'"Then who?"

'"My own ranks, of course. They see a target and they swarm like rats, because if they're doing it to you then no one's doing it to them."

'"Oh, my darling boy . . ." I said.

'His head jerked with his sobs. Now I did put my arms round him, and he didn't resist. I cradled his head against my chest, feeling the wetness of his tears through my blouse. "It's alright," I said. "It's alright."

'He pushed me away so violently and suddenly that I almost fell. I put out a hand to steady myself on the edge of the table, and his face was so contorted with rage that despite myself I tried to take another step backwards, not so much against the table as through it.

'"Alright? Alright? How is it alright?" He was screaming now, and I had this ridiculous fleeting fear that the neighbours would hear – well, of course they'd hear, everybody heard everything in this place. "Once you're marked, you're marked. You should hear them." He put on a sing-song voice, mocking them mocking him. "'Your dad's a war hero, your dad's a war hero. Why aren't you like him?' Why aren't I like him? Answer me that, mama."

'"You are like him," I said.

'"How? I get the shit kicked out of me for being soft! Why am I soft? Not from my father, that's for sure. From you. From you, mama! So this" – he jabbed at the weals on his chest – "is all your fault, you stupid, selfish old woman. All your fault!"'

6

Spring was on the way, if not actually here yet. The long months of the mercury struggling to get above zero were gone, and now it was warm enough at least to dispense with overcoats in the afternoon.

Min and Hyuk Jae walked through Moranbong Park, as they did every Sunday. It was always the same routine. Hyuk Jae would come and pick her up, they would head down to the river, walk along the bank, through the park, and be back home in time for tea. Every Sunday, without fail: every time the same walk, without fail; and every time pretty much the same conversation, without fail. The only difference from one week to the next was the weather.

Hyuk Jae would go through the motions of asking Min about her week, and as soon as was polite he'd change the subject back to himself. He spoke about his work at the *Bowibu*, as he always did, but only in the most general terms. Sometimes it felt to Min more like a lecture than anything else, as Hyuk Jae expounded on the importance of the *Bowibu*'s role in ensuring total national discipline and eradicating even the slightest traces of dissent. He couldn't, or wouldn't, tell her anything about what he did day to day. He didn't even want to talk about why he'd left the army for the *Bowibu*, other than to say it wasn't important and transfers like that happened the whole time.

Except, Min knew, they didn't.

She'd asked her mother, who had dealt with the *Bowibu* for many years. Han Na had initially been reluctant to answer – 'He's the right one for you, stop questioning it, and him, and me' – but Min had persisted, and eventually Han Na had admitted that no, she'd never come across someone who'd been in the army first. A couple of Min's school classmates who'd gone on to the army and whom she saw now and then said the same thing. She was sure Hyuk Jae had a good reason for not wanting to tell her, but the fact that he'd fobbed her off with something so demonstrably untrue irked her.

'Shall we get married?'

Hyuk Jae said it suddenly but unhurriedly, in his usual slightly nasal monotone, and for a moment Min wondered whether she'd heard him correctly. He could have been asking her for the time, or for directions. He hadn't even broken stride.

She stopped dead, because she hadn't expected him to ask. Well, of course she'd *expected* him to ask – that was the whole point of them having been introduced in the first place – but she hadn't expected him to ask so soon. That too was absurd, she thought, as six weeks was hardly 'soon' when compared to her parents' generation.

She realised, of course, that the only reason she hadn't expected him to ask so soon was that she hadn't *wanted* him to ask. She couldn't tell him that. Perhaps, she thought, he didn't want to be here any more than she did: but she knew that wasn't true either.

She ran to catch up with him. 'Let me think about it,' she said, and the words surprised her even as she heard herself say them.

Hyuk Jae shrugged and kept walking. Not embarrassed, not angry, not apparently perturbed in any way, as though asking women to marry him and being told they'd think about it was something that happened to him every weekend.

The silence stretched between them for the rest of the walk, elastic and distancing. Min cursed herself. Why hadn't she just said no? She knew the answer almost before she'd asked the question, of course. She hadn't said no because that was her default mechanism, to please people. That was why she did the job she did, that was what came from growing up in the shadow of a relatively famous father, that was the result of being shamed for making a simple mistake at the Arirang Games.

When they got back to the apartment, both Min's parents and Hyuk Jae's were standing stiff and formal in the living room. Min knew the moment she walked in that Hyuk Jae had announced his intention to them in advance, and that they were all waiting to congratulate the happy couple.

Only Cuckoo stood slightly apart. When Min caught her gaze, Cuckoo rolled her eyes in mild exasperation at this performance: and, for once, Min didn't want to laugh.

Both sets of parents embraced Min, and then Han Na and Hyuk Jae's mother kissed Hyuk Jae, and Chul Woo and Hyuk Jae's father shook his hand, and Chul Woo clapped Hyuk Jae awkwardly on the shoulder. The relief in Han Na's eyes sparked a sudden fury in Min, flaring fast and silent. Was it such a balm to Han Na that someone wanted to marry Min? Was Min that worthless, that undesirable?

Cuckoo opened her arms for Min to hug her, and in the softness of Cuckoo's shoulder Min felt a tear slide down her cheek, absorbed and gone into the fabric of Cuckoo's blouse before anyone saw it.

'I told him I'd think about it,' Min whispered in her grandmother's ear: but she could hear her mother bustling off to fetch the tea, and Hyuk Jae's mother suggesting propitious days on which they could get married, and she knew that even if she cleared her throat and told them all the truth they'd just ignore it and carry on as they were. Well, Han Na would say, you *have* thought about it now, so let's get on with it.

Suppression of one's emotions was the highest of all socialist ideals. Both excessively negative and excessively positive feelings were to be avoided for fear of their destabilising effect. Only those in full control of their emotions could advance in the Party, the government or the military.

Min detached herself from Cuckoo's hug and gave a small laugh as she exhaled. *Yes,* she told herself. *Hyuk Jae is a good man and he will do right by me. This is what I want. This is definitely what I want.*

Hyuk Jae came again the following Sunday, regular as clockwork.

They had hardly left her apartment block when she stopped and pulled his elbow to make him face her. She had a sudden urge to know who he was: properly, that was, not through his endless monologues which told her everything but also told her nothing. If they were going to do this, they might as well do it right.

'Why did you leave the army?' she said.

'What?'

'You heard me.'

'You can't ask these questions.'

'People don't just leave the army to join the *Bowibu*.' He opened his mouth to protest, but she raised a hand to stop him, and the astonishment in his face almost made her laugh: that she had dared, even once, to contradict him. 'They don't. You know they don't, and I know it too. So tell me.'

'I can't.'

'We're going to be married. You have to tell me things about yourself.'

Hyuk Jae looked around, as though seeking escape. Min stood her ground.

'I'll tell you while we walk,' he said: precautions against being overheard. 'But you must tell no one. Not even your family.'

'Why not? Is it so secret?'

'It is a protected matter under the regulations of both the Korean People's Army and the State Security Bureau.'

Silence in the tunnel, and darkness.

No, not quite. The soft, measured tread of slow footsteps, and twin beams of light which slashed through the black like swords. Mostly silence and mostly darkness, but not totally.

The beams played along the walls, up over the ceiling and down the other side. They moved as slowly as the footsteps, and their sweeping was methodical. At the narrow end of each beam, where the light was brightest and the motes of stirred-up dust danced most frenziedly, were two eyes, and the men to which these eyes belonged carried cans of spray paint to mark any parts that needed attention.

Hyuk Jae had been on tunnel detail for three years now, and he could assess damage and repair as though he were restoring fine art. He could look at two cracks that appeared identical and know the difference between them, know which one needed epoxy and which one urethane. He could tell whether leaking water was from moisture inside the concrete or groundwater above it. Sometimes, when he was alone, he would switch off his torch and try to ascertain structural irregularities by making clicking sounds and listening for variations in the echoes, as though he were a bat.

He wasn't alone today. Today he had been tasked with showing Sang Won the ropes. Sang Won was a *jungwi*, a second lieutenant, two ranks below Hyuk Jae. Hyuk Jae didn't mind that Sang Won was his junior, and nor did he mind showing him what to do. What he did mind was that the infernal fellow kept asking questions. And not the kind of questions Hyuk Jae felt comfortable answering, questions about structural loads or arch pressures or wall strains. No: the kind of questions Sang Won kept asking were the kind of questions Hyuk Jae couldn't have answered even if he'd wanted to.

How many tunnels ran under Pyongyang? Was it true that enlisted workers were blindfolded when being taken to and from construction sites? Were there secret doors leading from the metro lines to further tunnels? Was there really an underground network linking the Supreme Leader's palace with the port at Nampo or the airport on the outskirts of the capital?

Sang Won asked so many questions that for a while Hyuk Jae had wondered whether he was some kind of informer or agent provocateur, sent to test Hyuk Jae's loyalty and discretion. Every member of the First Brigade of the Korean People's Army Military Engineers knew that below Pyongyang was a netherworld of tunnels which had been begun during the Fatherland Liberation War: it had been the only way that those who had lived there could have survived the relentless bombard-ment from the air. 'The entire nation must be made into a fortress,' the Great Leader had said. 'We must dig ourselves into the ground to protect ourselves.'

But beyond that were only rumours and guesswork. So Hyuk Jae had said that he didn't know the answers, which was true, and he hoped that had been enough either to deter Sang Won from asking any further questions if he was on the level or reassure him of his bona fides if he wasn't.

At least now the man had stopped talking. The darkness suited Hyuk Jae, as it suited most people in the country. The darkness was where they kept their counsel, and the darkness was where they ended up if they didn't.

Hyuk Jae and Sang Won moved on in silence: sweep, mark, pace, sweep, mark, pace. The rhythm was therapeutic. Hyuk Jae would have happily stayed down there for weeks. But beside him he could sense Sang Won's restlessness, the constant needling suppression of his desire to break the silence and the darkness.

Darkness again, and tunnels again, but this time Hyuk Jae and Sang Won weren't beneath Pyongyang. This time, they were beneath South Korea.

The Korean People's Army had begun tunnelling beneath the DMZ pretty much from the moment it had been established at the end of the Fatherland Liberation War. Now, decades later, the tunnel network was vast and complex, an outsized rabbit warren with camouflaged airshafts and entryways disguised as filled wells. The tunnels stretched, rose and fell through multiple levels, and the deeper they went the longer and wider they became. The largest of all could accommodate tanks and move a brigade's worth of troops every hour. All in preparation for the invasion to liberate the southern brothers from the American imperialist yoke, which could come at any moment and would be lightning quick once it was ordered.

'Is it true that some of these tunnels reach as far as the Blue House?' Sang Won whispered. The Blue House was the presidential compound in Seoul, 50 km from the border. 'And that when the invasion comes, these tunnels will be blown up behind us to prevent retreat?'

Always with the questions, Hyuk Jae thought. 'Shut up and concentrate,' he said.

The slow, methodical sweep of the torch beams. Up, across, down. Back again the other way. Walls and ceilings briefly illuminated before sliding back into the gloom . . .

. . . and a shadow where there shouldn't be one.

Hyuk Jae killed his own light and, in the same movement, reached across with both hands: one to shut off Sang Won's torch, the other to clamp over his mouth.

'Not a sound,' Hyuk Jae hissed in Sang Won's ear.

They stood absolutely still. The darkness was velvet around them, heavy and soft. Hyuk Jae concentrated all his energies on listening: not a passive waiting for sounds to reach his ears, but actively seeking out the noise no matter how faint. This was how his predecessors had needed to be, he knew, when they had been hollowing the tunnels out from beneath the earth: so at home down here that they had almost blended into the walls, taking the senses from eyes temporarily useless and using them instead to keep both ears wider open than humanly possible, listening for the quick, deceptive tumbling of soil, which was the outrider to a cave-in, or the soft hiss from a pocket of gas inadvertently pierced by a careless pick, or the methodical tapping of the spades by men on the other side, hunting them.

Silence.

Hyuk Jae waited. He could wait indefinitely. With every second that passed, he became increasingly sure that, whatever had caused the shadow, it hadn't been more than one or two people. Several men – and he was always primed for the possibility that some South Korean soldiers had discovered an entrance and found their way down here – would have made a noise by now.

A soft scraping sound, almost a hiss: a shoe brushing across concrete. Then another, and another, a little fainter each time. Footsteps, going away from them.

Hyuk Jae turned his torch back on and aimed it in the direction of the footsteps. The light caught a man, lost him, caught him again.

He wasn't wearing a military uniform, but jeans and trainers and a T-shirt.

Hyuk Jae knew instantly who he must be, as he'd been warned about these kinds of people. Tunnel hunters, they called them: not South Korean soldiers, but regular citizens who kept seeking entry points to the tunnels. Just to show how foolish this was, some of these tunnel hunters had spent so much time and money on this pursuit that they'd ended up divorced and homeless. Why did they do this? Who knew? A madness visited on them by the strain of the Yankee occupation, no doubt.

The man began to run. Hyuk Jae knew that they had to catch him before he got back to the surface and escaped. If he knew where this entry point was, how many others did he know?

'Hey!' he shouted. 'Hey!'

The man dodged sideways, out of Hyuk Jae's torch line. Sang Won had turned his on again, and between them they tried to keep the man in sight as they chased him, their beams crossing and uncrossing like sabres.

A harsh metallic clanging sounded up ahead. Hyuk Jae found the gate still swinging on its hinges where the man had rushed through. He followed up a slope into which rough steps had been cut. Daylight high above, a circle that grew larger and brighter as Hyuk Jae climbed, his breath ragged, the man too far ahead . . .

Hyuk Jae reached the surface, with Sang Won a pace or two behind him. The man had vanished. Hyuk Jae looked wildly around, seeing nothing but green hills dotted with trees – and there was the man, briefly seen and gone again over the nearest crest.

Sang Won raised his pistol. Hyuk Jae slapped the barrel down. 'Don't be absurd! You'd never hit him from this far out, and even if you did, then what?'

'We could . . . I don't know. Take his body back with us?'

97

'You fire a shot here, you start a war. Listen, Sang Won. This never happened, you hear me? Our inspection of the tunnel was entirely routine and uneventful. Yes?'

'But we . . .'

'. . . don't want anyone asking questions. "We saw an intruder, but we let him get away." Is that what you want to tell them? Do you have any idea what would happen to us? If we didn't see it, it didn't happen. If it didn't happen, it wasn't our fault.'

Sang Won didn't answer. Hyuk Jae was about to repeat himself when he saw that Sang Won was staring out over the hills: not at anything in particular, Hyuk Jae realised, just at the landscape itself. The DMZ was no more than a mile away, and beyond it their homeland, but for a moment it seemed as remote as the moon.

Hyuk Jae knew what Sang Won was thinking, because he was thinking it too, just as the drop is what draws the man with vertigo to the edge of the roof: that here they were, south of the border, and if they wanted they could just walk to the nearest village and give themselves up. No one knew they were there. Oh, there would be repercussions for their families back home if they did, but they themselves would be long gone.

'You know what the South do with defectors?' Sang Won said.

'They torture them for months.'

'They give them money and a job, a car and an apartment.'

The man had to be a provocateur, Hyuk Jae thought: such talk was too blatant to be anything else. But what if he wasn't, and what if that were true, the stuff about money and a job?

No. Almost in the moment the thought occurred to Hyuk Jae, he batted it clean from his mind. He loved the Supreme Leader, and he was a sojwa in the greatest army on earth, and the very fact that he was trusted to come this far was in itself proof that he was too worthy to betray that trust.

'Come,' he said, motioning for Sang Won to follow him back down into the tunnel. And then, more firmly and tugging on Sang Won's arm when Sang Won didn't move, 'Come now.'

The debrief with their commanding officer had lasted two hours, and for most of that time Hyuk Jae had been afraid that Sang Won would suddenly blurt out what had happened the day before with the tunnel hunter from the South. Hyuk Jae had done his best to be professional and focused – listing the points in the tunnels that needed attention, making suggestions and recommendations, answering the CO's questions as fully as he could – but all the while he'd sensed rather than seen Sang Won's restlessness. It wasn't much, and if the CO had noticed then he hadn't said anything – and the CO hadn't noticed, because he was the kind of man to have said something if he had – but for Hyuk Jae, conscious of how they'd lost a man they should have caught, every one of Sang Won's hesitations in speaking, every jiggling of his knee, every look out of the window seemed freighted with some dreadful import.

The moment they were out of the debrief and Hyuk Jae was sure they couldn't be overheard, he turned to Sang Won. 'What the hell's up with you?'

'Me? Nothing.'

'That's not what it looked like in there.'

'I don't know what you're talking about.'

Hyuk Jae stopped walking and grabbed Sang Won by the lapels of his uniform. 'You just forget about what happened yesterday, all right? Just forget it.'

Sang Won nodded.

'Say it,' Hyuk Jae insisted.

'I don't even know what you're talking about.'

Hyuk Jae was about to repeat himself when he saw Sang Won's nervous smile, and realised what he'd meant by that last sentence. He let go of Sang Won's lapels.

'Good. I don't know what we're talking about either.'

They walked out into the sunshine, stepping aside to salute a senior officer. They were in Panmunjom, the only place in the DMZ where the two Koreas actually met: the peace zone, the demarcation line, the one they always showed on TV. The guard was being changed in the watchtower above them: a jeep braked heavily to a halt, tipping forwards and then backwards with the momentum before disgorging a couple of soldiers. A few kilometres away, across a strip of land bristling with barbed wire fences, landmines and searchlights, was the South.

Hyuk Jae and Sang Won were half the length of a football field, no more, away from the demarcation line when Sang Won began to run. He didn't just break into a gentle trot: he took off from standing like a startled rabbit, arms pumping and legs driving like a professional athlete, and he was three or four strides away before Hyuk Jae could react. Even then, Hyuk Jae didn't instantly realise what Sang Won was doing. In the second or two before his thought processes caught up with what his eyes were seeing, Hyuk Jae wondered whether Sang Won had seen someone in trouble and was rushing to help, or had been stung by a wasp he was trying to outrun.

Then he saw the purpose and determination in Sang Won's stride, and he remembered the way Sang Won had stared out at the countryside the day before when they'd emerged from the tunnel south of the border, and the way he'd had to drag Sang Won away, and Sang Won's nervy jitters in the debrief with the CO just now, and he knew.

'Sang Won!' he shouted. 'Sang Won!'

Sang Won didn't break stride, didn't look back. Sang Won was still running hell for leather, and Hyuk Jae could see the South Korean guards scrambling to as near their side of the line as possible so they could help him when he came near, and his comrades this side of the line looking at Sang Won or at one another, their brains still breast-stroking their way through the fog of astonishment.

Hyuk Jae running after Sang Won, though he didn't remember having started the chase. Hyuk Jae pulling his sidearm from its holster, trying to get a lock on Sang Won. Hyuk Jae feeling the heat of the air searing his lungs as he ran. 'Sang Won!' he yelled, and he heard the hard edge of determination in his own voice.

Sang Won slipped, hitting the ground hard. He bounced, rolled, pushed himself up and kept going, hobbling now, but in that time Hyuk Jae had closed to within a few metres of him: not yet near enough to tackle Sang Won, but near enough to know that he'd hit if he took the shot.

There were other soldiers in the periphery of Hyuk Jae's vision, all of whom would be interrogated whatever happened.

Comrade Hyuk Jae showed exemplary skills and presence of mind to neutralise the treacherous deserter Sang Won.

Comrade Hyuk Jae failed to take an easy shot and his cowardly incompetence allowed the treacherous deserter Sang Won to escape.

Sang Won was only a few strides from the demarcation line now. Hyuk Jae stopped, planted his feet, braced with his pistol in front of him, and fired. Three shots, one after the other, and Sang Won sprawled forward and lay unmoving face down on the ground. Hyuk Jae approached him, ready to fire again if necessary. Some of the South Korean soldiers were shouting, but to Hyuk Jae they sounded distant and muffled, filtered through gauze. He sensed some of his comrades at his shoulder.

Blood pooled viscous and dark beneath Sang Won's flank. Hyuk Jae squatted. Sang Won lifted his head with the greatest effort, and looked once more at the borderline, so near and so completely out of reach. When he looked back at Hyuk Jae, his eyes were already clouding over. He lowered his head again, and this time he did not move.

'And the next day, a man from the *Bowibu* came to me and said that they were very impressed with my devotion to duty and that I was being transferred.'

Min wondered whether it was true. Not Hyuk Jae's account of the incident – she believed that implicitly – but whether he had been transferred for the reason given or to hide the army's embarrassment that one of their men had tried to escape.

'Would you do it again?' she asked.

'Do what again?'

'Shoot a man trying to escape.'

'Shoot a traitor to the motherland, you mean?' When Min said nothing, Hyuk Jae continued. 'Yes. I'd do it in a heartbeat, thanks to the exemplary training which the Korean People's Army and the State Security Bureau have given me, to the unflinching loyalty to and love for the Great Leader and the Dear Leader which every member of those organisations holds dear, and to the guiding principles of Kimilsungism-Kimjongilism.'

His eyes glittered with the righteous certainty of the true zealot.

7

April 2016

'Can I walk the rest of the way?' Theo said.

They were a mile or so from the hotel. Yun Seok, eyebrows tilting towards each other in puzzlement, glanced at Theo in the rear-view mirror. 'Why?'

'It's a nice evening, I feel like stretching my legs. I've been sitting down all day.' Theo had been stuck at his desk checking the details of every fastening pin, bolt and nut he'd ordered: their grades, their torques, and their replacement or tightening schedules. His head was so fuzzy that when he closed his eyes the numbers kept scrolling down the inside of his eyelids like green coding rain.

Yun Seok and Min spoke fast to each other.

'I've been here three months,' Theo said. 'You must trust me by now.'

'We will walk with you,' Yun Seok said. 'Nam Il will meet us at the hotel.'

A vote of confidence, Theo thought. *About time too.*

Nam Il pulled over. Min, Yun Seok, and Theo got out.

Spring had well and truly come: no more freezing nights, and people walking in shirtsleeves when the sun was out. The air still held the last warmth of the day, and the poplars had just begun to bloom along the riverbank. Min, Yun Seok and Theo walked around and beneath them, and what little sound there was from the city became even fainter. The leaves, green hearts wavering on the end of swan-neck stems, shivered gently in the breeze. The trees were so tall and thick that even Pyongyang's vast buildings now appeared only in strobe beyond them, quick flashes of white through the canopy.

'These trees feel like they've been here for ever,' Theo said.

'Just since the reconstruction after the war. The Americans destroyed the originals, just like they did everything else in Pyongyang.' Min's tone was rock-solid neutral, and when Theo glanced across at her he saw that her expression was too.

'You speak such good English.'

'Thank you.'

'Where did you learn it?'

'At the Pyongyang University of Foreign Studies.'

Actually, Min thought, it wasn't quite true that she'd learned English there. Oh, she'd been *taught* English there, drilled in grammar and vocabulary until she was word-perfect. But she'd *learned* it, really learned it, through Sherlock Holmes books and ABBA songs.

She and her fellow students had been encouraged to read Sherlock Holmes because it showed the West for what it was: a toxic, polluted, crime-ridden, amoral cesspit where the police were so incompetent that they had to rely on a civilian to solve crimes for them. Every Sherlock Holmes story demonstrated the superiority of the revolutionary paradise which those in the Democratic People's Republic of Korea were so fortunate to enjoy. Crime was practically non-existent here, and the miniscule amount that existed was committed by mentally ill individuals and solved in double-quick time by the most skilled investigators in the world.

And they'd been encouraged to listen to ABBA because the group promoted family and community values in accordance with the revolutionary ideals of Kimilsungism-Kimjongilism. In general, that was. Three ABBA songs had been banned: 'Money, Money, Money' and 'The Winner Takes It All' for glorifying capitalist rapacity, and 'Gimme! Gimme! Gimme! (A Man After Midnight)' for encouraging illicit sexual activity.

Yun Seok had fallen back and was walking about five paces behind them. Min slowed, turned her head and said something to him. He gave a brief reply and a smile.

'Is he OK?' Theo asked.

'He says we walk a little too fast for him, but not to worry.'

Her smartphone rang. When she pulled it from her handbag a small pot with a screw-on lid came with it, and Theo moved fast to catch the pot as it dropped. Min glanced at the screen of her phone, pressed the button to ignore the call, and put the phone back in her bag. Theo handed her the pot.

'Thank you,' she said.

'What's in it?'

'*Kimchi.*' She thought suddenly of Cuckoo, and what she had said about there always being a reason why people behave the way they do. If Theo was going to make an effort after all these months, then the least she could do was reciprocate. 'Have you ever had some?'

'Yes.'

'In the hotel?'

'Yes.'

'Did you like it?'

'Not really.'

'That's not proper *kimchi. Kimchi's* only proper if it's made by Cuckoo.'

'Cuckoo?'

'My grandmother. I make it with her every November. We've done it for as long as I can remember. That's why November's the time of year I treasure the most.' The last days of autumn, and in the chill of the mornings, the closing in of the evenings and the wet carpet of wind-strewn leaves, the knowledge that winter was around the corner, but not yet, not quite yet. She treasured these days the most not for the weather but for what it meant: because *kimjiang* – *kimchi* time – meant she had Cuckoo all to herself. They'd done it every year without fail, even when she'd been a teenager, all coltish limbs and bashful awkwardness: that time in any girl's life when her body changes in fits and spurts, when the skin in which she's lived all her life suddenly feels as though it's not quite hers, when control over her extremities can seem intermittent and when hair and spots sprout in strange places. She could have been out with her schoolmates, but she'd told Cuckoo that there was nowhere she'd rather be and nothing she'd rather be doing, and both of those were the truth.

'How does she do it properly?'

'She just does. It's a whole process, *kimjiang*, and you have to pay attention to each part. We start at the market. Most people have cabbages delivered, as they're a key product and therefore subject to distribution, but Cuckoo's been around markets half her life and loves them. The crowds are thick and Cuckoo's tiny, but she pushes her way through like a, like a – what do you call those ships in the Arctic which break the ice as they go?'

'Icebreakers.'

'Really? Icebreakers! Ha! So simple. Like an icebreaker. You have to imagine the scene. There are piles of cabbages towering to twice a man's height, and scallions tied in bundles thicker than a water pipe. Cuckoo checks all the produce, because she knows the traders will try to get rid of the worse stuff first. She can spot a poor cabbage from fifty paces: they're too large and their leaves are packed too loosely. It's the smaller, tighter cabbages she wants, the ones with yellow leaves closely bunched in the centre. Then she haggles, not just because she wants the best price but because she enjoys it, you know? It's like a little opera, a sing-song, back and forth, back and forth. And eventually everyone's happy and she hands over money for the cabbages, and then we go through the whole thing again at the salted-shrimp stall and the dried chilli powder one, so we might be there for hours. "This is my grand-daughter," she used to say when I was younger, and while they were all fussing around me, she'd knock a couple of won off her bid price.'

Theo laughed, and Min smiled in appreciation of his amusement.

'Finally, with everything bought and paid for, we carry our prizes back to the apartment. There's so much that we have to do it in relays: first from the market to the foyer of our apartment build-ing, and then from the foyer up the stairs to the apartment.' They worked side by side in the kitchen, heads bent towards each other, their fluent dipping knives halving and quartering each cabbage, their conversation matching the rhythm of the work, speaking of everything and nothing, of school and friends and family, because all that mattered was being there and doing this with each other: a brief, precious moment of ritual. 'When we've quartered all the cabbages, we take them through into the bathroom and drop them in a large plastic tub, which Cuckoo's filled with water and salt.' The gentle splashes as the pieces landed, sunk, span and righted themselves: the water leaping up on Min's clothes and in her eyes, and her laughter as she wiped them clear. 'We get up four times in the night and turn the cabbages over in the bath, staying there long enough to do every piece but not so long that we're fully awake, and then we go back to bed until the next time. The next day, we cover the floor with newspapers—'

'Careful to make sure there are no pictures of the Great Leader or the Dear Leader—'

'Exactly! We cover the floor with newspapers, make paste from the scallions, shrimp and chilli powder, rub that paste into the cabbage leaves, and then pack the leaves into containers to ferment and become *kimchi*. We make enough to last through the winter, through the four months of darkness and cold until finally there's more day than night again. Until now, in fact. This is my last pot.'

She unscrewed the top and held it out to Theo. He took a piece, put it in his mouth and let it rest on his tongue a moment before beginning to chew.

'You like it?'

'It tastes of . . . It tastes of autumn, I think.' Sharp and red and tangy, a final flaring of brightness and rich colour before the monochrome. 'Oh, something else too. It . . . no. This sounds silly. But . . . it tastes of hands.' Human hands, with their lines and scars and dirt, and nothing so antiseptic as cutlery or machines.

Min beamed, and Theo felt suddenly as though he'd passed some sort of test.

'Yes,' she said. 'That's exactly what it tastes of. Her hands, and mine.' Her smile faded, lit up again, faded a second time: a strange flowering of happiness.

They walked again the next day, and again Yun Seok lagged a little behind, out of earshot if Theo and Min talked quietly. Theo opened his mouth to speak, thought better of it, and then thought better of thinking better and said it anyway. 'How are your wedding preparations going?'

She was so surprised she half-broke stride. 'Why do you ask?'

'Because I'm interested. Because I've been here for three months and I still know next to nothing about you or Yun Seok.'

She nodded as though this made sense. 'Preparations? Oh. You know.'

'Well, I've never been married, so no, I don't.'

'You seem quite old not to have been married.' Her mouth made a perfect 'O' the moment the words were out, and she grabbed at the air as though to catch them before they reached him. 'I didn't mean it that way! I meant . . .'

Theo was already laughing. 'I know what you meant.'

'If you're offended . . .'

'I'm not offended. I'm amused.'

'Really?'

'Really.'

She looked at him, trying to gauge how serious and sincere he was being. 'Have you ever been close to it?'

'No.' There was the arrangement with Sophie, of course, but Theo didn't think that really counted. Besides, Sophie seemed a long way away, in every way.

'Why not?'

'Just haven't. So tell me about the preparations.'

'Questions, questions, questions: that's all I'm asked about it.'

'I'm sorry. I'm just interested.'

She brushed his arm. 'I don't mean you. I meant everybody else. What about this dress? Which of these flowers do you prefer? This piece of food or that? Shall we invite him, or her, or them? All these people asking things, but they never ask me . . .' She gave a small laugh. 'Listen to me. I shouldn't be moaning.'

'They never ask you what?'

'It doesn't matter.'

They walked on in silence. The answer came to Theo, unhurried and unbidden. He wondered whether or not to voice it out loud, for the silence wasn't as easy as before. This time, he felt, it needed to be broken.

'They never ask you whether it's what you want,' he said.

It was a simple statement, but he fancied he felt the air shift as he spoke: not in the way a breeze may rustle leaves, but in a reordering of the molecules themselves. A simple statement, but one defined by the way she chose to answer it, by whether or not she chose to be honest or simply polite.

She gave an involuntary shudder, so quick and fleeting that he wouldn't even have seen it had he not been watching her closely.

They kept walking. She would give him an answer, Theo realised: he just had to wait for it.

The poplars all around, cocooning them in a soft, half-hidden world.

'They never ask me if it's what I want,' Min agreed finally.

'And is it what you want?'

Min glanced over her shoulder. Yun Seok was reading something on his phone. 'Why am I even talking to you like this?' She heard her voice, shrill and high, and recognised the fear that had made it so. 'I'm sorry, I don't mean to be rude, but . . .'

'You're talking to me like this because you can.'

'How do you mean?'

'You don't know me, not really. You don't have to worry that I know Hyuk Jae or what I think of him. That makes me safe. Your family know Hyuk Jae. Yun Seok's a colleague to you rather than a friend, which puts him in no man's land. But you can tell me what you want and know it'll never rebound on you. In a few months I'll be gone and you'll never see me again. I've got no skin in the game.'

'Skin in the game?' Min laughed. 'What does *that* mean?'

'I have no interest.'

'Then why did you ask me?'

'Not "interest" as in I'm not interested. Of course I'm interested. "Interest" as in I'm impartial. It's the difference in English between being disinterested and uninterested, and people always get it wrong.'

'And it annoys you when they do.'

He laughed. 'And it annoys me when they do.'

'I like that it annoys you.'

'Why?'

'I just do. It's you. Precise.' Min exhaled through her nose. 'Is it what I want? I don't know.'

'What's he like?'

'My parents are very happy with the match.'

'That's not an answer.'

'I know.'

'It's normal to question things, I think. And to be nervous.'

'It is?'

'Yes. When else do you make a decision which will last for the rest of your life?'

'He's a good man,' Min continued. 'Forget it. Forget I said it.'

He saw that her eyelids had a little fold in them when she blinked, that her cheekbones were high and her chin quite sharp, that she had a small gap between her front teeth, and that her mouth was small and full, a little plump bow of red. He saw her five days a week, and only now did he feel as though he'd actually taken the time to look at her properly: or perhaps it was only now, with spring, that she was beginning to unwrap herself from the long deep winter cold.

'This rollercoaster,' she said. 'It's quick, yes?'

'Of course.'

'And you're still looking for – what did you call it? – a theme?'

'Yes.'

'Then how about Mallima?'

'Mallima?'

'A winged horse. First there was Chollima, a horse that could travel four hundred kilometres a day. After our victory in the Fatherland Liberation War, the Great Leader introduced the Chollima Movement for the whole country to increase production in industry and agriculture. "Let us dash forward in the spirit of Chollima!" he would say. Mallima is ten times faster than Chollima, and is too swift and elegant to be mounted by any mortal man.'

Theo was staring at her. His eyes glittered. She waited for him to tell her what a terrible idea it was.

'You're a genius,' he said, and it was not just what he said but the vehemence with which he said it that made her start.

'It's just – well, it's just a suggestion.'

'No. It's more than that. It's a great idea. It's brilliant. Perfect. Thank you.'

It was as though she'd flicked a switch in him, unblocked something clogged deep.

The next morning, before going down to meet Min and Yun Seok, Theo stood at his window and let his gaze roam across the cityscape: the water flowing all around and beneath him as though he were high on a sailing boat's mast, the river spitting a single jet of water skywards over and over again beyond the boxy girders of an upstream railway bridge, the vast stadium fashioned in the shape of a flower head.

He'd imagine where he'd route a rollercoaster: not the one he was building, but an enormous city-sized one as long as an underground train line and as high as a skyscraper. He'd chug it up that bridge and down the other side so the riders would think they were going to plunge into the river. He'd bank it hard and tight past the twin bronze statues – no, not past them, *between* them, with what felt like only inches to spare on either side (there was always much more than that, of course, but the riders would feel it as being so close because speed scrambled the senses). He'd have a long flat section through that park over there, because you had to let people catch their breath from time to time. The peaks never felt so exciting without the lulls in between. Maybe a corkscrew round that weird outsize pyramid rising from the skyline like an Egyptian mausoleum. And a vertical loop right across the top of the gargantuan stadium he could see on the next island upstream from this one: up and over, with that delicious moment of weightlessness right at the top.

He went downstairs. Min and Yun Seok were waiting for him in the lobby. He wished them good morning, and choked down a sudden urge to thank Min for giving him himself back. It sounded trite, even pretentious, put like that, and he knew he couldn't bring himself to say it to her. It would feel impossibly, excruciatingly awkward. But he meant it anyway, and hoped that somehow she would sense it.

When they broke for lunch that day, he scrolled through the files on his computer before he found one full of old photographs: so old, the ones he wanted to show her, that they were actually photographs of photographs, printed pictures laid flat and snapped with a smartphone. He pulled up a sequence of him as a child, expression as severe as his haircut as he sat on the floor and assembled a plastic building set. Min laughed when she saw the first shot, and Theo understood that for what it was: the universal amusement at seeing someone's childhood pictures and trying to square the boy then with the man now. He glanced at her as she chuckled, and the distortion in her face was lovely.

Theo pointed to the building set. 'They were called K'Nex. "Building Worlds Kids Love": that was their slogan. I was eleven years old when they first came out, and that was it – me, hooked, instantly. Every birthday, every Christmas, all I'd ask for was more K'Nex. You could build almost anything with it.'

'And you built rollercoasters.'

'I built rollercoasters: the longer, higher and more complex the better. That's how I learned about gravity and friction, long before I studied physics in high school and learned about kinetic energy, potential energy, and the difference between the two. Every time we moved somewhere new, I'd find out where the nearest theme park was and beg my parents to take me there. In winter, I'd spend days shovelling snow to make banked turns so I could ride my sledge like a bobsleigh. One summer, I built an actual coaster in the backyard with all the stuff I found lying around. Planks, railway sleepers, some piping, bits of an old car: the seat to ride on, the battery to drive the winch up the first hill. I'd been doing carpentry classes all year. It was ten feet tall at its highest and took me two months working twelve hours a day. Best summer I ever had.'

Sometimes, when telling people this, he felt a curious sense of embarrassment, as if admitting to the simple, unfeigned joys of childhood was not what adults were supposed to do. But now he felt no embarrassment whatsoever: not the faintest trace.

The Korean Film Studios covered more than a million square metres – Yun Seok made sure to tell Theo this long before they'd arrived there – and in every single one of those square metres Chul Woo was treated as though he were an unpopular but feared general. People bowed their heads and greeted him respectfully, but they never lingered longer with him than they had to, and they let their strained smiles lapse the moment he had turned away from them. He walked round as though he owned the place: which in a manner of speaking he probably did, Theo thought, given all the films he'd shot here.

They'd come to see what they could use for Jucheland in general and Mallima in particular. Theo had designed the cars to be shaped and painted like Mallima itself, winged horses into which passengers would be strapped and in which they'd fly faster than they'd ever dreamed possible. The ride wouldn't just be a track: the ride would take them through the history of North Korea itself.

'Anything you want,' Chul Woo said. 'Anything you want, just say the word. Backdrops, pieces of stage sets, old props: this place has them all. You can take anything and everything you need. Have a good look round. Take as long as you want.'

Theo wondered why Chul Woo was being so magnanimous all of a sudden. Perhaps it was because he'd had his knuckles rapped by the authorities over the rollercoaster and told in no uncertain terms to give the American what he required. Perhaps it was because this place, these studios, were his home turf where he could afford to play the big man, and his expansiveness came from self-aggrandisement rather than generosity.

Theo watched the way the others reacted to Chul Woo, and watched also to see whether Min had noticed and, if so, what she thought: but her expression gave nothing away, and he couldn't tell whether she was genuinely oblivious or perfectly well aware and determined not to show it. She'd told him a few days ago, when Yun Seok had gone to the toilet, that she and her father had argued the night he and Theo had confronted each other over the length of the coaster. You took the American's side, Chul Woo had said. No, Min had replied: I translated, same for you as for him. But it shouldn't be the same, Chul Woo had said. Theo had felt obscurely pleased when Min had told him this: not that he wanted her to argue with her father, of course, but – well, he didn't quite know, but it pleased him anyway.

115

Two elderly women came up to Min and hugged her. One of them held her hand low, palm parallel to the ground, and they all laughed. Theo recognised the gesture as being the same the world over – 'last time I saw you, you were this high' – and realised that Min must have been here herself plenty of times as a child.

He decided to take Chul Woo at his word and walked unhurriedly through the lots, Yun Seok at his side. The studio seemed to be almost a small city in itself. A hangar large enough to house a passenger jet squatted low and wide away to his left. Heads bent over desks appeared like fairground coconuts in the windows of an administrative building. Iron dragons reared out from canopies on a street mocked up to look like Chinatown: facades of sushi and ramen restaurants jostled each other on a Japanese pavement. A woman in elaborate ancient Korean dress glided serenely past them and along a row of suburban Western bungalows, an effect slightly spoiled by the North Korean poster for *The Seven Year Itch* in which Marilyn Monroe looked more like Donald Trump.

A scene was being shot up ahead: four men standing in the open, arguing about something. Yun Seok pointed to the cameraman. 'Arriflex 535 video camera. Costs more than a hundred thousand dollars.' He nodded approvingly at Theo's surprise. 'As the Dear Leader said: "The cinema occupies an important place in the overall development of art and literature. As such it is a powerful ideological weapon for the Revolution."'

They slowed as they approached, careful not to spoil the take: but then the director called what Theo presumed was 'cut!', the cameraman lowered his officially approved six-figure apparatus, and the actors lost their positions in a sudden burst of laughter and conversation.

'Hey! Coaster guy!'

It was Peploe, Theo realised with a start: Peploe, detaching himself from the set, sidestepping the cameraman and coming over to Theo with a smile.

'You're an *actor*?' Theo said.

'My dirty secret.'

'Mr Peploe is a very big star in this country,' Min said. Theo hadn't even heard her arrive, but here she was: her father, too. Peploe batted away the compliment without much conviction. 'He has appeared in almost one hundred films,' Min continued.

'*More* than a hundred films, now,' Peploe replied. 'Got a captive market. Every film needs a bad guy, right? Only two kinds of bad guys here: imperial Japanese and contemporary Westerners. Got a lock on one of them.' The director called over. Peploe raised a hand, nodded, and turned back to Theo. 'He wants another take. Stick around and watch, if you like.'

Peploe nodded without warmth at Chul Woo – 100 films meant he was as much of a fixture here as Chul Woo was, Theo thought – and went back to his mark. Theo walked up to the edge of the set, keeping well off to the side to stay out of everyone's eyeline. Three North Korean actors in what looked like police uniforms took up position around Peploe, and when the clapperboard came down they began barking questions at him in quick-fire relays, with Peploe snapping back replies in Korean and doing his best to look defiant and unrepentant about whatever they were accusing him of.

The director called 'cut' again and beckoned the actors over. Chul Woo began to talk over the top of the director, gesticulating as to how he himself would have shot it.

'What was that scene about?' Theo asked.

'They are accusing him of a terrible crime against the Korean people.' It was Yun Seok who answered. 'He has tried to seduce a Korean woman. They are telling him that our nation has always considered its pure lineage to be of great importance, and it cannot

117

be sullied. This, our singular race, is our abundant natural beauty. This is the dark forest of our mother homeland, from whose bosom all true life and happiness springs. Not one drop of foreign ink in the Han River can be allowed.'

Theo thought of, and bit back, several possible answers before deciding on one.

'What will happen to his character? What's the punishment for doing this?'

Yun Seok looked at Min, and not for the first time something passed between them which Theo could see but not fathom: a silent moment where emotions and judgments flitted like shadows across their faces as they considered.

'Put it this way,' Min said eventually. 'There won't be a sequel.'

8

The concrete pour took all night. They were putting in the footers, the foundations, which would have to bear the entire weight of the rollercoaster's superstructure – of the support columns, the track and the train – and so it was emphatically not just a matter of pouring any old concrete into any old hole and hoping for the best.

Theo had spent days calculating maximum static and dynamic design loads: how many footers they'd need, how wide and how deep they'd have to be, how much and what type of concrete would be required, and so on. Rollercoasters were all about gravity, always working with it or against it: rising, falling, twisting. Concrete had great compressive strength, so it could resist the downward forces of the train on the descents: but its tensile strength was relatively poor, so Theo needed to reinforce it with steel to hold everything in place on the ascents when the train was effectively trying to pull the track up with it.

He stood by the workmen at each footer hole, not taking his eyes off the pour for a moment: checking, double-checking, triple-checking. He didn't know if they minded a Westerner bossing them around like this, and he didn't care. Building a coaster was like playing Sudoku: a small mistake at one stage put everything out of whack, even if it wasn't immediately apparent until later.

Min and Yun Seok stayed all night. Yun Seok took himself off to the hut to doze now and then, but Min stuck with Theo in silent complicity. He felt himself aware of her even when he was concentrating on his work: where she was, what she was doing, how she stood, the sound of her voice as she spoke. When he noticed her shivering in the pre-dawn chill, he took off his coat and put it round her shoulders.

'I'm fine,' she said. 'I'm wearing a coat already.'

'You're freezing.'

'I'm not.'

'Please.'

A beat before she smiled her thanks and wrapped his coat tightly around her.

They dropped Theo back at the Yanggakdo just after dawn. Shards of golden light jiggled on the surface of the river as the sun burned up the east. The dredgers were working their seams as they always did, night and day alike, sucking up the silt to keep the river flowing and to use for cement. Hills faded to grey in the distance.

'Maybe we could take you on an excursion?' Yun Seok said.

'Excuse me?'

'You said you have to wait for the concrete to settle and set.'

'There's other stuff I can be getting on with while it does.'

'It would be a nice break for you.' Yun Seok paused. 'And for us.'

'It only needs to be one day,' Min added.

They both looked at Theo expectantly.

'That would be nice,' Theo said. 'I can spare one day. Thank you.'

'Here,' Min said as Theo got out of the car. 'You forgot this.' She took his coat off and handed it back to him, and even in the solitude of the lift he had to resist a sudden urge to hold it to his nose and inhale the scent of her.

Min was late arriving at the Yanggakdo the day of the excursion: only by ten minutes or so, but enough for her to be embarrassed by seeing Theo and Yun Seok already waiting outside for her. They were talking, she saw, but not easily. She stood a moment unseen, watching Theo, and then she stepped forward and they both smiled as they saw her, in the way people do when a third party's presence lightens things up.

A crocodile of Chinese tourists was filtering on to a coach as Min got into the car. One of the guides assigned to the Chinese called across as they passed. 'The American behaving himself, is he?'

'The American's just fine,' she replied, and even though she knew Theo couldn't understand what she was saying, she still felt the urge to defend him.

She was humming to herself as Nam Il started the car.

'What tune is that?' Theo asked.

She smiled uncertainly, as though he'd caught her doing something she shouldn't have been. 'Just a song we were taught in school.'

'Min Ji has an excellent voice,' Yun Seok said.

'Comrade Choe is exaggerating.'

Theo cocked an eyebrow, and Min flushed slightly.

'Will you sing it?' he asked.

Once, at the start of this assignment, she would have thought this a taunt. Now she knew better. It was just a request, as sincere as it was simple. With the sudden quickness of a decision taken before it can be reversed, she burst into song.

Who is the partisan whose deeds are unsurpassed?
Who is the patriot whose deeds shall ever last?
So dear to our hearts is our glorious general's name
Our beloved Kim Il Sung of undying fame.

Theo clapped softly. 'That was beautiful.'

She looked at him and saw that he meant it. Something jumped just a little inside her. She gave him the briefest of smiles: a flicker on her lips, really, no more than that. When she glanced at Yun Seok, his expression was as unreadable as ever. She wondered how much he could see, and how deep: for if one didn't see everything, then in some ways one saw nothing.

She turned back to Theo. 'Oh,' she said. 'I almost forgot. You know you asked how much the statues of the Great Leader and the Dear Leader weigh?'

'Yes. And I wasn't asking to be difficult . . .'

'The weight of their statues is the weight of all the Korean people's hearts.'

Min watched Theo looking out of the window as they drove, and even though she must have travelled this road a hundred times – a trip to the DMZ was a staple of every foreign tour – she had never really paid attention to what was outside. The distance between Pyongyang and the DMZ had always been just that: a space to be crossed rather than an entity in itself, a place that was an absence, defined by what was forbidden rather than what was there. A place from which to avert one's gaze.

Now, Min looked.

The transition was as swift and abrupt as passing through a border control, with the high-rises on the city's perimeter as stark and delineated as a wall. The car passed beneath a vast concrete arch of two women leaning forward to hold up a sphere on which was marked a map of the entire Korean peninsula. 'The women represent the two parts of our glorious nation,' said Yun Seok. 'This is the Monument to the Three Charters of National Reunification.'

Min had heard him say those words over and over again, and only now did they sound stilted and rote, Theo next to her in the back of the car, and a six-lane highway stretching dead straight all the way to the horizon.

The moment they were out of Pyongyang, it was as if they'd entered a different country. The road surface was terrible. Nam Il sometimes had to drive the car in vast, arcing slaloms to steer between potholes the size of football field centre circles. The highway was completely empty. Every few minutes they might pass a lorry or a tour bus, or see a car coming in the opposite direction, but, those apart, they were alone.

'This is the Reunification Highway,' Yun Seok said. 'It takes us straight to the central military demarcation line, which will be dismantled when the Americans leave our brothers and sisters in the South and Korea can be one nation again.'

Tyres thrumming on the tarmac. A woman washing clothes in a river. Derelict factories with windows gaping empty and ragged. Soldiers standing guard over prison gangs working the fields. An old man, his face and arms burned umber by the sun, bent low to the ground under the weight of the cart he was pulling. A group of shoeless children sitting in the middle of the highway, their faces turning in unison to track the car as it went by. Two women in formal dress walking along the roadside. A man playing a grand piano in a field.

Min cast glances at Theo, and knew that in return he saw her following his gaze.

The checkpoints started coming thick and fast as they approached the DMZ. There were four in twenty minutes, and each time the same routine: Yun Seok handing over documents to a bored soldier with an AK47 who scarcely glanced at them before handing them back. At the final checkpoint, where the DMZ proper began, they stopped to register the car and pick up a soldier who'd accompany them at all times until they left. He took the front passenger seat, obliging Yun Seok to squash up with Min and Theo in the back. Min felt the press of Theo's thigh against hers, and she looked straight ahead and dared not move.

Nam Il continued to drive. There were more troops, and more, and yet more. To the side of the road was a vast mural of a single finger pointing skywards, with a slogan written in Korean beneath it. 'Korea is one,' Min said, and from the smile she sensed rather than saw next to her she knew she'd plucked the question from Theo's mouth.

The road became a narrow strip of tarmac between concrete brick walls. It was wide enough only for one car, and to Min it felt as though they were travelling along a drainpipe. When the walls stopped, even for a few metres, barbed wire or electric fences filled the gaps. Nam Il followed signs – not that he had much choice – until they reached a small collection of huts. He parked and switched off the engine.

'The tour buses from Pyongyang will be here soon,' Yun Seok said. 'This is the quietest time.'

They all got out of the car and went through a routine that Theo sensed was almost second nature to them all: seeing Kim Il Sung's signature on the armistice declaration; standing by the demarcation line set in the ground between the huts ('if you step across it you will be shot'); back to the car and another kilometre's drive to the conference room where the armistice had actually been signed and where for many years the division had been played out in self-conscious theatre, DPRK guards at one end and ROK ones at the other, the latter always wearing mirrored sunglasses and standing in tae kwon do stances with fists clenched at their sides, the place all the tourists loved, breathless with excitement at being front and centre of a nuclear stand-off; and then another forty-five minutes in the car to an observation point set high above rolling hills smeared thick green with trees.

They got out here and went to the edge of the observation point: a semi-circle of waist-high concrete beyond which ran a barbed wire fence hung with inverted red triangles marked 'Land Mines'.

Min usually explained what this place was to visitors as they arrived, but she felt – at least, she hoped – that with Theo it would be unnecessary: that he would instinctively know what it was.

Two birds wheeled high above their heads, calling to each other: wings outstretched like those of angels as the birds danced on invisible helices, the sun glinting off the white of their feathers as though they were shards of glass. A flash of black at their throats, another flash of red at their crowns. Min wondered what it would be like to be able to see air the way one can see water. She imagined thermals as fat trees, chaotic heaps of roots mushrooming into vast trunks edged with turbulence like old bark, and cold air falling slowly in parcels, which morphed as they turned and collided.

She looked at Theo. He was still watching the birds. She followed his gaze, and as she did so she felt a sense of great peace from just being here, with him, doing this. It was a warm spring day bursting with possibilities.

'Red-crowned Manchurian cranes,' said Yun Seok. 'They are a symbol.'

'Of what?'

'Good luck and long life.'

'Thousands of species live out there,' Min added. 'Not just birds. If we had longer, you might see deer or even bears. We call it the Peace and Life Zone.'

'How do they avoid the mines?'

Yun Seok and Min looked at each other. Yun Seok nodded.

'No one knows,' Min said.

An unexpected thought came to Min. There were thousands of species in the zone, but only supposedly the most advanced species of all, mankind, could be so blind as to create a shrine to war and watch it become a perfect nature reserve.

High above her and Theo, the cranes still danced and sang.

They stopped halfway along the journey back so Yun Seok could take a pee by the side of the road.

'We could just leave him,' Theo said. For a split second Min looked horrified before she saw that he was joking, and her laugh was three parts relief to one part complicity. 'Is that the kind of thing they do in your country?'

'Well, it happened to me once.'

'When?'

'When I was nine.'

The bottom row of her teeth were neat where her mouth fell open. 'Nine? It was an accident, yes?'

Theo hadn't told anyone this: not in years, perhaps not ever. He wondered why he'd brought it up now.

'No. No accident.'

Min looked at him and nodded, so slight that he could easily have missed it: *tell me if you want*. Her gaze went with his to Yun Seok, standing with his back to them. Yun Seok was whistling to himself, and he wouldn't hear what they said. Nam Il was still in the car, of course, but he spoke no English.

'It was on One Forty'

'One Forty?'

'Sorry. Interstate Forty, New Mexico. There's a criss-cross of motorways across America, and this is one of them. Boxes, that's what I remember. Always boxes, and the way the tape was so bright against the dull cardboard. Sometimes we hardly bothered to unpack them, because this time next year we'd be off somewhere else again. The station wagon was so full that the rear suspension sat hard on its stops. We'd been on the road for what seemed like days, and we were nearly there: at the Santa Rosa lay-by, a hundred miles or so outside of Kirtland. It was late August, New Mexico, high nineties and hot as hell. I'd had my face at the open window to catch the breeze and the seat leather sticking like a wet limpet to the back of my thighs. Wear trousers, my dad said. Wear trousers and it won't stick. Look at Neale. He's wearing trousers and his legs aren't sticking. Of course they weren't, because Neale always listened to Dad and did what he said. Me, I wore the shortest shorts I could find, just to piss my dad off. And this time, when we got out of the car and I had to unpeel myself from the leather, the seat took a piece of skin off. It was agony. There was blood, and I cried, and my mother rolled her eyes and my dad shouted, and we couldn't find the first aid kit among all the boxes, so they tried to stop the bleeding with paper towels from the toilets, but the towels just stuck to the wound and made it worse. And I refused to get back in the car until the bleeding had stopped, and my dad shouted that if I didn't get in they were going to leave without me. I stayed where I was. He told my mum and Neale to get in the car – "Why do you have to be such a pain in the ass about everything?" Neale hissed at me – and then Dad came up to me, towering over me, so close but not actually touching me, and said, "Last chance." It was more a growl than anything else. "Last chance." And I didn't move. I couldn't move. I thought he was going to drag me into the car, but no. He just got in and drove off.'

Theo felt a sharp pricking behind his eyes and a fluttering in his throat, and he would not, *would not*, succumb to either. Yun Seok was still urinating. The man's bladder must have been the size of Lake Michigan.

'But he came back for you?' Min said.

'Who?'

'Your father.'

127

'No.'

'*No?*'

'No.'

'Even though you were a hundred miles from home?'

'Yes.'

'What did you do?'

'I stayed there, waiting for them to come back. The bleeding stopped, and I thought that meant they'd be on their way, even though of course they couldn't have known that. The sun started to go down, and a few folk asked if I was OK and where were my mum and dad, and I said they'd driven off without me, and they were like "Oh that's awful, what a dreadful accident", and when I said he'd done it deliberately they rubbed my hair and said they were sure that wasn't the case. This was where I was going to have to live for the rest of my life, that's what I thought: here, at the Santa Rosa lay-by. And then a state trooper – a policeman, basically – turned up and asked where I lived, and I said we were just moving to Kirtland air-force base, and he drove me all the way there. He let me sit up front with him and gave me candy and let me play with the radio and the sirens, and he didn't mind if the cut opened up and I got blood on the seat – "Believe me, sonny, I've had a lot worse than that in here" – and I wanted to stay in that car forever. I burst into tears when we reached the base because I knew I was going to have to leave that car.'

'What did your father say?'

'That it had all been a misunderstanding.'

'And the policeman believed him?'

'I don't know. I remember the trooper talking to my dad, and he – the trooper – had his arms folded and was standing with his weight on his back leg, and even aged nine I somehow knew that this meant he didn't believe a word my dad was saying, but my dad got some senior officer to come over and eventually the trooper left.'

He crouched down in front of me before he got back in his car and said, "Look after yourself, son, and come ride with me any time", and for all the time we were at Kirtland I used to watch for his car passing on the perimeter road. But it never did, of course.'

The car door opened, bang on cue, and Yun Seok got in. Nam Il started the engine and pulled out without looking – no car had been past in either direction for at least ten minutes, so it wasn't that much of a risk – and the silence that followed vibrated very softly with confidences given and received.

The Juche Tower was still open, just about, when they got back to Pyongyang. They took the lift to the top, and from the viewing platform the city seemed to sprawl towards the horizon. The sun was going down by degrees, a slow suffusing of the clouds above the horizon, soft pink hardening and brightening to burned orange: the shadows lengthening, the world held between night and day. Sunset brushed gentle pastel glows on to apartment buildings: upturned oblongs like children's blocks of cherry blossom and canary, of duck-egg and mauve, and amidst them all the lush, almost violent green of trees and parks.

Over there was Jucheland, still a building site but with the various zones clearly demarcated by now: a work in progress, a gradual transformation. Theo let his gaze wander until he saw the city's railway station looming, the main entrance flanked by pillared facades, topped – inevitably – by twin pictures of Kim Il Sung and Kim Jong Il, and disgorging passengers half-hidden by the mountains of luggage they carried.

Of all the ways he'd travelled, Theo loved the night train more than any other. Even those two words together, night and train, came suffused with undiscovered frontiers and promises of secret assignations. Delicious half-sleep through the clickety-clack of the wheels and the distant whistles. India flashing endless changes at the window on the long westward haul across moonlit plains; the cabin he'd shared from Kazan to Moscow with a superbly drunk Russian wearing nothing but a pair of purple Y-fronts and trying to improve his English with an old copy of *Cosmo*; leaving London on a rainy February evening and waking up the next morning to an Inverness blanketed in snow.

From up here, the station seemed like something from a model railway set. In fact, the entire place looked like a toy town. In the vast expanse of Kim Il Sung Square across the river, men and women in uniform were marching in massed ranks – practice for the parade on the Great Leader's birthday, Min had explained – but even they looked no larger or more substantial than the kind of tin soldiers that spill out of a child's suitcase.

Theo remembered how grim and forbidding he'd found Pyongyang to start with. All it needed was a little sunshine and some familiarity: or perhaps that was all *he* had needed. Now it looked clean, bright and welcoming: sparse traffic meant that the buildings stayed clean, and as Min had said the other day, pretty much everything had to be rebuilt after the Korean War.

'Wondering what it was like before the bombardment?' she said.

He started, slightly, and saw that she saw it. 'Among other things.'

'It looked very different. The buildings were more traditional, and all these high-rises: they weren't here.' She pointed away to their right. 'You see that billboard? The two apartment blocks beyond it? That used to be the school my grandparents went to.'

'Cuckoo, right?'

'Right. And Kwang Sik. That's where they met. The Second Pyongyang High School.'

'What was wrong with the First?'

She smiled. 'I knew you were going to ask that. The First was Japanese.' Cuckoo had told Min all about the Japanese, the way they'd taken the best of everything during their occupation, the way their presence had squatted over not just the city but the entire peninsula like a malevolent umbrella. 'Kwang Sik hated the Japanese. He'd always hum a song about a balsam flower surviving a harsh winter before springing up to new life. The Japanese banned it after realising that its lyrics were actually a – how do you say – a way of expressing the Korean determination to resist?'

'A metaphor.'

'Yes. A metaphor. Kwang Sik's father applied to open a store – a general neighbourhood store full of groceries and essentials, nothing more – the same day as a Japanese merchant. The Japanese merchant got his permit the very next day. The permit for Kwang Sik's father took three months. Three months! And of course by that time the Japanese merchant had all the best customers and suppliers. Cuckoo used to go to Kwang Sik's father's store, even though it was more expensive, because she wanted to see Kwang Sik and do her part against the Japanese. Kwang Sik was – well, Cuckoo says he was one of those children who everyone knew, who everyone talked about. How he'd found the answers for an exam paper before they'd sat it, or let down the tyres on a teacher's bicycle, or tamped down night soil outside the front door of an unpopular policeman so that the man stepped in it the moment he came out of his house in the morning. Always aimed at authority, never at other children.

'There was one time during the war, when they were both about fourteen and already spending all their spare time together, when he made her hide in the attic of the store where his father kept all the spare stock. Through the window she heard Kwang Sik arguing with a Japanese policeman. The policeman was rounding up young women for the Voluntary Service Brigade and had seen

Kwang Sik talking to Cuckoo. When Kwang Sik denied it, the officer dunked him in a large tub of water. Kwang Sik was wearing white clothes, traditional Korean clothes which the Japanese saw as defiant. The water was dark and stagnant, and when the policeman lifted Kwang Sik out again he looked as though he'd been in a mud-bank. He made him repeat the oath of loyalty to Japan. "We are the subjects of the great empire of Japan. We shall serve the Emperor with united hearts. We shall endure hardships and train ourselves to become good and strong subjects of the Emperor. Long live the Emperor!" But the policeman never found Cuckoo, and that was the most important thing.'

'Why? What was the Voluntary Service Brigade?'

'They're better known as comfort women.'

'Sorry. I still don't know.'

'Everyone knew at least one comfort woman. So many were taken. The women – girls, really, many of them – were told they'd be nurses for wounded soldiers. Only when they got to the war zone did they discover the truth: they were there to have sex with the men. Each man was given seven minutes, no more. They lined up in queues, and if anyone took longer than seven minutes then the man behind him pulled him out of the way and took his own turn. The women were given a piece of chalk to mark the wall behind them at each changeover, so they could be paid for each man, but of course they never were.'

'What happened to them after the war?'

Min remembered what Cuckoo had told her: that when these women were back in Pyongyang, and everyone knew what had happened to them, most people had crossed the road when they saw them coming, as if the shame would have infected them if they got too close. A leprosy of the soul, an ostracism in the middle of a busy city. Sometimes these women had disappeared suddenly and only turned up a day or so later when their bodies had floated to the surface of the river or been found hanging from a stair rail: by their own hands, of course, because war could do that to you, could make you harm yourself worse than any damage inflicted by others.

It hadn't just been the comfort women, of course. There had been some people who had been there before the war and who were no longer there now, and not because they had been killed in action. There were those who hadn't just acquiesced to the Japanese, as everyone had been obliged to in the end, but who'd gone out of their way to help them: who had, unforgivably, taken the side of the Japanese over their own people. While the Japanese had been in power, these sympathisers, these imperialist running dogs, had been kept safe from reprisal: but the moment the war was over and the Japanese gone, such immunity had gone with them. Anyone deemed a collaborator had been left with only two choices, flee to the South or face a lynching, and if they hadn't been quick enough with the first then they could hardly have complained if they ended up hanging from a lamppost with a placard around their neck. In the South, it was said, they'd kept those who had been pro-Japanese in power because they wanted law and order above all else.

Min remembered Cuckoo telling her all this: remembered, too, the mixture in Cuckoo's voice of relief that she hadn't been either a comfort woman or a collaborator and of guilt and anger that others had.

'They just came back, I think,' she said, and even though she knew the lie was necessary it still caught momentarily in her throat. She hurried on. 'So Cuckoo and Kwang Sik got married a few years after the war. They were only eighteen.' Eighteen years old and all the time in the world, their lives unrolling in front of them like an endless carpet cascading down an endless staircase. 'The whole neighbourhood came, which would have been unthinkable before the war, when everybody had their place. But every young man had been sent off to fight. It didn't matter whether you were a servant boy or a member of the *yangban* gentry. And when they came back from that, even though things might have looked the same on the surface, they weren't really.'

'You know the Japanese have a word for that?'

'They do?'

'*Kintsukuroi.* I learned it when I did a coaster in Yokohama.'

'What does it mean?'

'It's when they use gold-seamed lacquer to repair broken pottery.'

'But surely you can see where the cracks are?'

'Yes. That's the point. All life is breakage and repair, so why not celebrate it?'

Min smiled. 'I like that.'

Yun Seok brought out the kind of Polaroid camera that Theo remembered from his own childhood, and motioned for Min and Theo to stand closer together so he could get a snap of them. They looked so discordant: Theo a head taller than Min, their hair russet and black respectively like unmatched shoes, his jacket open and flapping slightly while her uniform remained strictly buttoned. Their hands brushed for a moment as they got into position, and when a gust of wind whipped Min's hair into Theo's eyes she apologised and he laughed, which made her laugh too: and it was that exact moment Yun Seok caught, their eyes crinkling and their mouths stretched wide. They stood either side of him to watch as the photograph developed, a grey-white blankness gradually resolving itself into colours and shapes: and neither of them wanted to be the first to say that they liked the picture.

Yun Seok handed it to Theo. 'For you. A memory of this day.'

The soldiers they'd seen in the square weren't even the half of it, not when it came to parade practice. There were armoured cars, tanks, even rocket launchers, a procession as long as a freight train approaching at walking pace along the road below the Juche Tower as though martial law had suddenly been declared. Nam Il had moved the car – been moved on, more likely, from the look of it – to the other side of the road, and he was gesturing at them to hurry. If they crossed now they'd make it in time, but once the parade was on them it would be hours before there was a gap again.

Theo was down on one knee doing up his shoelace, and neither Min nor Yun Seok saw this before they hurried across the road. By the time Theo was upright again and they'd realised, it was too late: the first tank was clattering past, its caterpillar tracks bucking and juddering. He saw the expressions on Min and Yun Seok's faces shift seamlessly from surprise through concern to horror.

A second tank came through hard on the heels of the first, and a third, and a fourth, and when Theo looked down the line he thought the entire North Korean army must be here. Even if there had been a gap – which there wasn't – would he have risked it? A lone Westerner untethered amidst serious military hardware: he'd probably have been shot before he'd gone three paces.

Min's face strobed through the tanks: there and gone, there and gone. Theo cupped his hands to his mouth and hollered as loudly as he could. 'I'll go back to the hotel!' If she heard him above the noise, she made no sign. He yelled again and pointed towards the Yanggakdo. It was a straight walk along the riverbank.

Now came armoured cars three abreast, headlights cutting through the gloom of unlit streets, and Theo couldn't see Min and Yun Seok any more at all. He started to walk along the pavement, against the flow of traffic. The turret gunner of a tank turned his head as they passed to peer at Theo more closely, and a man riding the runner board of an armoured car started slightly when their eyes met, but no one shouted or leapt from their vehicles to wrestle him to the ground.

The procession snake turned away from the river, and in what seemed like no time at all the noise and light had faded and he was alone in the darkened city, the only man moving for what felt like miles around. No headlights cutting through the gloom, no street sweepers or fish-market workers or newspaper deliverymen or any other members of a city's traditional night tribe. Just him, as though he were lord of the manor taking a stroll around the estate with the night wrapped around him. The pyramid loomed ahead, larger and darker and more brooding than any other building, and beyond that the Yanggakdo with the river shimmering dark silver all around it. If any of the hotel staff asked him where his guides were, he would just have to explain what had happened.

And then the shout behind him, high and angry and scared all at once, and the unmistakeable metallic sound of a rifle bolt being cocked.

'Who is paying you to do this?'

The room was both windowless and airless: warm and stuffy, with a staleness which Theo could practically taste. The man in the jet-black suit sitting across the table hadn't told Theo his name: just asked him question after question with a politeness which Theo could tell was beginning to run thin.

'I'm here to build a rollercoaster.'

'Then you have been assigned guides.'

'Yes.'

'You must be with your guides at all times.'

'We got split up. I stopped to tie my shoelace . . .'

'. . . allowing you to get away from them. So I ask again: who is paying you, and what are you doing? Are you collecting information on the military capacity of the Democratic People's Republic of North Korea? Is that why you were so keen to see the parade? Perhaps you were plotting a terrorist attack? These are the actions of a spy.'

Even in the warmth of the room, Theo felt a droplet of cold sweat bloom between his shoulder blades and start the long crawl south.

'That's— I'm not a spy. I'm not.'

'You're working for the CIA.'

'No.'

'You've travelled all round the world. The CIA have always paid for you.'

'No.'

'Cooperate with me, please.'

'I am cooperating with you.'

'Things will be much less pleasant for you if you don't.'

'I'm telling you the truth. It was an accident. We got split up and I decided to make my way back to the hotel. I took the most direct route.'

The man cocked his head back a touch, as though he were a cobra preparing to strike. 'Would you like me to transfer you somewhere else? We have other sites, of course, where the facilities aren't as accommodating and the interrogation techniques are much harsher.'

'Please. Ask my guides. They'll vouch for me.'

The man got up and left the room without answering.

The twin faces of Kim Il Sung and Kim Jong Il gazed down on Theo from high on the wall, the same place where in Spain or Italy or Mexico there'd be a crucifix. Was it really so different? Theo wondered. It was easy to see North Korea as a gigantic prison, or a surreal theme park, or a nuclear-tipped Ruritania, and in some ways it was indeed all these: but it was also a real country with real people, and those people had real lives, real hopes and fears, real aspirations and problems.

Every country needed its own myths, Theo thought: every country bolted a superstructure of meaning and symbolism on to itself. Theo's American half had an atavistic reaction to Old Glory and Uncle Sam, to the Gettysburg Address and the Declaration of Independence, to motherhood and apple pie: his British half did similar to Buckingham Palace and the Houses of Parliament, to fish and chips, to red buses and black cabs.

The North Koreans – well, they weren't the ones who carved the faces of their favourite presidents into a mountain or who tuned in at the same time every Christmas Day to watch an old woman speaking from behind a desk, were they?

Hours crawled, minutes flew. Theo got up, walked round the room, sat down again: anything to keep his mind from turning in on itself. Accusing someone of espionage was the quickest way to make them disappear, he knew that much. Common criminals might get some help from their embassy, but spies were something else entirely.

Someone must have been telling lies about Josef K, he remembered. *Someone must have been telling lies about Josef K.*

The room grew hotter as the night wore on, and the silence was sheened with sweat.

'I suspect him of being a spy,' the man in the black suit said.

He wasn't sweating, despite the warmth which sat heavy and unmoving in the room. Min felt pricklings beneath her skin, a thousand tiny hosepipes waiting to gush. She blocked out the discomfort of the sensation and forced herself to think.

It had been a simple accident, a mistake, and on any other road at any other time it wouldn't have mattered. But she knew that this was only tangentially relevant. Whatever Theo had done would be seen by those who mattered as having happened because of some failure on her part, because she and Yun Seok had not sufficiently impressed on him what he could and could not do. She and Yun Seok had failed with the tourists and the photographs at the back end of last year, which was why they had been assigned to Theo in the first place. They couldn't afford another failure: they simply couldn't.

If it was decided that Theo was a spy, then the simple fact of associating with him would be an indelible mark on both her and Yun Seok. They would be deemed contaminated, suspect: sufferers of an infection which could spread to their families too. Theo absolutely could not be a spy, not if she wanted to survive. Somewhere else in this building, she knew that another man would be asking Yun Seok the same questions. Min hoped that Yun Seok would be as vehement in his denials as she was.

Most of all, she knew that Theo wasn't a spy. Well, she didn't know for absolutely sure – you could never tell exactly what was going on in someone else's head – but she was as certain as she could be. Nothing he'd ever said or done had given her the slightest impression that he was anything other than who he said he was. She didn't think he was a spy, and she didn't want him to be a spy: not just because of the trouble it would cause her, and not just because of the trouble it would cause him, but also because if he was then he would be taken away – gone to the mountains – and she would never see him again. Cuckoo apart, he was the first person who had ever listened to her: *properly* listened to her, that was, rather than just presumed that she wanted for herself what everyone else wanted for her.

'No,' she said. 'He's absolutely not a spy.'

'Why not?'

'We were told that this assignment has been authorised, arranged and funded by the SAC. They would have carried out their own extensive checks on him before offering him the post.'

Min saw the man nod – there was clearly sense in what she'd just said – and waited out his silence. She had a good idea of the calculations he was making. He was from the *Bowibu* – this was their headquarters she was in, though like most public buildings it carried no sign, logo or nameplate – and if he went against the SAC, and lost, that would be the end at least of his career and maybe worse. And if he was indeed thinking that, she had a good idea of what he'd do next.

'In that case,' the man said, 'you and Yun Seok are to redouble your vigilance on him, and report to me any violation, no matter how slight. You understand?'

She understood perfectly. He'd passed the buck back to her.

'I will go and tell him that myself,' she said.

The man nodded. Min got up, opened the door, and walked down the corridor to the room where Theo was being held.

'You're being released,' she said.

'Thank God. I wondered whether you lot would ever see sense.'

Later, she'd realise that he'd been just as scared as she was, and that the tone of his voice had been a way of both showing and masking that. But at the moment he said it, all she heard was complacency and arrogance, and her own fear came to a boil so sudden and furious that it took her by surprise.

'This is how we do things here. You don't like it? Then leave.' She caught a glimpse of her reflection in the one-way glass on the far wall. Her face was contorted by forces she hardly recognised, let alone ones to which she could give a name. There was fury there, of course, and fear too, but there was also something feral and visceral. 'I don't know how you do things in your country, and I don't care. I have a job to do, and that job is looking after you. I know you didn't mean harm. But I'm the one who suffers: me and Yun Seok, of course. Is that clear?'

'Yes,' he said. 'That's quite clear. And I'm sorry.'

She saw the realisation blooming within him of what he'd made her risk, and with that came the sense of a shift between them: *another* shift between them, perhaps, for she saw what, in an obscure way, he'd risked for her too.

'Comrade Park, what transgressions have you made against the Revolution these past seven days? What transgressions have you made in thought, in word, and in deed?'

'I have appraised the week that has passed. In order to correct my faults, I must cleanse myself of the repeated sins that accumulate and slow down our beloved Revolution. I have proved myself insufficiently grateful for the Supreme Leader's eternal love.

'First, I have been remiss in not helping my beloved mother as much I could have done with the preparations for my wedding, which is in itself one of the highest honours a person can have in this country, the opportunity to join in wedlock and start a family under the benevolent guidance of the Supreme Leader, father of the nation.

'Second, I failed to impress upon the American Kempe the importance of remaining with Comrade Choe and me at all times, which led to his unauthorised excursion the other night. Since then, however, his attitude has improved, thanks to the re-educational efforts of the skilled *Bowibu* operatives who questioned him subsequent to that excursion.'

'Do you take any personal credit for the change in the American's attitude?'

'I like to think that Comrade Choe and I have established a harmonious rapport with the American, which has helped to ease difficulties on both sides.'

'Describe to me the range of your discussions with the American.'

'I have missed no opportunity to showcase the shining example for international socialism which the Democratic People's Republic of Korea affords under all aspects of the Supreme Leader's glorious guidance.'

'Have you had any personal conversations with the American?'

'I'm not sure what you mean by "personal" in this context.'

'Have you told him details of your life or had him tell you details of his?'

'Only in the most general terms.'

'You have not shared inappropriate confidences with him?'

'If I had done, Comrade Choe would have reported them already. However, when I sang a patriotic song at the request of the American, I fear my voice was not good enough to do true justice either to the music or the spirit of the words.'

'These are sins against the Revolution in deed and word. Have you sinned against the Revolution in thought?'

'My thoughts are guided at all times by love for the Great Leader and the Dear Leader, and by my desire to study all their teachings.'

'You have had no improper thoughts at all this past week?'

'That is correct.'

'We congratulate you, comrade, for these admissions, which are so essential to the progress of each of us.'

It wasn't mentioned again. The next day they all assembled at the hotel as usual, and Nam Il drove them to Taesongsan as usual, and Theo worked on the rollercoaster all day as usual. Now and then his thoughts would drift away from engineering calculations and design options, and he remembered the way Min had looked yesterday, with her colour high and her eyes blazing and wide open, not just the lids but the pupils themselves, as though she had been looking not just at Theo but into him: through him, even.

The bloom on her forehead in the hot room and the quickness of her exhalations.

At the end of the day, Nam Il drove them back to the hotel. Theo wondered whether Min would suggest that they walk the last few minutes, or whether his transgression had ruled that out. He wouldn't ask, he decided, but if she offered then he'd say yes.

They were driving along the embankment when she leant forward and said something in Korean to Yun Seok. Yun Seok nodded, and Nam Il pulled into the side without apparently needing to be told.

Min turned to Theo with a smile and a raised eyebrow.

They began to walk, the three of them as before: and as before Yun Seok began to fall back, and Min and Theo walked on just out of his earshot.

'I'm sorry,' Theo said when he was sure Yun Seok couldn't hear.

'Why did you do it?'

'It seemed the best thing to do.'

'Why didn't you just wait for us? The parade would have ended sooner or later.'

'I don't know.'

'That's not an answer.'

No, Theo knew, it wasn't, but it was all he could give her. He couldn't give her anything that was anywhere near a truth he'd barely admitted to himself: that seeing her scared for him meant seeing that she cared for him, and the equal and opposite side was the thought that maybe they'd send him home and he'd never have to see her again. It was childish, of course: a juvenile, half-formed desire to test the boundaries of her tolerance and affection, just as he'd once ran away from Altus air-force base in order to see how long it would be before his parents came looking for him, and by extension how much they cared about him. His father had cared, enough at least to beat the living daylights out of him when he found him. A childhood memory replayed and re-enacted in the hope that it would end differently, better, the second time round.

There were two conversations going on here, Theo realised: the one they were having and the one they weren't. The gentle probing on both sides, the gradual, almost imperceptible slide towards the truth.

'Tell me something about yourself,' she said.

'Tell me what that place is first.'

'What place?'

'The pyramid.'

'The Ryugyong? It was a hotel, built for a world youth festival. One hundred and five storeys tall. But it didn't open in time, and then it didn't open at all, and then – well, it's just been sitting there.' The way she said it made Theo imagine a relic of some long-lost civilisation, this ghostscraper left abandoned in the face of some sudden and unspeakable disaster: an annihilated place,

Ozymandias' colossal wreck amidst its lone and level sands. 'It was for the same festival my parents met at, coincidentally.'

'Really?'

'The World Festival of Youth and Students for anti-imperialist solidarity, peace, and friendship. It was the year after our southern brothers and sisters had hosted the Olympics, but this was going to be bigger, better and more popular, of course. A week of sports, rallies, discussions on national liberation struggles throughout the world, musical performances, and so on. Chul Woo was in charge of filming the festival. Han Na – my mother – was his assistant. They were married six months later.'

'That's lovely.'

'Mmm.' She disguised her ambivalence as agreement, because Cuckoo had told Min the story and Min had left a lot of it out. She hadn't told Theo that Chul Woo had been ordered to destroy footage of the moment in the opening ceremony when the gun salute had followed on too quickly from the release of doves and the birds had either fled the scene or dropped lifeless from the sky, or that the first assistant whom Chul Woo had hired had left after three days as he'd been so rude to her, or that Cuckoo had been so desperate for Chul Woo to get married even though he was fifteen years older than Han Na that she'd basically set them up, and only then by pretending not to think much of Han Na. Chul Woo had always thought his judgment better than everyone's, so if his mother didn't like someone, that was for him a sure sign that they were worth pursuing. It had been the most basic of psychological gambits, but it had worked.

'OK,' Min said. 'Your turn.'

'I've told you lots about myself.'

'You haven't.'

'I've told you more than I tell most people.'

She shrugged. 'Then tell me something you haven't told me.'

Theo felt as though he was shuffling through a mental Rolodex. This one? Too flippant. This one? Too painful. Images held and hidden, curated and released: the stories we tell each other quite as much as we tell ourselves. Something he hadn't told Min? How about something he'd barely told himself? There would be safety in it: he'd be gone in a few months and they'd never see each other again.

'My mother has a scar on her arm. Just here.' He touched the inside of his right forearm, just below the elbow. 'She was holding a cup of tea when I came rushing through the door and knocked into her. I was, I don't know, eight or something. And in the summer, when it was warm enough not to wear long sleeves, she'd walk around with her arm turned a little outwards so people would see the scar and ask her about it. "Oh, that was Theo," she'd say, like I'd done it deliberately. "You do your best for them, and what do you get? Neale, though, he's a great kid." Then off she'd go, talking about Neale and how well he was doing at school. "Who's my favourite boy?" she'd ask him. "Who's my favourite boy?" She fussed around him the whole time. But when I fell from a set of monkey bars and knocked myself out, she didn't hug me or ask how I was. Just moaned that I'd messed up her day. Always making me feel like I'd done something wrong.'

'Or like you *were* something wrong.'

The damp, sticky scent of the leaves, low and asphyxiating. Her nearness and his awareness of it, both sudden and familiar as if it had been there all along and only now had he let himself acknowledge it. Her outline seemed to glow as she walked, a bright shining border beckoning him on. He felt the gap between them shimmer and reshape. When he swallowed, there was a catch in his throat. She heard it and turned to him. The pupils of her eyes were wide and dark. She touched his arm at the point where his mother's scar would have been and held her fingers there. He looked at her in surprise and she met his gaze, a silent acknowledgement of the risk she was running even with this most basic of actions, and Theo had to turn his face away with the sudden sharp pricking he felt behind his eyes.

They arrived at the hotel ten minutes later. Nam Il was sitting in the car, as silent and expressionless as a sphinx.

'Thank you for walking with me,' Theo said.

'Thank *you* for walking with *me*.' They both laughed.

She opened the car door and waved as she got in. The sun, bouncing off the windscreen, caught her eyes, and as Theo watched they flared from brown to gold, just for a moment. A line approached, but not yet crossed. A gesture, a look, a touch. A dawning, like a pale winter sunrise.

9

It had been unspoken but universally accepted that Cuckoo and Cuckoo alone would help Min prepare on her wedding day. Han Na and Chul Woo had gone off to meet Hyuk Jae's parents at the restaurant where the ceremony would take place: Min and Cuckoo would join them when Min was ready.

Hyuk Jae's parents had brought Min's dress round – it was tradition that the groom's parents gave the bride her dress – but Min knew the moment she saw it laid out neatly on her bed that it wouldn't suit her. The pink was too bright, too vibrant, all wrong for her colouring. She tried it on anyway. Cuckoo helped her, adjusting a bit here and a bit there, suggesting that Min wear her hair first one way and then another. But the dress fitted perfectly, and Min's hair wasn't the problem.

Min looked at herself in the mirror. Cuckoo shook her head. They both knew it.

'It doesn't matter,' Min said.

'It *does*.'

'It's the thought that counts.'

'It's every photograph of you on that day till the end of time. Everyone has a picture of their wedding up in their apartment. You have to look right. Especially you, my darling granddaughter.'

Cuckoo went over to the wardrobe. She was moving slowly now, but she could still get around so long as she conserved her energy, measuring it out in precise batches as one would do with ingredients for a recipe. Every day now she could feel her strength ebbing a tiny bit more. Today would be an effort and she would pay for it tomorrow, but she didn't care. What was a few days less at the end of a long life? Far better to see Min get married than just sit out the end and wait for the darkness to come.

At the far end of the wardrobe, untouched since they'd moved in here, was a plastic dress cover, and inside it was Cuckoo's dress in all its constituent parts. She unhooked the hanger carefully from the rail, pushed her other clothes aside so she could bring it out, and handed it to Min.

'Are you sure?' Min said.

'Let's give it a go, at least. Have we got time?'

'A few minutes.'

When Min went to unzip the cover, she saw that her fingers were trembling. Half a century kept protected in the darkness. She looked at Cuckoo. Cuckoo was smiling, and her eyes were wet. Min took the garments out one by one: the *chima*, the *sokchima*, the *jeogori*, all pressed briefly to her nose as she lifted them so she could smell the mustiness and the mothballs, so she could smell her grandmother from half a century ago and here today with her.

Cuckoo watched Min, layering sight upon memory: Min here, now, and Cuckoo herself all those years ago.

The school was almost closed when Cuckoo arrived. Ok Ja, the headmistress, was checking that everyone had left and that all the windows were shut. Not that there was any crime in the workers' paradise, of course.

'Comrade Park!' Ok Ja said. 'We wondered where you were.'

'I'm sorry. It was the quarterly meeting with the minister.' She left unsaid the second part, not just because she knew Ok Ja would understand but also because it was impossible to state out loud without implying criticism: that such meetings could take place with almost no notice and go on for as long as the minister wanted them to, which wasn't necessarily as long as they needed to. And if that inconvenienced Cuckoo (an inconvenience perhaps made deliberately, as she'd refused the minister's advances the previous year) and made her two hours late to pick up Chul Woo, well, that was her problem. They couldn't be expected to arrange everything around her schedule.

'Chul Woo went home with Comrade Lee.' Lee Song Si had a son, Song Su, who was Chul Woo's best friend, in as much as eleven-year-old boys had best friends: which was to say, right now they were inseparable, but this time last year they had barely spoken to each other and the same might well be true this time next year. Chul Woo and his friends seemed not so much to orbit round each other as crash about the place like the dodgem cars Cuckoo had seen in books about America, holding close for a short time before spinning off to the next place, a giddying maelstrom of friendships formed and broken and reformed.

'Do you have his address?'

Ok Ja reached into the pocket of her jacket and pulled out a slip of paper. 'Here. He wrote it down for you.'

Cuckoo took the paper and read it. Ponghwa Street. One of the city's main thoroughfares and a good address, which was as reliable an indicator of someone's status as any and more reliable than most.

The apartment was ten minutes' walk from the school, and in that time Cuckoo passed five separate building sites, apartment blocks rising from the ground like flowers seeking the sun. Less than a decade before, all this had been rubble, flattened by the bombs which had fallen like endless storm rain from the sky. Now, under the personal tutelage of the Great Leader, the city was being totally rebuilt, not as good as before but better. If ever there was proof that international socialism fostered solidarity, here it was. Volunteers had come from the Soviet Union and the German Democratic Republic, and many other countries had offered material assistance, all to help restore Pyongyang to its full glory.

Song Si's apartment was on the third floor. Cuckoo knew from the moment she walked in that no woman lived here. It was not so much what was there as what was not: no softness, no delicacy of touch, no wildflowers picked from the riverbank to add colour and scent. Everything was not just tidy but exceptionally so, as though the very act of perfect arrangement was in itself a silent scream.

Chul Woo and Song Su were playing on the floor, working through what looked like a hugely elaborate battle with tiny wooden figurines in army uniforms and toy tanks whose dull green paint was beginning to flake. Their red Young Pioneer scarves sat bright and bold against the white of their shirts. Chul Woo looked up, saw his mother, smiled and returned to the battle without missing a beat. Cuckoo had a sudden fierce desire to freeze him at this moment forever, when he was young enough still to hold on to childhood's innocence but old enough to be entirely his own person.

Song Si looked to be in his early forties, though trying to assess anyone's age after the privations of the war could be fiendishly hard. He bowed slightly to Cuckoo and offered her tea. When she apologised for being late, he waved it away.

'Think nothing of it. I know your job's important. I'm glad that today I was able to help.' He gestured towards the boys, rapt with concentration as they zoomed tanks around each other. 'Besides, it's been a pleasure. They play nicely together. It's not been easy for Song Su ever since his mother – ever since it's only been me and him – and he likes Chul Woo very much.'

Cuckoo would not have asked had he not alluded to it, but she sensed – more in the tone of his voice than the words he used – that he would not shy from talking about it: indeed, that he actually wanted her to ask. She mulled various ways of phrasing the question before opting for the simplest and most direct.

'What happened to your wife?'

'Tuberculosis. Six years ago.'

'It must have been dreadful.' Everyone knew someone who had died from tuberculosis, and it was never pretty: the awful wet coughing which spluttered up blood, the way the sufferer wasted away almost in front of your eyes as the disease ate them from the inside out, the fight for breath, the panicky rattle of not enough oxygen, and all the time drowning, drowning, drowning on dry land.

Song Si nodded. 'It was.'

Cuckoo put her hand lightly on his. 'I'm sorry.' She looked at the clock on the wall. 'Chul Woo, it's time we went.'

Chul Woo hopped to his feet without demur. 'Mama, can Song Su come and play at ours next time?'

'Of course.'

'He'd like that,' Song Si said. And then, after a moment in which he seemed to be weighing up whether or not to say it out loud, he added, 'As would I.'

Song Si with his kind, sad eyes. Song Si with his voice so quiet that sometimes Cuckoo had to lean forward to hear what he was saying. Song Si with tales of the 12th Tractor Factory of which he was general manager, and of their victory in the Chollima Works Tournament where they had exceeded their quotas by a greater margin than any other tractor factory in the country, and of the time the Great Leader had visited the factory to give the workers some on-the-spot guidance and how he, Song Si, had felt the great man's hand rest on his shoulder even for a moment and considered it the most astonishing privilege of his life. He had taken the jacket he had been wearing that day, placed it in a suit carrier and hung it in his wardrobe, never to be worn again in order to best preserve the mark of the Great Leader.

Song Si here in Cuckoo's apartment. It was the sixth, perhaps the seventh time they'd met, always with their sons, and in their respective apartments strictly in turn. Had they been younger then people might have gossiped, but then again had they been younger they would never have been permitted to meet like this, unchaperoned and behind closed doors.

Song Si cleared his throat. 'I was thinking, Comrade Park.'

'Yes?'

'Our boys, they're practically brothers now. It's good for boys to have brothers.' He cleared his throat again. 'And it's good for a man to have a woman, and for a woman to have a man.'

Cuckoo suddenly knew what Song Si was going to say, and she had honestly never thought for a moment, not a single moment, that he would come out with it, and she realised she had no idea how to answer.

'Comrade Park: perhaps you might agree to be my wife?'

She had told Song Si she needed time to think it over, not just so as not to embarrass him with an instant rejection but also because what he had said was true. It would be good for Chul Woo to have a brother – Song Su, that was, not another child that she and Song Si could have together. She didn't think of Song Si in that way at all, not at all. But she knew he would never hurt her, never raise a hand to her when he'd been drinking, never disappear for days on end with another woman and come back with neither explanation nor apology, and those in

153

themselves would make him a better husband than most of the men her friends were married to.

Those friends had told her time and time again that she could have any unmarried man she chose, widower or bachelor. She was beautiful, and still only in her early thirties. Women mourn, they said: men replace. And who was to say that the latter wasn't better than the former? Maybe in time she and Song Si would fall into some kind of pleasant companionship. It wouldn't be what she had had with Kwang Sik, but then nothing would be. She couldn't think about it as replacing a dead man, as no one could replace Kwang Sik. But if she thought about it as beginning a new life with a different man, that made more sense.

Song Su was a sweet boy, and it would be good for him to have a mother again: he could hardly have many memories of his own mother. And Chul Woo, of course, had no memories of his own father. Cuckoo did her best to bring Kwang Sik to life for Chul Woo, talking of him constantly, ensuring that photographs of him were on display in every room in their apartment, but it wasn't the same as Chul Woo having a real father.

For Chul Woo, Cuckoo knew, there was just a void in the shape of his father, perhaps even a void in the shape of the idea of his father, and all Chul Woo's questions and all her answers could not make that void flesh. He needed a father, she knew that. Every boy did. Fathers toughened boys up, showed them how to be men and how not to be men.

Two half-units, coming together to make a unit: the power of the collective at an everyday level.

She sat at her desk and wrote a note.

Dear Comrade Lee.

After consideration, I accept your kind proposal.

With best wishes, Comrade Park.

She sealed it in an envelope and put it in Chul Woo's schoolbag, reminding herself to tell Chul Woo in the morning to give it to Song Su, who would in turn give it to his father.

Cuckoo in her apartment, the morning of her wedding. Her friends had offered to help her get dressed, but she had declined with firm politeness. She wanted to be on her own for this. Even Chul Woo wasn't there: he was at Song Si's house, all boys together, with the people who would in a few hours be his father and brother. He had looked so smart when she'd seen him off this morning: shoes polished, clothes pressed, hair brushed into a side parting, which might just about last the ceremony, and his face alight with the excitement of finally having a family to call his own.

Her Chosŏn-ot, *the traditional costume that all women wore for their wedding day, was laid out on the bed in all its constituent parts. She turned the radio on and picked up the* sokchima, *a corseted underskirt.*

'The Soviet Union has secured a great victory in the Cuban missile situation. The Yankee imperialists have agreed not to invade Cuba: a humiliating climb down for the young, weak and inexperienced President Kennedy.'

Cuckoo adjusted the sokchima *until it hung off her just so. Her mouth was dry, but she did not drink any water: bathroom breaks were more or less impossible once the clothes were on. Over the* sokchima *came the* chima, *the skirt that ran down to her ankles and was deep red in hope of good fortune.*

'The Korean People's Army was delighted to welcome today an American soldier who of his own free will has come over to the Democratic People's Republic of Korea. Mark Peploe, twenty-one years old, was stationed at the Demilitarised Zone as part of the illegal Yankee occupation of the southern part of our republic and their subjugation of our brothers and sisters there.'

Now the jeogori *jacket, with its main panels and fabric bands and removable collar. Cuckoo put each part on without thinking, the movements routine.*

'I grew tired of living in a decadent society, said the defector. I wanted to contribute to juche, the self-reliance that is the basis for the socialist fatherland of Kim Il Sung. I realised that the USA has been defeated and just doesn't know it yet.'

She wondered what must have been going through that young Yankee's mind in the moments before he walked across the border. Cuckoo knew enough about soldiers to know that they did as they were told. To not do what you were told – more, to do what was strictly forbidden – was therefore an act of considerable courage. That Yankee had turned his back on everything he'd known and done something just because it was the right thing to do, because that was what his conscience, his heart, had told him to do.

Cuckoo stood stock still in front of the mirror, examining herself: not how she looked, as she knew that already, but how she was. She wasn't looking, she realised: she was listening, and in the thumping beneath her ribcage was the song of her heart.

How strange, that a man she'd never met – a man she'd only just heard about on the radio – should have made her think anew about everything. Or perhaps it was less that he made her think anew, and more that he made her see what had been there all along.

She thought of Song Si, and the smile he'd given her when he'd learned of her acceptance. It had been a smile of relief, and of a gratitude that had almost been pathetic. And in that moment she had realised something she had always known and had suppressed deep within herself: that Song Si would always be second best. It would be a marriage of three hearts and not two, and that was not fair on either of them.

Cuckoo was still standing in front of the mirror when Chul Woo came to find her several hours later, long after the allotted time for the wedding service had come and gone.

Min finished dressing and turned to face Cuckoo. The *Chosŏn-ot* looked perfect on Min. Of course it did. Cuckoo laid a hand gently against on Min's shoulder. 'You look so beautiful I can hardly bear it.'

'Thank you.'

They stood in silence for a moment, looking at each other: a reflection in Min of Cuckoo's past, a mirror back to times gone, a mantle passed between them.

Cuckoo nodded towards the bright-pink *Chosŏn-ot* which Hyuk Jae's parents had given Min. 'This is the only reason you can give that back to them: that your silly old grandmother wanted you to wear her wedding dress.'

Min looked down at the *Chosŏn-ot* she was wearing. 'And you're sure about *this*?'

'I've never been surer. Nothing would give me greater pleasure. I never got to wear it. Maybe that's because all the time it was waiting for you.' Min folded Cuckoo in a hug. 'Don't get it all creased!' Cuckoo laughed, and as she disentangled herself she turned away for fear that Min would read the expression on her face, would feel the remembrances held in every stitch that this dress was bad luck once, would remember what Cuckoo had said about her being too good for Hyuk Jae and wonder whether the dress was talisman or curse: because Cuckoo was wondering exactly that herself, and she didn't know whether she'd given Min the greatest gift or a poisoned chalice.

Min smiling at Cuckoo, and Cuckoo seeing that the smile didn't reach Min's eyes, and both of them knowing the truth.

'Maybe you shouldn't wear this dress after all,' Cuckoo said.

'The dress has nothing to do with it.' Min's voice was steady, and Cuckoo realised that Min wouldn't cry, just as Cuckoo hadn't cried when she'd backed out of marrying Song Si.

'You have to go through with it, you know,' Cuckoo said softly.

'You didn't.' An observation, not an accusation.

'Things were different for me.'

'How?'

'My parents were dead, so I didn't have to worry about what they thought. I had a child already. My life was – things weren't like they are today. And Song Si: it was a terrible thing, to do what I did to him. I should have said no when he asked me, or at least some way ahead of time. Leaving him standing there, the time ticking on and everyone knowing that I wasn't coming. I wonder if he ever got over the humiliation.'

'Did you ever speak to him again?'

Cuckoo shook her head. 'I was too ashamed. I don't have many regrets, darling girl, but that's one of them: not that I did it, but that I did it that way. It was the cruellest thing imaginable. It burned in me for years. I used to wonder what would happen if I saw him on the street. He moved his son to another school after that, you know. I wanted to see him, just once, and apologise. But maybe it's best that I couldn't. Don't do it to Hyuk Jae. He's a good man, you know that.'

'You told me he was a crashing bore and I could do better.'

'He is and you could. But that's not what marriage is about.'

Min rested a finger against the red thread that Cuckoo wore around her wrist. 'And this?' In Korean tradition you were linked to your true love by a red thread, no matter how far apart from them you might be.

'What about this?'

'Would I ever wear one of these for Hyuk Jae?'

'Would your mother ever wear one for your father? I got lucky, my dear. I got very lucky indeed. Most people never have what I had.'

'So I should just settle? Accept that Hyuk Jae will be as good as it gets?'

'We all settle in life. Get married, have children, go to work, bring up the children until they can get married, go to work, have children of their own, and on it goes. It's advantageous to marry Hyuk Jae, not just for you but for your parents too. But the really important things – the truth, the feeling, the rebellion – we keep in here.' She made a loose fist and tapped it against her breastbone. 'We keep it in here, locked tight so only we can find it and no one can take it from us.'

A bright May day, the sky almost unclouded and the warmth of the air suggesting that summer would soon be coming in.

Hyuk Jae was waiting for Min outside the restaurant. 'You look beautiful,' he said, but when he led her inside he did not take her hand. He walked a pace ahead, trusting that she'd keep up. She had a sudden flaring of dislike for his thoughtlessness: was it too much, on her wedding day of all days, to ask that he walked beside her?

When Min entered the room where the ceremony was taking place, everyone there turned to look at her. She made her eyes go fuzzy, not by much but so she wouldn't have to catch someone's gaze and wonder if her own expression betrayed her. Her friends were to the left as she walked down the aisle: Yun Seok, of course, and the other guides, plus her university friends and those she'd known since school. Pretty much everyone in her life, in other words.

Everyone apart from one person, of course.

There was no way she could have invited Theo, much as she'd wanted to: it was unthinkable for a foreigner to attend a wedding here, absolutely unthinkable. And even if it hadn't been, how would she have explained it? Hyuk Jae knew nothing of Theo's existence in any way other than the careful, neutral explanations in which Min had already mentioned him: that Theo was here to build the rollercoaster and that she and Yun Seok had been tasked with looking after him. Hyuk Jae hadn't asked any more than that. Hyuk Jae rarely asked any more than that about anything. Min wanted to bring Theo into pretty much every conversation she had, as even saying his name gave her a small thrill deep inside: but years of preserving her thoughts from the outside had inured her to the temptation.

There was a ceremonial table at the front of the room, and on it were a live hen and rooster wrapped in red and blue cloths, tightly enough so they couldn't move any more than their heads. A stern-looking woman in a grey jacket motioned for Min and Hyuk Jae to sit in the chairs placed at the table: Min on the hen's side, Hyuk Jae on the rooster's. Min smoothed her dress out as she sat. She and Hyuk Jae were too far away from each other to touch, and she knew that it was immaterial.

The woman in the grey jacket rattled through what she had to say, so fast as to stop only just short of insulting, as though she had half a dozen of these to do today and couldn't afford any slippage in the timetable. 'Welcome to you all and thank you for bearing witness to this man and this woman being joined in matrimony there is no more precious duty for any of us than to join with another as part of one great family under the guidance of the Supreme Leader there is no honour higher than to produce the next generation of that national family who will themselves bask in the love of the Supreme Leader just as we bask in it now and just as we did in the love of the Dear Leader before him and the Great Leader before him.'

Min listened to the woman, but her thoughts were with Theo: and she only just realised in time that the woman was asking whether she, Comrade Park Min Ji, took this man to be her lawful wedded husband.

'I do,' Min said, and the words sounded dry and hollow in the back of her throat.

When Hyuk Jae was asked the same question, his voice in reply was deep and sure, as though he'd been waiting all his life for this moment.

There was a smattering of applause from behind them. Min turned to see Han Na smiling at Hyuk Jae's father, and Chul Woo with his shoulders back and chest puffed out as though he were single-handedly responsible for all this. She dared not look at Cuckoo, the one person she wanted to see above all. Well, almost above all, and as the guests came up in turn to place flowers and dates in the hen's beak and red chilli in the rooster's, Min smiled and took their congratulations, the mask on so firmly that not a scintilla of her true feelings could escape.

Nam Il was waiting outside the Yanggakdo with the car. There were two guides with him, both men, and their uniforms were different from Min and Yun Seok's. An alternative organisation drafted in as cover, perhaps.

Theo had debated what to do all morning. Min had explained on one of their walks beneath the poplars that she'd have liked to invite him, but he had to understand how impossible that was.

He *had* understood, of course, and then he'd asked her to talk him through what would happen on the day so he could at least imagine what she was doing.

Perhaps it was for the best anyway, that he couldn't go. He didn't have especially good memories of weddings: the last one he'd been to had been his brother's, where he'd stood at the end of the line of groomsmen, a pace away from the next man, and thought that he'd rather have been just another guest than given the sop of groomsman. It had been his mother who'd insisted on it, of course, for fear of what the guests would have thought had Theo not been at least nominally among his brother's nearest and dearest. By the time the next formal family occasion, his father's funeral, had come round, the pretence had worn paper thin. His mother had sat in the front row with Neale and Neale's wife and children – who were too young to understand what was going on – and Theo had been placed in the second row next to a distant aunt and uncle. He'd contented himself with the thought that it was at least one row nearer the exit so he didn't have to spend a minute longer with the old bastard in the coffin than was absolutely necessary.

This morning, he'd tried to keep himself busy. He'd opened a book, tried to concentrate on it, realised he'd read the same page three times without taking in a single word, closed it with a sigh and rubbed at his eyes with his knuckles. Since he wasn't allowed to run, he'd done press-ups. Standard ones on the floor, incline ones with his hands on the end of the bed, reverse incline ones with his feet on the end of the bed and his hands on the floor, performing each set to failure, arms burning and jellified, until he'd been able to do no more even if he'd wanted to.

Min had confided her doubts in him: told him her secret, no matter how obliquely. He was curious about her family, her life. He wanted to know all about her, about the myriad of people and experiences that had helped shape her. Most of all, he simply wanted to see her. Even on the day when she was giving herself to someone else, he wanted to see her. Better in those circumstances than not at all.

He moved fast now, determined to go through with it before he changed his mind: into the corridor, down in the lift, and out the front of the hotel where Nam Il greeted him with a taciturn lack of enthusiasm so usual that Theo found it comforting.

'Can we go to Mansu Hill?' he asked the guides. 'I'd like to draw the Chollima statue to help me design the cars.' He held up a sketch pad and pencil.

They nodded and gestured for him to get in the car.

Theo made a show of drawing the statue – the horse rearing up and forward, and on its back a worker raising a document from the Central Committee of the Korean Workers' Party and a peasant woman holding a sheaf of rice, the worker seven metres tall and the woman six and a half, all of course lovingly detailed by the guides – but his eyes kept darting to the twin statues of Kim Il Sung and Kim Jong Il nearby. This was the very first place Min and Yun Seok had brought him when he'd arrived in Pyongyang, and today there was a queue of newly-wed couples laying flowers at the statues' feet and genuflecting in supplication for the blessing of their union. Theo knew enough by now to be aware that this was what marriage was in this country: not so much a man and woman's commitment to each other as their joint commitment to the nation itself, to continue the cleanest race of them all, and both nation and race were embodied by the men who stood bronze and eternal at Mansudae.

He sketched and waited and waited and sketched, and eventually – it was probably only a few minutes, but it felt like hours – Min and Hyuk Jae reached the front of the queue. Theo saw the way Hyuk Jae looked at Min and the way she looked back at him, the mismatch in their expressions. He knew that mismatch well: he'd seen it sometimes in photographs of himself with other people. In his case, it had been because the walls he'd built had become so tall and solid that there was no breaching them. But Min wasn't too scared. She was perfectly capable of feeling all the things Theo hadn't allowed himself to feel, but not with or for the man she had just married.

He watched her go up with Hyuk Jae to lay their flowers and bow low. When she turned, she looked straight at Theo, and it wasn't so much the half-smile she gave as the remainder of it she was trying so clearly to suppress that made him glad he'd come after all. Feeling suddenly and unexpectedly emboldened, he made three gestures: a wide sweep of his arm to take in all their guests, a tap to his chest, and an open palm indicating the statues behind her.

She understood immediately, as he'd known she would. *The weight of their statues is the weight of all the Korean people's hearts.*

Min smiled and held her hand to her own chest, and Theo knew in a way he could not explain that it was just for him. Her husband and family all around and the avatars of the nation loomed behind her, but still that moment was just for him: and his heart twisted and leapt like a wild salmon from a river in spate.

PART II

Revolution of Word

'We pardon to the extent that we love. Love is knowing that even when you are alone, you will never be lonely again. And great happiness of life is the conviction that we are loved. Loved for ourselves. And even loved in spite of ourselves.'

Les Misérables, Victor Hugo

10

It felt all wrong from the moment Hyuk Jae shut the door behind him.

They were in Min's apartment. More precisely, they were in Min's room, the one that until now she'd shared with Cuckoo. It was tradition that a newly married couple spent their first night at the house of the bride's parents and their second at that of the groom's. Only on the third night would they move into a place of their own.

So Cuckoo had gone to sleep with Han Na, Chul Woo was on the sofa – he'd been deeply unhappy about that, but even he wouldn't have dared suggest that his octogenarian mother sleep alone on the sofa or in the same bed as him – and Min's bed had been pushed right next to Cuckoo's to form a makeshift double.

If there was a scenario more perfectly designed to ensure that Min felt as little like a newly-wed as possible, she couldn't imagine it. This was the place where she and Cuckoo had talked and laughed night after night, conversations charting miniscule advancements in Min growing up and Cuckoo growing old. This was a room with walls so thin they'd had to keep their voices low to avoid disturbing Chul Woo and Han Na. This was her space, and Cuckoo's: no one else's. Certainly not Hyuk Jae's. He'd never even been in her bedroom before, let alone stayed over.

Hyuk Jae smiled. Min hoped that he was as nervous as she was, no matter how brave a face he might be putting on it. They would have to help each other through it. That was what married life was about, wasn't it?

She thought of Theo, and wondered what he was doing now, alone in his hotel room. She thought of him and wondered whether he was thinking of her.

'Let me take that off for you,' Hyuk Jae said.

He was all fingers and thumbs, clumsy in trying to remove what Cuckoo had been elegant in helping Min put on. He pulled the *jeogori* over her head, and when it got stuck he pulled harder until Min yelped with pain.

'I'll do it,' she said. Her fingers found his, and she realised that he was trembling. She was not the only one with no experience here. Premarital sex was a gross offence against revolutionary ethics. Sure, some soldiers boasted about their conquests, and there were rumours that certain *Bowibu* operatives had their way with suspects, but if so then Hyuk Jae was clearly not among them.

She got undressed slowly, not by way of seduction but in the hope that the longer she took the more she could delay the actual moment. She had never been naked in front of a man before. In front of other women, sure – everyone stripped at the neighbourhood bathhouse without a care – but never a man, and shame flushed hot and rising beneath her exposed skin.

Cuckoo had told her a little bit about what was going to happen, but Min hadn't really listened, hadn't *wanted* to listen. Listening would have made it real. Listening would have meant that it was going to happen. Besides, she'd been too embarrassed to take most of it in. If it wasn't shameful, then why hadn't her mother rather than Cuckoo addressed it with her? Cuckoo had had no answer to that. She'd tried to talk to Min, and Min had just dissolved into creases of laughter until Cuckoo had rolled her eyes and given up.

Hyuk Jae took off his shirt and trousers. His body was like his face, all angles and sharp edges: elbows and kneecaps sticking out, skin stretched taut and hairless over the boat shell of his ribs. When he removed his underpants he had to pull them out first, away from his waist, and then down. Min clamped a hand to her mouth, just so she wouldn't scream. That thing was coming nowhere near her, not if she could help it.

'Take off your underwear,' Hyuk Jae said, and when Min glanced towards the wall in a mute entreaty for him to keep his voice down, he laughed. 'What else do you think they think we're doing?'

With a sudden determination to get on with it and get it over with, Min took off her bra and knickers, dropped them on the floor beside the bed, and lay back. She felt both hot and cold, shivering even though the room was warm and her skin burned to the touch. Hyuk Jae pushed her legs apart with his knee and lay on top of her. Min turned her head to the side, not just so she could breathe but also to reduce the smell of him: the high scent of sweat and cheap aftershave, the hint of animal that brought to mind the odour of a goat on a collective farm in South Hamgyong Province.

She remembered the other couples waiting their turn at Mansudae, and how she'd tried to discern how far the brightness had stretched behind their smiles. For most of them she hadn't been able to tell – everyone was adept at hiding their true feelings – but there'd been one woman in a light-blue *jeogori* whose smile hadn't reached anywhere near her eyes, and she'd returned Min's gaze with a look that had been equal parts understanding, complicity, and sympathy.

Hyuk Jae's mouth, rough and abrasive, was on her neck, her cheeks, her mouth. Min tried to kiss him back, but now he was burying his head in her shoulder. She felt a sharp pain between her legs: his hand, not his hand, his hand again. She made a little meow, trying to keep her voice low while asking him to be more gentle – she imagined her parents and Cuckoo listening on the other side of the wall: was this what it had been like for all of them too? – but Hyuk Jae did not or would not hear her. He kept pushing harder and harder, trying to force himself past her dryness, and when she tried to adjust her hips to make it easier he was too heavy on her and she could not move. *Please*, she thought, *please slow down, please look at me, please talk to me, maybe that will make it better*, but the smell and feel of him were all wrong and she wanted nothing more than for it to be over. She reached down to help guide him in, but he batted her hand away with the back of his, a quick petulant flash of male pride. The pain was becoming clearer and sharper, Min biting her own hand to stop herself from crying out and punish herself for not enjoying this, Hyuk Jae rutting joylessly like a frantic dog until Min felt a warm wetness and heard him groan so deeply that she wondered whether it had hurt him as much as it had hurt her, and if so then whether he'd be angry, as she wanted to at least please him in this aspect of married life.

Hyuk Jae rolled off her and propped himself up on one arm.

'Move to one side,' he said.

Min did so. He looked over her body at the spot where she had been lying. Min followed his gaze. There was a patch of blood there. Min absently realised that it was the same shape, more or less, as the map of Australia they had been shown in school.

Hyuk Jae looked at the blood, and nodded in what looked like approval. 'It *was* your first time, then.'

He pulled the sheets up over him, turned away from Min and went to sleep.

She lay awake for hours, her fury and shame crashing in waves against his oblivious back. In the moment he'd said that thing about it being her first time she'd really hated him, not just for doubting her but also for having said so in such a careless, self-satisfied fashion.

This man will never hurt you. That's what she'd thought when she'd first met him. But there were more ways than just one to hurt someone.

Breakfast the next morning was awkward from start to finish. It wasn't just that Min was worried her parents and Cuckoo might have heard her and Hyuk Jae making love – if that was what you could call it – or that Han Na made three separate but uniformly unsubtle remarks about expecting grandchildren. It was, Min realised, something deeper than either of those. It was that Hyuk Jae's presence had unbalanced everything here. This little unit of four had been there for so long, with everyone in their roles and a role for everyone: and now he'd come in and knocked everyone out of their orbit.

Cuckoo shot Min a glance that spoke endless, wordless volumes, and as they passed while clearing the plates away, she leant into Min and whispered simply: 'It gets better.'

Min and Hyuk Jae left for his parents' apartment before lunch. If Min found the second night more bearable than the first, it was not by much, and even then only because of two things: that here it was not her role that was being pushed off kilter, and also that Hyuk Jae fell asleep without trying to have sex with her again.

On the third day they moved in together: a furnished one-bedroom apartment more or less equidistant between the two sets of parents, not quite near enough for them to pop round unannounced but not far enough for visits to be a chore either.

'This is great,' Hyuk Jae said.

'Looks to be,' Min replied, conscious that neither of them knew enough other than to be pleased with the apartment: she had never lived anywhere but at home, and this was several steps up from the barracks accommodation he had been used to in the army and the rundown guest houses in which he was billeted when on *Bowibu* business outside Pyongyang.

'Aren't you going to carry me across the threshold?' she said.

'What?'

'You carry me in through the door. That's what newly-weds do.'

'Who told you that?'

'Everyone knows that.'

'But we're inside now.'

'So?'

'So what's the point?'

'The point is' – Min could hardly believe she was having to spell all this out to him – 'that this is an adventure we take together.'

'An adventure?'

Min walked back out of the door and stood on the landing. Hyuk Jae looked blankly at her. 'I'm going to stay here until you carry me across the threshold,' she said.

He stared a few seconds more, and then came towards her. For a moment Min thought he was going to shut the door in her face, but he stepped through the doorway and stood in front of her. She put her arms round his neck and felt the biggest fool imaginable. Why should she have to be the one to initiate all this? Why couldn't he have the gumption to do it? He bent stiffly, put one arm beneath her shoulders and the other behind her knees, hoiked her skywards, walked back into the apartment, and set her down with all the care and grace of a man dumping the groceries on the floor.

'Happy now?' he asked.

Min gave him the most non-committal smile she could muster. *Happy now?* She couldn't even begin to answer that question honestly. And the worst thing was this: that Hyuk Jae really was happy, she could see that full well. She was the most beautiful woman he'd ever seen: that was what he'd told her when he'd first met her, and several times since, and for him that was so obviously enough. Not just beautiful, either: beautiful and untouched, which was clearly important to him.

And now he had his wife, and a new apartment, and when they went to bed that night it was a tiny bit better than the first time: a little less awkward, a little less painful, and there were even a few brief moments when she felt as though this was something that one day she might be able to enjoy rather than simply endure.

But when it was over and he went to sleep, Min once again lay awake in the darkness for a long time, unable to shake a feeling of acute claustrophobia, a belief that somehow she'd narrowed her life rather than expanded it.

Theo had been determined not to miss Min when she was gone. It was only a few days that she'd be off – when he'd explained the concept of a honeymoon to her and Yun Seok in the car one day, they'd both laughed as if this was the stupidest thing they'd ever heard – but it felt to him all wrong that she wasn't there. He wondered how she was finding being married, and felt a little bereft and inadequate that he had nothing in his own life against which to compare it: no memory of those early days as husband and wife, of embarking on a journey together, of arranging yourselves face to face with each other and back to back against the world.

He wondered whether she still doubted that she was doing the right thing, and found with a jolt that he hoped she was still doubting and she would once more confide in him. No, he chided. It was wrong to want anyone to be unhappy, let alone someone you cared about. He corrected himself. He didn't want her to be unhappy with Hyuk Jae, but he *did* want her to continue being happy with him. He wondered whether the difference was merely semantics. Was this a zero-sum problem? He found the same thing when designing coasters: that each time there came a stage beyond which he couldn't make one part better without making another worse.

And he remembered the moment at Mansudae when she had held her hand to her chest, and that she had done that just for him.

Peploe had taken Min's place in the car, just for today. How Peploe had known where to be or had got himself on board this trip, Theo had no idea. They were on their way to the port at Nampo, where the parts for the rollercoaster had been delivered. Theo needed to check they were all present and correct, and he hoped to God that they were both: there would be a fearful delay if they weren't, and in terms of the schedule he was up against it as it was.

There was, he tried to convince himself, no reason why they shouldn't be. They had been made in a factory that Leuschner Piesk had used many times before without a problem, and shipped using a carrier with whom the relationship had been equally fruitful. The issues, if there were any, would come during construction, when Theo would have to be on his game every minute the site was open.

The highway to Nampo was as empty as the one to the DMZ had been. Nam Il drove, with Yun Seok alongside him and Peploe with Theo in the back. In the rear-view mirror Theo could see Nam Il's eyes, as watchful as he was silent.

'Bet you're wondering why I wanted to come out today,' Peploe said.

Theo had indeed been wondering that, but he didn't want to give Peploe the satisfaction of saying so. There was something about Peploe that brought out the pettiness in Theo, and he wasn't quite sure what. Perhaps it was Peploe's minor but incessant bragging, the way he traded – like now – on his prized status as the outsider in the belly of the beast.

'Truth is,' Peploe continued without waiting for Theo to answer, 'it beats kicking around the house all day. You married?'

'No.'

'Sensible fella. Keep it that way. Third time round for me. You'd think I'd have learned my lesson by now, wouldn't ya? Maybe that's what happens when they're chosen for ya.'

'Chosen?'

'This is not an appropriate conversation,' Yun Seok said.

'Ah, it's perfectly appropriate,' Peploe replied. 'I ain't telling him nothing he can't work out for himself.' He shifted in his seat so as to see Theo better. 'I can say what I like. They can't do nothing to me. First one was Romanian. Doina, her name was. So much peroxide in her hair, it turned white. Should have dyed it red, she was such a commie. Then Farhana. Malaysian. Didn't last too long. Now I got me a Japanese, Nobuko.'

'I really must . . .' Yun Seok sounded momentarily like a peeved English butler. 'Especially after the incident with the parade. Theo, this is not . . .'

Peploe ploughed on as though he hadn't heard. 'You see the pattern, don'tcha? Even back in the day when I was the model

175

defector, their big propaganda tool, they never let me near any of *their* women.'

Theo remembered the scene he'd seen Peploe filming at the studio outside Pyongyang. 'Not one drop of ink in the Han River.'

Peploe laughed and leaned forward to nudge Yun Seok. 'You see? Nothing he couldn't work out for himself. That's right. Nothing to dilute the nation's racial purity. What you have here is the biggest bunch of racists on God's green earth.'

'Racists?' Yun Seok said.

'Your national commitment to racial purity,' Peploe said.

Yun Seok looked unconvinced, but said nothing. Peploe smirked at Theo, and the complicity made Theo feel uncomfortable.

They spent three hours at Nampo. Theo had a full inventory of what should have been delivered, and he went through it methodically, insisting on opening every container to see that what they said was inside was actually inside. He took steel support columns and track segments at random and measured the bolt holes for the mating components, not to check they were all the same size but to check that they *weren't*, not exactly. He'd designed some of the holes to be slightly larger than others to account for other measurements not being completely millimetre-exact, so there was some tolerance for a hole that was fractionally off-centre, or not a perfect circle, or not completely flush to the mating surface. Tolerance stack-up, engineers called it, and like all engineers he'd been bitten by a failure (a very expensive failure, given the amount of parts that had to be remade) to incorporate it in one of his early projects and had never made the same mistake again.

Only when every item on his inventory sheet had a big black line through it did Theo sign the parts off as having been delivered correctly. They would be put on army flatbed trucks and brought to Taesongsan tomorrow, he was told, and then construction could begin.

The car on the way back from Nampo. Theo looking out of the window, seeing the same kind of sights the trip down to the DMZ had offered: exhausted locals toiling in the fields or pushing carts as though they were treading molasses. It wasn't the poverty that really struck him, but the energy: or, more precisely, the lack of it. Almost everywhere else he'd been, even the poorest people – *especially* the poorest people – had some zip about them, a sense either that they might as well eke what joy they could out of life or that with enough work and luck they could haul themselves out of the quagmire. Not here. Here, the poverty was poverty of the soul.

And then the pastel-coloured high rises were glowing in the late afternoon sun and they were back in Pyongyang, and for the first time Theo saw the city for what it was: the country's own Xanadu, the Capitol from a real-life *Hunger Games*, a pleasure dome so faded by Western standards but so vibrant by their own, a place that could spend millions of dollars on a rollercoaster when outside the walls people still worked and lived in conditions not far removed from those of medieval peasants, a vampire squid that sucked up everything from the rest of the country and gave nothing, *nothing*, back, and he remembered what Sophie had said and hated himself for being a part of this, but he knew too that he couldn't leave.

'Did you miss me?' Min said.

She addressed it to both Theo and Yun Seok, but it was only Theo's answer that she wanted to hear: and even as she spoke she wondered whether he'd give her an honest reply, because it had hardly been an honest question. She'd asked it as the inverse of her own thoughts, flipped around and with a question mark popped on the end: for 'I've missed you', read 'Did you miss me?'

'Of course,' Theo said, deadpan in the face of both Min's smile and Yun Seok's equally deadpan examination of Theo's expression.

'How are you finding married life?' Yun Seok said.

'It's everything I thought it would be,' Min said.

The briefest of moments between her and Theo: the memory of their discussion beneath the poplars, the complicity and under-standing of what she really meant behind the bland formalities of what she'd said, the knowledge that this was a layer Yun Seok didn't know existed and couldn't access.

The parts had arrived on site, and so Min spent all day out in the open with Theo, translating for him when need be and watch-ing him otherwise. She loved the way he became so absorbed in what he was doing, the depths of his immersion and concentration: and even though she knew he was aware of her the same way she was aware of him, it gave her a curious thrill to see how he could shut out not just her but everyone and everything else not germane to the task at hand. In his obliviousness she could marvel at the things about him which were at once basic and thrilling: the way he chewed slightly at his lower lip when he was thinking, the slight kink at the bridge of his nose where it had been broken many years before, the curl of his hair against the very top of his collar.

The steel supports went up one by one. It was happening now, she saw: all the things that had once been just Theo's imagination, and then had been merely images on his computer, had become solid, and real, and *here*. The supports rose like the riverbank pop-lars, and Min had a sudden thought of walking with Theo through these metal thickets, the two of them alone in the playground of his creation. With him she felt light, both weightless and bright. Hyuk Jae was heavy, darkness. Theo was neither.

She'd heard some of her fellow guides moan sometimes about the work when they'd thought nobody was listening, especially when they'd been assigned to long tours and could be away from home for weeks at a time. Min had never felt that – she'd always loved her job – but home was no longer where she was used to, and she realised that for her the opposite of those complaints was now true: that home was something to be endured until she could go to work again. Hyuk Jae was home and Theo was work, but she thought of them the other way round: one a chore, the other a pleasure.

They went back to the hut late in the afternoon, as Theo wanted to check a few things on the computer. It would take about half an hour, he said.

Min reached into her bag and brought out a sketch pad and drawing pencil. Yun Seok glanced up, saw the pad, and smiled. He was used to her sketches. There was always time to while away on any excursion, let alone when cooped up in a prefabricated cabin, and he'd often said he wished he'd been born with her artistic talent, or in fact any kind of artistic talent whatsoever. He'd said it with warmth but regret too. I'd draw what's out there, he'd said, and not what's in here, tapping at his temple. He'd seen her sketch the city skyline, and some of the tourists they'd looked after, and the statue of the Three Revolutions, and a dozen other things besides. She'd even sketched him once, and she could have sworn he'd become a little emotional – the only time she'd ever seen him that way – when she'd given it to him. That's how you see me? he'd asked. Yes, she'd replied, knowing that she'd captured both his kindness and his wariness. That's the nicest thing I've ever received, he'd said.

Yun Seok turned back to his newspaper. Min watched Theo's hands as he continued to work on the computer. She'd only ever sketched one person's hands before, and that was Cuckoo. She'd spent so much time holding Cuckoo's hands, and knew them as well as she knew Cuckoo's face, that it had seemed only natural. They'd been out one day and Cuckoo had been leaning on her walking stick, and the way her hands had curled and wrapped round that stick had drawn Min's eye: the momentary illusion that hands and stick were one, each rooted in the other. Min had remembered all the things those hands had done, all the events they'd lived through: a life woven into and scored on Cuckoo's hands quite as much as her face. People spoke of hands showing lifelines, but for Min the lifeline was not the one they always meant, the one scored across the palm. The true lifelines weren't a guide to how long your life was, but to how you'd lived that life: experiences rather than predictions, pasts rather than futures.

Faces were obvious. Faces were the first place you looked, both at someone and for someone. Hands were different. Hands had their own intimacy.

Shifting position slightly to give herself a better angle, though not so obviously as to draw his attention – she didn't want to make him self-conscious – she began to sketch Theo's hands.

He had long fingers: a surgeon's, perhaps, or a piano player's. He moved them with deft precision, never once looking down at them as they conjured up the constantly morphing images on the screen. Min saw, and drew, the veins that ran in large 'H' shapes, and the thin raised weal of white scar that ran across the back of his left hand, and the hairs that rose like reeds between the first and second joints of his fingers, and the tiny square of loose skin at the edge of his right thumbnail at which he picked with his index finger now and then without even seeming to realise.

Yun Seok kept reading the paper. Theo kept working.

The sketch appeared line by line, black on white. Shading a patch here, strengthening a line there, erasing small areas with her finger and starting again. Tiny things, teased out little by little, until the lines became a shape and the shape became a drawing.

Min worked fast, the paper turned away from Yun Seok so he wouldn't see what she was sketching if he looked up. It wasn't that she feared his reaction: she was doing nothing wrong, and he would think nothing unusual in it.

It was, she realised, because she wanted to keep this to herself.

As it was, Yun Seok was still on the penultimate page of the newspaper when she finished. She closed the pad and put it back in her bag. Maybe she'd go back to it later and tidy up a few rough edges. Maybe she'd leave it as it was. Maybe she'd never look at it again.

'Done,' Theo said.

Yun Seok smiled. 'I suggest that we all go to dinner.'

'What's the occasion?'

'The supports have gone up. Miss Min Ji has fulfilled her first working day as a married woman.'

'Mrs Min, then,' Theo said, and the recognition cut her even though she knew he hadn't meant it to: he'd just been being precise, same as he always was.

'Of course,' Yun Seok said. 'Either way, we have cause for celebration, surely?'

They went to the Yanggakdo. Min wondered whether Theo would have liked a change of scene, but the food was better here than in most other places in Pyongyang, so she and Yun Seok wanted to use the perks of their job when they could. They ate and drank, talked and laughed. Min was at pains to include Yun Seok in every aspect of the conversation, as though by compensating to this degree she could hide the undercurrents which only she and Theo could see.

Yun Seok was drinking heavily. Min had seen this before sometimes, when they'd been out with other tour groups, but it had rarely been a problem. Alcohol made him more loquacious than usual, more amusing, and thankfully he wasn't a bad drunk: he didn't get melancholy or violent. She watched his intake, but there was nothing she could do about it even if she'd wanted to.

After dinner they all went downstairs to the bar in the basement. Yun Seok took a large swig of beer, smiled beatifically, and slumped sideways on to the banquette. It was curiously elegant: upright one moment and horizontal the next, with the perfect arc of a falling tree.

'Does this happen often?' Theo asked, as Yun Seok began to snore.

'Sometimes.' Min smiled, and knew it did not reach her eyes.

'Are you embarrassed?'

'I want only to show you the best of our glorious country.'

'You are. But it works both ways. How much of other countries have you seen?'

'World geography was an integral part of our school learning programme.'

'Min.'

'What?'

'Talk to me properly.'

She laughed. She wondered whether she too was a little drunk. 'Sorry.'

'So?'

'So?'

'So how much of other countries have you seen?'

'I've lived all my life here.'

Theo glanced at Yun Seok, asleep to the world: and then took his laptop from its bag – he hadn't yet been up to his room – opened it, moved the cursor to the icon of a globe in the dock at the bottom of the screen, and clicked on it.

'What are you doing?' Min said.

'I'm taking you round the world.'

It was only Google Earth, but for Min it might as well have been magic. Theo, as a foreigner, could – with special permission from the authorities – still access a site from which Min, like the vast majority of North Koreans, was strictly barred. From the moment he started the programme and began to spin the globe, she was transfixed. Flying high above the parched brown of the Middle East and diving low over the Empty Quarter, an expanse of dunes and wadis so vast that the track across it seemed endless. Pulling up and back so fast that she half-staggered with the reverse vertigo. Theo shifting in his chair so she could take the cursor, laughing as she skimmed round and round the Pacific before she got the hang of how it worked. Down again towards Manhattan, the skyscrapers clustered and thrusting from the screen like quills on a porcupine, and now skimming low across the rooftops and down on to FDR Drive and up again and along and down, oblongs of grey resolving themselves into city blocks, into streets, into buildings, into cars and people frozen at the moment the picture was taken. Fly with me, take my hand and fly with me: we are birds, we are angels. Spinning and twisting down through the minarets of the Taj Mahal, and into the forest of symbols laid over Tokyo's sprawling cityscape. The kaleidoscope of coloured roofs cascading down to the waterfront in Reykjavik and the messy white glacier splodges. Lake Baikal, a thin reclining sliver of aquamarine.

Min held her arms out either side of her.

'Flying?' Theo asked.

'Stopping myself from falling.' Her eyes were wet with tears. 'I never knew – I never knew any of this.' And even as she said it she glanced around to check whether anyone could have overheard, for their education system was the greatest in the world under the guidance first of the Great Leader, then the Dear Leader, and now the Supreme Leader.

The barman was too far away to have heard, but Min's holding her arms out had attracted his attention. He came out from behind the bar and walked over to them, suspicion narrowing his eyes.

Theo spun the computer round so the barman could see it. A computer-generated rendition of Mallima filled the screen.

'I'm just showing Comrade Park the latest design for the rollercoaster,' Theo said.

The barman peered at the image, grunted, and went back to his station. Min gave Theo a watery smile of gratitude. Theo span the laptop back towards them and switched tabs so Google Earth came back up again.

'Will you show me where you live?' Min asked.

'Sure.'

Theo typed in the name of his street, and once more the virtual magic carpet carried them across the rooftops and down to the ground. A lorry unloading and a cyclist with a pixelated face: an ugly post-war council block on one side of the road and Victorian conversions on the other, black railings flanking black doors.

'There,' he said, pointing to the third house along. 'That's where I live.'

'In all that house?'

'No. An apartment in it.'

'What's it like?' She felt a need to know everything about where he lived, to try to imagine his life when he was not with her: his normal life, his real life, the life to which he'd said he'd return without a second glance when his stay here was over.

'It's, er . . . it's nothing special.'

'That's not an answer!'

'It's four rooms. Bedroom, bathroom, living room, kitchen.'

'What can you see from the windows?'

'The other side of the street.'

Min laughed, rolled her eyes and reached for the laptop. Her hair brushed against his, just for a moment, and she neither prolonged the contact nor shied away from it.

'Where do you work?' He began to zoom out again, but she put her hand on his. 'No. Take me through the streets. Tell me what you see.'

They scooted down virtual roads, the city arranging itself on either side. 'Here, Kensington High Street, I once saw a woman walking eight dachshunds in perfect formation, four either side and ahead of her like a miniature snowless husky train.' Through a pair of gates into Kensington Gardens. 'A soldier in camouflage trousers and a hi-vis vest – make your mind up, mate, do you want to be seen or not? – opening the gates of Hyde Park Barracks for half a dozen of the most beautiful horses you could ever imagine.' Out of the park. 'Nike and her chariot above me and Constitution Hill framed perfectly in the proscenium as I go through Wellington Arch.' Past Buckingham Palace and on to the Mall, dark red and flanked with flags. 'The Eye rising above Horse Guards Parade with the sun in its spokes. A thin line of ducks crossing the road into St James's Park and taking the stopping of cars and pedestrians alike as their right.'

'You never saw ducks!'

'Of course. They come from the lake in St James's Park.'

'Really?'

'Promise.'

She looked at him, doubtful, and saw the sincerity in his face. 'Then I'll believe you.'

'Good.'

'How about one of the places you grew up? One of those bases?'

'Which one?'

'Any one. The one where you made the rollercoaster when you were a teenager.'

'Ah. Offutt. OK.'

The globe span again. Grey blocks in the vastness of browned Nebraskan plains. He zoomed in on them, talking half to himself. 'The accommodation area was over here, and we were near the perimeter fence on the north side, end of a row . . .' The image hovered, moved a little, hovered again. 'There. That's it. That garden. Definitely that garden. It had two sheds. Look.' He pointed to two small squares. 'And this is where I ran the coaster. A big figure of eight, basically. Started here, went round here, up over itself here and back to the start.'

'What happened to it? When you moved, why didn't the next people just keep it?'

He swallowed. 'It got burned.'

'Burned? How?'

'By Neale.'

'Your brother?'

'Yes. Him and his friends.'

'Why?'

'Why not? Because he could. They'd been drinking, even though they were underage, and Neale found a petrol can and some matches, and that was it. His friends held me down while he went round pouring petrol on the coaster, taking his time and really drawing it out, making a big song and dance about it. My parents were out at some function, and they had to come rushing back because of course the fire service came when someone saw the flames, and I got in big trouble.'

'*You* got in big trouble?'

'Neale's friends had all left by then. He told our parents that I'd done it. Set light to it myself.'

'And they believed him?'

'Of course. They always believed him. He said I hadn't been happy with the end result and burned it because it wasn't as good as I'd wanted it to be.'

'Even though you'd spent all summer working on it?'

'Even though I'd spent all summer working on it.'

'That doesn't make sense.'

'It does if you were them. One time, when I'd been much younger, I smashed up a K'Nex model I'd built because that really hadn't come out right. A childish tantrum, nothing more. And of course you could always rebuild a K'Nex. But every time after that, Neale would wait till I'd finished a model, smash it up, and then say that I'd done it because it hadn't come out right. Sometimes he *wouldn't* smash it up and that was almost even worse, because I kept waiting for him to.'

Theo zoomed out quickly, back high above the plains where the hurt couldn't get to him. The only coasters Neale hadn't been able to destroy were the ones in actual theme parks, which was why Theo had sought out the nearest rollercoaster the moment they'd arrived anywhere new: an anchor, a safe space, a place where he could take himself, the sole spot he felt happy, and free, and alive. His father had gone with him once, on the Texas Tornado in Amarillo, and the rollercoaster had made him sick. Food poisoning, his dad had said, to cover the shame of chucking up on something his son could ride without problems: but the lie hadn't fooled Theo for a second, and anger had come hard on the heels of his old man's embarrassment.

It had been a small triumph in the midst of what Theo had hated, which had been pretty much everything else. The fronts, the appearances, the masks, the uniforms: he'd hated all of it, and buried that hatred in the same place as the pain, deep below ground and marked by flags only he could see. The only capital offence had been truth, which was also the only weapon he'd had. His parents' marriage had been disintegrating, at first in patches and then altogether, or maybe it was just that he'd become better at seeing it the older he'd got.

'What about friends?'

'What about them?'

'All those times you moved, you never kept in touch with the friends you'd made in the places you'd been before?'

'I didn't really make many friends. "Let's stay in touch", people say. But they never do. I used to say it back to them, just to be polite, until I realised what a load of shit it was. So now I spare them, and me, the trouble. I just go. Break camp and get out.'

He wondered whether she would ask the obvious question, and if so whether she'd try to make it light-hearted to soften it: and she did both.

'You're going to leave here when you've finished the rollercoaster without a backwards glance?' A smile as she said it, and it fooled neither of them.

'Sure am.'

'I bet you don't.'

'I know I will.'

A fluttering inside him. *Don't need anyone. Everyone needs someone.* Intimacy desired and feared in equal measures.

He knew what she was thinking: that living like this meant that he only gave a snapshot of himself to others rather than an entire film of change and growth. When with your shiver of alienation you always have one eye on the nearest door, what else can your life be but an eternal present, washed away and dissolved and reconstituted with every move?

'That's why you make rollercoasters, isn't it?'

'How do you mean?'

'To stop things from disappearing altogether.'

For a moment Theo thought, he honestly thought, that she'd reached out and punched him in the chest. That was what those words were: a physical blow, a statement that laid him waste in the simplicity of its truth. A legacy, a small proof that he'd been there. It was so obvious, but he had never articulated it for himself, never thought to turn the light upon himself, not to this degree. Oh, he'd thought of his coasters in many ways, but mostly in terms of the effect they had on those who rode them. He'd thought of them as their end product rather than their genesis, as their omegas rather than their alphas: he'd thought of what they were, but never of why they were. A grabbing at time, an analgesic on the wound of transience, an imposition of stability on the flux.

He held up his hands: *maybe you're right.*

'Doesn't that make you lonely?' Min continued.

'I'm alone,' Theo said. 'I'm not lonely.'

He hoped she wouldn't ask the question twice, as he didn't want to lie to her twice.

'I think you're the loneliest person I've ever met,' she said, and her tone was suffused with concern and affection: an offer of succour where others would have judged, if only he chose to take it.

He said nothing, and she filled the silence.

'My turn. Can you come back here, to Pyongyang?'

Again the image retreated and approached, until they were looking down at the roof of the hotel they were sitting in. Min used the trackpad to follow the line of the river south until she found what she was looking for.

'You see that bridge?'

'Sure.'

'That was the last place Cuckoo ever saw Kwang Sik.'

Cuckoo had told Min the story so often that Min half-felt she'd been there herself, even though it had been almost half a century before she'd even been born. She looked round the room, but the barman had gone and they were the only ones in here: no one to overhear what she was about to say. But she leant in close to him anyway and kept her voice low, just in case.

'It was December the fourth, 1950. The Fatherland Liberation War.'

The bridge pulsed and swarmed, a living thing. People covered every part of it like ants, a colony on the move. The north side was still intact, great swooping iron trusses marching across the river, but the bombs had hit at the midpoint, and after that the piles had crumpled and the lattice arches had slid down towards the water with a drunkard's languid grace.

It was here that the ant people moved, studding the high girders in silhouettes of dinosaur spikes, crabbing across the struts with cloth sacks strapped tight to their backs, easing their way round torn flanges, which gaped blindly at the sky. And all this without speaking, almost without sound: just the quick shallow breathing of refugees desperate to reach the south bank and the odd muted splash as someone lost their footing and went under, a fast freezing death, plumes of breath and bubbles and nothing.

Kwang Sik tested a piece of decking under his weight. The water lapped to the edge of his boots. He smiled as reassuringly as he could and held out his hand to Cuckoo. She looked at him with wide eyes. He nodded and beckoned her. Trust me.

Cuckoo slid the last few feet down from her girder, spinning slightly as a rivet half-caught her in the stomach and tore the fabric of her red coat. Kwang Sik caught her and pulled her close.

Carefully now on the decking, trying to get across to the next lateral brace. Trying to keep out of everyone else's way: the tired, the disorientated, the panicking, the ones who could tip them into the Taedong without even realising.

It was Cuckoo who saw the vessel first: a patrol boat painted as grey and forbidding as the sky, churning up thin floes of ice as it glided towards them. An officer dressed in black stood at the prow, eyes flitting beneath the peak of his cap as he watched this silent exodus.

Cuckoo raised an arm to him.

'No!' Kwang Sik hissed. 'Don't.' He grabbed at her, pulling her hand down, but it was too late. A gently curving wake stream frothed behind the boat as it changed course and headed for them. Kwang Sik looked round, trying to find somewhere to hide or a place to climb, but there were too many people and it was too late and the boat was on them.

Three old men made as though to board. The officer raised a pistol, and the old men shrank back as one.

The officer gestured with his pistol to Kwang Sik. You. Here. Now.

Kwang Sik took Cuckoo by the waist and helped her over the gunwales. He followed her on to the boat, and scarcely had his feet left the decking of the ruined bridge that the patrol boat was arcing away again.

Back to the north side of the river, Cuckoo noticed. Back to Pyongyang. She looked at the officer's collar insignia. Four silver stars and a yellow stripe on a black background: a taewi, *a captain.*

'Papers,' said the taewi.

Kwang Sik dug inside his coat with cold-numbed hands and brought out two sets of documents: one for him, one for Cuckoo. The taewi *took them and flipped through: first Kwang Sik's, then Cuckoo's.*

'Born 1930, both of you,' he said. He read some more. 'Married two years.'

They nodded. Cuckoo opened her mouth to speak, but the taewi held up a leather-gloved hand and turned to Kwang Sik. 'You are twenty years old. Age of mandatory conscription into the Korean People's Armed Forces to fight in the Fatherland Liberation War against the imperialists is seventeen. Either you have exemption papers or you are a deserter.'

Cuckoo listened as she always did, with her head on one side. That was how she'd got her nickname, from someone who'd thought the pose reminded them of the bird.

And now, too late, she understood. The patrol boat hadn't been there to help: it had been checking for men of fighting age. Most men on the bridge had been too old to be called up. Not Kwang Sik. He had been with her, and they had seen him.

Cuckoo felt the cold clutch of panic deep down in her gut: that one single mistake could be so catastrophic, so terminal.

'We are medical students.' Kwang Sik pointed at a section on his identity document. 'I can show you. In my bag I have basic equipment, to help these people.' He gestured back towards the bridge.

'Where are you heading to?'

'Kaesong.' Kaesong was the country's southernmost large city, not far from the border. 'We have arranged places at medical school there.'

The taewi looked at Kwang Sik, and at Cuckoo, and at Kwang Sik again. His pupils were very dark: as black, almost, as his uniform. He gestured with his hand, and in the wheelhouse an unseen helmsman adjusted the tiller. They glided towards a jetty.

The taewi found the section that identified Kwang Sik as a medical student and tore it off. It fluttered as he held it high in the wind. 'Your wife can use her skills in Pyongyang. She won't be short of practice there. As for you – you are hereby enlisted under conscription and will be taken to the barracks at Onchon for basic training.'

He opened his hand with a flourish, and Kwang Sik's certificate whirled and span across the water. The cold seemed to have settled in Cuckoo's head as she watched it go. She could not formulate any thought other than this one. *It's over. It's over.*

She buried her head in Kwang Sik's shoulder. 'I'm sorry,' she said. 'I'm sorry.'

He pulled her close to him, looking over the top of her head at the taewi, who stared back without expression. 'It doesn't matter. It would have happened one day.'

The boat bumped slightly as it came alongside. A rating leapt nimbly on to the jetty and twirled a rope round a bollard with a circus artist's quickness. Cuckoo disentangled herself from Kwang Sik. The taewi jerked his head towards the jetty. 'Off.'

She saw the darkness in his eyes, and knew better than to argue. He would shoot her as easily as breathing if she disobeyed. Was this what war did to men, or was it something in them – in some of them, at any rate – which was always bubbling beneath the surface and which needed only the slightest tug to be brought out?

From the place in her coat where the rivet had torn it she pulled a long thread, held it up and bit it halfway across to make two pieces. She tied one piece around her wrist, quick despite her frozen fingers, and handed Kwang Sik the other. 'The red thread connects those who are meant to be together, no matter how far apart they are. Wear it for me, and come back to me.'

He took it from her and wrapped it round his own wrist. 'I will, and I will.'

The taewi barking at her to move, and the splashing as another person fell from the bridge into the cold wet death, and Cuckoo and Kwang Sik with their faces together, committing each other to memory. Her demand and his promise. *Wear it for me, and come back to me. I will, and I will.*

She stepped on to the jetty and watched as it set off again, tears smudging and blurring her vision until all she could see were ink blots of grey. She wiped her eyes with the back of her hand and saw KPA soldiers moving to shut off access to the bridge from this side.

The only way was back to Pyongyang and the merciless bombardments from the vast metallic birds of prey, which circled above the city and rained down firestorms of death. The only place she could go, and yet no place for anyone like her: young, and alone, and with a child already three months grown inside her.

Nine months later. The heat pressing down, low and clammy over the ruined city. Dusk, and only now did the people dare emerge from the tunnels and cellars and basements where they spent their days, listening to the roaring overhead and wincing when the ground shook nearby. Everyone knew someone who'd been buried alive in the rubble: then again, everyone also knew someone who'd been caught in one of the infernal firestorms which the bombers hurled down.

The bombs didn't fall to earth intact: they broke into small pieces while still in the air, so that when they hit the ground they started dozens of small fires that licked and grew and ran after those who tried to run from them, the napalm flames catching and burning their skin to blackened pus and leaving them begging not to be saved but for a quick, final mercy, because those fires bent iron bars out of shape and left bodies so disfigured that even their sex couldn't be determined.

Cuckoo had seen more than enough of these cases, which was to say that even one of them was one too many, and every time she tried to do her best with her woefully inadequate supplies and hoped against hope that they understood and that her tenderness in their last moments was humanity enough.

Cuckoo adjusted Chul Woo slightly in his sling as she came up above ground. She kissed the top of his head, nuzzling against the dark soft hair and inhaling hard as she did so: nothing, not even this hell, could obliterate the smell of a new baby. Six weeks ago she had given birth by torchlight in a dank tunnel so humid that even the walls had seemed to be perspiring, her hair drenched and lank against her forehead, her screams blending with the wailing of the missiles outside, and suddenly there he'd been, all purple and scrunched, and through her agony she'd felt this surge not just of love but of protectiveness too; now they were two, and she would keep them both alive until this was over and Kwang Sik came back as he'd promised. What a time to bring a child into the world, and what a place to do it: but life itself did not stop during war, no matter how many people might not make it through.

'Look, little one,' she whispered as they walked. 'Look around you.'

She knew he couldn't see much, pressed against her chest, and knew too that it didn't matter. There was little worth seeing, as there was little left of the city. From where she stood she could see two, perhaps three buildings left untouched. The rest had been destroyed: not a few glancing blows here and there but annihilated, entire blocks reduced to rubble, houses pancaked down on to themselves with spilled bricks and tumbled roof beams and the odd wall still standing as if lonely and surprised.

In the early weeks of the bombing, when the air-raid sirens had sounded thick and fast and there had been some ruthless Darwinian winnowing of those too old or slow or infirm to get to shelter in time, people had wandered such ruins with faces shocked into blankness, perhaps with thin streams of tears carving paths through the dirt on their skin: people who'd taken shelter for an hour or so and returned to find that everything they owned had been obliterated. But now there was nothing left to obliterate. Not that it stopped the bombers, Cuckoo thought, for they just came round again and again, simply pounding the rubble into smaller pieces of rubble as though mere destruction was not enough and only total atomisation would do.

She wiped her brow and wondered what was worse: this enervating heat or the brutal cold of winter, when a meal could be nothing more than frozen cabbage roots dug from beneath the snow, and dead children lay frost-white as though sleeping.

Two men were picking their way through the devastation towards her. She smiled as they approached, because at times like this there was an unspoken communal pretence that this was an evening promenade, families all together and the sun setting, as though they were in one of those old European cities she had been taught about in school: Lisbon, perhaps, or Madrid. Even army officers, as these men were – their uniforms were threadbare and oversized, but they wore them as smartly as possible – liked to stop and chat, to ask the baby's name, to forget for a few moments.

And then Cuckoo saw that one of the men was carrying a small box and the other was clasping his cap in front of him as though for protection against her, and they were both trying to arrange their expressions into the requisite mix of stoicism and regret, and even before they spoke she knew, she knew, and then there was just her screaming and her fists beating on the men as they held her up and the heavens above her as uncaring and merciless as the abyss.

She wasn't aware of anything they'd said, nor did she feel anything beyond the slashing pain in her chest, her heart cracked open and seared. When she came round it was to the concerned faces of her neighbours and a few lost hours she'd never get back. Her first thought had been for Chul Woo, panic rising fast and unbidden as she remembered him wrapped in a sling on her chest, and as though reading her mind one of the neighbours said, 'He's OK, he's safe, don't worry.' The written notification was still in Cuckoo's hands: she'd been clutching it all that time without realising.

On 18th August 1951, Comrade Park Kwang Sik died a glorious death in service of the fatherland on Hill 983. In a locale entirely denuded of vegetation cover by artillery fire, Comrade Park used grenades and a trench knife to take several of the enemy, American imperialist bastards and their dog-like French lackeys, with him as he died. His sacrifice helped the Korean People's Army secure a famous victory, and the Supreme Commander Kim Il Sung extends his personal gratitude and condolences.

A red thread bound her and Kwang Sik together for all eternity, and death was not even a bump in that particular road. A red thread the colour of his blood, the blood he'd spilt on that razorback ridge, the blood that ran in Chul Woo and kept Kwang Sik alive for her still.

Theo said nothing for a long, long time after Min had finished. 'Thank you,' he said eventually, and it felt both totally inadequate and completely appropriate.

'I've never told anyone that,' she said. 'It's always been between me and Cuckoo.'

'What about your father?'

She shook her head. 'He's not interested.'

'Even though that's his own father who he never knew?'

'Maybe that's why.'

Min typed something, too fast for Theo to see what it was, and the globe span again. Down she went, to another bridge across a wide, grey river, but when she zoomed in she looked disappointed.

'What is it?' Theo asked.

'This bridge . . . the pictures always make it look much better than this.'

Theo looked. It was a nondescript bridge, six lanes of highway, the kind you could find in any large city in the world, and for a moment he thought Min must have got the wrong place: and then he realised where it was.

'That's because they usually take pictures of it at night,' he said.

Her smile was half-pleasure, half-incredulity. 'You *know* it?'

'I went there when I was in Seoul.'

'It's the most beautiful place I've ever seen.'

'Maybe w— maybe you can go there one day.' A pause, a catch over the word, and she knew he had been about to say 'we'.

Min shook her head. 'That's not possible.'

'Why not?'

'No members of the DPRK can go there. Only those who betray the motherland.' She paused. 'Tell me what it's like.'

'It's a place for lovers,' he said without thinking.

'Really?'

'Really. I saw lots of couples when I was there. They go at sunset, to watch the lights as the darkness falls.'

'And you?'

'And me what?'

'Who did you go with?'

'I went on my own. I was designing a coaster at Everland. I had some time off.'

She looked at him for a moment and then she laughed: a throaty sound coming from a place that seemed to take her by surprise.

Yun Seok was still asleep. When Min shook him gently awake, he batted her arm away before suddenly sitting bolt upright and staring at her.

'Are you OK?' she said.

'What time is it?' His voice was very slurred, and his breath was high and sweet from the *soju*.

She checked her watch. 'Just after ten. Come on. Let's get you home.'

'I can get myself home.'

His smartphone dropped from the pocket of his jacket as he sat up. Min caught it before it hit the floor. 'Shall I call a taxi for you?'

Yun Seok snatched at the phone. 'I said I'm fine.'

He stood, planting his feet wide to keep his balance. Min saw his eyes trying to focus on her. After a moment, he grinned lopsidedly, saluted, turned, and weaved his way unsteadily towards the door of the bar. She waited for a minute or so before following him, in case he'd fallen over again and needed picking up, but there was no sign of him in the lobby or outside. He was a grown man, she thought: he could look after himself.

Theo had gone up to bed. An image popped into Min's brain, so quick and fleeting that it had bounced out again almost before she'd registered it: a wall where the mortar was coming away in flakes and the plaster was shot through with hairline cracks.

She walked out of the hotel and through the darkened streets. She took the long way back to her apartment, just so she could stay out alone for a little longer with her thoughts of the things she'd seen on Theo's computer: of all the places she had never known existed, of his own apartment on one street among thousands, and of flying the way the red-crowned cranes would, the world laid out beneath them as they called to one another.

11

It was properly hot now, summer squatting over the city and asserting its residency for the next few months. The days were becoming ever more humid, and the nights so warm that sleeping was sometimes difficult until the small hours brought both exhaustion and a sufficient cooling of the air.

Mallima was taking shape. Once the supports were in place, the workmen started laying the tracks on top of and between them. There were two pipes, or rails, where the wheels would ride, and between them a third pipe, the spine, through which the track was connected to the support columns. The steel was thin around what would be the station area, where speeds and stress would be low, and much thicker at the base of the drops where the coaster would be coming through at high velocity.

These pieces of track were not just metal to Theo: they were individual miracles of precision engineering, tubular rails heated and bent and moulded, and beneath the smoothness of their surface he knew there would be strong and weak points equally unseen, places where forces both dynamic and static would gradually worry away the metal's strength to the point of failure.

This was physics, invisible but ubiquitous, and it had fascinated Theo for as long as he could remember: that there is so much in life that we cannot see, and yet it governs everything we do. He would leave the operators with everything they needed to test for fatigue and to replace the track before anything catastrophic happened, but he would be long gone by the time they either did so or chose not to.

The welding torches threw off angry sparks. Theo inhaled the high scent of their burning as though it were frankincense, and listened to the cacophony of hammer on steel as rapt as an opera-goer. He walked each section when it was up, sure-footed like a mountain goat and unbothered by either the height or his lack of harness. There was no logical difference between walking along a surface six inches above ground and one sixty feet up. The first was so simple as not to require thought: the second was just a matter of controlling one's mind enough to override the fear.

He heard Min gasp the first time he placed a ladder against a support column and went up it two rungs at a time, and he gave her an insouciant grin, which hid the quick thrill of knowing that she cared about him enough not to want to see him in danger.

He was, he realised, overriding a very different sort of fear.

'Don't worry,' he called out. 'I won't fall.'

'You'd better not.' Her turn to grin. 'Imagine the trouble I'll be in if you do.'

He made a face. 'And there was me thinking you cared.'

'Don't be silly.'

Slowly unfolding in front of someone he adored, open and almost reckless: 'almost' because Yun Seok was the only one there who could speak English and he wasn't within earshot. There could have been others, Theo supposed, agents secreted among the workmen, but he took his cues from Min and if she didn't seem concerned then neither would he be. He had never declared anything to Min, nor she to him, but he knew it with the same certainty he knew his Newtonian laws. How far could he push it? Right now it was stasis, and they could go neither forward nor back, bound by the parameters of her marriage and his inevitable departure.

Theo turned back to the rail. Sure-footed did not mean complacent, and he needed his full attention up here. He went along the track, inspecting every bit through sight and touch. His focus was fully on the task at hand, but in the background was Min, constant and permanent: Min in his head and also in the place between them, the wordless place that was neither her nor him but somewhere outside them both and yet within them both too. He saw her grin, and a thought of delicious warmth came to him: *I did that. I made her smile like that. That smile was at me, for me, by me.*

It was almost sunset by the time Theo decided he was done for the day, but when they reached the main gate they found that it was locked and they couldn't get out. The three of them were the only ones left on site: all the workmen had already gone home.

'There must be a security guard about,' Yun Seok continued. 'I'll go and find out.'

He began to walk along the inside of the perimeter fence. Min watched him go for a few moments before looking up at the coaster in all its gap-toothed promise.

'What are you thinking?' Theo asked.

'I'm trying to imagine what it will feel like to ride Mallima once it's finished.' There were looped coasters at the Mangyongdae Funfair, but she'd never ridden them.

He was already off, walking towards the coaster. 'Come.'

'Where?'

He smiled. 'Just come.'

Min followed. Yun Seok was nowhere to be seen.

Theo stopped at a point where the track wasn't much higher than their own heads. 'This is where the ride stops and starts. This is where you get in.' He motioned with his hands. 'You pull the restraint bar down, hear and feel it lock into place. The moment the car starts moving, there's no getting out. You're committed.'

Min smiled. 'I'm ready.'

He gave her a look that was nine parts open and one part unreadable. She saw the light dusting of stubble on his jaw, and wondered what it would feel like beneath her fingers: very few Korean men grew their facial hair.

They began to walk beneath the track as it rose high and away from them. 'You start slowly. A long, long climb up to the top. Two minutes, perhaps.'

'That doesn't sound long.'

'Trust me, it is. It is when you're going higher and higher, and you're waiting for the moment you get to the top, the moment you half-want to come now and half-want not to come at all. The anticipation's part of the suffering. The ground's getting further and further away below you, and the higher you climb the more you can see of the city. You look around you, at the track and the supports, at all this, this – this danger temple of towering spires and twisting spindles, and you think: "I hope the guy who built this knew what he was doing."'

Min laughed deep within her throat, low and hoarse. She could feel the fear just from the images he was conjuring up, but alongside that was an equal and opposite sensation of safety. She knew he wouldn't be doing this to her – to anyone, in fact – if the fear was really justified. He would keep her safe even while thrilling her, and she thought fleetingly of the conversation she'd had with Cuckoo about Hyuk Jae: safety there too, but no excitement.

'And finally you're at the top, almost as high as the top of the Yanggakdo, and the wind feels like it's getting up a bit, and you're terrified, and the only thing scarier than being up there is when you see how steep the drop is, and the car's edging closer and closer to that drop, and you can hear everyone catching their breath . . .'

They were right under the highest point of the track now. Min glanced at Theo. His eyes were shining, and she knew hers were too. He broke into a run, sudden and fast beneath the descending support columns, and she hurried to keep up with him. His words came staccato through quick breaths.

'. . . and suddenly you fall and it's pure terror, pure white terror so blinding that for a few seconds you can't think of anything else, that sound you can hear is your own screaming whipped away by the wind, you're going faster and faster, the ground rushing up to meet you, you're being pushed and squashed back into your seat, it's not speed you're feeling, humans don't feel speed, we feel acceleration, it's acceleration gathering and gathering, the support structure flying past your face, so close you think you can touch it and just when you think you can't take any more you pull out of the dive and the track begins to level off and you start to slow down again.'

Theo slowed to a walk. Min's face was tingling, and she felt a little dizzy. The track sections above them levelled off and then began to rise and fall gently.

'Now the camelbacks,' Theo said, hands moving in the shape of the coaster as he spoke. 'Up and down, up and down, highs and lows. Every time you go over a crest you feel you leave your stomach behind. For a moment at the top of each one you're weightless, you've escaped gravity. That split second when you can fly. If you're in the front car, you get the quick plunge into every trough: if you're at the back you get the whiplash thrill of being yanked over the top of the camelback hills.'

The columns tilted right in a long curve. Min put her hand on Theo's elbow to steady herself as they followed them round.

'This bit's tilted: not the riders, but the track. It rotates around your heartline.'

'Heartline?'

Theo tapped his heart. 'Heartline, centreline. Means the acceleration takes you to the outside of the bend not the inside, so it's smoother.'

'Heartline,' Min said again. *This is your heartline*, she wanted to say to him. *This is your heartline, isn't it? All this, the coaster and the park and what they are. This is what you love.* But she hesitated, wondering whether or not it would be appropriate, and the moment was gone.

'Then we straighten up. Into a tunnel here, so it's suddenly dark and you just have to feel rather than see, and then another camelback to get up enough speed for the coup de grâce.' He gestured towards a stack of balloons clustered close together. 'The inversion.'

'Inversion?'

'Loop the loop. You go upside down.'

'You don't!'

'You do.'

'That's impossible!'

'It feels like that, for sure. The world spins around you and your brain's telling you this is impossible, but by the time you've realised that you're through and out the other side, and the coaster's slowing and coming to a stop, and you have a little start of surprise when you realise you're right back where it all began. And the restraint bars lift and you get out, and the people waiting their turn see your faces and they know that in a few minutes' time they'll be feeling that way too.'

'Alive.'

Theo smiled. 'Alive. That's exactly what you feel. Like you've looked death in the eye and stared it down.'

'And then?'

'You tell me.'

Min thought for a moment, and knew even as she said it that she had the right answer. 'And then you want to go and do it all over again.'

The sky sheened, shimmering. The pores of his skin opening, leaking.

The stands rose high and vertiginous all around them. Soldiers sat in wide banks of deep green; civilian shirts made vast blocks of perfect white. The arched roofs above them unfolded like the petals of a flower.

These were the Arirang Mass Games, they'd told Theo, and to him they seemed equal parts Busby Berkeley and Leni Riefenstahl. Far below, down on the pitch, small armies of women dressed identically in yellow dresses opened up golden fans to make a vast, burning sun emerging in a triumphant blaze over snow-clad mountains. Thousands of schoolchildren held up coloured cards to make the national flag, and in giddily slick transitions flipped those cards round to form the faces of the Great Leader and the Dear Leader, and to make a map of a unified Korea, and to show a square-jawed soldier with flamethrower and bayonet: and each time the crowd clapped, their hands batting back and forth in such perfect synchronicity that it sounded not so much like applause as volleys of gunfire.

Now the cards made a turtle and an octopus. Flip, and the octopus reached for the turtle: flip, and the turtle retreated inside its shell; flip, and the octopus withdrew.

'It's our desire for reunification,' Min whispered in his ear. 'We reach out to the South, but the Yankee imperialists there ensure that they behave like the turtle.'

He felt rather than saw her smile over the words 'Yankee imperialists'. It may have been about reunification, but Theo felt it deep within himself: that for so long he had been the turtle, seeking shelter in his shell whenever anybody had come too close, and doing so again and again not in the hope that one day things would go differently but in the expectation that they would always turn out the same way, because even a warped comfort was better than no comfort at all.

Schoolgirl gymnasts came on from all four corners at once, criss-crossing in lines of split-second perfection. They tumbled through blazing hoops and formed giant pigs which in turn gave birth to dancing piglets: they cartwheeled over and round one another, springing from hands to feet to hands to feet with dizzying speed and slickness.

Min leant into Theo again to be heard over the applause. He felt her breath against his ear, and kept his face expressionless in case anyone was watching them. 'I was one of those once,' she said.

'Really?'

'We trained for six months: two hours every day after school, no exceptions. Sometimes I'd come home with red welts on the backs of my calves where the coach had flicked a bamboo stick at me for making a mistake. Sometimes I was so tired that I just fell asleep at the table.'

He leant into her in his turn. 'What did your parents say?'

'Oh, this was Arirang. Nothing was more important. If the coach had punished me then I must have deserved it: that's what they thought.' Cuckoo it had been who'd consoled Min, who'd held her while her body shuddered with sobs, who'd whispered that tears weren't a weakness. 'And then I got it wrong.' He raised an eyebrow. 'Don't make it look like I'm telling you something strange,' she said. 'Pretend I'm explaining what's going on.' He nodded. 'That's better.'

'What happened?'

'I turned left when I should have turned right.' It had been a second, no more, and in that moment she had made herself the blemish, the sole point of imperfection in a flawless sea. The panic had bloomed fast and grabbing on her face as she'd forced herself back into the routine, and her eyes had shone wet and bright with terror. She'd followed the rest of the routine perfectly, but the damage had already been done. Afterwards, the coach had bawled her out in front of everyone, spittle-flecked and caring nothing for her humiliation as he screamed in her face. Neither Chul Woo nor Han Na had spoken on the way home: not a single word, a silence so heavy and oppressive that even an eruption of rage would have been better. Min had gone straight to bed without bothering to get changed. She'd pulled the covers tight over her head and hadn't moved, not even when Cuckoo had come to sit on her bed and pressed her hand against the Min-shaped sheet.

'You should be proud,' Theo said.

'Why?'

'Because it shows you're an individual.'

She laughed. 'That's exactly what Cuckoo said to me too.'

The following day, Cuckoo had taken Min to Mount Taesong. The funfair had been closed, so they'd sat beneath the tallest tree they could find, and their silence had been not fraught and oppressive but serene and contented. There'd been whispering in the apartment block where they lived – did you hear about the Park child? Ruined the whole display, she did. So terrible for her parents

– but Cuckoo had told Min to pay them no mind. She was a child. Children made mistakes. What was so hard to grasp about that?

When they'd finished their picnic Min had leapt up to catch hold of the lowest branch, hauled herself up, and began to climb. Cuckoo had watched as Min climbed, and climbed, and climbed. Min had climbed all the way to the top, and she hadn't looked down once.

Peploe had assembled a few people in the bar of the Yanggakdo to celebrate the Fourth of July. It couldn't be marked as such, of course – no Stars and Stripes, no Springsteen, no hot dogs – but the usual Benetton ad array of expat workers drawn to far-flung locations hardly needed an excuse for a party. French NGO workers chatted with Egyptian telephone engineers and German bottled-water salesmen, conversational groups shaping and reshaping themselves like wax clouds in a lava lamp.

Theo drank and chatted, and chatted and drank. Was it only a few months ago that he'd had to leave the awards ceremony because all the small talk was exhausting him? He still felt himself the outsider at events like this, though he figured that everyone here was an outsider in some way: people who in normal circumstances would never have met one another and had almost nothing in common, but who had found themselves thrown together, strangers in a strange land, and therefore clung to one another like shipwrecked men to a life raft. Everyone here was an outsider apart from Peploe, but then again Peploe was in most other ways the biggest outsider of them all.

Theo kept an eye out for Min and Yun Seok, trying to include them in the conversations as much as possible, but they seemed happier talking to each other. He understood: they had been assigned to him and no one else, and keeping an eye on him didn't necessarily mean talking to every other Westerner there too. But still he knew instinctively where Min was at any one time. He never had to look for her in a room: he knew where she would be even before he turned his head towards her.

When everyone was drunk enough to have cast off their embarrassment, Peploe wheeled out an ancient karaoke machine and plonked it on the bar. He grinned at the cheers and whistles, and kicked off proceedings himself – Theo got the distinct impression that this was something of a tradition, and no one dared or cared enough to spoil his fun – with a rendition of 'My Way'.

If Peploe's choice of song was predictable enough, defiant and pathetic in equal parts, he sung it pretty well. He had a good voice, Theo thought, especially given his age and the amount he smoked.

Others took their turn. One of the Egyptians got 'Kung Fu Fighting' out through a fit of giggles; the German water salesman gave 'Rhinestone Cowboy' plenty of oomph and a little dance routine too. Faces became flushed and sweaty and creased with laughter. Peploe called out for Theo to come and do a song, and Theo shook his head.

'If you won't do it,' Peploe shouted, 'how about Yun Seok?'

Yun Seok giggled and shook his head too. He was drunk again, Theo saw, though not as drunk as the other night: that was, he was still conscious, though Theo reckoned another glass or two of *soju* would probably send him over the edge.

'No?' Peploe held the vowel in mock disappointment, a wheedling auctioneer. 'How about you then, miss? Defend your nation's honour?'

Theo turned towards Min, both to check that she had taken Peploe's words in the drunken but good-natured spirit in which they were intended and to tell her she didn't need to do anything she didn't want to do, but before he could say a word he heard the squeak as she pushed her chair back, the smile in her voice as she said 'sure', and the volleys of whooping and applause that accompanied her all the way up to the bar.

'You got any particular track you wanna do?' Peploe said.

Min shrugged and shook her head. There was a brief silence, the drinkers waiting while the machine cued itself up, and for Theo it was a pause in the flow of time itself: a sense that came from somewhere he couldn't name but which he knew to be as true as the rise of the sun, that whatever song came up she would sing not just to him but for him.

The lights were bright and harsh, but in Theo's head the room had narrowed to the two of them: a bubble skin of time that could extend forever and ever, a tunnel of light between them, and nothing beyond other than the fade into darkness.

She was singing now, the others clapping in time, but Theo hardly heard them, and he was sure that Min didn't either. He was amazed at her boldness, for surely everyone here could see what was between them, but if she didn't care then he wouldn't either.

Perhaps Peploe was shooting him warning glances, perhaps Yun Seok was looking thunderous. Theo didn't know and didn't choose to look. He looked at Min and her alone: at the way the microphone grazed her mouth as she sang, at the way she smoothed a strand of hair with the heel of her hand, at the hollow that nestled at the base of her throat.

She sang, and it was the most delicious thing he had ever heard. He listened to her voice and watched her lips shape the words: saw the desire in her eyes and knew that she would see the same in his.

I want you. I want you, I want you, I want you. I. Want. You. Unsaid. Screamed.

12

'I'm being transferred out of Pyongyang.'

This was one of the things with Hyuk Jae: he said everything in the same mild monotone, irrespective of what it was. He'd asked Min to get married in the same tone as he'd said it might rain later, and now he said he was being transferred as if this was akin to one of the metro trains running a minute late.

No, Min thought. *No*. If he was transferred she'd have to go with him, her own career be damned. If she went with him she'd never see Theo again. The shock prickled wet behind her eyes, and she dabbed at them with the knuckles of her forefingers and tried to damp down the panic in her voice.

'Where?'

'Chongjin.' Chongjin was in the far north, a blackened hellhole of pollution forested in scrap metal. No one wanted to go to Chongjin. But right now that mattered less to Min than the simple fact that Theo was here and she would be there: 'there' in this case being anywhere he wasn't, and all options therefore equally ghastly.

'When?' *Please let it be after Theo has gone. We only have a couple of months left. After that, I'll go anywhere you want.*

Hyuk Jae laughed. 'Oh, don't worry. It's not permanent. Just a few weeks, starting from Sunday. Some investigation into theft from the kaolin mines there.'

'Why can't the local branch do it?'

'Why do you think?'

The harshness in his tone gave her the answer. The local branch of the *Bowibu* couldn't do the investigation because the local branch of the *Bowibu* was almost certainly responsible for the theft in the first place. Hence the decision to bring in the outsiders, untainted, to get to the truth.

'You said "transferred",' she said. 'As if it was permanent.'

'You know me. I'm not very good with words, am I?' He gave her a lopsided grin, slightly goofy: and she felt an affection for him that she knew wasn't enough. 'Like I said,' Hyuk Jae continued. 'Two weeks. Three, maximum. You'll be OK without me?'

Peploe was waiting in the hotel lobby when Theo got back one evening. It had been a long day, and the last thing Theo wanted was to have to listen to yet more tales from the Pyongyang frontline, but Peploe held up a hand even before Theo could open his mouth.

'Don't you worry. I ain't gonna detain you. Just came over to say one thing.'

He gestured for Theo to walk back outside with him, into the warmth of the evening air where the microphones couldn't hear them and where no one was in earshot: but even so he kept his voice low. 'Don't try it.'

'Don't try what?'

'What I said in the car on the way to Nampo. Three wives, and not a single one of them a local. Don't try it. Not once, not with anyone, not while you're here. For you, it would be dangerous. For her, it would be catastrophic.'

And he was gone.

Hyuk Jae and Min in the darkness. Hyuk Jae and Min moving together but not together: awkwardly, without rhythm. Smoke and beer on Hyuk Jae's breath, stale and sweet all at once. Hyuk Jae burying his face in Min's shoulder as he thrusts. Min lying beneath him, waiting for it to be over. Hyuk Jae thrusting harder and faster. Hyuk Jae emptying himself with a low whimper. Hyuk Jae propping himself on his forearms above Min, staring down at her. Hyuk Jae rolling over, giving Min his back. And then the snoring, long and even.

Min got out of bed, pulled her nightshirt back down, and went into the bathroom. As always, she'd filled a bath with cold water before going to work as a precaution against the water supply going off along with the electricity. When she turned the tap, nothing came out. She scooped a cupful of water from the bath and used it to help clean her teeth, wetting her toothbrush with it, swilling it around her mouth once she'd finished, and cleaning her toothbrush with the remainder.

There were three things, and she knew two of them. She knew what she wanted to do, and she knew too that she shouldn't do it. But which way between those two she would eventually jump: that was the part she didn't know.

A small street market had sprung up on the route that Theo and Min usually walked, with Yun Seok a few paces behind as per usual.

'That wasn't there before,' Theo said.

'They're called frog markets.'

'Why?'

'When they started they were illegal, so when the authorities came along the traders would leap up like startled frogs and scatter: but the moment the authorities moved on, the frogs would come hopping back again. Cuckoo used to take me to them as a baby, strapping me to her chest while she bought and sold things.' Nowadays the markets were at least tolerated, but back then they'd sprung up anywhere and everywhere – outside train stations, on waste ground, in tram depots. News of their existence had spread as fast and invisible as whispers on the wind, absorbed into the communal knowledge almost by osmosis: a hive mind floating just out of the authorities' reach. Wherever there'd been a market so too had there been Cuckoo: day or night, calling out *sasseyo!* – 'come and buy!' – as though it were an ancient tribal incantation, eerie in a blackness broken only by the dancing yellow light of pencil torches as customers inspected wares and merchants counted money. The money changers had arrived too, offering Chinese *yuan* at black-market rates, and even the doctors, who'd charged for medical diagnoses they'd once given for free in the days when the state had paid and fed them (though they hadn't charged as much as they might have done, as the doctors were men and the markets were run by women, and even the hardiest doctor had quailed in the face of this).

'Had she always done that?'

'Been a market trader?'

'Yes.'

'No. Before that she used to work for the Ministry of Agriculture. She became a trader after she retired.'

Retired. Now there, Min thought, was a word that covered a multitude of sins. Of all Cuckoo's stories, this was the one over which she'd most sworn Min to secrecy, the one about which she'd never breathed a word to either Han Na or Chul Woo. Cuckoo had only told it to Min in the past year or so, even though the events had taken place more than two decades before: that was the depth to which she'd buried what she knew.

Cuckoo had checked her figures, and double-checked them, and triple-checked them. She had collated reports from all round the country, compared them to historical yields – the miles of shelving in the basement of the ministry building held records going back 45 years – and cross-referenced with the State Hydro-Meteorological Administration. She was the nexus, the only one who'd put all the information together and could therefore see the whole picture. There was no possibility that she had made a mistake, none at all. This left her only two options. There was the sensible one, which was to fudge the figures, or the honest one, which was to present them to the minister as they were, in full knowledge of the consequences for her.

Perhaps when she was younger, with much of her life and career still ahead of her, she'd have chosen the former. She could fudge it, and no one would ever know. But she was sixty-three now, and she hadn't got to be one of the few women in senior positions in the ministry without both possessing and exhibiting a certain amount of backbone. Besides – no, not besides: most of all – this wasn't the kind of thing that should be fudged. Every day and in every way she was exhorted to do good for the collective, and sometimes doing good meant telling people what they didn't want to hear: for this was a matter of life and death, and on a vast scale.

She went to see the minister. His office was grand, a corner room with views all the way up and down the Taedong, and it was as neat and unostentatious as he was.

Her report was just three pages long. The minister did not, initially, invite her to take a seat while he read it: but he was no more than halfway through the second line of the first page when she saw his eyes widening and the colour draining from his face, and he gestured distractedly towards the chair opposite him, already aware that he would need to read it twice in order to grasp its full import.

He said nothing for a full minute after finishing, and she heard the dry clicking of his tongue as he tried to work some moisture back into his mouth. He had taken credit for her work on many occasions, but somehow she doubted that this would be one of them.

'You know that I can't present this to the Great Leader,' he said eventually.

She was pleased that he hadn't questioned her figures, even by way of shock rather than genuine disagreement. Her work had always been of the highest quality, and they both knew there was no way she would have brought this before him without being totally sure.

'Then this country's going to starve,' she said simply.

She had written it right at the top of the report, directly under the title, so there could be no hiding it or mistaking its severity.

Unless current food production and distribution measures are drastically overhauled, and produce is allocated across the nation according to nutritional requirements rather than as a reward for political loyalty, the Democratic People's Republic of Korea is facing a humanitarian disaster on a scale not seen since the end of the Fatherland Liberation War.

She had been determined not to hide it in the text. Write it down, say it out loud, make it so.

The minister looked at her with distaste, as though she'd committed a faux pas of dreadful vulgarity. Cuckoo did not lower her eyes: and it was he who looked away first, covering his discomfort by pretending to check something in the report.

'Have you told anyone else?' he asked.

She hadn't, of course, but she couldn't say so. She needed some insurance, no matter how flimsy. 'I have confined distribution to those I deemed appropriate.'

Would he take the chance that she was calling his bluff? No. She had contacts here, and he was a timeserver. He would make this go away.

'I will take the appropriate action,' he said. 'Thank you, Comrade Park, for the diligence of your work.'

She knew, then, what that meant.

The following morning he called her in. 'Due to unavoidable reallocation of departmental resources,' he said, 'your position has been discontinued. And since you are only two years away from mandatory retirement, there is little to no chance of your gaining another position commensurate with your seniority and experience in that time. I am therefore advising you to take early retirement.'

'No.'

'No?'

'You are not advising me to take early retirement. You are obliging me to do so.'

He did not dispute the point. Nor, however, did he voice what they both knew to be true: that people had been shot for less.

The famine came, and it bit deep and hard. No official figures were released – it may have been that no official figures were even kept, and if they were then it was at several levels above the one Cuckoo had reached – but Cuckoo had developed contacts all over the nation during her time in the ministry, and the whispers came to her like hisses on the wind.

She heard of people scavenging for berries and mushrooms in the countryside, or eating bark and sap from the trees, or grubbing in the dirt for mice and rats. She heard of people falling down dead as they shuffled along the street, or hacking at corpses for what little meat there was left on them, or preying on others out alone at night and selling the meat the next day. Every city and every province had stories like these, and even allowing for fabrication, exaggeration and score-settling, some of them had to be true: the simple mathematics of nutrition ensured that.

Cuckoo still met with former colleagues, and they told her of campaigns hatched behind closed doors in anonymous buildings. Officials had devised the slogan 'Let's only eat two meals a day!' on the grounds that the food thus saved would go to their starving brothers and sisters in the South: the double whammy of a noble cause and a pop at the Americans. Bureau 39, the most secretive of all government departments, had drastically increased their production and distribution of methamphetamines to help suppress people's appetites.

There were constant references to this being a new Arduous March, after the guerrilla campaign against the Japanese that the Great Leader had headed (and, of course, triumphed with in the face of overwhelming odds). Even the words 'hunger' and 'famine' had been banned from future use and redacted from official documents already printed, as though these things would not exist if they were not named. In a country where things happened because the government decreed so, the obverse should logically also have been true.

But when the problems were mentioned – and they had to be mentioned, even in this place – they were referred to only in the vaguest terms, and always as a result of events beyond the Dear Leader's control, even though his control was thought to be omnipotent. After all, it had been only two years since the Great Leader's death, a tragedy that had sent the whole world into paroxysms of tear-stained grief: state television had shown crowds mourning his loss in cities across the globe.

'We have experienced more upheavals than people in other eras faced in a whole century. The Soviet Union, which had seemed eternal, splintered into several capitalist nations, and almost all socialist countries collapsed in succession and reverted to capitalism. Our socialist fatherland is under siege from global imperialism. In the midst of all this, our nation suffered an enormous trauma as the Great Leader, the founder of socialist Korea, left our side. And now we have suffered destructive natural disasters – earthquakes, flooding, landslides, hurricanes – as though nature itself has formed an alliance with the imperialists and their policy to isolate and choke us with a blockade.'

Cuckoo read all this, and she knew the truth. Hundreds of thousands of people, perhaps millions of people, sacrificed at the altar of the minister's fear and the Dear Leader's ego. But she knew too that it was more than her life was worth, and more than those of Chul Woo and Han Na too, to say so out loud. Three generations could be punished for one person's crime, and there was now a third generation: Min, her first and only grandchild, after Han Na had all but given up hope of being a mother and had attributed the pregnancy to a miracle willed by the Great Leader in the last moments of his glorious life.

If it had just been Cuckoo, she would have been more inclined to be fearless and speak her mind, but it wasn't just her. It was very rarely just one person. That was what the system was counting on, of course.

Cuckoo saw all this, and she knew. She knew what this country was, knew what it had become. But she knew too that Chul Woo, Han Na, and Min were all she had, and that if they chose not to know, if they chose not to see, then that was their choice, and who was to say that it wasn't the right one? People needed to eat, even in Pyongyang which always had the best of everything and was spared the worst ravages of the blight.

Min couldn't tell Theo this: he was still a foreigner, and the urge to show the best of her country had been burned deep within her.

Besides, there was something else she wanted to ask him. She took a deep breath.

'Hyuk Jae has to go away. I was wondering . . .'

Theo looked at her, and the realisation of what she was saying spread across his face as sunlight spills over a field.

'Yes?'

'I was wondering if you'd like to come over to dinner?'

'In your apartment?'

'Of course.' It was the only place they could meet. No one was allowed to stay in a hotel in their hometown: what possible reason, other than a nefarious one, could a citizen give for doing something like that? It was also totally and utterly insane. No foreigner could visit a local's apartment, supervised or otherwise, and had this been put to Min even a few weeks ago she would have thought that whoever had made the suggestion had taken leave of their senses. But here she was, now, offering Theo the very same, which meant that she too must have taken leave of her senses. She thought of herself as not the kind of woman who would ever do this, have another man round to dinner when her husband was away: but she knew too that she couldn't say she wasn't that kind of woman when she went ahead and did it anyway. She knew only that she wanted to be in Theo's company, to show him something of her life outside the repetitive parameters of funfair and hotel.

The dance between them, nudging their way towards what they both wanted more than anything else.

'I'd love to,' Theo said.

They arranged it with the careful intensity of two people who knew one thing: this was so insanely risky that nothing could be left to chance. Every step had to be foolproof and they had to place implicit trust in each other, for if they got caught . . . well, if they got caught they would be in such deep trouble as to be almost unimaginable. That was no idle turn of phrase: a literal truth, rather. It was why people spoke in euphemisms about going to the mountains, as the reality was too far beyond the conceit of all those fortunate enough not to have experienced it. If anyone knew, really knew, what would happen to them once they'd transgressed, there would have been no misdemeanours at all, not a single one. The fact that people still fell foul of the system was not just a sign that the system was imperfect, but more importantly that human imagination was limited – mercifully, perhaps, in cases like these.

No: if they got caught, there would be no possible explanation, no excuse that would hold water. So there was only one thing for it. They would have to ensure that they couldn't, wouldn't, didn't get caught.

Min was on her way home when her mobile rang.

'Hello?'

'It's Theo. I've left my laptop at Taesongsan and need to get it.'

'Can't it wait?'

'I'm afraid not. I really need it.'

'OK. I – I don't have Nam Il's number, but I've got Yun Seok's. I'll ring him, he'll ring Nam Il, and we'll come and get you.'

'Thanks.'

She ended the call, dialled Yun Seok's number and felt his phone vibrate in the depths of her handbag. He often put it on top of the compartment between the front seats when they were in the car, and it had been the easiest thing in the world for her to brush it into her bag, accidentally on purpose, when she'd got out of the car after they'd dropped Theo back at the Yanggakdo. It was the kind of mistake anyone could have made, and since Yun Seok always had his phone on vibrate – 'That way I can tell my wife I didn't hear her ringing when it suits me,' he liked to joke – Min wouldn't even have to explain why she hadn't heard it ringing when she'd dialled his number.

She left a voicemail, asking Yun Seok to call Nam Il and go to the Yanggakdo. He wouldn't get the message until the morning, but that wasn't the point. In this country, the best way to hide – perhaps the only way to hide – was in plain sight. So Theo had dialled her from the hotel front desk, not only knowing that the receptionist would overhear but actively intending him to do so (and besides, there was no other way of getting through to her: neither the phone in his room nor any SIM card on sale to foreigners allowed connection with local smartphones). Min would come back to the hotel to pick Theo up, ostensibly waiting for the others to arrive: and then she would walk with Theo across the bridge and off the island, telling the security guards that they were going to wait on the main road for Yun Seok and Nam Il. With the sun now set, Min and Theo could make their way through unlit streets back to Min's apartment. Like all the most convincing lies, it stuck as far as possible to the truth: apart, of course, from the small matter of them having gone back to her apartment rather than to Jucheland.

And now here they were: darkness outside, the ruse having come off perfectly, and Theo's presence in her apartment so huge and overwhelming that he seemed to fill the place, stretching up to the ceiling and squashing into the corners.

Min poured two glasses of wine with a shaking hand. The liquid sloshed in air-filled gulps on to the table. Theo took the bottle from her, found a cloth and poured with one hand while wiping with the other. It's fine, his smile said. Relax.

But how could she relax? It wasn't the fear of being caught that worried her, catastrophic though that would be, because for the moment at least that remained an abstraction. It was him, and her, here: a declaration of something that until now had been unspoken, a narrowing of the divide they had kept between them, a surrender. Not totally, of course: or maybe it was, because it was as much what they thought as what they did. Thoughts were still the one sacred place here.

Min smiled back at Theo, and sipped from her glass: twice, three times, until she felt the warmth in her veins and the diminution of her anxiety.

She showed him an advert, a crudely printed flyer rather than something from a glossy magazine: before and after pictures of a woman's face.

'What's that for?' he asked.

'Basic eyelid surgery. They put a fold of skin in there.'

'Why?'

'To make you look more Western.'

He looked at her. 'Don't tell me you're thinking of doing that.'

'Why not?'

'Why would you want to change who you are?' When she opened her mouth to reply, he cut her off. 'Seriously. You're – you're fine just as you are.'

And Min knew from Theo's expression that he had been about to say 'perfect' instead of 'fine', and the joy bubbled in her as she turned away and busied herself in the kitchen.

She cooked *onban*: the same dish, she remembered, that she'd made with Han Na and Cuckoo the night before she'd learned of this assignment. *Onban* in the winter to warm you up, and *onban* in the summer to cool you down. *Iyeol chiyeol*, as the saying went: fight fire with fire.

She cooked it by rote, and ate it by rote, and tasted none of it. A parody of domesticity, with a man here who was not her husband but who was already to her in many ways much more than her husband. A parody of a domesticity they could never have. Theo sat across the table from her, and once more Min told him about Cuckoo and the red thread she wore for a man she'd never see again. Min saw Theo's lips move as he talked, and she didn't hear a word he said. She wanted him to go and never return: she wanted him to stay and never leave.

One day, and it would come on her sooner than she wanted to admit, Theo would indeed go and never come back, and it would be her who could never leave. Or perhaps she could. Perhaps she could transfer to a job with the diplomatic service and find herself sent abroad. It would mean that Hyuk Jae would have to give up his career, or maybe he too could move jobs, could join the Reconnaissance General Bureau, the foreign intelligence service.

They could go to London and she could find Theo again: the two of them in the same city, just as they were now, and maybe that would be enough, two souls lost amidst millions but only a few miles apart. You could run into each other now and then if you lived in the same city. You couldn't if you lived on the other side of the world from each other. They could make time for snatched meetings, a few precious moments on those streets he'd shown her. She could never imagine wanting to know Theo less rather than more: could never imagine being bored by or indifferent to him.

I want to see you naked, she thought. *Not unclothed, but naked, properly naked: without the lies we all tell each other and ourselves, without the fear that leads to those lies, without the barriers and the shields. I want to see you naked, and vulnerable, and true: and I want you to see me just the same way. In a world of concealment, this is the only truth.*

Her hand was on the table between them. He touched it while making a point, and he didn't move away: the tip of his finger on the back of hers, a circuit connected. Min looked at the point where they joined, and up at Theo, and all she could hear was the hammering of her own heart and the jagged loudness of her breathing.

She thought of the science she'd been taught in school. She thought of the physics that explained why the world goes round, of the biology that explained why people were alive, of the chemistry that explained how atoms reacted with each other: and she realised that all of them were at play here, and yet none of them could adequately explain the truth of what was happening.

Theo finished what he was saying. The two of them now perfectly still and perfectly silent: plates cleared, glasses empty, the lightest but most charged of touches between them. A moment held in time, the last safe point, a perfect equilibrium at the centre of opposing forces from all points on a sphere: desire and decorum, want and need, recklessness and self-preservation, sanity and madness, possibility and impossibility, the road taken and the one not. The tiny nudge needed for a heart to lose its balance, and the longing for the chance to fall.

'What are we going to do?' he said. Not as in 'what now?', because they both knew what now, but as in 'how can we possibly manage this, the enormity of what we feel?'

Min smiled and said nothing. She had no answer. There was no answer. She dared not move, but she knew that nor would she resist.

The deep green of Theo's eyes, so close to hers now.

And in the silence, the sudden intemperate bark of a knock at the door.

There were four of them: the *inminbanjang* and three members of the *Bowibu*. The *inminbanjang* reminded Min so much of Han Na that it would, in other circumstances, have made her laugh: but now it just gave her a cold, slow chill, as though the resemblance was not coincidental but actively sadistic.

'Spot check,' the *inminbanjang* announced unnecessarily.

Min stepped aside so they could come in. Concentrate, she told herself. *Shut out everything else and concentrate.*

The *inminbanjang* consulted a sheet of paper attached to a clipboard. 'You live here with your husband?'

'Yes.'

'Where is he?'

'Chongjin.'

The *inminbanjang* nodded towards the *Bowibu* men. 'He's one of them, right?'

'Excuse me?'

'Your husband is a member of the State Security Bureau.'

'Right.'

Min did not expect any special treatment on account of Hyuk Jae's job, and she certainly wouldn't ask for it. They would be as zealous with her as with anyone else: even more so, perhaps, because the first place anyone looked for corruption in this country was as close to home as possible.

The three men took a room each: one the bedroom, one the bathroom, one the living room. The *inminbanjang* herself began to search the kitchen. Han Na did the same on her spot checks, Min knew. Women knew the hiding places in a kitchen the way men never could.

'You've had company?' the *inminbanjang* said.

There was a moment, no more, when Min thought she'd be stuck mid-swallow with a mouth so dry that it would choke her. Then she dredged up just enough saliva to complete the swallow and get the words out. 'No. Why?'

The *inminbanjang* gestured towards the crockery in the sink. Two plates, two glasses, two knives, two forks.

'I didn't wash up last night,' Min said.

The *inminbanjang* peered at the plates. 'You're telling me you ate the same meal two nights running?'

'Of course.'

'Don't take that tone with me.'

'I'm sorry. But – yes, I did. I cooked enough *onban* for a few days so I wouldn't have to do it each night when I was tired.'

The *inminbanjang* stared at Min for a moment before nodding. 'Very sensible. I do the same thing myself sometimes.'

One of the *Bowibu* men came in. 'Key to the balcony doors?'

'I was looking for it earlier.' It was amazing, Min thought, how easily the lies came when they had to. She almost felt as though she were watching herself from above, a member of the audience attending the play of her own life. 'I think Hyuk Jae might have taken it with him by mistake when he left. It's not ideal on hot nights like this.'

The man turned and left the room. Min watched him go over to the balcony doors and look through the panes, his face pressed up hard against the glass and his hands on his temples to block out the light.

She watched and waited, and waited and watched. She was dimly aware that she was holding her breath somewhere between her breastbone and her throat, and that if she didn't start acting normally pretty quick then the *inminbanjang* – who was going through the kitchen drawers with fast fingers – would be suspicious.

Min leant against the kitchen table and folded her arms, pressing the backs of her hands hard against the insides of her elbows to stop them from shaking. Waiting for the shout, the outraged commotion, the other *Bowibu* men to come running. Waiting for the swift, headlong, total destruction of not just her life but her entire family's too: Hyuk Jae, Cuckoo, Han Na and Chul Woo, all burned for what she and she alone had chosen to do. The last safe point indeed, but in a totally different way from the one she had been imagining: entire lives pivoting on this moment, and the enormity of it all impossible to comprehend.

The shout never came, nor the commotion, nor the destruction. The *Bowibu* man took his face away from the balcony doors and continued searching the living room. The one who'd been in the bedroom came to help him, and Min caught enough of their exchange and the cackle of their laughter to know that they were discussing how much use a newly-weds' bed was seeing.

They were there half an hour in all. They did not apologise to Min for the time it was taking, and they did not thank her when they left.

She closed the door behind them and slumped against the wall. She didn't move for a few minutes, and that wasn't just because she wanted to be sure that they weren't coming back. When her legs had stopped shaking long enough for her to stand, she fished the key to the balcony doors out of her pocket and opened them.

Theo was crouching in the far corner, out of sight not just of anyone looking from inside but anyone looking up at the building from the pavement below too. She took his hands in hers and pulled him upright, watching him stagger from cramp and fear in equal measures.

Neither of them said a word. When Min heard the *Bowibu* clumping around in the apartment above hers, she and Theo went downstairs again, fast and keeping close to the shadows on the walls just in case, and back through the shadows to the Yanggakdo. Silence between them: a whole raft of might-have-beens, an unspoken mutual recognition of how close they had both come to total disaster.

At the hotel, Min told the receptionist that they'd waited for hours on the road before giving up and returning. Yun Seok must not have got her message, and she didn't have Nam Il's number. Ah well. It happened, didn't it, this kind of thing? No harm done, she said, and knew that the receptionist had no idea how apposite those last three words were.

13

Nam Il stopped the car in the usual place so Min, Theo, and Yun Seok could walk the rest of the way as they usually did. It was an unspoken rule now, that this was the way they liked to do things.

'Let's just keep going,' Theo said. Yun Seok turned in his seat and raised an eyebrow. 'I've been on my feet all day,' Theo continued. 'And out in the heat too. I'm tired and just want to get back to the hotel.'

Next to him, Min didn't move.

Nam Il looked at Theo, and then at Min, and then at Yun Seok, and finally indicated carefully before pulling out into non-existent traffic.

Crouched in the corner of her balcony, curled up into as small a ball as possible. The shame, the humiliation. Become invisible. Become nothing. The fear, hot and yellow in his stomach. Hearing the sound of a man pressed up against the glass, looking out into the darkness where Theo squatted hidden. His father on the warpath and Theo hiding on the balcony with Offutt military base all around him. His crime? To steal a bunch of fireworks earmarked for the Fourth of July and set them off a day early. The consequences? The promotion for which his father had been earmarked going to someone else. If a man couldn't control his son, it was reasoned, he wouldn't be able to control his men either. That was why Theo had done it, of course. That had been his power, to break his father's career: to say that no one had ever asked him whether he wanted this life, that he'd just been presented with it. And now his father yelling for him to come out and take it like a man. Fight, flight, freeze. Unseen. Not just Theo himself but inside him too, all his emotions at absolute zero. Should have come out. Shouldn't have cowered away. The thinnest of lines between safety and exposure. Peploe's words looping like a hamster wheel in his head. For you, it would be dangerous. For her, it would be catastrophic. Then the relief and the sickness at how close they'd come. The way she made him want to play with fire.

He could ask for her to be reassigned, of course, but there was no way of doing so without arousing suspicion. He wasn't worried about her being offended – he knew she would understand the reason, and indeed would probably welcome it – but Yun Seok would wonder why Theo wanted a new guide when he and Min seemed to be getting on fine. Yun Seok was no fool. If he wondered long enough, he would soon work out the truth, and Theo would have brought about precisely the outcome he was trying to avoid.

If there was no way of getting her to leave, then there was only one thing for it.

'Theo! How's it going?'

'I need to come home, Moritz.'

'Man, we've been through all this.'

'I know. But things have changed.'

'How?'

'I— I just need to come home. You can get someone else to cover for me. The design's done, the track's being installed. It's a supervising and testing job more than anything else now.'

'I can't get someone else to cover for you.'

'Why not? It's only a couple of months, if that. Six weeks.'

'Everyone else is booked up on their own projects. Please, Theo.'

'I can't stay here.'

'Why not? Why can't you stay? How have things changed?'

What could Theo say? Even if there weren't listeners on the line, what could he tell Moritz that wouldn't make him sound like the worst kind of love-struck, hormone-addled teenager? He could barely articulate it to himself, so how would he explain it to someone else?

'Ah, don't worry,' Theo said, silently cursing his own weakness but knowing there was no other way. 'I'm just tired, that's all it is. I'll be fine. Don't worry.'

His room was a respite now, a place of sanctuary. He had to steel himself every morning before going out to the front of the hotel and getting in the car. He wanted to be with Min so completely that he could barely stand to be with her. In the flesh she was too much, a presence of disruptive longing that overwhelmed him and threatened to suck the very air from his lungs. Only when they were apart did he find it tolerable. When they were apart and all he had was the thought of her, he could manage that: he could keep the thought where he needed it to be, twist and spin and pirouette it like a design on his CAD programme. She was real enough to him when she wasn't there and too real when she was.

Theo liked order and control, and these were the very things she was taking from him. It was disorientating: a coaster with no rails, a compass unable to find its azimuth. To desire the very thing that sparked such fear, to be understood without being vulnerable: it was impossible, and only now did he realise that, only *here* did he see it, in a place where for once he could not flee and where he had to trust that she would not abandon him. She was a light above the porch. She had seen through his awkwardness and loneliness, and in making him less awkward and less lonely had made him more than he had imagined possible. He could not deaden once more the parts of him that she was bringing to life, and in turn he knew she could not unsee what she was seeing with eyes he was helping to open ever wider.

The brief, delicious twilight just before sleep, when he drifted and she swirled.

Theo was everywhere all the time, and Min couldn't reach him. He wouldn't talk to her: at least, he wouldn't talk to her the way he had done before. He would still go through her when he needed things translating, and he would at least be civil – for fear that Yun Seok would notice something was amiss, probably – but that almost made it worse. She wondered whether he hated her now, or regretted having let things get as far as they had, even though in some ways they hadn't gone far at all.

She was acutely aware of how little she knew about any of this. She was a blind woman in a strange country with no map. Was this the way people behaved when love got in the way? Was this how he had been with other women? Was this what he was used to back in his own country? At least with Hyuk Jae she knew where she stood.

Every day she and Yun Seok picked Theo up as usual, and took him to Taesongsan as usual, and dropped him back at the Yanggakdo as usual: and yet nothing was usual about it any more. Every day she wanted to scream at him: look at me, talk to me, tell me what you're thinking. An entire country where no one told the truth, and he had now been here long enough to become infected too.

Min caught herself when that last thought came to her unbidden and blasphemous, but it was too late. What was the truth if no one ever told it? What was the truth if she could feel the way she was feeling? It was as if she were being dismantled piece by piece, and if she could ever be put back again it would not be quite in the same order.

She found herself holding on to things, literally, to remind herself that the world was still there: sitting in the car with her hand on the grab handle, leaning against one of the support columns on site, letting her hand linger on a table or chair as she moved. She needed anchoring, tethering. She was a compass whose needle never settled, a boat that had capsized and could not be righted. It was not the world that was off kilter: it was her. Her baseline was gone.

No one could know, not just for her safety but theirs too. The nation was a family, and anything that harmed that family was a crime, no matter how slight and inconsequential that harm might seem. If everyone behaved like her, what would be left? If everyone took a chisel to their tiny part of the edifice, it would soon crumble. It wasn't even enough just to leave that edifice alone: it needed to be built upon and reinforced every single day.

But then Min remembered something she'd been taught in school: that for many centuries people had believed that the sun revolved around the earth rather than vice versa. Perhaps, she thought, that was what she was discovering now: that it was not her who was wrong, but everyone else. In a world of lies, perhaps this was not the biggest lie of all. In a world of lies, this was the only truth.

In the quiet and the solitude of her apartment, the place he had filled to such an extent that it felt as though he was still here in the dust and the echoes. In the silence came an understanding of sorts, born from the same strictures that governed all life here: that what you thought was not what you said, and what you said was not what you did. It was an insight she would not have had without him. She understood that Theo was behaving like this not because of animosity but because of fear. He was scared, just as she was. How else could they be, in the face of what was happening to them? That he chose to turn his face from her made him no less scared.

And that he would not even give her an explanation was, she realised, a strange form of compliment. He trusted her enough to take his behaviour not at face value but at the opposite: to scramble through the thickets of silence and obfuscation to get to the truth beneath. He trusted her intelligence to see this and her understanding not to hold it against him. He wanted her to read his mind, because only that would prove they had the connection he thought they had.

And she did read his mind, and she did know that the connection was real.

In the quiet and solitude of her apartment, Min smiled.

Hyuk Jae came back later that night, a few days earlier than he'd said he'd be. Min was already in bed, and his return annoyed her. She wanted to be here alone with her thoughts of Theo, not having Hyuk Jae clumping around.

Hyuk Jae answered her questions in quick, staccato bursts as he undressed. Yes, they'd sorted the factory theft out. No, he never wanted to go to Chongjin again. Yes, he hoped the success would go on his record and lead to a promotion. No, he wouldn't have to leave Pyongyang again for a while.

He fumbled at her nightshirt when he came to bed. She took it off herself, to spare him the bother and her the annoyance. She was tired, but she knew it would soon be over, so she pushed her hips against him and smiled to convince him that she was enjoying herself.

Theo in this place, in this apartment. Theo with his finger against hers. Theo here in her head and all around her.

Min pushed Hyuk Jae off her, sudden and rough. He opened his mouth to protest, but she was still pushing him, on to his back now so she could straddle him. He reached up for her, but she took his wrists and pinned them back against the pillow, either side of his head like the man who'd looked through the balcony window for Theo. Min guided Hyuk Jae inside her and began to rock against him: her rhythm and not his, her pleasure for once, and she cared nothing for Hyuk Jae's surprise or his inability even to begin to understand what was happening to her or anything other than the image of Theo behind her closed eyes and the fire he had lit in her.

Work was piling up, just the way Theo liked it. The opening of Jucheland was only a few weeks away now, and even though the entire site was still a mess, Theo knew – he *hoped* he knew – that they would be ready on time. It had been like this on pretty much every project he'd ever worked on. Sometimes the place still looked like a bomb site with less than twenty-four hours to go, and still it turned out OK. Perhaps it was the way of all humans, to push hard up against any deadline no matter how generous or ludicrous it was. When Chul Woo panicked, which he did more than once, it was Theo who calmed him down and told him it would all turn out right.

An extra detachment of soldiers was assigned to the site to help with construction. They worked through the infernal heat, day after day, and by the evening they looked as shattered as a chain gang in a Texas summer: but the next morning they were back again, and the morning after that, and the morning after that. Theo asked for Min and Yun Seok to come earlier every day and leave later and later. If he had to work eighteen-hour days, so be it. Sometimes he found one or other of them dozing in the hut that was his office, but he was too consumed by the project to care.

The track was in place now, and he could start adding the parts that would turn it from a long trail of metal into a proper coaster. There were lift motors and drive wheels, chains and brakes, gates and tyres, control systems and electrical work: a multiplicity of plates he had to keep spinning, making sure that everything was done in the right order, finding that solving one problem meant causing another one further down the line.

He loved it, not just in itself but because it allowed him to cut out all distractions. He could reduce his life to simple, easily understood essentials, a tripartite existence in which everything had a single, specific reason. Work for necessity, food for fuel, sleep for rest. Work harder. Eat quicker. Sleep less. Fill every minute until there was no room for the messiness of the human heart.

But still Min wormed her way into his head. Through the cracks of his fatigue and round the sides of his resistance, seeking his weak points like water: flowing, dripping, testing, eroding. Little by little, imperceptible to anyone but him.

He was a cartoon character off the edge of a cliff, convinced he could keep running if only he didn't look down. He began to make mistakes: small ones, sure, but he never made mistakes, not usually. He ran a test circuit without checking that the block systems were operational, and it was luck rather than judgement that meant a car coming off the switchbacks at speed didn't crash into one up ahead which he had stopped in order to work on the brakes. The cars were empty, so no one would have been hurt, but still. Failing to check the block safeguards was total amateur hour.

He went out in the sun without a hat, and refused to put one on: a childish stubbornness, a determination to punish himself in the great furnace of his shame. He had a blinding headache that night, and the next morning he couldn't get out of bed.

It wasn't that he didn't want to: it was that he couldn't. He could move his head, hands and feet, but the rest of him felt as though it were being crushed beneath some great unseen weight. The phone rang – Min and Yun Seok wanting to know where he was, no doubt – but he couldn't answer it.

The next thing he knew, they were gingerly entering his room, and beyond them was a doctor who was opening his case and the hotel manager who looked almost ecstatic in his relief that Theo wasn't going to die on his premises, at least not today.

14

Min had never been in an aircraft before, so a Soviet-era turboprop airliner in a summer storm was hardly an ideal first time. Yun Seok didn't look much keener on the whole idea either, clutching the sick bag with the white-knuckled zeal of a child seeking solace in a favourite teddy after a nightmare.

Only Theo didn't bat an eyelid. It had been ten days since they'd found him motionless and broken in his hotel room, and the doctor had signed him off work on the spot. There'd been arguments back and forth about this, and at one stage the SAC had even become involved – the rollercoaster needed to be finished, on time, and nothing could stand in the way of that – but the doctor had stood his ground. If you let this man keep working the way he has been, he said, he will die.

Something had dropped very fast and heavy in Min's stomach when he'd said that.

Theo, of course, had been determined to return to Jucheland as quickly as possible. He'd kicked up the most enormous fuss and had only relented when they'd reached a compromise and flown his colleague Moritz out to take temporary charge. Even then, Theo had resisted even this until Yun Seok had presented him with the transcript of his last call to Moritz, when Theo had said, 'You can get someone else to cover for me. The design's done, the track's being installed. It's a supervising and testing job more than anything else now.'

The doctor had told Min and Yun Seok to take Theo away: a change of scene and some fresh mountain air would do him good. Deep down, Min had felt, Theo had wanted a break as much as she did: he just hadn't known how to say so. Once it had been taken out of his hands, he'd surrendered himself: to it, and to the prospect of being with her.

The plane lurched as though it had hit a speed bump. Min swallowed a shriek of fear and dug her fingernails into Theo's forearm.

'It's OK,' he said. 'Flying's much the safest form of transport. You're five thousand times more likely to be killed on the way to the airport than in the air itself.'

'Not in Pyongyang traffic, you're not.'

He laughed. 'That's true. Think of something different. Take your mind off it.'

Thinking of something different was easy enough. He was right next to her, and that alone was enough to make her happy.

The air up on Mount Paektu was crisp, pure and cool. For the first time in what felt like months, Min didn't feel the sweat beginning to prickle the moment she was outside. It was a sweet, unexpected relief: the delicious sensation of knowing that when the sun went down she would need an extra layer and would be able to see her breath against the night sky.

'This is the most sacred place in the country,' Min said. 'At school, we were taught to sing songs about Mount Paektu and draw pictures of it. This is where the Dear Leader was born. At the moment of his birth there were two rainbows in the sky and a swallow descended from heaven to announce the birth of a general who was going to rule the world. The sight of the rainbow and the swallow filled the Japanese interlopers with awe and terror. They knew they could never defeat the brave Korean partisans with such a personage to inspire them. Indeed, those partisans killed so many Japanese occupiers that they thought it only possible through the art of land contraction, which in turn made the Japanese fight among themselves and kill one another.'

He stopped walking, waiting for her to turn and look at him. 'Really?' he said, when she did.

'Yes,' she said, but her reply was a touch too quick, her voice a touch too loud.

'The Dear Leader was not like other three-year-old children,' Yun Seok said.

'Clearly.'

It was what they'd always been taught, Min knew: the rainbow, the swallow, the land contraction. It was one of the founding myths of this country. She'd never even considered whether or not it was true. Of course it was true. But now, when she heard herself saying it, her voice sounded hollow. She wondered if Yun Seok had noticed. She wanted to grab Yun Seok and say, 'Don't you get it? Don't you see?' But how could Yun Seok see without going through what Min was? Only something so seismic could open one's eyes when they had been shut so tight for so long.

They arrived at a collection of huts, behind which trees climbed up the hillside. 'This is Secret Camp Number One,' Min said. 'This hut here, this is where the Great Leader founded the Party.' It was simple, wooden and clean. A kitchen, a sitting room, and a bedroom, all spartan but modern. 'As you can see, it is exactly as it was when the Great Leader was here.'

'Exactly as it was?'

'Exactly as it was.' And now it was a game they were playing, just the two of them. The challenge in her voice: *call me out if you dare.*

Yun Seok nodded approvingly at Min's answer. Min herself caught Theo's eye, just for a moment, and on her lips was the hint of a smile. It was reckless, foolish.

There was one hotel, the Pegaebong, in the resort: indeed, the hotel pretty much *was* the resort. A group of students apart, the three of them were the only guests there. The mountain itself reared high in the distance.

'It is a ninety minute drive to get to the base of the mountain itself,' Yun Seok said, 'and another ninety minutes' climb to the summit from the base. The views from the top are spectacular.'

'Can we go there?'

'No.'

'Why not?'

'It's a military area.'

'We could ask,' Min said.

'It's a military area,' Yun Seok repeated.

'And we're here as part of an SAC project. This would be good for Theo's health, which is in turn vital to the success of that project.' She held Yun Seok's gaze, challenging him to dispute the logic of her position.

'I'll ask,' he said.

Min tried not to smile, and when she glanced at Theo she saw that he was doing the same.

Permission to climb the mountain came through late that afternoon. Two soldiers would come and pick them up at two o'clock the following morning: sunrise was just after five, so with the drive and climb they should reach the summit at round about first light. The soldiers would be with them at all times, from the moment they left the hotel to the moment they returned.

'I did not expect them to agree,' Yun Seok said. 'Certainly not so fast.'

'Theo is clearly a matter of national importance.' Min's expression was deadpan.

Yun Seok got drunk again at supper. They put him to bed between them. He giggled as they led him upstairs, his arms draped over their shoulders. Min unlaced his shoes while Theo lowered him on to the bed, and Yun Seok giggled again and pulled Theo close in a drunken headlock, saying something over and over again that Theo couldn't make out.

Min had the room next to Yun Seok, and Theo the one opposite. The rooms were at the end of a corridor, and between them was a fire door, which led out on to a balcony. Through the glass panel in the door, framed so perfectly it could have been a painting in a gallery, Mount Paektu's flanks were stroked silver by the moonlight.

Theo opened the door and stepped on to the balcony. Min followed. Their breath bloomed into the cold air. Keeping their distance but wanting to be close: not daring to do anything so public, but wanting the other to know. She was so aware of him, of every part of him, that she could hardly bear to be this close, to hold this space.

'You know that sunrise over Mount Paektu is the first of this country's ten natural wonders?' Min said.

'I didn't know that. But I do now.'

'You're teasing me.'

'A little.' He paused. 'What are the others?'

Min laughed. 'You think I don't know them, don't you?'

'I'm sure you know them. I want to hear them. I want to hear you say them.'

'OK.' She opened her mouth to begin, and he held up a hand.

'Wait. When you say them: take me there.'

'Take you where?'

'To them. To all of them. Each of them in turn. Take me there with your words. Fly with me to them.'

She smiled. 'OK. Ready?'

'Ready.'

'The winter pines at Dabak, with their branches bending so low under the weight of the snow that it looks like they'll snap at any moment. When the sun's low in the sky the shadows flee from it in stripes as long as railway tracks. When the fog comes it's as though the whole world has turned black and white, and only a flash of red on the sleeve of your jacket reminds me you that the world is still coloured in.

'The azaleas at Chulryong, carpets of red and pink. The reds are as bright and vibrant as a starburst, a forest fire stretching across the hills, the pinks so lush and deep that the landscape seems to be swathed in a vast *jeogori*.

'The view of Jangja mountain at night, ridged and jagged against the moonlight. The mist collects in wisps of grey, and the sky fades from blue to indigo as it soars away from the earth. You might hear a lynx scream, shattering the stillness, or you might just hear the wind as it circles the peak and comes rushing down into the valley.

'The echo of the Oolim Falls, a low rumbling thunder, which you can hear from miles away. Perhaps you don't so much hear it as feel it, a vibration passing through you, but as you approach the sound fills your ears until it's all around and within you, and the spray hangs in the air as the light makes rainbows of it.

'The horizon of Handrebul field, two pure stripes: the blue of the sky and the yellow of the field. No matter how long you look for or how much you squint, neither colour ever bleeds into the other, not even the tiniest bit. It could be a painting: a flag, even.

'The potato flowers from Daehongdan, strips of purple and white marching into the distance like scarves laid out in the market for a woman to admire: to buy if she has the money, to dream of if she doesn't.

'The village of Bumanli, where man works in tandem with nature: men and women working the fields in a silence that is instinctive, knowing what to do and how to do it just as their fore-fathers did and as their descendants will too. The soil is so deeply ingrained in the lines of their hands that no amount of washing will ever get it out.

'The rice harvest in the town of Migok, where sheaves are left on frames to dry in the sun, upturned with their bases tied and then the stalks spreading out across the wood, rows and rows of little pyramids.

'And the Ryongjung sturgeons, which swarm to the sea as birds fly to the sky, darkening the water with the mass of their bodies: a great gathering, a migration, so close that they could touch one another but so graceful that they never do.'

She knew she was conjuring the images for Theo as she spoke. He batted his hands together softly in applause, and in the moments of silence between claps she fancied she could hear the beat of her own heart.

'To see and be seen,' he said.

'What do you mean?'

'To see and be seen. To understand and be understood. To want to show someone things and see the things they show you. You get that so rarely in life.'

She knew what he was saying, and the ground beneath her feet seemed to shake slightly as if from a distant tremor. He released the brakes that held her back, made her overflow and feel dizzy with the flare of his excitement.

'What's that?' she said. He followed her finger. A light was moving high and fast above them. 'An aeroplane?'

Theo shook his head. 'It's the space station.'

'Are you sure?'

'Yes. It's moving too fast to be a plane, and the light's solid, not blinking.'

'We were taught about it at school.'

'What I showed you on the computer the other night: that's what the astronauts up there see for real, every day. The earth laid out beneath them.'

Min didn't take her eyes off the light as it sped across the vault. She thought of riding so high as to see everything the lowly terrestrials could not: the earth glittering vast and sapphire, the Mediterranean painted in vivid ultramarine, Africa mottled like the skin of a leopard, fleeting twilight belts of clouds sprayed pink by the setting sun as it circled endlessly round the planet, dawn after dawn of flashing rainbow hues above the whirling horizon, and the stars shining as bright as love itself.

The dual life: one public, the other private. The fracture, and within each half another fracture. The first half, the public half, splits between the face you show the world and the face you show one particular person. And the second half, the private half, also splits: between what you hide from that person, and what you hide from yourself.

Min and Theo met in the corridor at ten to two in the morning. He'd wondered whether she'd be there and, if not, whether he dared enter her room to wake her. He liked to think she'd wondered exactly the same thing.

'Is Yun Seok coming?' Theo asked.

'I can knock on his door and find out.' She phrased it as a question.

'Or we could just let him sleep last night off.'

'He's probably a bit old to be climbing mountains anyway.'

'You won't get in trouble?'

She shrugged. 'I don't know.'

'You could always say that you tried to wake him and he didn't respond.'

'Wicked imperialist, encouraging a pure Korean to lie.' He saw her teeth flash white in the gloom as she smiled. 'I'll say that we'd arranged to climb the mountain and that I couldn't let you go on your own with the soldiers.'

'Which is true.'

'Which is true.'

It was cold – deliciously, gloriously frigid, the kind of chill that sears the lungs on every breath and makes nerve endings tingle. One soldier took the lead and the other brought up the rear, with Theo

248

and Min in the middle. They all had torches, but the moonlight was quite enough when their eyes had adjusted.

There was a path cut into the mountainside: steep in some places and shallow in others, sometimes well marked and other times indistinct, but always there. Their boots crunched on the stones. Around them the silence, and above them the stars.

A memory came unbidden to Theo: sitting in an Alpine refuge during a white-out. The entire morning he'd stayed there, twitching to get out and keep walking: he'd taken himself off hiking in the Alps – alone, of course – and hiking meant just that, hiking, not sitting around staring out of the window at a featureless bank of fog.

At lunchtime he'd decided to go, white-out or not: just got up, shrugged on his pack, and walked out of the door, letting the disbelieving cries of the other hikers bounce off his back. For half an hour he'd walked along a path of which he could only see the next six feet, and then the fog had lifted with the ease and quickness of a curtain being drawn back, and he'd realised three things at once.

First, that there was a more or less sheer drop on either side of the path, hundreds of feet down over unforgiving scree. Second, that he could see for what felt like a hundred miles in every direction. And third, that in all those hundred miles, in all those thousands of square miles, he was the only thing moving.

He felt like that again now: not just that they were the only things moving in a world of otherwise perfect stillness, but also that same sense of being alone on a high wire, that one step the wrong way to either side would lead to a headlong, bloodied tumble.

The creeping glow to the east as the sun stirred and began to lighten the sky, as slowly and gently as a man might awaken his lover in the quiet of the dawn.

The wind beat about them as they reached the top. Theo turned to help Min up the last few paces, and saw her eyes – the only part of her face visible between a hat pulled low and a scarf pulled high – flash with amused defiance. She set herself next to him without taking his hand for support, and for long moments he stood there, marvelling at everything within and without: the delicious ache in his legs, the sunrise spraying gold across the rise and fall of the land, and the simple pleasure of being with her. There was nowhere he'd rather be and no one he'd rather be with: twin dustings of perfect satisfaction.

The landscape folded and creased, reared and fell, welcomed the long sunrise shadows and hid from them.

Min said something that Theo couldn't make out. He gestured for her to uncover her nose and mouth. She lowered her scarf, and just before she opened her mouth he saw her, saw her properly: not for the first time, of course, nor even for the hundredth, but in a way he had never done before, for she was always revealing herself to him anew. He saw the olive of her skin and the wisps of night-black hair snaking from beneath her hat, he saw the way her eyes were coloured like almonds, he saw the promise in lips plumped as delicately and lightly as scatter cushions. She could have been a Biblical queen brought early to her throne.

He saw all this, and felt it sink into him with a jolt: something alien, something unexpected, something that could hurt him in the hardened hollows deep inside.

He didn't care. It would hurt, and he would endure it.

Heavenly Lake was a marbled bowl below them with birch trees clinging to the shoreline. The water was so calm and so blue as to appear almost solid, a vast block of lapis lazuli rather than something that would yield to the slightest touch.

Min raised her voice so Theo could hear her above the wind. 'The surface is at 2,190 metres above sea level.' When he laughed at the deliberateness of her monotone she smirked, evidently pleased that he'd heard it for what it was. 'It covers an area of 9.16 square kilometres and has a depth of 384 metres, making it the deepest mountain lake in the world. When the Dear Leader died, ice cracked on the lake so loudly that it seemed to shake the earth, and a mysterious glow was seen. They say that the lake can help you know your own mind. When things are reflected, when they're turned upside down, then you can see what the lake wants you to see.'

Theo had a sudden vision, a vivid burst of imagination which sprang to mind fully formed. *He and Min were down by the lake, the scree rising above them. A tree's bare branches, the peak of Paektu itself, a cloud the shape of a zeppelin scudding across the sky, each of them caught and held in the implacability of the lake's reflection. They were stripping off, him giving her his back as they undressed, not for his sake but hers. He knew how deeply transgressive this was for her, to be like this in front of a man who wasn't her husband, and knew too that she needed to hear things from him, even silently: I won't hurt you, I won't tell anyone, this is just for you and me. Turning to face each other in their underwear, seeing her look at him, a quick glance that took in everything: the ridge of muscle on his thigh as he balanced on one leg to remove his sock, and the red worm of the scar that skirted the edge of his shoulder blade. She was coming alongside him, and he saw her eye drawn to the way his hair spread in tight curls across his chest and in downy lines towards his waist.*

The water felt even colder than the air, and at the very first touch of it his breath quickened. He forced himself to go in. One step, and then another, and another, the water rising around his knees and thighs. He splashed his face and chest, and gasped reflexively. Hands below the surface, already feeling numb.

The cold was piercing, a razor blade: it was lightning jagging black against a white night, it was a silver strip on the nerve ending of a tooth. The cold was all there was, and he felt the first stirrings of a strange exhilaration. He got his breathing back under control and let himself sink beneath the surface.

And suddenly he was swimming, slicing through the water, and he realised that the strange noises he could hear were coming from his own mouth, and were his trying to laugh through snatched breaths. His skin was burning, frost become fire, and every cell in him felt not just alive but supercharged. Water all around and in him, holding him up and dragging him down, churned by the frothing of his limbs. Water does not strive. It flows in the places men reject. Bubbles rose from the depths beneath him, and when he looked down it was on to ever-deepening shades of blue extending to total darkness. He felt himself held in suspension over a strange, hazardous, beautiful world.

Min was shrieking: not in pain but in delight, yelling her head off in happiness at this lunacy. She disappeared under the water like a seal, kicking her legs hard, and when the ripples she'd made bounced against Theo's face he fancied that they kept on going right to the very heart of him, and that the shore against which they eventually spent themselves was not the one on which he'd left his clothes but the one on which he'd left his soul.

15

It was getting near, Cuckoo knew. She was moving more slowly by the day, and she found the dog days of summer even more enervating than the long winters. She could always wrap herself up warmer against the cold, but there was no escaping this heat. All she wanted to do was sleep. She was ready now, to go on whenever the time came.

Han Na was preparing dinner when there was a knock at the door.

It was unexpected, but that in itself did not necessarily make it unwelcome. There were plenty of reasons someone could be calling, especially since Han Na was the apartment block's *inminbanjang*: to report something or someone, or to hand over a permission slip for an overnight stay.

'I'll get it,' Cuckoo said, when Chul Woo didn't move.

Cuckoo went over, her pace so glacial that another knock sounded before she got there. She opened the door. A woman in her forties was standing there, and the first thing Cuckoo noticed about her was the thick armband round the upper part of her left arm. It was white with a large red cross, and the woman was standing slightly at an angle, as though she wanted the armband to be the first part of her that Cuckoo saw.

'Comrade Park?' said the woman.

'Yes.'

'I'm from the Red Cross. May I come in?'

'What's this about?'

'It'll be easier if I can come in.'

Cuckoo stood aside, a little uncertainly: though, when she thought about it later, she realised there was no way she could have known what was coming, and that her uncertainty had simply been a natural reaction rather than a harbinger of anything remotely momentous.

The woman walked past Cuckoo and into the living room.

'My son, Chul Woo, and my daughter-in-law Han Na,' Cuckoo said.

'I'm sorry to intrude on your time,' said the woman, eyeing the food Han Na was preparing, 'but please, could you all stop what you're doing?'

It wasn't the armband that made them acquiesce, but her manner: a no-nonsense briskness which intimated that, whatever she was there for, it wasn't to waste their time, or indeed her own. Han Na put down the chopping knife and Chul Woo got up from his chair. The woman gestured for them to sit at the table, as though this were her apartment and they were the guests. Chul Woo bristled at this, but Han Na was more circumspect. Everyone in this country understood authority, and this woman, whoever she was, had just that.

'Is it Min?' said Han Na. 'Has something happened to my daughter?'

The woman came and sat down at the table with them, unslinging a satchel from her shoulder and opening it as she did so.

'Please,' she said. 'I have done this many times. Let me do it the way we know through experience is best.' She looked at Han Na. 'It's nothing to do with your daughter, I promise you that.'

'What, then?' said Chul Woo. Cuckoo put her hand on his arm. He shook it off irritably.

The woman took a cardboard folder from her satchel and placed it on the table, squaring it off so it sat perfectly straight in front of her.

'I don't know how much you know about the Red Cross,' she said. 'We work in several different areas – flood relief, health-care programmes, food production – and in the aftermath of the Fatherland Liberation War we provided many people with clothing, bedding, and medical services.'

'After the imperialists had attacked without cease,' Chul Woo said.

The woman gave him a short, single nod. 'Indeed. And, as you know, the effects of that conflict are being felt even today. Millions of families were split by the war. Husbands and wives, parents and children, brothers and sisters, all of them displaced by the fighting, stranded on either side of the line when that fighting stopped, and condemned in a flash never to see each other again.' She glanced at Chul Woo. 'Due to the Yankee occupation of the South, of course, which prevents our people being reunited in one Korea.'

It was Chul Woo's turn to nod.

'We work with our counterparts in the South to identify family members affected in this way,' she continued. 'Although our countries have yet to be reunited, sometimes it's possible for a few people to meet up with loved ones from across the border. A hundred people each time, maybe two hundred. You've probably seen these meetings on television or in the newspaper. In fact, the next meeting is a fortnight from now.'

Cuckoo felt a strange awakening, as though time was running slightly ahead of itself. She knew why the woman had come and what she was going to say, even though it simply wasn't possible: a state of total acceptance and utter rejection all at once.

The woman took Cuckoo's hand in hers. 'This is going to be a huge shock, I know, since as far as I understand you were told that your husband Kwang Sik died a glorious death in service of the fatherland on Hill 983. But things get mixed up in war, records jumbled, people confused.'

No, Cuckoo was thinking, *no, this isn't possible* – and she was vaguely aware that she was squeezing the woman's hand as hard as she could, just to anchor herself against the feeling that she was tumbling into a sudden but endless fall.

'Kwang Sik did not die on Hill 983, nor at any time afterwards. He will be at the reunion meeting on the second weekend in September, and he would very much like to see you.'

Alive. That was all Cuckoo could think. *Alive.* One word, over and over again. After all this time, Kwang Sik was alive.

She plucked at the red thread around her wrist, the one that anchored her soul to his and had been a way of keeping his memory burning . . . and all this time he'd been here, there, somewhere.

The questions tumbled over each other like acrobats in her head – why now? Why hadn't he tried to get in touch before? What had he been doing? Had he remarried? Was it even really him? – but even if she'd wanted to grasp at any one of these questions it was out of reach, gone and replaced by the next one. It was as though she were looking at the world through a fog, as though she were a child reaching for bubbles that popped the moment before she touched them.

Not once in six and a half decades had she even considered this. It was a magic trick, the whipping away of a tablecloth so all the cutlery and plates and ornaments stayed upright – but this was her life, and it wasn't upright any longer. It was tumbling through space, and she with it.

'Breathe, comrade,' said the woman, still holding her hand. 'Breathe deeply. In through your nose, out through your mouth. That'll relieve the pain in your chest.'

Cuckoo hadn't even mentioned the pain in her chest, but the woman had still known. That reassured Cuckoo that the woman knew what she was talking about. Cuckoo breathed as instructed, and the pain began to recede.

'Many people react this way,' the woman said. 'It's quite usual.' She turned to Han Na. 'Maybe some tea?'

The woman would stay for as long or as short a time as they wanted, she said. Some people hurled questions at her for hours; others preferred to absorb the implications on their own. She had seen both reactions plenty of times, and had no personal preference.

Was she sure that it really was Kwang Sik?

Yes, absolutely. That had been checked, double-checked and triple-checked by her colleagues in the South.

Where was the meeting taking place?

At Mount Kumgang, a tourist resort down near the border. The bus would leave Pyongyang on the Saturday morning and return on the Sunday morning. They would stay there overnight.

Why hadn't they been given more notice?

There had been no time. This was how meetings were arranged. Coordination between the two sides was always difficult.

Did Cuckoo have to go alone?

No. All reunion participants could take someone with them for practical and moral support. Perhaps Chul Woo would like to accompany his mother? This wasn't just her husband, of course, but his father too.

Thank you, Chul Woo said. I think we need time to discuss this between us.

The Red Cross woman gave Cuckoo a card. 'That's my number, there. If you could give me an answer within seventy-two hours, that would be very helpful. Places are limited, and if you choose not to take yours up then there are others we can ask.'

Chul Woo escorted her to the door, only just remaining the right side of polite in his eagerness to hurry her out of the apartment. The moment she was gone, he went back to the table, poured three glasses of *soju*, drained his in one swallow and urged Han Na and Cuckoo to drink theirs.

'We can't go,' he said.

Cuckoo and Han Na looked blankly at him. 'Why not?' Han Na said.

'Am I the only one still thinking clearly?' he snapped. '*Songbun*. That's why. Nine. Twenty-two. Are you getting me?'

In the simplest terms, *songbun* was a person's social class dependent on their political loyalty. There were three main classes: core, neutral and hostile. The core – the Party, the military, those trusted by the state – made up perhaps a quarter of the population (and, high Party officials apart, few people were revered as much as those who had given their lives against the imperialists). The neutral, such as peasant workers, were around 55 per cent; and the hostile (defectors, criminals, prisoners and subversives) made up the other 20 per cent.

As with most systems of classification, however, the devil was in the detail, and the detail was graded into shades as deft and defined as a painter's colour palette. The detail was not between the classes, but within them. The three classes were divided into fifty-one categories, and it was not just your class but your category that would determine everything about your life: where you lived, where your children would go to school and university, what job you could and couldn't have, even your access to food and medicine.

Their current category was nine: that was, the families of soldiers killed in the Fatherland Liberation War. Nine was core class, of course: high Party officials apart, few were revered as much as those who had given their lives against the imperialists. Twenty-two was those who'd surrendered to or worked for the South during the war, and they were to be considered in the same way as those removed from the Party: that was, as implacably hostile.

Cuckoo had always thought it a ludicrous system. Small merchants. Hired people from the families of labourers. Administrative clerical workers. Revolutionary intellectuals. Nationalistic capitalists. Practitioners of superstition. Tavern hostesses. Economic offenders. Reactionary bureaucrats. And on and on: people's lives whittled down and locked into what they did rather than who they were. What about chance? What about the myriad of random ways in which life's dice fell? Look at who had survived the wartime bombing raids and who had perished. Blind luck, nothing more or less: a single wrong turn taken on a long, long highway. But totalitarian states could not abide any notion of chance. Chance led to rebellion, rebellion led to overthrow, overthrow led to anarchy. If the state could control every aspect of every individual's life, then by definition it could control the collective too.

There was no way of fighting this, Cuckoo knew, not overtly, not without losing your *songbun*, and there was no way back from that. If you did something bad enough to lower your *songbun*, it wouldn't be just you who suffered: your entire family would have theirs lowered too. The rationale behind *songbun* was that it suffused pretty much every aspect of life in the country, and each citizen assimilated it in their own everyday existence as deeply and easily as eating or breathing.

'We can't know that,' Han Na said eventually.

'What else could it be? He was a soldier. He was reported dead, but he wasn't. He never came back, not even after the war when prisoners were swapped back. Therefore he must have switched sides.'

'He would never have done that,' Cuckoo said. 'He would have come back for me, and for you.'

'Well, he didn't, did he?'

'Why not wait till we see him? Then he'll tell us what happened.'

'Don't you see? Don't you *understand*?' The force of Chul Woo's anger battered against Cuckoo like waves on a sea wall. 'If we go to this reunion, our lives are over. Your husband, my father, will be revealed as a traitor, and our *songbun* will be ruined. We'll be stripped of residency rights in this city, at best. And at worst . . .'

He didn't finish the sentence. He didn't need to. 'At worst' meant the vanishing, going to the mountains: those who were here one day and gone the next.

'Then what do you suggest?' Cuckoo said.

'Easy. We say he's an impostor, he's mistaken, it doesn't matter. He's not your husband, he's not my father, so we're not going.'

Pyongyang felt even hotter and more humid than it had done before. Min stood on the aircraft steps when they landed and wondered how it was that only a couple of days before she'd subjected herself to obliterating cold.

Something had changed between her and Theo again: or perhaps it was not so much that it had changed again as that it was reasserting what it had long been. They were like the ocean and the shore, always reaching forward and falling back. The memory of how close they had come to disaster still bubbled near the surface, but the gravitational pull of his orbit dragged and warped everything else. She trembled with their nearness and the knowledge of what they held massive and unseen between them: the angles they now took when they faced each other, the intoxicating silk of their secret. Everything risked in every glance, and every night she would scuttle home to Hyuk Jae and exult in his obliviousness to everything she was feeling.

All she had to do was negotiate the final few weeks of Theo's stay: then he would be gone and she would be safe. That was all she had to do.

All.

'Comrade Park, what transgressions have you made against the Revolution these past seven days? What transgressions have you made in thought, in word, and in deed?'

Min knew now what she had not done a few months previously, or rather what she had not dared let herself know: that this whole thing was a farce. Everyone had to confess to something, and the trick was to pitch that confession just right. Too facile and it looked like you weren't taking the whole thing seriously; too grave and you could find yourself in big trouble. Now it was all Min could do to stop herself yelling out 'Can't you *see*?', but that it was a charade could never be publicly acknowledged. No one dared so much as joke about it. If by chance someone ever did, they would find no response for fear that they were a provocateur, an enemy of the state.

'I have appraised the week that has passed. In order to correct my faults, I must cleanse myself of the repeated sins that accumulate and slow down our beloved Revolution. I have proved myself insufficiently grateful for the Supreme Leader's eternal love. I failed to wake Comrade Choe for the trip up to the summit of Mount Paektu. I should have done so, but he was sleeping so soundly that I did not want to disturb him. Therefore I went solely with our military guides and the American, who had expressed such a great desire to go and who badly needed the exercise after the way he had overworked himself.'

'What did you do on the climb?'

'We went to the summit, looked down at Heavenly Lake, and then returned.'

'What did you talk about?'

'I impressed upon him the beauty of the mountain and the lake, and the importance of both in our national fabric.'

'Do you have any other transgressions to confess?'

'On the plane up to Paektu I exhibited unmistakeable signs of fear, which in turn may have suggested to the American that I had insufficient faith in the expertise of those who fly and maintain the aircraft. I had never flown before, so the experience was entirely new to me. If my unfamiliarity came across as fear, I apologise and pledge not to let it happen again. I would like to think that no such weakness was apparent on the return journey.'

'Do you have any other transgressions to confess?'

'No.'

'Your thoughts have been pure in the service of Kimilsungism-Kimjongilism?'

'My thoughts are as pure as the snow atop Mount Paektu and the air around Heavenly Lake.'

'Thank you. I congratulate you, comrade, for these admissions, which are so essential to the progress of each of us.'

When Min went round to her parents' apartment, she found everyone there fixed in their emotions as though they were toy figures frozen in a tableau: Cuckoo disbelievingly happy, Chul Woo broodingly furious, Han Na unusually flustered. It had been a day since they'd received the news, but to all intents and purposes it may as well have been a minute.

They went over it all again for her, picking apart what the Red Cross woman had said, talking over and contradicting each other until it all dissolved into shouts and tears. Finally, Cuckoo turned to Min and said simply: 'What would you do?'

'Go and see him, of course.' Min turned to her father. 'You too. To look after Cuckoo, if nothing else.'

It was as though she'd been set a test, Min thought. Cuckoo, all hugs and tears, clearly thought she'd passed it: Chul Woo's scowl showed exactly the opposite. Pass or fail, of course, Min still had all the questions the others did too. A grandfather she'd never met, a father her own father had never met, back from – well, if not the dead, then at least somewhere near outer space. Sixty-five years! That was practically three times as long as she'd been alive.

It would, she knew, take some time to accept. You couldn't just think someone dead all your life and then shrug your shoulders when they turned out to have been alive all along. But then again, there were plenty of ways in which her life was turning out to be the opposite of what she thought it was. She'd never imagined sitting at a computer with a man she'd been told was her mortal enemy and flying around the world with him, or seeing him smile at her when the flying was for real and so was the terror, or feeling compelled by something she didn't fully understand to defend him when the *Bowibu* wanted to take him away to a prison camp.

She'd known nothing.

'I found this the other day.'

Min and Hyuk Jae were in bed. Hyuk Jae was holding something between his thumb and forefinger. It caught the light as he rotated it, and Min saw what it was: a button.

'I'll sew it back on,' she said. 'Just leave the shirt out for me.'

'It's not from any of my clothes. Must be one of yours.'

'I'll have a look. Where did you find it?'

'On the balcony.'

Min was conscious that she must be gawping stupidly at Hyuk Jae, but it was as though the connection between her brain and her face had suddenly decided to run at half speed. She was trying to remember not so much what Hyuk Jae had said but the way in which he'd said it. 'Must be one of yours': had that been loaded with sarcasm and suspicion, or was her guilt making her hear things that had never been there to start with?

'Are you OK?' he asked.

She shook her head quickly, as a dog might do when stepping out of a river. 'Yes, fine. Sorry.' A lie slid smoothly into her consciousness, and she grasped at it before it could vanish. 'I was just wondering if I'd signed my weekly confession paper, and then I remembered that I had.'

'I haven't seen you out on the balcony.'

'Oh, I sat out there a few evenings when you were in Chongjin. It's about the only place in the apartment with a breeze, and some of those nights were so hot.'

'It doesn't look like one of your buttons.'

'You're a clothes designer now?' She smiled both to leach the sting from the words and to stop herself from screaming. 'Maybe it belongs to whoever lived here before us. Here.' She took the button from him. 'I'll have a look through my clothes, and if it's not from them then I'll just keep it as a spare. Let's sleep. Today has worn me out, one way and another.'

She turned her light off, and soon enough heard Hyuk Jae's rhythmic snoring start up. He couldn't have been that suspicious, she thought, if he'd fallen asleep so quickly: but she knew it would be a long time before she joined him in slumber, and that she'd be lying awake for hours with Theo's button pressed into her palm like a talisman, a tiny artefact holding his essence, a breadcrumb leading her back to him.

The track was complete: a vast, beautiful metallic beast which reared high above the park. Theo allowed himself a few, brief moments of savouring it: its shape, the way it swooped and soared, the artistry in it that was so visible and the engineering that wasn't. He had designed it, plucked the pieces from the ether and put them together, starting on a slate-grey January day with the ground frozen solid hard beneath his feet and ending in sledgehammer heat and the track too hot to touch once the sun was high.

But he knew too that a rollercoaster track was not there just to be gawped at. It was there to be ridden on, and all its height and depth and curves would count for nothing if the ride was not the experience Theo had designed it to be.

The cars had been delivered last week, and he had kept the covers on them even while fixing them to the track. It wasn't just so they wouldn't get scratched or damaged, but also because he wanted to give them a big reveal.

Now he made sure that all the workers were watching, and then he pulled the cover off the first car with the flourish of a magician doing the tablecloth trick. There was the briefest moment of silence – *please*, he thought, *don't let them be disappointed* – and then he heard the gasps and the applause, and he figured he'd been here long enough to know genuine wonder when he heard it.

The cars were as beautiful as any of those on his other coasters. They were dark red, almost russet, a colour so rich and lustrous that the paint seemed to glow from within. At the front of each car was a horse's head thrust upwards and forwards, and beneath it the front pair of legs tucked in on themselves mid-leap. Wings ran

265

down either flank, and when Theo ran his hand over the ridges and feathers he fancied that he could feel the skeleton and musculature of a living thing beneath his fingertips. And out of the back of each car trailed a rear pair of legs thrust out straight as they drove forward with all the power they possessed.

He smiled and made a bow that was half-serious.

It was time to test the cars.

He took the covers off them all, and started them off empty. The long clacking of the ratchets as they climbed the first hill: two minutes from station to summit, not just because that was the speed they could go at given the anti-rollback mechanism, but also because it would allow the anticipation and the fear to build and build. Coasters were not just art and engineering: they were psychology too.

Theo watched in silence. This was where he found out whether all his calculations had been correct or not. If they hadn't been – well, he'd have to go back and amend them, even though there was hardly enough time left for that. They called it T & A, Test and Adjust – yes, they'd heard the more risqué version a thousand times – and it was something that every rollercoaster designer hated. It sounded so simple: three short words, test and adjust. But there was lots to test and sometimes not much less to adjust. And with the testing and adjusting came two immutable truths: that the schedule would slip, and that the opening day wouldn't change.

Min was standing next to Theo. He felt her hand squeeze his, brief and unseen, and he took it for what it was: a gesture of solidarity and a recognition of so much more. He squeezed back. He did not look at her. His eyes were on the cars at the top of the hill now, inching towards the long drop.

Here we go.

The cars plunged down the drop, gathering speed almost as quickly as they would have done in proper freefall, and Theo knew from the moment he saw them go that things would be fine. He could judge a coaster's speed to within a couple of miles per hour just by watching it run, in the same way that professional athletes can hit a given lap time to within a tenth of a second without needing a stopwatch. When one did it often enough, one could sense these things as accurately as a racing pigeon knows which way to head for home.

The cars zipped over the switchbacks, twisted elegantly through the heartline curves and looped the loop in a beautifully flowing ellipse. When they came to a halt back at the station, the entire construction crew burst into applause: not the weirdly synchronised thunderclaps that Theo had heard at the Arirang Games, but proper spontaneous applause, which sounded like falling rain. He waved and bowed, and hoped they could discern how genuinely touched he was.

He ran the test a few more times with empty cars, and then with sandbags to approximate the weight of passengers. Each time he'd examine the system feedback and make tweaks where needed. He read strain gauges and accelerometers with the easy familiarity of a concert pianist reading sheet music. He tested hardware, electrical systems, and software over and over again. He set electromagnetic proximity switches and photo-eye sensors to deliberately fail in order to ensure that the cars would stop safely even when the usual systems were disabled. He adjusted brake systems to make the decelerations as smooth as possible, and he went round and round with break beams and pressure mats to ensure that the ride would stop instantly the moment a passenger was where they shouldn't be.

Theo ran the sandbagged cars for 101 separate cycles – 100 as standard and one for luck – before pronouncing himself satisfied enough to go on to the next stage.

'What's the next stage?' Min asked.

'We run it with actual passengers.'

They took Moritz back to the airport.

'Thanks for coming out,' Theo said. 'You saved my ass.'

'Your ass is my ass. In this case, at least. See you again soon. It won't be long now.'

Those last five words cut Theo to the quick. Moritz hadn't intended to, of course, hadn't even known that they would or why they could: but he could hardly have flayed Theo more accurately if he'd tried.

'There's something different about you, you know,' Moritz continued.

'Like what?'

'I'm not sure. Just – different.'

'Good different or bad different?'

'Oh, good. Definitely good.'

On the way back into town, Theo asked whether they could return to the film studios soon. There were still a few items he wanted to secure, things that would help the coaster tell the story the precise way he wanted it to.

'We can go tomorrow,' Yun Seok said.

'I was going to ask.' Min cleared her throat. 'My grandmother's had a shock, and she's very old, and she needs me to help her with something. I was going to ask if I could take tomorrow off.'

'That's fine,' Theo said before Yun Seok could answer, and he saw the look of hurt surprise on her face.

'It's not for you to decide,' Yun Seok said.

'No. But we have only ten days left, and I need these things as soon as possible. So I'm happy to go just with you.'

He didn't look at Min again.

The apartment was quiet, warm, and still: a perfect repository for Cuckoo's thoughts, which squatted low and heavy over her like a great toad.

She was thinking about Kwang Sik, of course. She'd thought about nothing else since the woman from the Red Cross had called round, and had in a few minutes ripped apart everything that Cuckoo had thought to be true. It was more than sixty-five years since she'd last seen him. Sixty-five years was longer than some people got for their entire lives. Sixty-five years, day after day, and all the while he'd been out there somewhere, hidden from her in the seething billions of people going about their business in every country in the world. What had he been doing? Where had he been living? Why hadn't he tried to get in touch? Why now? Why so late in their days?

There was only one person who could give her these answers, Cuckoo knew. She could ask the questions until the end of time, but she didn't have the answers, and nor did the walls of this apartment, and nor did anyone else in Pyongyang. If she wanted the answers, she would have to go to Mount Kumgang.

If. If she wanted the answers.

Cuckoo pressed her wrist to her nose and inhaled the smell of the red thread she wore. It wasn't the same thread she had tied around her wrist that day on the banks of the Taedong river, of course – that one had frayed and snapped, as had the many she'd put on since then – but every time one broke she replaced it immediately, because it wasn't the thread itself that mattered but what it represented.

The thread she'd given Kwang Sik hadn't been in the box they'd returned to her all those decades before. It had been the first thing she'd looked for, of course, but all she'd found were possessions from his time in the army: a handful of brass badges, a water bottle, some webbing, a soldier's handbook. She'd recognised none of them, as they had all come from the time after she had last seen him. As far as she'd been concerned, these items could have belonged to anyone: they hadn't been his, at least not as she'd remembered him.

Remember him she had, and remember him she did, every single day. When Chul Woo had still been a small boy Cuckoo had almost felt as if Kwang Sik was still there, and that at any minute he'd come through the door, smiling as he always had, and sit on the floor with Chul Woo and ask him about school, and then later he'd read to Chul Woo before bedtime and he'd look up and see Cuckoo standing in the doorway looking at her boys and her loves, and it would be as if those two soldiers had never found her that day in the ruined city and given her the news that had almost destroyed her in turn as well.

But all the while life had swept on without him. Pyongyang, which had been flattened during the war – literally flattened, entire city blocks pancaked to rubble time and time again – had sprouted up like spring shoots: cranes and workers everywhere, buildings rising day by day amidst the exhortations for the nation to produce more, practise economy, and over-fulfil the Five-Year Plan ahead of schedule: a grand march of socialist construction galloping at the speed of Chollima, smashing passivity, conservatism and mysticism about technique.

There'd been plenty of times those first years when the grief had come without warning, pushing Cuckoo off kilter and making her clutch at the nearest sturdy object in order to anchor herself. She could be walking down the street or cooking in the evening, and it would rear up in an instant. Once it had knocked her clean off her bicycle, so sudden and forceful that she'd thought even as she'd fallen to the tarmac that she must have been hit by a car: but no, it had just – just! – been this wave of longing. *Go gentle with me,* she'd begged the intruder. *Floor me if you must, but at least do not press down on me when I try to get up.*

Its power hadn't dissipated, not for a long time. It had been a living thing, nourishing itself off her reaction to it. She hadn't just lost Kwang Sik that day when she'd first found out: she'd lost him anew and afresh every day, sometimes several times every day. She'd lost him with a scent that had brought to mind the smell of his skin against her nose, or a sound that for a brief, luminous moment could have been the low rumbling of the laugh from the cave of feeling that had echoed inside him, from the place where he had stored his zest and sorrow, his intelligence and diligence, all those contradictions he had worn lightly but which had never been far from the smiling surface. She had lost him last thing at night when she'd gone to bed alone with no one to tell about the day just passed: she'd lost him first thing in the morning when she'd woken with an empty space beside her, and for a half-moment in the dawn light there had been no bridge, no air raid, no war.

Then, now, always, she carried Kwang Sik everywhere she went. She could summon him at a moment's notice, an echo as pure and sharp as the reality of him had been: as pure and sharp as the sensation of falling in love with him had been too, as though grief and love were mirror images or twins swaddled close together. How could that be legislated away into a category and a box? How could the best *songbun* in the world protect you from something like this?

Sometimes she wondered whether it would be easier to let go, to watch that memory slowly fade like a photograph left on a window-sill for the sun to bleach with slow inexorability: but when she tried it made no difference, and if she could have tried harder then she didn't or wouldn't know how. She knew at some level that she *chose* not to let him go, because to let him go would be to betray him. She never wanted to not miss him. And he would have done the same thing, she was sure of it. Maybe he would have gone to other women – men had needs, didn't they? That's what everyone said – but that would have been to soothe his body only, not his heart.

She had let life carry her onwards, but she could never bring herself to turn her face completely forward and lose Kwang Sik from her sight entirely. She was his sole custodian, and it was an honour that she guarded with a tiger's ferocity and a priest's appreciation of the sacred.

And now he was back.

Cuckoo held Min's hand in silence and ran the red thread under her fingernail. She was not an impulsive person, and liked to be considered and calm when making her decisions: to turn things over, to arrive slowly but surely at any fork in the road. She would not be browbeaten by Chul Woo or anyone else on this one. She had spent a lot of time protecting her own feelings, and other people's too. This one she would do for herself first and foremost.

Perhaps it would be better not to know. Her memory of Kwang Sik was still from the day he'd left, young and handsome and doing his best for her and the baby inside her. This was the memory that sloshed and spilled with the love they had held for each other. But who was to know how he might have turned out since then? He could have been injured in the war, or suffered an accident afterwards. Perhaps he'd fallen victim to some kind of debilitating illness. That vitality she remembered so vividly might have long drained from him, leaving him twisted and bitter about how his life had turned out. He might be nothing like the man she had known – nothing like the man he would have been if she had still been with him – and once she saw that, there would be no way of unseeing it. Nothing could be worse than knowing how much he'd suffered without her.

No, she realised. That wasn't quite true. There was one thing that could be worse, and that was seeing quite how little he'd suffered without her. What if he'd never given her another thought after leaving? What if he'd stayed in the South not because he'd been made to but because he wanted to? What if he'd fallen in love with someone there? It was supposed to work the other way round – southern man and northern woman, that's what people always said was the ideal match, since southern men were thought more handsome and northern women more beautiful – but that was just an old saying. What if he'd found another wife, and had a family with her, and raised his children and worked hard and in time had dangled his grandchildren on his knee, and only now, when perhaps his wife was dead and he was on his own again, had decided to look Cuckoo up again? What if it was nothing more than an old man's whimsical curiosity, a long-forgotten itch to be scratched, an ordering of his affairs in the twilight of his life? What if he, deep down, wanted little more than to peer at her as though she were an animal in a zoo?

Cuckoo thought of all the things she'd done in those decades: thousands of days, tens of thousands of days, lived dawn to dusk and dusk to dawn. She thought of the men she'd turned down because none of them could have matched up to Kwang Sik. She thought of Lee Song Si with his sad eyes whom she'd jilted on the morning of their wedding, and Pak Yong Chol from the ministry, and old An Il Gwang. They, and doubtless some others too if she'd bothered to notice. What had Chul Woo said? The memory of a ghost, that was it. They had all been up against the memory of a ghost, and because of that they hadn't stood a chance.

A ghost who turned out not to have been a ghost after all. A memory cleaved to throughout a lifetime of love, and now the chance – unexpected, almost inconceivable – to make new memories. An absence both heartbreaking and sustaining: a perfect love never to be sullied by reality's harsh toll. A man who might prove himself unworthy of decades of self-abnegation, or a man who might prove himself all too worthy of those decades. A walk through the fire, either way.

Cuckoo thought back to what she'd been like when she'd last seen Kwang Sik. Different in almost every way, sure, but deep down where it really mattered she was still the same. People didn't change that much, did they? Take Chul Woo. How he was now was the way he'd always been: guarded, suspicious, quick to blame others rather than himself, looking first in any situation for what could go wrong. What he'd said about the *songbun*, that was typical of him: more concerned with his own standing than with the prospect of meeting a father he'd never known.

Well, Cuckoo thought, she was too old to worry about *songbun* or anything like that. If she was still the same as she'd ever been, then Kwang Sik would be too: and if that was the case then she simply couldn't bear not to see him. Even the knowledge that he was out there and that she'd chosen to turn her back on him would finish her.

'What do you think?' she asked Min.

'You know what I think.'

'But if your father's right, and this affects your lives . . .'

'Then let it affect our lives. I'll take the risk.'

'You will?'

'Of course.'

It was as much the way Min said it as what she said that intrigued Cuckoo: but she had too much to think about as it was.

She dialled the number on the card the Red Cross woman had left with her.

'Red Cross.'

'This is Comrade Park. You visited me . . .'

'. . . I remember. Have you decided whether you want to come to the meeting?'

'Yes, I have, and yes, I would.'

'I'm so pleased.' She really sounded it too, Cuckoo thought. 'You won't regret it.'

The start of live running – that was, cars with actual human riders as opposed to sandbags – was always a big day.

'I'll go first,' Theo said. Min knew that he did this on every single coaster he built: not through ego or a sense of ownership, but because if something was going to go wrong when it came to taking actual passengers then he wanted to be the one to whom it happened.

'I'll come too,' Min said.

'You don't have to.'

'I know.'

A few of the construction workers were milling around near the station, clearly unsure whether they should put themselves forward or not.

'Can you tell them that it's best just to start with two people and then increase it from there next time round?' Theo said.

Min spoke fast to the construction workers and tried not to be worried when they looked relieved that their services would not be required. Theo let her step into the car first and sat down beside her before reaching up and pulling the restraint bar down. Min heard it lock into place, but even so he shook it hard to test that it had caught. A designer's instinct: always build in the redundancy, the failsafe.

'Was that true?' Min said quietly.

'Was what true?'

'About starting with just two people.'

'Not in the slightest.'

She felt the smile come from deep within her. 'Is this going to be scary?'

'Terrifying.'

'Worse than the plane?'

'Different.'

'How?'

'In a plane, you just feel freaked out that you're not dropping from the sky. What you *don't* feel is speed, because you've got no landmarks to measure it by. Remember what I told you before: humans don't sense speed. They sense acceleration. That's what you'll feel, and that's what you'll find scary.'

Min remembered the day, a few months and several lifetimes ago, when Theo had walked with her beneath the tracks and told her how it would feel. She remembered the first stirrings in her that day, something felt rather than known, as animals will sense the approach of a distant storm and seek shelter: a change in the air, a weightening, a darkening, a quickening. An acceleration: from inertia to flux, from order to chaos.

She settled herself. She was petrified, and she trusted him implicitly: twin poles orbiting each other and finding their equilibrium deep within her centre.

The car began to move.

'Is it supposed to make that noise?'

'Yes. That's the anti-rollback mechanism. If for some reason it fails – which it won't – then we can only roll back a short distance rather than all the way.'

Min looked round and back at the station: at Yun Seok and the construction workers gradually becoming smaller as the car climbed. She reached for Theo's hand, and found that he was already reaching for hers, high up here where no one could see.

The city revealing a little more of itself with each increment of the climb, and the wind getting up a little, and Min feeling the lurch in her stomach as she realised how narrow the track was and how long the empty drop either side.

'Don't worry,' Theo said. 'There's no way we can come off.'

'How did you know that's what I was thinking about?'

He smiled. 'There are three types of wheels keeping us secured to the track: road wheels bearing the load, guide wheels running on the inside of the rail, and upstop wheels under that rail.'

She loved the pride in his voice and the precision of his speech. 'I believe you.'

'I should hope so too.'

They were almost at the top. Min moved closer so she could nestle against Theo. A moment, no more, when they were right on the edge: the last safe point. Min could see all the way across the city now, right to the perimeter where the buildings stopped and gave away to bare countryside. Jucheland was laid out below her, and just as they began to drop she saw what Theo had done, and when she squealed it wasn't just the rush of the fall but the sheer sunbursting joy of his work.

Remember, he'd said: every rollercoaster tells a story.

He'd spaced them out sufficiently far apart so she had time not just to see but to relish them as they approached. First up were tall metal sculptures shaped and painted like poplar trees and placed either side of the track so the car passed through and beneath them. The coaster began to level out into the camelbacks, quick plunges into the troughs and quicker flashes of weightlessness on the peaks as they passed two more sculptures, smaller ones this time: red-crowned Manchurian cranes, reaching for and calling to each other. Pressed tight against the radius of the heartline curve. A vast billboard on which was painted the summit of Mount Paektu, and beyond that another one with the Heavenly Lake. The inversion loop approaching, and more billboards spaced left and right like slalom gates, the ten wonders she'd told him about on the balcony the night before they'd climbed Paektu: the sunrise, winter pines, azaleas, a night mountain, the falls, a field's horizon, potato flowers, a village, a rice harvest, sturgeons swarming to the sea. Up and over the inversion loop and out the other side, and as the car glided to a halt at the station it passed under a bridge from which jet nozzles squirted water prismed in all the colours of the rainbow.

Yun Seok and the construction workers were waiting, expectant, just as Min's parents had waited for her to return from the walk on which Hyuk Jae had proposed to her. Min didn't, couldn't, dared not look at them. She was vaguely aware of Theo lifting the restraint bar up and off them, but all she could think about was the ride, the way Theo had made it the story of them without ever telling her that he was going to do it. She looked at him in wonder, her eyes streaming.

'That was why I went to the studios the other day,' he said, close up to her ear. 'To get the ten wonders and complete the story.'

No one else would know, that was the beauty of it. A million people could take this ride and not notice, or if they did notice they would just think that the displays were typical national vistas, and what could be more appropriate than that in a place called Jucheland? But Min knew, and Theo knew, and they would always know: hiding in plain sight while the world went on its way around them, and the two of them holding a secret so luminous that she wondered whether its light would spill from the corners of her eyes and realised that she no longer cared even if it did.

PART III

REVOLUTION OF DEED

'The aim of the Party was not merely to prevent men and women from forming loyalties which it might not be able to control. Its real, undeclared purpose was to remove all pleasure from the sexual act. Sexual intercourse was to be looked on as a slightly disgusting minor operation, like having an enema. The sexual act, successfully performed, was rebellion.'

Nineteen Eighty-Four, George Orwell

16

September 2016

It was close, as it always was, but he made it, as he always did. The ninth day of the ninth month, and Jucheland was opened in grand style. The Supreme Leader himself came, beaming as he walked round and trailing flunkies like a comet leading its tail. All who followed him had notebooks, and they wrote down every word he said. He admired the tripartite revolving statue of himself, his father and his grandfather at the centre of the park, and he nodded approval at the park's zones: post-war reconstruction, *The Flower Girl* movie, *kimchi* making, and all the others. Chul Woo stayed by the Supreme Leader's side throughout the opening, introducing him to various members of the design team and smiling benevolently at their consequent rapture.

When they reached the rollercoaster, however, Chul Woo ushered the Supreme Leader into the car without even acknowledging Theo.

'It's a matter of national pride,' Min whispered. 'Don't be upset.'

'I'm not.' He watched as the car began to move: the Supreme Leader and Chul Woo in the front row and a phalanx of bodyguards in the one behind. 'Not at that, anyway.'

He sensed rather than saw her nod. Today was Friday. The park was open, the rollercoaster was running, and his job was done. He had no more reason to be here. His flight out was scheduled for Monday morning, and after that he knew he would never see her again. It was a truth he'd always known, of course, but until this moment it had felt faintly abstract. Now, with the park open, it was all too real.

The car climbed to the top of the coaster. Theo watched it drop, and figured that if it crashed and killed the Supreme Leader then he would at least get to stay in North Korea a while longer, even if it was in a prison camp.

Min and Yun Seok would be with him on his last weekend here, and they'd take him out for dinner on his last night to say goodbye, but there was no way he could find any time alone with her.

The car ran over the camelbacks and through the heartline and up and over itself in the inversion, uncomprehendingly moving through the story he had made for Min and her alone, and as it slowed to come into the station the Supreme Leader grinned with the uncomplicated happiness of a small child and demanded to go again, *right now*. There was no greater compliment to any rollercoaster designer than that, but for once Theo didn't care. He'd made all his previous coasters for everyone who rode them, but not this one. This one was different, and always would be: the most beautiful and most painful one he'd ever constructed. He thought of Penelope in *The Odyssey*, every night undoing part of the burial shroud she was making in order to forestall the moment she'd have to choose a replacement for her husband, and realised that he'd been doing the same thing in reverse, more or less. Every day he'd been making this coaster had been another day with Min, but equally it had been another day nearer the end, sands trickling through an hourglass with every support erected and piece of track laid, and he'd always known he couldn't spin it out indefinitely.

He remembered telling Min how he'd walk out of here without a backwards glance, the same way he always had before: and he wondered whether he'd ever been so wrong about anything in his life.

Cuckoo had packed. She'd been packed for days. She was trying very hard to be calm about it, not least because she knew that, though revitalised by the prospect of seeing Kwang Sik again, she still only had a finite amount of strength and needed it all for the reunion itself. She couldn't afford to dissipate it in worry and anxiety beforehand.

Min and Chul Woo came in together. Min looked exhausted. Chul Woo was shining.

'How was the opening?'

'A triumph,' Chul Woo said. 'An absolute triumph! The Supreme Leader was full of compliments, and personally congratulated me many times on the work I'd done there. We began at the centrepiece of the statues, of course . . .'

Min came over and put her hand on Cuckoo's. Cuckoo smiled at her, an unspoken message that she knew Min would understand: *he'll talk all about himself anyway, so just let him.*

'Don't mind me,' Cuckoo whispered. 'I don't know which way's up at the moment. One minute I'm bouncing round the place and can't wait to get there. The next minute I start thinking of all the things which could go wrong, and I wonder . . .'

'It'll be fine.'

'What if it's all a huge mistake? What if I wish afterwards that I'd never gone?'

'Better to regret something you have done than something you haven't.' Min looked towards her father. 'And Papa will be there with you.'

Chul Woo stopped talking. He looked half-surprised and half-outraged that they weren't giving him their full attention. 'What did you say?'

'I said you'd be with Cuckoo this weekend,' Min replied.

He made a noise like the escape of air from a puncture. 'I'm not going.'

It was something that vexed Cuckoo every day: that no matter how much you tried to mould a child, you were in the final analysis merely a conduit for their entry into the world, and there were aspects to their personality that came with them during that entry and which were, to all intents and purposes, ineradicable.

'We've been through this, Chul Woo,' Cuckoo said. 'I know you're worried about—'

'I'm not going. I've told you that time and time again.'

'I know, but I thought—'

'You thought I was just being wilful and would come round in the end.' Cuckoo didn't nod: she didn't need to. 'You thought if you treated me like a child, which is how you always treat me, then I'd behave like one. And now you see. I'm not going.'

'But he's your father.'

'That makes it even worse. He cares so little that he's only turning up now? I've lived all my life without knowing him. I can live the rest of it the same way.'

'I can't go on my own.'

'Why not?'

It wasn't just the words that stung Cuckoo – she was an old woman about to subject herself to an earthquake, that was why not – but the callousness with which he tossed them out.

'I'll go,' Han Na said.

'No,' Chul Woo replied.

'Why not?'

'Because you're no relation of his, that's why. You have no blood ties.'

That was true enough, Cuckoo thought, but Chul Woo had no need to say it as hurtfully as he did: a dart twisted and screwed to inflict as much pain as possible.

Cuckoo looked at Min. Min looked back at her, and on her face was the strangest look: not just love for the old woman – Cuckoo took that for granted – but the pain of a terrible dilemma. It lasted a second, perhaps two, and in that time emotions flitted across Min's face like seasons. Cuckoo wondered what could possibly have triggered such feelings in her granddaughter, what could possibly have had such a seismic effect on her, and felt at some level she couldn't properly articulate that, whatever it was, it was a good thing.

'I'll go,' Min said. The smile Cuckoo gave her would have illuminated the Rainbow Bridge. 'He's my grandfather. I'll go.'

'Impossible,' Chul Woo said. 'You have to look after the American.'

'Yun Seok can do it.'

'Foreign visitors must be accompanied by two guides at all times.'

'He's going home on Monday. What's he going to do before then? It doesn't matter. This is more important.' Min swallowed, composed herself. 'This is more important.'

If Cuckoo hadn't known better, she'd have thought that Min was trying to convince herself of what she was saying.

'I have to go with my grandmother.'

'I understand.'

'I'm sorry. I really wanted to . . .'

'It's fine. You must go.'

'I'll be back tomorrow.'

'I know. I'll see you then.'

'Yes. You too.'

There were three buses, each of them holding around thirty people and an untold amount of anticipation alike. Fathers who had been sundered from their daughters and mothers from their sons, husbands from wives, brothers from sisters. No one spoke, though everyone seemed bursting to do so. They would, Min thought, all have the same worries and questions that Cuckoo did, all have the same kaleidoscope of emotions mutating and spinning slowly.

It was the strangest thing, she thought, to have believed someone dead for so long and then find that they were not. Kwang Sik had been an absence all her life: no knee on which she could have sat as a toddler, no hand to hold while walking through a park, no mildly risqué stories once she was old enough to be told them.

She understood why her father hadn't wanted to come, though she still thought that he should have done so, for Cuckoo's sake if not for his own. But when she thought further about it, she realised she was glad he hadn't. Min had been Cuckoo's favourite, and vice versa, all her life. If anyone should have been here with Cuckoo it was Min, and she realised that Cuckoo would have wanted her to come all along. It was right that Cuckoo had asked Chul Woo first: it was even more right that Min was here now. This, too, was a gift Theo had given her, to know herself worthy of this when previously she might have doubted. It was the last, best thing she could ever do for her grandmother.

The bus rattled on the highway. Min rested her head on Cuckoo's shoulder, just as she had done so often in childhood when anxious or tired: and Cuckoo inclined her head so it was touching Min's.

Min thought of Theo, left with Yun Seok for the weekend. Maybe she'd be back in time to go out to dinner with them tomorrow night, and she'd certainly be there to take Theo to the airport on Monday: again, with Yun Seok, of course. She knew it wasn't Yun Seok's fault, and she knew she was entirely in the wrong here, but she felt a sudden, vicious spike of resentment against him. If it wasn't for Yun Seok then she and Theo could have spent more time alone. Even as she thought it she knew that it was both true and irrelevant. They'd been alone in her apartment, and on Google Earth, and in a manner of speaking beneath the poplars and on top of Mount Paektu too, and it wasn't Yun Seok who was stopping them, it was the entire system, the way life was set up in a hundred different ways. The system that shamed her even for thinking what she did: the system that meant her beloved Cuckoo had to wait sixty-five years to see her husband again. Maybe it would be sixty-five years before Min saw Theo again, the two of them wrinkled and wizened beyond recognition.

No, Min thought. *I will not be shamed, not even in the secret corners of my own mind. Not any more.*

Through the touch of their heads, she could feel Cuckoo's life force, burning more fiercely than it had done for a long time.

'Whatever happens,' Min said, 'be glad you did it.'

'I hope so.'

'Even if it's terrible, better to know that than not to have gone and always be wondering what you missed.'

Cuckoo smiled. 'When did you become so wise?'

'Probably around the time I started listening to you.'

'Ha! I've given you love, my dear, but the wisdom is all your own.'

'That's not true.'

'It is.'

'Anyway. I'm here with you all the way. These things, this kind of thing, which can rock your life on its hinges – they don't come along very often, and you have to grab them when they do.'

Min wondered even as she said it whether she was trying to convince Cuckoo, or herself, or both: and she didn't wonder very long, because she knew the answer full well, and knew too that she didn't want to admit it to herself.

Theo at Jucheland, watching Mallima: the queues, the excitement, the high flush on the faces of the riders as they came back in. Theo hearing the screams of fear and delight, and knowing that it was the age-old sensation of never feeling more alive than when you think you've cheated death. Theo knowing all this, and knowing that on every other project this was the bit he loved most, the pleasure that his skill gave to other people. Theo knowing all this, and knowing too that it was no longer enough.

Theo walking through the rest of Jucheland, silent amidst the chatter and laughter of the crowds. The industrial zone, the agricultural zone, the intellectual zone: the hammer, the sickle, the calligraphy pen. People all around him, apart from the only person he wanted there. Why, of all of them, did it have to be her? Why her who had got under his skin in a way no one else ever had? When had it become inevitable?

The line had been heat haze on a summer road. It had shimmered, seductive and deceptive, a way up ahead of them, and again behind them once it had passed and gone, but at the exact point they'd crossed it there'd been no sign. They had neither sought nor forced it. It had just happened, so slowly and gradually as to have been almost imperceptible until there it was: the immoveable certainty of what they were to each other.

Theo knowing that she'd made the right choice, to go to Kumgang with Cuckoo this weekend, and loving her all the more for it, for her loyalty and kindness. In another time and place he could have shared in Min's love for Cuckoo. He could have watched them making *kimchi* together, could have joined Cuckoo in telling stories against Min that would have made all three of them howl with laughter and Min protest that they were beastly: yes, they, the two people she adored most in the world. But as it was he had no hold on Min's heart that could match this. He was an interloper, a temporary madness.

Theo knowing that she'd made the right choice, and finding that the knowledge didn't deaden the pain by any fraction measurable to man. Before all this he would have wanted her to go in order to absolve himself from making a decision, but not any more. He'd lived all his life with a steering defect that he'd had to constantly correct, almost without thinking. She hadn't helped him correct it: she'd gone beneath the bonnet and fixed the defect at source.

Theo walking the streets of Pyongyang with Yun Seok in silence. Theo telling Yun Seok that he just wanted to have one last feel of the city before he went home. So close and hot and humid it felt as though it would break at any moment, the final bloom of summer before the air began to chill and the shadows began to lengthen again. The sweat pricking at Theo's temples and plastering his shirt to his back.

Theo walking, because if he walked long enough then his footsteps would coincide with hers: he would be treading places she had done long ago, in a time before he had come here, before they had even known of the other's existence, let alone of the other's love. He imagined her in all these places he was now, tiny echoes of dust and sound held here for him. Perhaps one day she would do the same in places he had been: not here, not in this country, but places all over a world just waiting for her to come and explore. Everyone imprinted their stories in the places they trod, and their footsteps were heavy with the weight of their lives.

Theo walking and walking and walking, as though for fear of what would happen if he stopped. Theo alone beneath the poplars, the clandestine emerald world where he and Min had first shyly and haltingly declared themselves to each other, perhaps without even realising that they were doing so. Theo feeling her absence in a way he had never imagined possible: as an excision, a photographic negative, something flipped and torn from him so violently as to make the world itself seem different.

Theo knowing that her being here all weekend would have in its own way been some kind of exquisite agony, and that perhaps fate had done them both a favour. Theo wondering whether if he told himself this often enough he'd start to believe it.

Theo walking, and walking, and walking.

Mount Kumgang was a tourist resort down by the border with the South. It had technically been a joint project between both halves of the peninsula, though in effect North Korea had leased the place to the South Korean Hyundai Asan conglomerate, which in turn had built the entire infrastructure. It was a place designed both to anticipate and symbolise the reunification to which both governments cleaved as an article of faith. Cuckoo remembered its early days, as they had coincided with her last days at the ministry: different departments, sure, but news like this circulated anyway.

And if reunification seemed as distant as ever, so too did the gap between what Kumgang was and what it wanted to be. The endless coachloads of tourists from the South remained a mirage, not least because Kumgang was in no real way a look inside the North: it was sealed off on all sides, and only those with proper authorisation could get in. When, some years before, a woman from the South had inadvertently strayed outside the designated areas, DPRK soldiers had shot her dead. Not great for the tourist trade. But the resort did at least still exist, and was still maintained at something more than a basic level. Min herself had brought European tour groups here before, though they used a separate hotel from the one earmarked for reunions. There were meeting rooms and bedrooms, restaurants and grounds. As a place for reunion meetings, it was as good as any. Cuckoo knew how these kinds of places worked. They stood empty for all but a handful of days every year, but they could not shut altogether in case they were needed. Wasteful, sure, but that was just how it was.

The Red Cross representative who had come to Cuckoo's apartment stood up at the front of the bus as it pulled through the main gates of the resort.

'Here we are,' she said. 'Soon we will be arriving at the hotel building. Please follow these instructions carefully. You will be allocated a bedroom first, where you can freshen up and leave your luggage. It is now just before one p.m. Lunch will be served at one thirty p.m., and at two thirty p.m. you will be escorted into the conference room to meet the member of your family. You will be given three bottles of blueberry liquor and a tablecloth, which you will give to your relatives. You must declare any and all gifts you receive, and the authorities will decide which ones, if any, are appropriate for you to keep. You will be allowed two sessions today with your family member – a public one and a private one – and another public session again tomorrow morning, but you will not be permitted to spend the night with them. You will find a timetable in your bedroom. There is no departure from this timetable or any of these restrictions, and any attempt to subvert them will result in your immediate removal from the resort and the cancellation of your reunion.'

She neither invited nor received questions, and Cuckoo realised this was not because she was unkind – quite the opposite – but because it must have been impossible to accommodate everyone and everything.

Whoever had thought of putting lunch immediately before the reunion should have had their head examined, Cuckoo thought. She was too nervous to eat, and by the look of it she was far from alone. Even Min was only picking at her food, distractedly chasing half a hardboiled egg round the edge of her plate. Cuckoo remembered how they had been told that, when the Americans had first landed on the moon, the astronauts had been scheduled to sleep before going out to explore the lunar surface – as if they'd have been able to switch off and relax like that! Well, this wasn't much different.

Min had helped Cuckoo get ready, just as Cuckoo had helped Min on her wedding day. The nicest dress she owned, even a little bit of make-up: she wanted to look good, not just for herself but to show Kwang Sik what he had been missing. If this was vanity, then fine: Cuckoo was not above it, and she had never thought herself to be. Kwang Sik would be making an effort, too. He had better be. A man couldn't come to see his wife after six and a half decades and not bother to dress up.

'You look wonderful,' Min said.

The clock ticked round with infernal slowness: every minute seeming to last a year, and the hour feeling about as long again as the decades they'd been apart.

Please let it be him, Cuckoo thought. *That's all. Whether it's wonderful or disastrous, please let it be him. Please let there not have been a mistake or a mix-up. I can deal with anything apart from that: that the man who they think is my husband is not him at all, but instead a complete stranger, that all this will have been for nothing. The only thing more cruel than getting my hopes up would be to see them dashed again.*

The Red Cross workers took them in at two thirty on the dot. Cuckoo and Min were given name tags and a number: forty-four, the table at which they should sit.

The conference room was vast. There must have been fifty tables in there: all circular, all with eight chairs arranged at precisely equal points around them. A schematic of the room layout told Cuckoo that table forty-four was on the far side of the room, hard up against a wall. She reached for Min's hand, and found that it was shaking quite as much as her own was.

'What a pair we make,' she said: and they clung to each other all the way across the room until they found the table and sat down. There were flowers, and bottled water, and hope and trepidation and a million other things besides.

It was clear that the northerners were being brought in first. Cuckoo watched as the others she'd seen on the bus and at lunch found their own seats: mothers with daughters, husbands with wives, brothers with sisters. It wasn't just spouses being reunited today, of course: it was people who'd been sundered from their own families in several different ways. There would also be those who hadn't seen their children or their siblings in all this time. The war had cut a vast weeping gash not just across the peninsula but across all those who lived there too.

The Red Cross staff moved briskly through the room like airline staff, checking that everyone was in place.

A moment of perfect stillness and quiet. The cusp.

One of the Red Cross staff went to a door, opened it and said something to whoever was on the other side. Cuckoo caught her breath as the southerners began to come in. She vaguely noticed how much taller they were, and better fed, and better clothed, and how much younger they looked – they weren't, of course, they'd just led

293

easier lives – but none of that was either surprising or meaningful to her. She was watching for Kwang Sik and Kwang Sik alone.

And would he be alone? Would he have come with someone? A child of his own, perhaps? Not a wife, Cuckoo thought – no wife would want to come and meet her predecessor – but a child, very possibly: a living, breathing representation of all the life he'd had after her. Without her.

They came through, flowing left and right as they found their tables and their loved ones. Cuckoo saw the long, rocking hugs out of the corner of her vision, and she heard the tears and wailing and exclamations, but she never took her eyes off the door. At the sight of each man who came through, she would start slightly. Was this one him? Or this one? Or this one? She scanned their faces as though to find the Kwang Sik she had last seen hiding there, as though by sheer force of will she could discern him still. Would she recognise him? Would he recognise her? Would she have to work it out from his features, or would she somehow *know* at a level so visceral it would bypass eyes and brain completely?

Was that him, coming through the door now? It could be, Cuckoo thought, it could be him: he was certainly handsome enough . . . and then the man moved towards another table and fell into the arms of two women who were themselves clinging on to each other. She watched them for a moment, and by the time she'd turned her eyes back to the door another man was halfway across the room and heading for her table.

He was stooped, his back hunched over. He smiled and raised a hand that was clawed in on itself. As he did so, his sleeve slipped a little way down his arm, and Cuckoo saw what the man was wearing around his wrist.

A red thread.

A red thread, just like hers.

17

It was a long, long time before either of them said anything. They just held each other, and for Cuckoo it was as though sixty-five years had simply fallen away. Kwang Sik smelt the same and felt the same as she remembered: the way his body curved round hers as they hugged, the slight roughness of his chin against her cheek. Now and then she would hug him a little bit harder, if only to check that he was real and that she hadn't somehow conjured all this up through the force of her imagination, a dying woman's hallucination appearing flesh.

She sobbed and sobbed, and felt his hand stroking the back of her head, the way he had done in the early days of her pregnancy when the hormones had made her vomit over and over again. There was weeping all around the room, scores of families going through their own versions of this scene, but to Cuckoo it all faded out. It was just her and Kwang Sik: one to the last, as she had always said. One to the last.

Eventually they disentangled, still keeping hold of each other as though through fear that without touch they would simply vanish. Kwang Sik's suit was rumpled, his tie askew and his shirt collar turned over on itself. Cuckoo straightened them for him, and his laugh set her off crying again.

Cuckoo turned to Min, who'd been sitting there all this time, letting them have this moment while the tears rolled down her face too.

'This is your granddaughter,' she said. 'This is Min. My favourite person in the whole world.'

Kwang Sik opened his arms for Min, and she came to him like a child.

There was so much to say, and they could have spent all day talking over each other in the rush to get it all out. No, Kwang Sik said, we have to do this properly. You tell me about your life, and then I'll tell you about mine, and then we can let the conversation go where it will. And Cuckoo laughed, because this too was the Kwang Sik she remembered, orderly and practical and always working out how to do things most efficiently.

She told him everything she could remember: about how they'd told her he was dead, about the men who'd wanted to marry her, about Chul Woo and his films, and Chul Woo and Han Na, about the famine and her sacking from the ministry (she spoke in a low voice during this part so no one else could hear, and he had to lean in close, but that wasn't a problem: everyone was leaning in close, everyone wanted to somehow try to compress themselves into those they'd missed for so long), and about Min, of course. Lots about Min: Cuckoo with one hand on Min and the other on Kwang Sik, and giggling at her own indecision when she wanted to drink some water and didn't know who to let go of first.

Kwang Sik listened, and his eyes brimmed, and filled, and spilled. Cuckoo knew what he was feeling, because she would feel it too when it came to his turn. All this he'd missed out on, all that should have been his too, and he must both have wanted to hear it more than anything and yet also felt that this was something from which he would always be excluded: a life that belonged to someone else and which he could see only through a thin layer of gauze, endless forking pathways, which he'd never had the chance to take, which he'd never even known existed.

Cuckoo talked and talked and talked until her voice was hoarse.

'Your turn,' she said.

He hadn't been killed on Hill 983: that was the first, most obvious thing to say. It had been a shitfight, days on end of nine parts boredom and one part terror, and in the end he'd been one of those rounded up and corralled into a prisoner-of-war camp. Some of his mates had run themselves through with bayonets rather than face the indignity of surrender, but that had never occurred to Kwang Sik. He'd figured to last out the war in the camp, where he could put his medical training to good use, and when the war was over he'd find his way north again to Pyongyang, and to her and their baby.

That thought had been his guiding light, his polar star, every day and every night of those two years in camp. Get through to sunrise, get through to sunset, and it would be another day closer to the time he saw her again. In the sledgehammer heat of the summer, when only for an hour or so just before dawn had it been cool enough to sleep, and in the arch biting cold of the winter when slumber had come fitful and through chattering teeth, that had been all that sustained him: her, Cuckoo, like the first call of spring.

Then the war had ended in 1953, and they'd gone through every man's discharge papers and matched them with what they'd heard from the North. He'd waited patiently in line for three hours, and when he'd got to the head of the queue they'd checked his documents, consulted a list, and taken him to one side, where they'd told him that his parents' store had been destroyed with them inside in October 1951, and that Cuckoo had been killed in an air strike barely six weeks before the armistice had been signed.

The pain in his chest had floored him, literally: knocked him off his feet and pinned him to the ground, where he'd clutched at his breastbone and thought, hoped, begged that he would die too. It had lasted a few minutes before subsiding, and within a few hours it had gone entirely. A cardiac arrest, he'd thought, but one he'd been young and healthy enough to see off. The octopus tentacles of grief had come in place of the chest pain, and they'd wrapped themselves around him so tight he knew they'd never let go.

They had shown him a picture of his parents' store, so he had known that was for real, but there had been no such evidence for Cuckoo's death, nor indeed for most deaths in Pyongyang during the bombardment. How had the mix-up happened? How had Cuckoo been declared dead when she was still alive? He didn't know, though he'd met others who had been through similar experiences. War was confusion, and so many had died on Hill 983 – some of them right next to him – that bodies had become unrecognisable and identities muddled. When the time had come for his officers to go through the carnage, they must have simply thought that someone else was him, and of course he hadn't been there to put them straight: he'd been in a camp hundreds of miles away.

And how had he been told that she'd been killed when she hadn't? The same kind of thing, presumably: an attempt to impose order, names and statistics on a situation that mitigated against all of them. His own erroneous death had been one thing: he could have lived with that, pardon the pun, if only he'd been able to find his way back to her and convince her that he wasn't a ghost. But to be told that she was gone, too: that had finished him. And since he hadn't known that he'd been reported dead, he hadn't presumed they could have made an error like that. How could he have guessed?

They'd offered him no condolences, no sympathy. Why would they have? The war had numbed everyone to everything. All they'd offered him was a simple choice: stay here in the South or go back to the North. It hadn't been a hard decision. He'd had nothing to go back for, save the possibility of being punished for having been captured, as if two years in a prison camp hadn't been punishment enough. So he'd chosen to stay in the South and try to build a new life there.

He gave Cuckoo a box, beautifully wrapped in blue and gold. When she took it, it was surprisingly heavy.

'What is it?' she asked.

'Open it and see.'

The ribbon looked like ears on a headband. She pulled at it until the ears vanished and the ribbon fell away in waves. The wrapping paper came next. Cuckoo wanted to tear at it as a dog would, but she took her time, savouring the anticipation. She had waited sixty-five years for this. She could wait another few moments longer.

The box was full to the brim. Envelopes, Cuckoo saw, bulging and plump with the paper inside them.

'One a year,' Kwang Sik said. 'I wrote you a letter every year, on the anniversary of the day we were parted. I wrote them for me, not you, of course: I thought you were dead. But I kept them all. Whenever I moved house, they were the things I kept safest. They'd have been the first things I rescued in a house fire. I wrote them for me, but they're yours.'

Cuckoo's tears, and Kwang Sik's too, and the touching of the red threads around their respective wrists as they reached for each other's hands.

4th December, 1954.
My darling,

I'm leaving for America. Seoul is no place for me, though maybe anywhere's no place for me without you. There's such hostility to northerners now. The scars of the conflict run so deep, and everywhere I go people hear my accent and either back away or come in too close to tell me what they think. I've been spat at in the street, attacked by three men outside a bar late one night. I've got a job in a hospital and hoped that would help, and it has to a degree, but not enough. There are patients who refuse to let me treat them and colleagues who change their shifts to avoid having to work with me. So now the hospital's advertised a programme for doctors to go and work in the United States, and I didn't need a second invitation. Sure, they're the ones I was fighting against just a few years ago, but I bet most of their soldiers wanted to be there quite as little as I did. My job is to help people, that's all. I don't care who or where. I do care that America has by far the best facilities for what I want to do, and maybe people there will be more welcoming.

I cross the ocean and it takes me further from you, but how can it? You're in my heart, every day and in every way.

4th December, 1962.

Precious Cuckoo,

I didn't know, at least to start with, why I
have such an affinity with the heart. I thought
perhaps it was something to do with what happened in the camp when I'd been told you were
dead, but that seemed too simplistic. Surgeons are
strange people, you know. We're attracted to very
different and very specific parts of the body, and
most of us could no more tell you why than fly to
the moon. A liver specialist can't see the attraction
of the spine: a man who lives for kidneys finds
himself left completely cold by lungs.

For me, it's the heart. Even as a general doctor,
before I specialised, I found myself drawn to it:
the way it thumps and gurgles through a stetho-
scope, the feeling of an artery jumping against my
fingertips as I take a pulse. When I listen to music
it's the drums I hear loudest, because their rhythm
is also that of the heart's ventricles.

I'm in Honolulu. It's hot and volcanic, the air
heavy with humidity, which plucks sweat from
my pores and slicks my skin the moment I step
outdoors. There are lots of Koreans here, so I don't
feel too isolated, and there's plenty of work for a
heart surgeon too, since so many Hawaiians eat
badly and don't do enough exercise.

I love everything about the heart. I marvel at
how small it is, how powerful, how reliable. Any
two of those three would not seem unreasonable,
but to have all three at once is surely where science
becomes a miracle. I fancy myself a mechanic, an

engineer: observing, examining, deconstructing, repairing. Every heart is different and every heart teaches me something, no matter how small or insignificant that thing might seem: a brick in the wall of my knowledge, a tiny accretion, something I didn't know the day before.

And with each heart comes a person. It's a rare and precious thing, to know that I hold someone's life in my hands – quite literally, sometimes, when they're on the operating table being kept alive by a machine while I dig and pull and cut and join. I can stop a heart at will and start it again the same way. When I hold one in my hands, I feel as if I'm holding the secret of life itself.

To start with, like all doctors in their early days, I found myself becoming too attached to my patients and their families: sharing their hopes, feeling the sunburst of their triumphs and the agony of their despair. But I soon realised that I couldn't do that and do my job properly too. Surgery is surgery, and it works only if the surgeon is dispassionate and completely focused. When I'm in theatre, I think of nothing other than the problem with which I've been tasked. If I think of the patient at all, it's only in relation to the specific condition of their heart. The body is invisible beneath blue drapes, reduced to a small rectangular window of breastbone and heart.

There are patients I like and those I don't, patients who thank me and patients who curse me. I've hardened myself against both. I'm kind to all those who come to me – I never forget that what's either routine or challenging to me is unique and terrifying to them – but equally I keep them, and my kindness, at arm's length.

I've lost patients, of course: we all do. I'm a surgeon, not a miracle worker. Some hearts are simply beyond repair, and neither sublime skill nor blind faith can alter that. For those left behind, death's a tragedy. For me, it's an opportunity: to see what I could have done better, to identify a mistake I won't make next time. My patients need courage to put themselves under my control: I need the courage to fail them now and then.

In the crux of a fourteen-hour-operation, arms slick to my elbows with blood and pus and bone dust, having to piss into a catheter, simultaneously listening for and shutting out the voices of my colleagues, the hissing of the ventilators and the shriek of the alarms: that's where I find my grace. The moment of knife to skin is the point of no return, each and every time. I love the excitement, the adrenalin, the pleasure of working with a well-drilled team: instruction and obedience, call and response. I love the tidiness of neat stitching and no unnecessary steps: models of efficient organisation, trimming fat and minimising waste. I love the speed and dexterity of my fingers and the way they work with my brain quicker than thought itself. I love the feeling of taming a beast: a heart doesn't just submit passively to being cut, it bucks and swells and sprays, it's a living thing in every way, and it demands that a man beat and coax it into surrender.

This job, this calling, this vocation: it's like quicksand, sucking me further and further in. When I'm on call I hope and pray for operations to happen. Losing myself in them means I don't have to lose myself in me: the aching loneliness, the sense that too much of my own life has been buried in the rubble of the air strike that they told me had killed you. Sleep's a waste of time. Sleep means missing something exciting. There's no risk in sleep: no reward, either.

There are women, of course there are. I'm not a monk. But none of them ever amount to anything serious, because I never let them. Every day before surgery I carefully untie the red thread from my wrist, and every day after surgery I equally carefully tie it on again. And when it breaks, which inevitably it does, I simply find another piece and start again with that.

A surgeon's life isn't one for a happy marriage: the stress, the long and uncertain hours, the intensity of the work, which creates fierce but short-lived affairs between staff members. Divorce rates among the surgeons run at more than 100 per cent, with each surgeon on average being divorced more than once. I don't want any of that. I've found and lost once already. I don't want to find and lose all over again.

There's money, too. Heart surgeons are the best paid of all, and many of them flaunt it with enormous houses and fast cars. I keep what I need and give the rest back to the hospital, not because I'm especially virtuous but because none of that stuff really interests me. I don't need a big house as I've only got myself to consider, and I don't need a fast car because the traffic's woeful.

Above all, my darling, I know two things. First, that I'm wedded to the idea of saving people because to do so is in some small, inadequate way an atonement for not having been able to save you. Second, that though the heart is the strongest muscle in the body, there's one heart I can never fix, and that's my own.

4th December, 1974.
Darling Cuckoo,

This comes to you from Los Angeles. I loved it in Honolulu, but I was getting serious island fever. It's a tiny corner of America hived off and tucked away from the main country itself. This is a big city full of energy and noise and a certain madness.

A colleague examined me the other day, more as a test of skill and diagnosis than anything else. I thought the examination was just routine, but then he called me back and asked me to undergo another one.

Is there a problem? I asked.

No, no problem.

Then what is it?

Your heart: it shows evidence of cardiomyopathy. The left ventricle, look at it here. It's distended and misshapen. You know what the Japanese call it? *Takotsubo*. It means a trap to catch octopuses in, because that's the shape your ventricle is now.

How did it happen? Have you ever felt sudden, intense emotional stress? That can stun your heart enough to make it change shape, and it can never change back again. It works fine, but the scars are always there.

The kind of sudden, intense emotional stress you might feel when told that your wife and child are dead?

Yes. Very much that kind of stress.

The Japanese might call it *takotsubo*, but the Americans have another, more prosaic, name for it: broken-heart syndrome.

4th December, 1993.
My sweetest petal,

This is my last winter in Los Angeles. I've been here almost twenty years: happy ones, mainly, down in Koreatown on my days off and working with some of the best specialists in the world. But last year there were riots everywhere and the city burned, and nowhere burned more than Koreatown. It didn't directly affect me – I live in Brentwood, an upscale neighbourhood far from the flames of South Central – but I felt the pain of my own people more than I did that of my own patients, if that makes sense. The TV footage of Korean men half or a third of my age on the rooftops firing blindly down at the looters ransacking their shops below – that knocked at something deep within me.

I gave money and time to the reconstruction efforts, but this place doesn't feel like home any more and that's not coming back. I heard my people being called 'gooks' and 'chink-asses'. The police department left Koreatown to burn, that's how it felt. They sealed off the border of Koreatown at Crenshaw Boulevard and left the Koreans to fend for themselves amidst the falling ash of a burning city. I've dedicated my life to helping people, because that's the job I've chosen, and I feel very strongly that the same should go for those who've sworn an oath to protect and serve.

4th December, 2011.
My love,

My eighteenth year in New York City. Journey upon journey, and going further from home with each of them: because Korea's still 'home', no matter how much I might try to pretend otherwise. You know I've never called the United States 'my country'? Not once. Just 'America' or the 'US': a temporary holding ground which has somehow lasted me almost sixty years.

I've kept working, because what else can I do? I'm in my eighties, but I'm still good at it: hell, I'm one of the best in the country, and students come from all over to hear my lectures or have the chance to follow me on my rounds. But the decades of work have been relentless and punishing, and they're taking their toll. My right hand's begun to claw over itself, the legacy of hundreds of thousands of metal instruments being slapped into it by thousands of nurses across tens of thousands of operations. My fingers have begun to arrange themselves in the positions they took up to clasp those instruments, as though they're just waiting for the next occasion. My spine, too, has become so used to bending over an operating table that it's become increasingly reluctant to straighten itself up again. It's as though my entire existence has been reduced to this, a tableau of surgeon at work, which has now translated into every other aspect of my life.

And so, against my will and to my intense frustration, I've begun to scale back my work. The less I've worked, the more time I've had to look around. There's a big Korean community in New York, just as there was in LA and Honolulu, and I've been struck by the way the younger family members take in their elders as death approaches. Not all of them, of course, but most of them – certainly more than is usual here, where old people are farmed out to nursing homes and left there with minimal visits from their families.

'Even death can be better met together' goes the saying. We're all far from home, we Koreans in our diaspora, but our culture has never left us. *Godoksa*, we call it: not just dying alone, but dying so alone that it's some time before one's body is found. A disconnected death, a severed death. Shame, that's what it is, to die like that: but that is how I will die, for I have no family.

I read an article in the *New York Times* a few months ago about these reunion meetings they have, bringing together families divided by the war. There was a line in the article, near the end and easy to miss, about one of the participants who'd been declared dead during the war when they were still alive: a mistake that had only come to light when they'd applied to take part in the next meeting.

It was a million to one shot, perhaps more, but it was worth a go. I flew to Seoul – it was totally unrecognisable from the city I'd left in 1954, so much so that I checked with both the taxi driver who took me from the airport and the receptionist in the hotel where I was staying that yes, this really was Seoul – and went for an interview with the Red Cross. They heard my story, took my details and told me they'd do what they could: but even if you are still alive, I should know how many people wanted to take part in these meetings. There are 66,000 registered, only 100 places available at any one time, and half those places are reserved for people over 90.

I could, as the Americans say, do the math. It's vanishingly unlikely, but it's not impossible. If there's even the smallest chance you're still alive, I want to find you. I might not be able to die with my family, but I would at least die with your memories imprinted on my heart.

'For almost five years I waited,' he said. 'Five years, trying to put it out of my mind but never quite succeeding. I felt it as a siren call from across the ocean. And then the phone call came, telling me that they'd found you and that I'd been selected for the next reunion meeting. The night before I left New York for Seoul again, four days ago, I sat down with a map of the world and plotted every place I've been in my life. It took me hours, savouring the memories of trips taken and experiences enjoyed, and when I finished I looked at the map and saw another truth, as inescapable as my acts of atonement and my inability to heal my own heart: that a man travels the world, and in doing so he ends up tracing the shape of his own face.'

The crying. So much of it and for so long that Cuckoo wondered where all the water was coming from. Not just a slow, silent leakage of tears, but proper heaving sobs, the kind that rack the body, puff the eyes, and stream the nose. Sobs so seismic that it was hard to breathe during them, and when they abated Cuckoo laughed in relief and mockery of the way she must look. But what else could she do? What else could anyone do in this situation but cry? Tears were equal parts sadness and happiness, and in their mingling Cuckoo could no longer tell the difference.

Two simple administrative errors had condemned them to a lifetime apart: now it was administrative procedure that had brought them back together again. Yes, they were here together, but they were not here together too. They had grown older without each other but with all the subtle and gradual changes that ageing brought. They didn't know each other, not truly, and a few hours here could no more than scratch the surface of rectifying that. Growing older separately had denied them the chance to shape each other, no matter how often Cuckoo had spoken to Kwang Sik's ghost or Kwang Sik had written her letters he'd never sent. Their love was real, but it was also an abstraction, adhered to not just for its beauty but also through loyalty and stubbornness. They hadn't been with each other when they'd been sick or suffering.

The best of love, Cuckoo thought, was to give the strength and courage to share the burdens of the man she loved, to carry them herself in his place where she could. To choose herself to suffer, not him. To laugh and cry with him, to listen to him when he was feeling low and have him listen to her: to love him, in short, in all the myriad of messy, imperfect, heartfelt and quotidian ways by which humans loved each other. To have this love and not be able to do these things was an aberration. She realised now, holding Kwang Sik fast, how much she had needed to touch and be touched, how much she had aged and crumbled to dust without him, no matter how much she had pretended otherwise.

And still she knew for a certainty that even this, as exquisitely short and painful as it was, was better than not having it. The Red Cross woman had told her she wouldn't regret it, and the Red Cross woman had been right. A lifetime apart could not undo the truth for them both: that they were loved, they had been missed, and they mattered.

Min lay in the darkness and listened to Cuckoo's snoring. At another time she would have gone over to the old woman's bed and nudged her to make her stop, but Min wanted Cuckoo to sleep. What she had been through would have been exhausting enough for someone half her age. Besides, Min knew that she wouldn't drop off for a while, snoring or no snoring.

They had eaten dinner together, the three of them. Strangely, given they all had so much to talk about, there had been several periods of silence during which the words had stuck in their throats and they had just gazed at one another, wanting to drink in every last detail. Min had, totally without self-consciousness, taken her grandfather's claw hand in hers and held it to her chest: she had stared at his face, memorising the lines scored deep and the trans-lucence of the skin in certain places. Cuckoo had spoken so often of him, and now here he was.

Min had wondered what kind of relationship she would have had with him: whether it would have been closer than the one she had with her father, how it would have impacted on her closeness to Cuckoo. She and Cuckoo would never have shared a room for so long if Kwang Sik had been around, but she hoped they would still have had the special bond they did. She wondered how Chul Woo might have turned out with his father around. Perhaps he'd have done something different with his life, which in turn might have meant that Min wouldn't have been assigned to Theo, and on it went: all these unknowables, ripples cast and left uncast.

So much to say, and think, and feel, and so short a time in which to do it. It was as though she were cramming all her words and thoughts and emotions into a jar and screwing a lid tight on it before they could escape. Tomorrow she and Cuckoo would leave here, and on the way back to Pyongyang they would think of a hundred things they wished they'd said and which they would now never get the chance to say again. Did it matter? Kwang Sik would feel the same way too, surely. Everyone here would. There were things Kwang Sik had said that Min was sure she'd already forgotten, just because she hadn't been able to take in everything at once, and if it was like that for her it would be ten times worse for Cuckoo.

Min had left them to each other during the late afternoon, and had gone for a walk through the grounds of the resort. Kumgang was wild and mountainous, and sometimes the trails were half-swallowed by undergrowth. She had walked for what felt like hours, knowing where she wanted to go but also happy to take her time getting there. She had savoured everything around her: buttercups strewn across fields like drawing pins thrown by hand, bullrushes bending their heads to murmur to each other in the breeze, streams smeared with sun and creased by wind, birdsong drowning out the distant eruption of a chainsaw.

Finally she had reached her destination. It was called Monggyong, Mirror Rock: a great boulder that looked like a split mirror and was reputed to read the minds of those who saw it. There had been no one else around. Min had sat facing the rock and let her mind go blank. It had been a while before she'd settled, before she'd stilled the thoughts racing round her head, and deep down she'd known what was in her mind and what the rock would read: but she had done it just the same, just to be sure.

Breathing, quietening. The noise and haste of her life receding. Cuckoo and Kwang Sik and all the others reunited back at the hotel. Theo, Yun Seok and Hyuk Jae back in Pyongyang. Min here, all alone: with her thoughts, and her blossoming, and the growing knowledge of what she had to do. She had encouraged Cuckoo to come here because it would have been too awful to have that chance and not to take it.

Her thoughts spinning, forming, crystallising.

Cuckoo and her, back when Min was ten. Min at the Arirang Games, missing her cue and finding herself out of step. Cuckoo saying that it showed she was an individual.

Arirang itself, the meaning of the word: from the Arirang Pass, an imaginary rendezvous of lovers in the land of dreams.

The following day. Min climbing the highest tree on Mount Taesong: her eyes bright and trained on the sky, her hands and feet finding grip and leverage without conscious thought, her whole being wanting only to get higher and still higher without a thought of how she'd get back down.

These three thoughts forming a triskelion in her mind, reaching for one another and revolving in a slow, indivisible dance.

Mirror Rock, reading her mind indeed. Min had walked back to the hotel with a sense of purpose at once light in its joy and heavy in its import.

And now she was here, in bed, with her grandmother and her resolve. She remembered the day Theo had arrived in Pyongyang nine months before, and how much she'd disliked him on sight. She hadn't been able to sleep that night. Cuckoo had heard her tossing and turning in the darkness, and had said, 'You know something? When you can't sleep, it's because someone is thinking of you.'

It had been that night, too, that she'd got out of bed and seen the Rainbow Bridge on the TV for the first time.

Min felt the smile on her own face as though it were something plastered there. She got out of bed, careful not to wake Cuckoo, and padded softly to the window. The moon was high and the night clear. Silvered lawns stretched away below her. A zephyr shivered her nightshirt, very gently, and stilled.

She could conjure his image at will now: his eyes, his hands, his passion for what he did, the way he carried himself. She felt him here with her, and she dared not move for fear that he would vanish. He was a wanderer who left his mark in metal and wheels, and like all wanderers he would be gone too soon.

She stood at the window, looking out: and she knew with a certainty she could not explain that Theo was at that very moment both here and there: standing at his own window and reaching across the darkness for her, just as she was for him.

Theo wanted nothing more than to be left alone – actually, of course, he wanted nothing more than to have Min there, though that wasn't an option – but Peploe was in the bar and insisted that they have a drink together. 'Say goodbye, you know. You sit. I'll bring them over.'

He appeared a minute or two later with a beer in one hand and a glass full of clear liquid in another. He gave the beer to Theo. Theo nodded at the other glass. '*Soju?*'

'Water.'

'*Water?*' Theo heard the surprise in his voice and worried that it sounded rude.

Peploe laughed. 'Water. I don't feel like drinking tonight.'

'Why not?'

'Because I want to tell you something, and I want to be sure that I'm clear.'

The cold, high clutch of fear in Theo's stomach. 'What do you want to tell me?'

Peploe gestured: you drink. Theo took a sip of his beer and turned it into a glug, conscious that he wanted the fizz of alcohol in his bloodstream while listening to whatever Peploe was going to say.

'You remember I told you that getting involved with someone here would be catastrophic?' Peploe didn't wait for an answer. 'I told you that for your own good, just as I'm telling you this for your own good. There's a place called Camp 25, though officially it doesn't exist. It's in the far north of the country. They call it a Total Control Zone. It's a place of all the horrors you can imagine and plenty more that you can't. It's a place where love cannot exist.

'I could tell you a thousand stories about it – they leak out, no matter how hard the authorities try to keep them from doing so – but I'll choose just one. A family arrived one day. A husband and wife in their early thirties, with two small children and the husband's parents too. Six people, three generations of one family. They were from here, Pyongyang, of good stock, high *songbun*. Now they were class traitors, anti-Party, counter-revolutionary factional elements and despicable political careerists and tricksters: worse than dogs, perpetrating thrice-cursed acts of treachery in betrayal of such profound trust and warmest paternal love. They arrived in their city clothes, straight from where they'd been arrested. It was winter, a long way below zero. They had to relinquish everything, they were told. Everything? Everything. Their futures, because they had none, not any more. Their pasts, because they were from another existence entirely. There were no beds there, no pillows, no spoons, no toilets. Food was what they could find, and if they were lucky it tasted of nothing. Vision and hearing? Better off without, because that at least would let them block some things out.

'There were only three colours there: the grey of the buildings, the brown of the ground, and the black of dried blood. And there was pain of all sorts: pain ramped up to inconceivable levels, shifting, muscular rivers of pain, pain to create such a rift in their identity that those who made it to the far shore would be nothing like those now starting the crossing.

'The grandfather was the first to die. There was a mine where the prisoners used to dig coal, and it collapsed when he was down there. Scores of people died that day. The guards just sealed off the section they'd been in and made the survivors keep digging.

'One of the children, a small boy, was next. He got dysentery. Then his sister too, from pellagra. People would catch and eat rats because they contained protein and niacin, and pellagra came when they didn't have enough of that. But there weren't enough rats, and she was so small and broken by her brother's death that she never stood a chance. Her skin peeled off in strips, clean off her body, and her tongue swelled in her throat until she couldn't eat, couldn't drink, couldn't breathe.

'Next came the wife. She got pregnant, not from her husband – men and women were segregated – but from one of the guards.

That was strictly illegal, and she was blamed for it. She was taken outside and tied to a wooden pole: two sets of ropes, one round the chest and the other round the knees. Her husband was made to watch as the firing squad – including the guard who'd raped her – fired three rounds at her: the first at her chest to break the ropes binding it and make sure her body sagged forward; the second at her head to make sure she was dead; and the third at her legs, to break the second set of ropes and make her fall prostrate and defeated to the ground.

'So now it was just the husband and his mother left. She committed some infraction – maybe she complained about the conditions, something as simple as that – and she was put in the sweatbox: a tiny space not big enough to stand or lie down in, no ventilation and blazing hot, because by now it was the summer. She was in there for three days. No food, no water. Maybe she was deliberately left out there that long: maybe she was just forgotten. Either way, the result was the same. By the time she was brought out, she was dead.

'Imagine you're this man. You've had to watch your wife, your children and your parents all die. What do you do? I'll tell you what he did. He tried to escape. He made a break for the perimeter fence one day when he was on work detail, and one of the guards saw him and gunned him down.'

Peploe finished speaking. He drained his water. Theo hadn't touched his beer since Peploe had started. Peploe indicated Theo's glass. 'May I?' Theo nodded. Peploe drained the rest of the beer too, wiped the back of his hand across his mouth, got to his feet, and held out his other hand for Theo to shake.

'Been a pleasure knowing you, rollercoaster man. Go well.'

'You too.'

Peploe was halfway to the door when Theo called out. 'What had they done?'

Peploe turned back, and Theo saw from the look on his face that he had meant Theo to ask this question all along.

'No one knows. That's the point.'

Theo lay in bed and let it all wash over him. He thought of bodies sagging from poles and pulled desiccated from punishment rooms. He thought of Min: in her apartment, on top of the mountain, on the rollercoaster. He thought of a zone whose aim was to eradicate love. He thought of the secret hollows in a heart where the pilot light of that love would still flicker, come what may. He thought of how fickle time was, and how little love had to do with time. He had lived for years without being touched, not deep down where it mattered, and then when he had least expected it, when he had certainly not gone looking for it, it had come both slowly and all at once. He thought of the tattered, ragged parts of him, and of Min, and knew that loving those rather than just the shiny surface was the hardest and most important thing of all.

He wondered idly if he'd been asleep, because the force that tugged him from his bed seemed to be half-imagined, the kind that makes total sense in dreams but vanishes at the moment of awakening. It wasn't a violent force nor an uncomfortable one: more a gentle propulsion, a nudge, almost a floating.

He crossed the room and stood at the window. As ever, the only light that burned was the electric flame on top of the Juche Tower: but as he looked across the darkened city he knew with a certainty he could not explain that Min too was standing at her window hundreds of miles away, and that the thread between them ran invisible and unbreakable.

18

Cuckoo ran her hands over Kwang Sik's face, trying to commit him to a memory more visceral than the one that comes through eyes and brain. She kissed him again and again, as though she could somehow inhale him, consume him. There was breakfast on the table in front of them, but it was untouched. Breakfast? She could have breakfast any time.

She wanted to lie down here and die with him. The only thing worse than finding and losing someone was to find and lose that person for a second time. They were limpets, barnacles: epoxy, adhesive. They clung to each other so fiercely that the Red Cross workers had to separate them: gently at first and then, when they would not let go, more firmly. Slowly, with tear-stained resistance, they unpeeled from each other until the only parts touching were the tips of their fingers: and when that too was gone Cuckoo howled like an animal caught in a trap, a creature crushed beneath the weight of a misery too terrible to be borne.

The southerners boarded their buses first. Cuckoo stood on tiptoe to touch her hand to the window where Kwang Sik was, and he did the same, both of them pressing so hard that the blood fled from their skin and it seemed that the pane itself might shatter. All the way down the buses, on both sides, the same thing. The wailing, high and primal, of those who could not bear to be left again. The buses beginning to move, the passengers inside standing unsteadily to keep their loved ones in sight for as long as possible. What were a few more seconds after sixty-five years? Everything, that was what, for those seconds were a few more precious segments of time eked out against eternity. The palms turning into fists to beat against the glass and the metal: no, no, no, no, no. The Red Cross workers ushering the northerners gently but firmly away, and holding them up to stop them from collapsing in shuddering agonies on the tarmac. Here, let's go back inside, have some tea. The bittersweet cruelty of a second chance, the distress where there should have been peace of mind.

The total, annihilating emptiness when the buses back to the South had disappeared from sight.

Cuckoo and Min joined the others filing back on board the buses that would return them to Pyongyang. No one spoke. No one had spoken on the way here this time yesterday, weighed down as they'd been with anticipation and apprehension. Now the silence was harder, more ragged. Whether they'd been reunited with husbands or wives, mothers or fathers, daughters or sons, brothers or sisters, they all had one thing in common: they would never see that person again. They could not go and live in the South, and the southerners could not come and live here: and no one got a second reunion, no matter who they were.

Cuckoo sat heavily in her seat. She felt drained, as if someone had pulled the plug. She was not in pain and she felt no distress: she was simply exhausted, not just physically but spiritually too. Tired, that's what she was. Deeply, profoundly tired.

Min sat down next to her. Cuckoo rested her hand on Min's. 'Thank you,' Cuckoo said. 'Thank you, my darling girl, for coming with me.'

'I wouldn't have missed it for the world.'

'And I wouldn't have wanted anyone else to share it with me.'

320

There was a sudden scream from behind them: a woman standing, raging, choking out her anger at having come in the first place and made it all worse. The Red Cross workers came over and calmed her down. Min and Cuckoo listened.

The bus had been on the road for half an hour when Cuckoo next spoke.

'You know what's funny?'

'What?'

'Kwang Sik and I, we spent all that time telling each other about our lives: what I'd done, what he'd done. The one thing we didn't talk about – perhaps because it was so obvious, perhaps because it would have been too painful, perhaps both – was the life we could have had together, where we wouldn't have had to tell each other those things because we'd have known them already. Somewhere there's a life in which Chul Woo would have had a brother or sister and in which you would have had some cousins: a life in which I wouldn't have left Lee Song Si waiting for a wife who would never be, or gone through year after year trailing my widowhood like cloth in the water behind me. I've lived a good life, don't get me wrong, but we all have other lives which never were, and that was mine.'

'I know.'

'Good.'

'Are you still glad you went, though?'

Cuckoo turned towards her. 'Yes. Absolutely.'

'You're sure?'

'I've never been surer.'

'Even though it hurts?'

'Especially because it hurts. The depth of your love today is the depth of your wound tomorrow, darling girl. Be brave enough to break your own heart.'

It was late afternoon when they arrived back in Pyongyang, the air malevolent with a distant storm. Min took Cuckoo home, and stayed long enough to answer the questions Chul Woo and Han Na asked about the weekend and to help settle Cuckoo in bed. Chul Woo was already working out his strategy for the *songbun* committee – he would argue that since Kwang Sik hadn't settled in the South, and had probably thought his family to be dead, then he should still be classed as a war hero – but Min wasn't really listening. Something had gone out of Cuckoo during the journey back from Kumgang, she thought. She seemed deflated, a popped and wrinkling balloon. Min knew how much Cuckoo had been holding herself together for the reunion, how resolute she'd had to be to steel herself for the joy and trauma of seeing Kwang Sik again. Now it was over, in every way.

Cuckoo reached out from under the bedsheets for Min's hand. 'Thank you.'

'You don't have to thank me.'

'I know I don't. But I choose to anyway.'

'Are you all right?'

Cuckoo's skin, translucent and stretched by her smile. 'I'm very much all right.' She squeezed Min's hand with surprising strength. 'Go.'

Min was halfway to the door when Cuckoo said something else, quite quietly. Min only half-heard it, so she couldn't be sure if she was right, but when she turned it over in her head as she walked back down to the street, she was more and more convinced that Cuckoo had said, 'Do what you have to do.'

She found Theo and Yun Seok having coffee at the Yanggakdo. Nine months Theo had been here, Min thought, and still he and Yun Seok seemed stiff and formal with each other. They didn't see her immediately when she walked in, and for a moment she stood in the doorway just looking at Theo, drinking in everything about him, fixing in her mind the way his hair sat and his teeth flashed as he spoke. A waiter pushed past her, a posse of tourists too, and she was oblivious.

It was Theo who saw her first, and the look of sheer leaping pleasure on his face made something somersault deep inside her. He stood and came over to her. She wanted nothing more than to bury herself in his arms, but this was a public place and Yun Seok was watching, so instead she patted him awkwardly on the shoulder, and saw that he didn't know what to do with his hands either.

'How was it?' he asked, and at that exact moment she said, 'I'm sorry I had to leave.' The two of them, speaking both at once and over the top of each other before dissolving into laughter. He ushered her over to the table, his hand hovering just next to her elbow but not quite touching it.

Min sat and told them all about the reunion meeting, and already it seemed as though it had happened to someone else: this great, seismic overturning of everything her beloved grandmother had ever known, and the same thing was happening to Min right now with a man who tomorrow would be gone and whom she would never see again. Cuckoo had left Kwang Sik for the last time this morning, and tomorrow morning Min would leave Theo just the same way. Her breath came in quick shallow pants, as though her throat was constricted.

Yun Seok clapped his hands when Min had finished talking: an announcement rather than applause. 'I suggest we give Theo a couple of hours to pack, and meet him back here at eight o'clock for our final supper.'

We give him. We meet him. Yun Seok, her eternal chaperone: the eyes and ears not just of the Party but of her own conscience too.

Min was wearing a thin red sweater. Her arm brushed Theo's as she stood up, and for a moment she felt resistance and thought that he had grabbed her hand, brazen and careless in his desperation. Then she looked down, and saw that her sleeve was caught on the wristband of his watch. She pulled her arm away as slowly and gently as she could, and it trailed a red thread: the fabric of her sweater trapped and unwinding, and with it all her hopes and fears too.

She didn't know where to go. She couldn't go back to her apartment and see Hyuk Jae, not just because it would have felt treacherous but because he of all people couldn't even begin to understand this. She couldn't go back to where her parents and Cuckoo lived: Cuckoo had been through enough this weekend already, and she didn't want to face her father's obsessive worrying about *songbun* and the like.

For a brief, terrifying moment of total insanity she wondered whether the Juche Tower was open today, and if so whether she could go up to the top and throw herself off. It would be so simple, so easy: the final answer to her overwhelming desire not to feel anything ever again, not to be unhappy any more. There were places on the observation platform where it would be the easiest thing in the world to stand trembling on the thin edge, all interdiction and seduction and repulsion, and to take that final, single step over.

The regime hated suicide, for it was the ultimate defection. If she jumped, her family would be punished. She could not do that to them, Min told herself: but even as the thought came to her she knew it was an abstraction, a justification in which she didn't truly believe. She had been prepared to do something as bad when Theo had been in her apartment for supper that night.

It wasn't because of her family that she wouldn't jump. She wouldn't do it because she wouldn't have the courage. That was all it came down to: the courage, and whether she had it or she didn't. The fall would be quick, and brutal, and painful. The fall wouldn't kill her, but the impact would.

She had already fallen. She didn't know how much further she had left to drop.

There was an old Korean tradition. What could you do when you had a secret that was burning you up from the inside, which you felt you could no longer keep without corroding your very soul, but you didn't feel able to share with anyone else? Whisper it into a hollow, that was what. Go to the top of a mountain, make a hollow in a tree, pour out your secret into it and cover it with mud when you had finished.

She went to Mount Taesong. It loomed high above Jucheland, and for the past nine months Min had seen it practically every day: the rollercoaster and the park itself going up piece by piece in the lee of its great flanks, the treeline tracing the gentle swell of the summit like a cockscomb. Nine months she had seen it, and in all that time she had never climbed to the top: until now.

Thunderheads rolled on the horizon as she walked between the trees. Any tree would do, she thought, but still she scanned each one, trying to discern which would be best, which one offered itself up: *here, take me, talk to me, pour the contents of your heart into me and I will seal them up with sap and bark.*

She found one with a small hole in the trunk. When she went close enough to lean against it, she realised two things. First, that the hole was exactly at the height of her mouth, so she would neither have to stoop nor stretch to speak into it. Second, it was the tallest tree around, which meant it must be the one she'd climbed aged ten after messing up the routine at the Arirang Games, when she'd come here with Cuckoo and Cuckoo had told her that making mistakes showed that she was an individual.

Yes: this tree was the one.

Min scrabbled in the earth around the base of the trunk. The soil was dry and crumbling, though in a few hours' time when the rains came it would become mud, thick and viscous. She gathered as much as she could in her hands and closed them into fists. The soil was warm and gritty against her palms.

There was no one around. She could hear birdsong and the distant screams of the rollercoaster riders, but here it was just her and the trees. The leaves melded into a canopy high above her head. Min leant her head to the hole and began to speak, so close up against the trunk that sometimes her lips brushed the bark, felt its abrasion and tasted its bitterness.

She spoke without knowing what she was going to say. She didn't censor her thoughts or try to organise them, didn't automatically arrange them to portray herself in the best light. She just spoke: of her, and him, and all the vast, wild, forbidden things she felt. She spoke of the ways in which she had not so much got to know him as remembered him, that he was not so much a parcel to be unwrapped as an etching whose faded lines she knew how to colour and revive. It was impossible, of course, but still she felt it: that they had known each other before, loved each other before, for how else could she explain this familiarity? In a different time, of course, perhaps even a different plane of existence, but there nonetheless. She spoke of how in those lives they must have promised themselves to each other in this one, just as in this life they would be promising themselves to each other in the next one: a hall of mirrors, an endless reflection through time and space. It was more than one life could hold, what they had. It was more than this life could hold, that was for sure: this life of which she had been so certain, this life, which had been so well and impregnably built, a fortress around her heart. But even the strongest fortress was only made of bricks, and bricks could be knocked down. It wasn't about the number of bricks that were knocked down, but the placement of them. The ones at the base, which supported and underpinned the others, they were the ones that Theo had come and chipped away: brick by brick, slab by slab. Foundations poured from concrete that had turned out to be quicksand: a trumpet call, a clamour, and down had tumbled the whole lot. The castle gone, demolished by the earthquake of his love, and with it everything she had ever known.

This was the truth, her and the tree, because she had to lie to everyone else about everything else. What do you do when you find that everything you've ever known is a lie? You go insane. Worse: you go sane. You tell the truth in a world of deception, and it sounds like a pistol shot: you become yourself in a world that demands you be anything but. This bright shining light of truth, so incandescent that it shrivels and burns everything else in its path; and tomorrow it would be gone, and in its place would be a darkness she had never noticed before, but which she knew now she would never be able to unsee.

She talked and talked and talked. It came gushing out like dam water on to a spillway. She talked through her tears and her sweat: she talked through swells of heaving sobs and flatlands of perfect calm. *Hold it all*, she told the tree. *Hold it all, because I have told you everything: I have trusted you with the contents of my heart, precious and agonising as they are. Hold it all.*

Min eked out the last drops of her confession. She was spent. She felt a little better for the purging, but the ache still hummed within her. When she looked down she saw that her hands were muddy, and it was a moment before she realised that she must have opened them without realising, and her tears had dripped on to the earth and made it mud, warm and gooey against her skin. She took this mud and pressed it into the hole, using her fingers to ensure that not a single air pocket was left before smoothing it flush against the bark when the hole was full.

She looked at her watch. An hour! She'd been here a whole hour. It had felt like only a few minutes. It was almost time to head back to the Yanggakdo, if she could bear it. Maybe she could just walk the streets all night, placing her footsteps where she knew his had been: imprint her story on his as he had imprinted his on hers.

Min turned to walk out of the copse, and stopped dead. There was a man standing there, close enough to have heard what she'd been saying. She blinked away the tears, and he swam into focus.

Yun Seok.

He didn't say a word to her: not when she asked in a voice high with fear how long he'd been there, or how much he'd heard, or what he intended to do now. He didn't say a word as he turned his back on her, or as he walked quickly and jerkily through the trees back to the car park, or even as he opened the rear door of Nam Il's car for her before getting in the front himself.

Nam Il drove through empty streets. Min opened her mouth to ask Yun Seok again, and then thought better of it. It was funny, she realised. On the surface she was almost in full panic, trying to find out what Yun Seok knew while knowing that he could very probably ruin not just her life but those of her entire family in the time it took to click one's fingers. But deep down she was very calm, extraordinarily and perversely so. That was Theo, she realised:

the courage he had given her to turn her face to whatever would come and to accept it, to allow herself to be bloodied but always unbowed. The *Bowibu* would interrogate her. Maybe Hyuk Jae himself would do the questioning.

Let them, Min thought. Let them do their worst.

The storm clouds were so low over the Yanggakdo now that Min thought the building could almost puncture them. The three of them were going to go through this farce of a last supper, Min thought, and Yun Seok would eke out her agony for as long as possible, because she had betrayed everyone: not just him, not just Hyuk Jae, not just her parents, but every single person in this country, because she had betrayed the country itself. That was how he would view it, because he was one of them, he was part of the system.

That was how she would have viewed it too, before all this had happened.

Nam Il turned left at a set of traffic lights, away from the Yanggakdo. Again Min thought about asking Yun Seok where they were going, and again she decided to stay quiet and wait him out. She glanced at him. The edges of his nostrils were white with the effort of whatever he was holding in.

Min looked at her watch. They were going to be late for Theo.

Nam Il pulled up outside an apartment block. Yun Seok got out of the car, gesturing that Min should follow suit and Nam Il could go. Min followed Yun Seok as he walked to the main entrance and went inside. For a moment she thought that he was going to shut the door behind him before she could reach it, but he held it open without looking at her until she was inside. As she turned to watch it close, Nam Il's car was nowhere to be seen.

Up three flights of stairs they went, and into an apartment.

'This is mine,' Yun Seok said. His voice was loud in the silence. 'Look around.'

The apartment was spartan. The kitchen was one half of the living area: the bathroom was tiny and the bedroom not much bigger. A single bed, she saw. There were only a handful of books. The walls were bare save for four framed pictures: the ones of Kim Il Sung and Kim Jong Il, the sketch Min had done of him, and a photograph of Min herself.

No: that wasn't quite correct. Min looked closer, and saw that though the woman looked very like her she was in fact someone else entirely.

Min had a sudden flash of memory: Cuckoo telling her about the first time she had been to Lee Song Si's apartment, and how she'd known from the moment she'd walked in that no woman lived here. It had been not so much what had been there as what hadn't been: no softness, no delicacy of touch, no wildflowers picked from the riverbank to add colour and scent. Everything had not just been tidy but exceptionally so, as though the very act of perfect arrangement had in itself been a silent scream.

And so it was here too. Yun Seok's apartment was, like Lee Song Si's had been, defined by absence rather than presence: in particular, of course, by the absence of anyone else, by the absence of the wife and two teenage children to whom Yun Seok had gone home – to whom Yun Seok had *said* he'd gone home – every night and every weekend since Min had known him.

He saw that she'd worked it out. He cleared his throat and clasped his hands behind his back, as though he were a scholar about to embark upon the presentation of a detailed thesis on an obscure aspect of Kimilsungism-Kimjongilism.

'There are things you don't know about me,' he began. 'Many things, in fact. Most of them are not important now. But this is important.' He unclasped one hand, gestured vaguely round the room, and returned it to its position behind his back again. 'I have always wanted a normal life. And I have never had one.'

'Why?'

He gestured towards the picture of the woman who looked like Min. 'Her name was Hei Ran. Graceful orchid, that's what it meant, and that's what she was. Never was someone more perfectly named. We were engaged to be married, and we already knew that we would live in the eastern part of the city and have two boys: we'd discussed all that, and neither of us had needed to persuade the other, we'd both wanted the same thing without being asked.

'One night, a week or so before the wedding, Hei Ran was crossing the Okryu Bridge when a car hit her. She was carrying the papers confirming our ceremony and giving us official permission to get married, and they were dark brown and stiff with her blood. I sat beside her hospital bed for that entire week, and on what would have been our wedding day the doctors said there was nothing more they could do.'

'Oh, Yun Seok. I don't know what to say.'

'There's nothing you can say, my dear.'

'What happened to the driver?'

'It was a black car that hit her.'

There was a compound in central Pyongyang that was walled off from the rest of the capital. It was called the Forbidden City, and only the highest-ranking Party officials lived and worked there. Their cars were all black, purring in and out of the compound through gates that lifted silently as they approached and lowered again the moment they were past, and their occupants were untouchable. A black government car could have driven along a pavement for a kilometre or two, scattering pedestrians like ninepins, and it would have been as if the whole thing had never happened: no report in the newspapers or on television, witnesses and relatives alike not breathing a word if they knew what was good for them. A lone woman on a bridge after dark would scarcely have registered: the briefest of ripples, if that, and then things would

331

have gone on as before and Yun Seok left alone to deal with the unfathomable crater in his life.

Yun Seok continued. 'To be different is to be suspect, as you know. So I invented what I did not have, what I was *expected* to have, what I would have had.' His *inminbanjang* would have known the truth, Min thought: but an *inminbanjang* was responsible only for a single building, and would have had no reason to know any of Yun Seok's friends or colleagues, let alone fraternise with them. 'It was easier that way: to fit in and opt out all at once, to make people think I was like them and yet have an excuse not to join in every social occasion going. And with you . . .' He paused, swallowed. Min saw that he was trying not to cry. 'With you, it's because I never wanted you to feel threatened by me, not in any way.'

'Threatened by you? I've never felt threatened by you.'

'That's good.'

'I mean: I've never felt threatened because I never would. You've never given me cause to think that. We're colleagues, friends. Why on earth would I feel threatened?'

He gave a smile so weak it was hardly visible, and Min saw that it was not only her heart that was breaking tonight.

'Because I love you.'

He explained it all in a soft voice, and didn't look at her once as he spoke. Every day had been a gentle flowering, being with her: and every night he had withered. A slow, quotidian death, loving someone who not only didn't love him back but didn't even know the first iota of how he felt. Of course there was supposed to be no love in this country other than that for the Supreme Leader, and the Dear Leader, and above all the Great Leader, but what there was supposed to be and what there actually was were two different things.

He'd known from the moment she had been assigned to work with him that he loved her. Within the first few minutes, literally: the first time he'd seen her smile, the first time she'd stood up in the training session they were at and performed a word-perfect welcome without a hitch. Yes, she looked so like Hei Ran, but that wasn't the reason: he loved Min for who she was rather than who she wasn't. He'd seen her patience and her goodness, and had marvelled at her beauty, and had known that she would never, ever feel the same way about him: not even a fraction of that amount for a fraction of that time.

It had been easier that way, strangely, for he had never had to worry about what she might think of him or how best to make her feel attracted to him. Partially requited love was worse than totally unrequited love, that was for sure. And that was why he always used her full name, Min Ji, when talking to her: because to maintain that distance was also to keep his sanity.

And then Theo had arrived, and he'd watched her fall in love with him little by little. Oh yes, of course he had noticed, no matter how much she thought she had hidden it. Why else did she think he had got so drunk those few evenings they'd all been together? To blot out the pain, of course, but also to allow them some time on their own: for he knew what it was like to feel the way she did, and he too liked Theo. Passing out drunk had been one of the few plausible ways he'd been able to absent himself: that, and letting her walk ahead of him with Theo beneath the poplars, and pretending to oversleep the morning they'd climbed Mount Paektu, and even lingering over his comfort stop on the way back from the DMZ.

Min stood, and listened, and said nothing, for there was nothing she could say.

Yun Seok looked at his watch. 'We said we'd be there by now.'

'Then we'd better go.'

He shook his head. 'You go.'

'But . . . ?'

'What do you expect me to do? Report you? You know what that would mean. Gone to the mountains. Why would I do that to you? Why would I do that to myself? This' – he tapped his heart – 'this, all this, I've learnt to live with it. It's dreadful. But I get to work with you, and see you five days a week, and be your colleague, and that's not nothing. That's something. To condemn you for something your heart feels . . . no. I can't feel that myself and then expect you not to. The sun shines on me when I'm with you, and that's enough. I'll come to the hotel tomorrow morning, and we can all go to the airport together. What you do between now and then is your business. I won't tell. You don't need to be careful of me. But you *do* need to be careful of others: the hotel staff, the listeners. You know that as well as I do. Be careful. Tomorrow he will be gone, but you will still be here.'

'I don't know . . .'

'Yes, you do. I love you, so I give you this.'

She kissed his cheek and was gone.

Min stood on the street outside Yun Seok's apartment. A freight train was moving behind the buildings opposite, carriages pushed and pulled through the windows of space as though by unseen puppeteers: a slow trudge along tracks already set.

Life was not just about what one did, Min thought, but what one did not do: the paths ignored, the opportunities spurned, the things unsaid. Life was positive spaces and negative ones too. Cuckoo had chosen to go to Kumgang: Yun Seok had invented a family who never were. Hearts and minds had borders quite as much as nations did, sealing off the past and choking off the future.

Min had a chance now, if only she chose to take it. How much was she prepared to risk, not just of her life but of those of others too? And how much was she prepared to risk in other, less tangible ways? Tomorrow Theo would be gone, come what may, and it would all but kill her. She could regret what she had done, or she could regret what she hadn't.

Cuckoo had faced the same choice. Cuckoo had made her decision. Min wondered what Cuckoo would do if she were her now, and she wondered what Cuckoo would want her to do, and she knew the answer to both. All the stories Cuckoo had told her – standing up to the minister, refusing to go through with her marriage to Lee Song Si, celebrating Min's mistake at the Arirang Games – all these had given Min the tools to rebel, and only now had she realised. Cuckoo had planted the seeds, and they had needed nothing but someone's sun to come and shine on them. Cuckoo had been the wind, and now Theo was the whirlwind.

Another life, if only for a night. Another story, if only between her and Theo. A possibility seized and cherished rather than deserted and discarded. A step off the edge into the unknown, and the trust that there would either be something solid underfoot or that she would soar. A refusal to be cowed any more. Convention. Freedom. Gravity. Flight.

She pulled out her phone and dialled Hyuk Jae.

'Hi,' he said. 'How was Kumgang?'

'Emotional. Very, very emotional.' She forced out a small laugh. 'Listen, I think I'm needed here tonight.' *Here*: suitably ambiguous, and so easy to use that ambiguity when Hyuk Jae trusted her so completely. So easy and so degrading, but she was long past caring about that.

'Of course. Do what you have to do. I'll see you tomorrow.'

He hadn't meant it as a blessing, of course, but it was one all the same.

The Yanggakdo stood like a beacon, calling her. The air sagged with moisture all around, and in the distance came the delicate growling of thunder.

Min was still a few minutes from the Yanggakdo when the rain came. Big fat drops hurled from the sky and bouncing up off the tarmac: a dark curtain sweeping over her, plastering hair to scalp and clothes to skin. She began to run, not in hope of getting to shelter sooner but from the sheer childlike pleasure of being soaked. She heard it hammer on the rooftops, felt sudden puddles splash warm and wet up her legs. Rivulets sprang, eddied, rushed. Buildings folded themselves into the downpour: waterfalls hurried from eaves. Min opened her mouth to taste the rain on her lips and tongue. She ran her hands over her face, and sweat and dust came with them. A car sprayed a puddle at her as it passed, and she just laughed. She was cleansed and purified: the flood, lifting her up as it swept her away.

The lobby of the Yanggakdo was full of Chinese tourists shaking umbrellas and peering gloomily through the windows. There were no lights on, even though the evening was dark outside with the clouds and the storm. The power was out. Min skirted round the edge of the tourist group, knowing that their chatter would distract the receptionist, and headed for the stairs. Up she went, fast and urgent and oblivious to the effort of the climb. Her feet squelched in her shoes, and when she looked back down the flights of stairs she saw that she was leaving dotted trails of water.

She came out on to Theo's floor, went to his door, and hammered on it. Looking up and down the corridor, seeing it empty.

'Hello?' Theo's voice from behind the door.

'It's me. Min. Open up.'

She was through the door the moment it opened, pushing it shut again behind her and seeing how his brief confusion gave way to the realisation of why she was here.

'It's not safe,' he said.

'Yes, it is.'

'It's not.'

'They can't listen when the power's out.'

'Peploe told me—'

He stopped dead, words frozen as he saw how the light ran wild within her.

The depth of your love today is the depth of your wound tomorrow. Be brave enough to break your own heart.

He ran his fingers over hers, lifted her hand and kissed it. He pushed a wet strand of hair back behind her ear.

Then he moved his lips to hers, and she was destroyed.

19

It was soft and slow, tender and nudging, their mouths barely touching. Why rush, when they'd waited so long for this? Not a smash and grab kind of lust full of tongues and limbs, but deeper, gentler. She cupped his cheek very lightly with her hand, and she felt as though she was holding on to something delicate and precious – not just him but them, their togetherness, what they had.

A rain-greyed darkness in the room as the storm raged outside. No lights to brighten, no microphones to eavesdrop. Her fingers tracing his skin, the brush of her hair as he kissed the hollow at the point where her throat met her chest. Infinity beyond his eyes, and Min felt she could travel every inch of it with him. She was not just seeing him: she knew too that she was seeing him seeing her, seeing her properly, bringing her to her own attention and giving her new eyes, and with that came bravery and wonder and a giddying exhilaration. It was the riskiest, most certain thing she'd ever known.

Leave no corner of me untouched, she whispered.

Shadows and heat as they took the clothes off each other. His hands in her hair, scrunching it up around the base of her neck. She lay back and let his fingers on to her and inside her, and when they kissed now there was no hesitation or reservation, it was two people who wanted only to be consumed, totally consumed, by each other.

She raised her hips to his mouth, felt the press of his hands on her flanks as he tasted her.

Lying on a beach with the tide coming in, the sea rising up her legs, retreating, rising higher, retreating, rising higher still. The thousand sharp needles of tingling in her feet, a hot wave of chills spreading and building. Her head going light and rushing, the moment at the top of the rollercoaster before the drop. Dominoes toppling beneath her skin, the flame inside turning from orange to red to white. A river of consciousness between them, and suddenly she was pulling him towards her, tightening herself around him to ride the shivering wave so that at the moment of avalanche there was no separation. She shuddered in great leaping spasms, the shock rippling through her body entire: a seizure, a vanishing. She tried to speak but could not: she tried to gulp down air, but all she could do was pant like a dog. The rip through her, again and again as it demanded her surrender.

Then, suddenly, she felt herself spat out back into the room. She was on the bed, glowing, and Theo was looking at her. Her limbs were clouds and her core was honey.

.

The rain had stopped, and the evening sun slanted through the room and striped the floor. Min got out of bed, stumbling on jelly legs and having to hold on to the wall to stop herself from falling. Adulteress, faithless, cheat. Lover, adoring, adored.

When she was sure she could support her own weight, she padded over to the window and looked out. The entire horizon was banded pink, and there were purple and orange flares around the sun itself.

Theo came over and wrapped himself around her. They watched together as the sun dipped below the horizon for good, and at that moment it was as though the entire city exhaled.

'Think of me at sunset,' he murmured. 'Every night when the sun goes down, think of me.'

'Will you think of me too?'

'Wherever I am and whatever I'm doing. Always.'

His face was above her, and she was losing herself in it. She never took her eyes off him, not for a second, watching as his expression changed and changed and changed again: the way he looked at her with mild bemusement as though he could not quite believe she was here; the way his eyes opened, not just the lids but the pupils themselves, as he marvelled at his own hunger; then the way they half-closed, his mouth curling almost into a snarl with the quickening and the ferocity. He covered her, pressed down on her: smothering, consuming, protecting. She found his mouth with hers and chewed at his lip. When he raised himself again she saw the ridged lines of muscle on his upper arms, and she wiped the sweat from his brow and smeared it across her own chest, and she looked down at where they were joined, and she could hardly get the words out.

'Look at us,' she said. 'Look at how perfectly we fit.'

They did fit, and that could neither be faked nor undone. This was their biggest joy and their biggest tragedy, that they moulded so well to each other's contours and yet they could not be. It made this night almost like a dream, and even in the middle of it Min knew both that she'd remember it with crystal clarity for the rest of time and also that it would seem ethereal, hard to believe that it had ever happened: no evidence, no photographs, no tickets or receipts or reports or minutes of meetings or any of the other ways humans like to note events.

The world had disappeared. It was just her and him, just them, and it was so rare and precious it made her want to sing and cry. Their bodies moved beautifully together but they were also a barrier: two people trying to devour each other's flesh and bones so as to reach what lay beneath. She wanted to burrow her way into him and find her hiding place, somewhere she could keep from being found by everyone bar him, the one person by whom she wanted to be found.

In the lulls, wrapped around each other. This was also where the intimacy was, in the troughs as much as the peaks, in the stillness as much as in the motion. He was her safest sanctuary and her greatest adventure; he was her stillest day and her most raging hurricane, and she loved him tender and reckless just the same.

'Did you ever come looking for it?' she asked.

'No. Never.'

'Why do you think it is? Why do we have what we have?'

'Because our souls are the same shape, that's why.'

She heard that and burned it on her soul, the same shape as his.

She would have ripped shreds in the delicate fabrics of space and time if she could: slipped behind the curtain with him and quietly away. All the places they could never go together: cobbled cities with backstreet wanderings all day and each other all night, sun-scorched hikes in wildernesses and stripped bare in mountain lakes. Whitewashed rooms at dusk. Swarms of butterflies. The scent of lavender. Cool paths through forests. Aching legs, white minds, spontaneous laughter. Shimmering roads leading on. The taste of an orange.

In some other life, she thought, they would be laughing at the fact that in this life they would end up apart.

Out of the window, far away across the darkened cityscape, the solitary flame burned atop the Juche Tower. Min saw the light, and felt her head resting on Theo's shoulder and her leg thrown across his. *This is the place I should not be*, she thought, *and yet there's no other place I'd rather be: here, with you, unashamed.*

Theo half-woke at dawn. The sheets were down by their ankles, and all night it had been too hot in here even to have them against his skin: but now, finally, there was a delicious window of coolness, and in his groggy semi-consciousness he pulled the sheets up and Min across towards him. A moment of drowsy warmth, of safety and belonging: and he wondered as he drifted off again whether he had ever felt so happy.

She was still asleep when he woke again. Their hands were locked together and their legs intertwined, and for long moments Theo lay there as still as a stone crusader, listening to her breathing and with his nose pressed so close to her skin that her smell was all around and within him. He would stay like this forever if it were allowed, entwined with her like the skeletons found in Pompeii: two people who had seen the end of the world coming and had instinctively chosen to face it with each other.

Slowly, so as not to wake her, he disentangled himself, propped himself up on one elbow and gazed at her. She was lying on her back, one arm above her head and the other flung out towards him. Sleep softened her face, marked out its vulnerability. Her hair was sprayed out across the pillow, and he remembered it wild and whirling over him.

He had a plane to catch. He woke her with vagabond hands and pilgrim lips.

Afterwards, he lay on his back and she on her stomach, at right angles to each other so he was looking up at her face. Her hand rested against her cheek, and her hair cascaded over it. Her throat was exposed in all its delicate lines and her mouth slightly open, as though she was about to speak, about to smile. He saw the arch of her eyebrows as they curled down and became the sides of her nose. Her face was at rest and yet full of motion, sated and still flushed with temptation. The monochrome light of dawn gave no colour, no distraction. This was how he would remember her: a face in black and white and endless shades of grey, the revelation of her soul.

He had never tried before to find someone in which to lose himself. He had always been too scared, and had passed it off as being too self-contained. Only now did he realise that he had always been lost, and that she had given him the most precious gift of all. She had been the one in whom he had found himself.

Time crawled, time raced. This room, the two of them, was the world entire. They lay together and said nothing, for words were only a distraction now. Theo breathed her in, trying to take as much of her with him as he could: with him, inside him, beneath the texture of his skin. He was a man with a talent, he knew, but deep down he was an ordinary person living an ordinary life, just as she was – and for this moment they had something extraordinary, something between and outside them both.

Theo packed. When he closed his suitcase, Min came up behind him and pressed herself against his back. In the silence was her soft sobbing and the high tinkling of his breaking heart. He turned to her, put a finger beneath her chin and lifted her face up so she had to look at him. Her eyes were swollen red and her features elongated and distorted by her pain, and she was the most beautiful thing he had ever seen.

The stray piece of thread was still hanging from the sleeve of her red sweater where she had caught it against his watch yesterday. She pulled at it, twisted it round her finger and yanked it until it came away. She folded it on itself, bit it at the halfway point, gave one half to him, and began to tie the other half round her own wrist.

His fingers on hers, taking it from her, tying it for her, and then holding out his wrist so she could do his. It took her three tries, she was fumbling so much.

They went downstairs separately, of course: Min first, then Theo, and a good few minutes between them. Min was waiting with Yun Seok and Nam Il by the car when Theo emerged. Nam Il lifted Theo's suitcase into the boot of the car, waited until everyone had settled themselves in their usual seats, and set off as though this final journey was just like any other.

Theo looked out of the window as the city flashed images at him, just as it had done on the trip in from the airport when he'd first arrived nine months before. What he would give now to reverse that time, to push against the axis of the world and make it spin backwards: to give himself nine more months here with Min, even if that meant knowing her less and less each day, to see their relationship diminish rather than grow until they were back here on a cold January day with her telling him he couldn't turn tail and go back to the airport. Even that would be worth it, for he would still know how their story had ended: still have that single precious night to tuck away in his memory, to keep safe from harm and out of reach of life's quotidian banalities.

Theo went through the motions at the airport. He shook Nam Il's hand, but managed to prise neither sound nor smile from him. Yun Seok gave him back his passport, and Theo laughed at the idea that Yun Seok might have lost it and that Theo would therefore be obliged to stay here: laughed briefly, that was, until the idea made him want to weep. Theo checked his suitcase in, and received his boarding pass, and then they were standing there, the three of them, and on the departures board above them the stark confirmation that he really was leaving. JS151 to Beijing, on time.

Yun Seok put out his hand. 'It's been a pleasure. Really. It has.'

For a moment Theo wondered whether he should hug Yun Seok, but Yun Seok had never seemed the tactile type.

He shook his hand. 'Thank you. Thank you for everything.'

Yun Seok turned to Min. 'I need a coffee, I think.' He indicated the café on the far side of the concourse. 'I'll be there when you're ready to join me.'

There was so much still to say, and yet nothing left to say. A public place, the antiseptic sterility of a transport terminus: this was not the place for anything more than a perfunctory confirmation of what they both knew. This was the only way. She had her life, and her life was also that of those around her. To take her with him, even if that had been possible, would have been to ruin what they had, to discredit and dishonour the purity and beauty of their love. They deserved what they had because they knew both the limitations and the luck of what they had. She could not disappear and abandon those she loved: he could not be responsible for making her do that. It wasn't just about balancing one choice against the other. It was that they would both become different people, worse people, if they made the leap. The act of decision would also be an act of change. The only place and time in which they could be together was in a place outside of time: in their heads, in their memories, in the ether where they would always abide.

This was how he would keep it forever, Theo knew: pure, untainted. This was how he would love her the way he did now for the rest of his life: knowing that they had done the right thing, and that even the short time they had had together was better than none at all. Love was not about time. There were years in his past that he could scarcely remember, and there were the hours of last night that he would never forget. He and Min had in that time been children, ancients, immortals.

He looked at her. 'What am I thinking?'

'That you told me once that you would leave here without a backwards glance or a second thought.'

He laughed, because that was exactly what he had been thinking: and he laughed because it was all that would keep him from howling at the heavens.

'I'll tell you what else I'm thinking,' he said.

'Go on.'

'The best thing of all was waking up with you.' He pressed his wrist to his chest, red thread against the fabric of his shirt. 'And this: this thread is unbreakable. Whatever happens, there'll always be a small quiet place that belongs to you and you alone, where I carry you and can talk to you. There'll always be a current that runs deep and high, somewhere way out of reach of the rest of my life. Even on a really rough day when the only person I want is the one I can't have, I will still have something special because I have you.'

Min nodded, and Theo knew that for the second time in a few hours she could not speak even if she'd wanted to. They hugged, brief and tentative with the airport workers all around. 'See you at the Rainbow Bridge,' she said.

'Go back to Mount Taesong at sunset. Go there and walk with me, be with me.'

'I can do that anywhere.'

'It has to be there.' She looked quizzical. He smiled. 'Please. Tonight. Do it for me.'

He pressed his hand to her cheek, just as he had done when she had come soaked and determined into his hotel room the night before, and then he walked quickly towards passport control before either of them could change their mind.

The plane pushing back from the stand, taxiing across the apron, swinging in a wide arc to line itself up on the runway. The sudden acceleration, and Theo by the window watching the landing lights rush by, faster and faster. Humans don't feel speed, he'd told her: they feel acceleration.

The point of no return. The nose lifting, the wheels rising up and off the ground. Grass and buildings below, Jucheland and Mallima, wider and smaller as the plane climbed until they looked no larger than miniature toys. He pressed his face to the glass and felt his tears warm against the pane, secret and hidden from the man next to him and the stewardess watching from her jump seat.

Goodbye, my love, goodbye.

It had been the right thing to do, the only thing to do. His departure was Min's protection, was her whole family's protection, and he knew that somewhere, hidden beneath the searing of its pain, was the glow of its virtue. He remembered Min's fear on the plane to Mount Paektu, the way in which he'd reassured her when she'd dug her fingernails into his arm. Life was little moments of protection and love, and though he couldn't be there for those, he could at least do this one thing, this one vast, overarching thing, to keep her safe.

To say goodbye is to die a little, but I have lived so much more because of you. Goodbye and thank you for what you let me give you, but much more for what you gave me.

Only now he'd done something so seismic for someone else did he feel how threadbare and lukewarm it had been looking after, and out for, himself alone. It was she who had done that, she who had made him capable of it. He remembered what he'd said that night at Paektu: 'To see and be seen, to understand and be understood, to want to show someone things and see the things they show you.' To be accepted, not despite his flaws but because of them. She was the first person ever to have done that: that was her gift to him, and it was as priceless as anything and everything he'd done for her.

He took out the photo Yun Seok had taken of him and Min atop the Juche Tower and pressed it to his heart. He closed his eyes, and he and Min were still together.

20

Cuckoo was waiting for Min to come. That was all she wanted, to see Min one final time. Chul Woo and Han Na were out at work, and she might be gone before they got back. That, she didn't mind, but she did want Min there with her when it was time to cross over. She wanted that very much.

She had slept most of the time since returning from Kumgang yesterday, and she hadn't eaten. That was one of the signs, she knew, when the body decided it didn't need food any longer. Her body knew. It had hung on this long. Maybe it had known Kwang Sik was out there all along, at some level she could feel but not understand: a hum in the ether, a resonance, a connection, beyond the ken of her comprehension just as a dog's whistle is beyond the range of the human ear. And now she'd found him, her body knew too that it could renounce the fight.

Her skin was pale and mottled in blue and purple, but she did not feel cold. She was sleeping most of the time, and sooner rather than later she just wouldn't wake up. She had Kwang Sik's letters, and even though the words swam in front of her eyes it was enough just to feel the paper and know how much of himself he had poured into them.

There was movement in the room. Her vision fuzzed, stabilised, brightened, defined, like an old TV set coming to life. Min was here, just as Cuckoo had known she would be. Min was here, and she was with another woman, someone older: like Han Na but not her, someone Cuckoo did not recognise.

'Can you hear me?' the woman was saying.

She did not look like a doctor. Cuckoo wondered who she was. She nodded: *yes, I can hear you.*

'I am the *inminbanjang* for this young woman's apartment block. We conducted a routine check last night, and she was not in her apartment. Her husband said she was here with you, and that she had accompanied you to what must have been an emotional reunion meeting at Mount Kumgang over the weekend. It is legal for a person to stay with members of her immediate family without permission providing that they live in the same city, but it is also incumbent on me to check that this was indeed the case.'

It was just as well, Cuckoo thought, that her lips were so dry as to be stuck together, or else she wasn't sure that she could have resisted the temptation to cheer Min from the rafters. She tried to open her mouth, but it was as though there was glue all around her lips, sticking them fast to each other.

Min came forward. There was a glass of water beside Cuckoo's bed. Min dipped her finger in it and dabbed at Cuckoo's mouth, wetting her lips just enough to unstick them. Cuckoo watched her as she did this, and Min's face told her all she needed to know. It was not the face of the woman she'd last seen yesterday afternoon when they'd returned from Kumgang. It was the face of someone different: someone transformed, transcended, and whatever had happened to make her that way – and there was only one thing it could be – had gone off like an earthquake in her life.

'Yes,' Cuckoo said. Her voice was so quiet that the woman had to lean close over the bed to hear it. The woman had no odour, but then again nor had Min, and Cuckoo realised that her sense of smell had gone. 'She was here with me all night, in that bed right there.' She moved her eyes towards the other bed in the room, the one that had indeed been Min's for so long. 'Just like old times.'

'That's fine. Thank you.'

Min left the room with the woman, and when she came back a few moments later she was alone. She sat on the bed and took Cuckoo's hand.

'You're cold,' Min said.

'Tell me,' Cuckoo replied.

'Tell you what?'

Cuckoo smiled and tried to put as much mock gravity into her voice as she could. 'Comrade Park, what transgressions have you made against the Revolution these past seven days? What transgressions have you made in thought, in word, and in deed?'

There was so much Cuckoo wanted to say when Min had finished.

She wanted to tell Min that you could love someone so much that a lifetime was both too short and too long for that love: that some loves were so condensed and heightened that you had to pack a lifetime's worth into a fraction of that time.

She wanted to tell Min that some people just aren't meant to stay forever, that they come into our lives for a season, for a reason, and that the only thing to do with people like this is to love them while they're here and accept that one day they'll be gone.

She wanted to tell Min that she would carry Theo so deep within her that her love for him would filter through like water finding its way through strata of rock: that it would morph and change, but that the pure bright kernel of it would remain constant and undimmed.

She wanted to tell Min to let the hurt come in and come through her, because it would only eat her from the inside out if she didn't.

She wanted to tell Min to let it all fall apart inside her, and trust that the love that was bleeding her dry would one day be the love that would start to heal her, and that the pieces now shattered and scattered in their thousands would spell out their patchwork truth as she put them back together.

She wanted to tell Min that love was all there was, and that the only thing more worthwhile than loving hard was loving harder.

She wanted to tell Min that she would never be the same again, and that was good, that was right, that was how it was supposed to be.

She wanted to tell Min that everyone dies, but not everyone truly lives.

She wanted to tell Min that in time she'd forget what Theo had done, or said, or even looked like, but that she'd never forget how he'd made her feel.

She wanted to tell Min not to breathe a word of this to Hyuk Jae, for that would be the most selfish thing she could ever do: to hurt him, to double the pain rather than halve it. This was her secret and she must take it to her grave, just as Cuckoo was now taking it to hers.

'Theo will be with you always. And so, my darling girl, will I.'

Min's hand on hers, pressing down in desperation to stop Cuckoo unravelling. Min's tears and the howling of her anguish that Cuckoo and Theo would both leave her on the same day, and not seeing that it was best and right this way, the two people who had helped forge her into what she was today. Cuckoo looking at her granddaughter with a love both infinite and unconditional, and being happy beyond measure that Min's face was the last thing she would ever see.

Cuckoo breathed hard through the fluid in her lungs, and though the rattle sounded harsh it came with no pain. She could no longer see, but she could feel Min lying next to her, just as she'd done as a child growing up in this room with her. She felt as though she were taking off a tight pair of shoes, as though she were a leaf floating in the breeze. Her course was marked by stars now, back to a place where this whole world would seem just a dream, fragile and elusive and half-forgotten, just as a dream is a dream to the person who wakes.

It was a step across to the other side, nothing more: a doorway, a skip through the clover, a falling about in green fields. She had found Kwang Sik once, and a second time, and soon for a third and that would be all eternity.

The world seemed changed, at once greyed out and coloured in. The sun was almost below the horizon, and the grass where Min sat was alternately glowing and darkened where the light and the shadows fell. Below her, Jucheland was closed: the rollercoaster arching against the fade of the sky, the triple statues surveying empty spaces until it all began again tomorrow morning.

Go back to Mount Taesong at sunset.

So here she was, waiting for she knew not what. The loss pulsed deep within her, as though the zenith of her life was already past and the rest of her days would be a slow cold ride down to death.

She'd known Cuckoo was dying, of course she had. She'd stood in death's doorway alongside her and had thought she'd be prepared for it, but only now did she realise that the door slammed shut behind the one who had passed through. Cuckoo had been the one constant in her life: her north star, her cheerleader, her confidante, her warrior. Without her, Min felt unanchored. She had Han Na and Chul Woo, Hyuk Jae, and Yun Seok, but none of them would ever be to her what Cuckoo had been, not properly.

Cuckoo had died happy: that much Min knew. She had died with Min there and Min alone, and her soul had been long gone by the time Han Na and Chul Woo had come back and the doctor had arrived. The body left in the bed had no more been Cuckoo than the grass that Min felt beneath her: a collection of cells and atoms, no more.

Min knew that Cuckoo had understood. Close on her bed, telling her all about Theo, not pouring it all out the way she had into the hollow of the tree here yesterday evening – had it only been a day? It felt like several lifetimes ago – but measuring it more slowly, more considered, determined to convey to Cuckoo the sheer starburst joy of it through her tears. Min had seen Cuckoo and Kwang Sik together: a love that Cuckoo had kept aflame over long decades without any expectation of reward, just because that was what one did, that was what one had to do, that was the only thing one could do with a love that burned so bright and came so rarely.

Min would go on, she knew that. She would go to work and do her job, go home and be a wife, have Hyuk Jae's children and bring them up. She would do all this, and she would do it well. And inside her every minute of every day would be a double helix, twin swirling vortices locked together: the joy of Theo's love and the agony of its loss, her need to remember every part of it and her desire to forget it had ever happened. It wasn't just that she and Theo had found each other: it was that in finding him she had found herself. She was different, but more herself than ever. The Min she had thought herself to be, the Min everyone else still thought she was – that Min was dead, and she could no more be

354

revived than a butterfly could turn back into a caterpillar. He had made her life come to life. She had been a lock waiting for his key, a rosebud waiting for his sunshine: and she'd never even known it until he'd arrived. There was no coming back from what they'd had: not now, not ever.

There were two ways she could look at it, she knew. She could rage against all the things it wasn't – wasn't right, wasn't possible, wasn't fair. She could rise in fury at how terrible it was to love and not possess, and how no less terrible it was to possess and not to love. Or she could stop trying to stuff it into boxes that it didn't fit and find herself left with what it was, something so glorious that she had never imagined it might even exist.

Would she return to that first day back in January and turn away from him, back to a time when they hadn't known each other? Would she have asked that one of the other guides take the job? She knew the answer before she'd even fully formed the question: all the pain, every time, because she was worth it, he was worth it, they were worth it. She would hold her pain high and proud. She would wear it around her neck like the grandest of diamonds, and below it her heartbeat would spell his name over and over again. This city would be his now too: the places he'd walked, the air he'd breathed, the echoes of him, which only she would hear. When she woke early in the moments before dawn, she'd bring him from her dreams and lie with him there in her head, a time for the two of them and them alone. His soul had woken hers, and she knew it would never fall asleep again.

She had watched his plane as it had climbed, a silver sun-splashed tube tiny and vanishing against the vast blue. *Take anything from me*, she'd begged, *but leave me this one thing. Leave me him: leave me the man I love.* She had watched not only until the plane had gone from sight but also until the plume of its contrail had faded away into nothing too, and through the silence of her rage and begging had come the realisation that he was still with her, and that she could let him go not in the hope that they would one day be together but in the knowledge that, in the places where it really mattered, they already were. He had changed what she thought, what she said, what she did: given her the freedom never again to be blind or ashamed, and to shine not just with the truth of love but also with the love of truth.

It was incredible, she realised, that in a world so vast and populous they had found each other: that he had come to her and she to him, that two strangers had been in the right place at the right time. They had beaten the odds. They were the lucky ones. They lived in the flicker, and for one brief flash they had been together. A man she loved had loved her back and found magic in her, and that would always be enough.

It was getting dark now, and a little cold. She pulled the sleeves of her sweater down as far as they would go and wrapped her arms around herself, seeing the place where she had torn the thread off to wrap around his wrist.

There was a sudden flare in the gloom. A single red light had come on in Jucheland, and then another one right next to it, and another, and another: curving all the way up Mallima's inversion loop and over the top and down the other side to make a circle without beginning or end, a red thread that the whole city could see but only Min would know. Min looked, and saw, and the fat tears she laughed were everything at once, and she would have had it no other way, no other way at all: her, and him, and their circle of light against the darkening sky.

ABOUT THE AUTHOR

Boris Starling is an award-winning author, screenwriter and journalist who has appeared on *The Sunday Times* bestseller list for both fiction and non-fiction. He has written seven crime novels, five full-length non-fiction books (including, as a ghostwriter, the autobiography of British and Irish Lions rugby captain Sam Warburton), and twenty shorter non-fiction books. He created the *Messiah* TV series, which he adapted from his first novel and which ran for five seasons on BBC1. His other screen credits include *The Kid*, *The Defector* and *Blood Over Water*. He lives with his wife, children, greyhounds, and chickens in West Dorset.

Did you enjoy this book and would like to get informed when Boris Starling publishes his next work? Just follow the author on Amazon!

1) Search for the book you were just reading on Amazon or in the Amazon App.
2) Go to the Author Page by clicking on the Author's name.
3) Click the "Follow" button.

If you enjoyed this book on a Kindle eReader or in the Kindle App, you will be automatically offered to follow the author when arriving at the last page.